"Why didn't you tell me that everyone knew we were married, Rachel? Why did I have to figure it out on my own?"

She stared at him. "You really don't know?"

Wyatt said he didn't, but as soon as the words were out, he wondered if he'd lied. "You wanted to avoid this."

"This?"

"This." Edging closer, he brushed her lips with his. "And this." His fingertips ran along the length of her thigh, his palm came to rest on her hip. "Is that right?"

"Yes."

He had to strain to hear her. "But you didn't leave when you woke."

She shook her head. "I seem to be of two minds."

"Which one wants to kiss me?"

"This one."

Then she leaned into him and gave him her mouth.

Books by Jo Goodman

THE CAPTAIN'S LADY
CRYSTAL PASSION
SEASWEPT ABANDON
VELVET NIGHT
VIOLET FIRE
SCARLET LIES
TEMPTING TORMENT
MIDNIGHT PRINCESS
PASSION'S SWEET REVENGE
SWEET FIRE
WILD SWEET ECSTASY
ROGUE'S MISTRESS
FOREVER IN MY HEART
ALWAYS IN MY DREAMS
ONLY IN MY ARMS
MY STEADFAST HEART
MY RECKLESS HEART
WITH ALL MY HEART
MORE THAN YOU KNOW
MORE THAN YOU WISHED
LET ME BE THE ONE
EVERYTHING I EVER WANTED
ALL I EVER NEEDED
BEYOND A WICKED KISS
A SEASON TO BE SINFUL
ONE FORBIDDEN EVENING
IF HIS KISS IS WICKED
THE PRICE OF DESIRE
NEVER LOVE A LAWMAN

Published by Zebra Books

NEVER LOVE
A LAWMAN

JO GOODMAN

ZEBRA BOOKS
Kensington Publishing Corp.
http://www.kensingtonbooks.com

ZEBRA BOOKS are published by

Kensington Publishing Corp.
119 West 40th Street
New York, NY 10018

All Kensington titles, imprints, and distributed lines are available at special quantity discounts for bulk purchases for sales promotion, premiums, fund-raising, educational, or institutional use.

Special book excerpts or customized printings can also be created to fit specific needs. For details, write or phone the office of the Kensington Special Sales Manager: Attn.: Special Sales Department. Kensington Publishing Corp., 119 West 40th Street, New York, NY 10018. Phone: 1-800-221-2647.

Zebra and the Z logo Reg. U.S. Pat. & TM Off.

ISBN-13: 978-1-4201-0175-1
ISBN-10: 1-4201-0175-7

First Printing: September 2009

10 9 8 7 6 5 4 3 2 1

Printed in the United States of America

This one's for every girl that crossed my path at Brooke Place.
I'm telling you now,
you inspired me more often than you made me nuts,
but some days it was really, really close.

Prologue

Sacramento, California, June 1881

He could hear them arguing. It wasn't the first time their voices carried as far as his bedroom. He tried to dismiss them, counting the gold tassels that fringed his bed curtains so that numbers occupied his mind, not words. That diversion had served him well in the past, but it was no longer as successful. Once he had counted and confirmed there were ninety-six tassels, divided them, factored them, identified the prime numbers, summed the digits, and finally calculated the square root to the ten thousandth place, he discovered that repeating the mental manipulations was not satisfying in the least, and more to the point, did little to suppress the voices. He considered placing one of the thick pillows that were stacked around him squarely over his face, but it was a childish gesture and the last thing he wanted was to be surprised in so infantile a response.

His distress would worry her. She would blame herself, convince herself there was something she could have done to put the argument away from him. There was, but it meant she would have to leave the house altogether. He hoped for that day, dreaded it all the same. Once she was gone, he would be profoundly alone. She knew that. It weighed heavily on her decision to remain, and he'd never found the words that could move her.

It was not that he was unafraid, but that his fear was not for himself. He feared for her, could not help himself, and she knew that, too.

He turned carefully on his side and raised his head a fraction. Her voice was muffled, insistent but not loud. The other, deeper voice remained unmodulated. Volume substituted for a well-constructed argument. Heat and anger underscored every word. She remained adamant. Her opponent threatened, then pleaded, then threatened again.

He imagined her circling the room, keeping her distance, blocking an advance with an end table, the divan, an armchair. She would be wary, rightfully so. She would be scanning the room for a potential weapon. A candlestick. A book. A crystal decanter. Not that she would use any of those things. These were the missiles that might be thrown at her head. She was the one who would have to duck and dodge.

The servants would not interfere. They knew what place they occupied within the house and no one would dare overstep, no matter that they were fond of her. Feelings of affection paled in comparison to their collective fear of the man she faced. There was probably none among them that didn't wish for the courage that would permit them to come to her aid. It was common sense that kept courage on a tight leash.

Experience had taught him this. There was a time he would have cocked his head toward the outer door, hoping to hear the approach of footsteps, a preemptive knock down the hall. A diversion would have been welcome, but it never came. After a time, he understood that it would fall to him to save her, and that saving her meant she would have to leave him.

Now he waited, wondering if tonight would be the night she surrendered to the inevitable.

The crash startled him. He felt the vibration as a tremor in the bed frame. What had toppled? A chair? A table? A stack of books? There was a brief silence. He closed his eyes and envisioned the combatants catching their breath. Another sound, this time more of a thud. Heavy. Jarring.

He tried to rise and got as far as pushing his elbows under him. He willed his legs to move, imagining that he was pumping them vigorously while he watched the blankets to see if they shifted. There was a twitch, nothing more, and it was possible that even that small movement was only wishful thinking.

Falling back on the bed, he closed his eyes and concentrated on what he could still hear. It was only then that he realized there was nothing to hear. Silence had finally settled.

He waited it out, conscious of holding his breath as though the mere act of respiration would somehow influence the outcome. Had she won or lost? The pressure in his chest was heavy now, but he refused to surrender to it. He waited it out, nose pinched, lips pressed tightly together.

It was the footfalls that told him what he wanted to know. He lost track of the progress of her light tread in the hallway as he emptied his lungs and drew in a great, gulping breath. It was a mere moment, though, and he was able to steady the rise and fall of his chest by the time she reached his door. He opened his eyes and waited.

The bedside lamp lent just enough light for him to make out the turn of the handle. It occurred to him that perhaps he should pretend to be sleeping, but there was no time to consider it properly and just as little time to act on it. He kept his gaze fixed on the door as it opened only those inches necessary for her to slip into his room. Her entrance wasn't stealthy but representative of the economy she practiced in all things.

Extravagance and excess had never impressed her favorably, and he was reminded of that as she closed the door quietly behind her and made her way to his bedside.

She was simple elegance in a room given over to every sort of indulgence, from the Chinese silks and Italian vases, to the Gothic-like imposition of the massive marble fireplace imported from a sixteenth-century French chateau.

Wearing a voluminous ivory cotton nightgown, she moved toward him like a wraith. He would not have been surprised to learn her slippered feet never once disturbed the intricately patterned Persian rug beneath them, and the fanciful notion stayed with him as she seemed to hover at his bedside.

It was a long moment before she spoke.

"It's time," she said.

He nodded. Even though he had been expecting it, in some way even hoping for it, he was robbed of his voice.

"You'll forgive me, won't you?"

It was more to the point that she would have to forgive herself, but saying so seemed deliberately hurtful, and she would never accept that there was nothing to forgive. Instead, he reminded her of what was true.

"It was my idea," he said, and saw her smile a little at that. He recognized the smile for what it was. She was indulging him, not accepting it as fact. He saved his breath for what was important. "Did he hurt you?"

"No."

Her answer was too perfunctory to hide the lie. He saw she had the grace to blush, but the rosy color did not conceal the deeper stain along her jawline.

"No worse than I've known," she amended.

As a description of her injuries it left a great deal to his imagination and filled him with sick dread. "You should leave now."

"Yes." But she didn't move.

"Before he comes around."

Looking down at him, unable to look away, she only nodded this time.

"At his best he's impatient. Intolerant at his worst." He saw her smile again, this time as if he'd said a profound truth. She surprised him then by seating herself at the edge of his bed and angling herself toward him. She lifted the covers enough to find his hand, drew it out, and placed it between both of hers. He wondered if it felt as small and frail in the cup of her palms as it seemed to him.

"I don't want to leave you," she said. "You should never believe that I wanted to leave you."

He said nothing for a moment, absorbing the truth of it, concentrating on the tender fold of her hands around his. "I know."

She did not offer to take him with her. That was an impossibility and discussing it as if it could be otherwise was painful beyond what any person could bear.

"You mustn't be afraid that he'll bully you," she said.

"I'm not afraid of him."

"Of course you're not. I only meant that he won't bother you once I'm gone."

He knew she believed that, and he said nothing to contradict her. He could have told her that while he wouldn't be bothered, he would also no longer be of any use. There was nothing to be gained by reminding her.

"You'll do what's expected, won't you?" she asked.

"Yes." She meant the nurses. She would have already given instructions to them, made certain they knew what he should eat, his likes and dislikes, how often he should be exercised, how to care for his linens, what he enjoyed reading, how he cheated at cards and chess if you let him, and how to respond when the mood of the moment was fair or foul. She would have done all this gradually over time, all of it in the course of mothering him, smothering him, and without once raising suspicion that she was preparing for the possibility of abandoning him.

"I'm depending on your good sense," she said.

"I won't disappoint you."

Her smile was gently mocking, tinged with genuine humor. "I am almost convinced."

He smiled in return and grieving was pushed to the back of his mind. He felt her hands slip away from his. She braced herself on either side of his narrow shoulders and bent down to kiss him. He felt her lips settle lightly on his forehead. It only lasted the narrowest margin of time, but he knew the feather-soft sweep of her lips on his brow would remain with him long after she was gone.

When he opened his eyes, he was alone.

Chapter One

Reidsville, Colorado, September 1882

Watching her was a pleasure. A mostly secret pleasure. Wyatt Cooper braced his hands on the wooden balustrade and leaned forward just enough to make certain her progress down the street remained unobstructed. His second-story perch lent him a particularly fine view of her gliding toward him.

Give or take a few minutes, she was right on schedule. He didn't have to look away from her to confirm that he wasn't alone in his appreciation. He could safely predict there were upwards of a dozen men loitering on the wooden sidewalk between Morrison's Emporium and Mr. Redmond's Livery. Abe Dishman and Ned Beaumont were almost certainly glancing up from the checkers game they played every afternoon in front of Easter's Bakery. Johnny Winslow would have set himself to sweeping out the entrance of Longabach's Restaurant just about now, whether or not Mrs. Longabach needed him scrubbing pots or hauling water. Mr. Longabach, too, generally found some reason to wander outside the restaurant, even if it was only to remind Johnny not to dawdle.

Jacob Reston managed the bank and employed two tellers,

both of whom had surely moved quietly from behind their cages to crowd the doorway. Jacob had the best view, a consequence of the position of his desk, the window, and the convenience of a chair that swiveled. Ed Kennedy had likely stopped pounding out a shoe in his blacksmithing establishment long enough to watch her take her daily constitutional, and because Ed liked to impress the ladies, he'd be standing almost at attention, making the best of what God and hard work had given him: broad shoulders, upper arms like anvils, and hands as big as dinner plates.

Wyatt's fingers tapped out the steady cadence of her walk as she passed Caldwell's Apothecary and the sheriff's office. She slipped out of his sight when her path took her under the sheltering porch roof in front of the Miner Key Saloon, but Wyatt kept tapping, and she reappeared at the precise moment he predicted she would, just as his index finger hit the downbeat.

She was within moments of reaching her destination when he was joined at the rail. He didn't pretend he was doing anything but what he was, and the fact that he didn't try to hide it brought a throaty chuckle from his companion.

"I don't suppose you have a jealous bone in your body, Rose," Wyatt said.

"And I reckon I don't have any reason to be jealous. Purely wasteful emotion." She matched Wyatt's pose at the rail. The ruffled hem of her petticoats fluttered as a light breeze was funneled down the street. Small eddies of dust rose and fell between the bordering sidewalks, but they were no kind of nuisance compared to the muddy puddles that appeared after a rainstorm. "Are you fixin' to court her?"

"No."

"Why not? You watch her the same as every other man in town."

"Maybe I think she's setting up to rob the bank."

"She's not setting up to do any such thing, and you know it."

"Do I?"

"Course you do. Folks that rob banks come and go. Fast. She's been here a year now."

"Fifteen months."

"There you go." Rose belted the loose ties of her bloodred silk robe, then turned and leaned back against the rail. She glanced sideways at Wyatt. "She does all right for herself without robbin' the bank. She made this robe for me."

"It's a fine piece of work."

Rose snorted. "Like you would know. You hardly looked at it."

"Like you better out of it."

"Ain't that just like a man?"

"I hope so."

Rose allowed her glance to slide over Wyatt. He was taller than many men of her acquaintance, and it was a plain fact that she was acquainted with many men. In profile, he was all smoothly sculpted angles and edgy watchfulness, more than a little aloof but not so cold that you could see his breath when he spoke. He was surely the most contained man she knew, not exactly comfortable in his own skin, but making the best of the fit. From where she stood, she had no complaints about the fit. He'd dressed carelessly: loose fitting trousers, half-tucked shirt, and bare feet. Only one suspender strap was hitched over his shoulders. The other dangled in a loop at his side. The clothes, though, did not make this man. He was narrow-hipped and tautly muscled across the chest and abdomen. The stiff brace of his arms made them as hard as iron rails. He had long legs, tight buttocks, and, damn him to hell, prettier feet than she'd seen on most women, including her own.

He never exactly issued an invitation when you came at him straight on. He'd tip his hat, nod politely, always say hello, yet you got the sense it was all form and no feeling. At least she got that sense, and the improbably named Roseanne

LaRosa counted herself as a fair judge of such things. Her profession demanded it. Her life could very well depend on it.

Impulsively, Rose reached out and brushed back a few strands of hair that had fallen across Wyatt's brow. Her fingers lingered a moment, separating threads of sunshine gold from his thick thatch of light brown hair. He cocked his head to look at her, one eyebrow slightly raised, and she whipped her hand away as if she had reason to feel guilty—or in danger.

"You ought not look at a body like that," she said sharply.

"Oh?" His eyebrow kicked a notch higher, and he made a point of looking at her body exactly like that.

Rose's mouth twitched. "That isn't what I meant, though I suppose you think you're flattering me. As if you could with eyes like a wolf's."

"A wolf's? Because of the color?"

"Because when they're not all still and watchful, they're squinty."

"Squinty."

"Yes. Don't say it like you don't know. There you go again. Squinty-eyed and accusing. I didn't do anything wrong."

"I didn't say you did."

"You don't have to. I'm telling you, it's there in your eyes."

Wyatt turned his attention back to the telegraph office near the end of the street. "If you say so."

"I do."

Wyatt shrugged. "What do you suppose she's doing in there today?"

Rose glanced over her shoulder at the now empty sidewalk. "I expect she's takin' delivery of some packages. Artie Showalter picks up her things at the depot and brings them to his office. She's been expecting three yards of Belgian lace and a bolt of peacock-blue sateen. She says she gets it faster if she places the order herself instead of asking for it at Morrison's."

"Really?"

"You couldn't be at all interested, so why bother asking?"

"Just making talk, I expect."

"Are you sure you're not fixin' to court her? Seems like every other single man's fixed his eye on that prize. Now that I recollect, a couple of married men spun that notion around in what sadly passes for their minds—until their wives spun it back."

"I say again, I'm not fixing to court anyone, let alone Miss Rachel Bailey."

"Why not? She's handsome enough, ain't she?"

"Handsome enough?" It wasn't how he would have described her, but coming from Rose, it was a fulsome compliment. "Yes. She's that." And more, he thought. A pure pleasure. He nudged Rose with his shoulder. "Who are you trying to marry off? Me or her?"

"Don't see that it matters either way. You're not exactly keeping me in silk and silver, and she's a nice enough lady. A little sad about the eyes, if you ask me, but not so much that you think she's about to burst into tears if you look at her sideways."

"Huh."

That was enough of a prompt for Rose to go on. "I never heard anything that wasn't gossip and speculation because Miss Bailey likes to keep to herself, but my girls spin a good tale about her pining away. They're fanciful in that regard, especially on a slow day."

"Is that right?"

Rose ignored that. "Anyway, if you came around more, I might not like seein' you go, but the way it is now, it'd be all right if you put your hat in the ring for Miss Bailey's affections. She's not going to stop making dresses just because she gets married, so I'm thinkin' that'll be all right, too. And she *does* keep me in silk and silver, though, God knows, I pay a pretty price for it."

"You're the best-dressed woman in Reidsville," Wyatt said. "Probably in Colorado."

She laughed. "When I'm wearing clothes."

"There's nothing wrong with your birthday suit, but Miss Bailey does right by you."

Rose thought it was an odd thing for him to say. Not the first, but the second. She'd never have guessed his watchful, predatory eyes noticed the cut of a woman's gown or the color of her threads. "You're a peculiar sort of fellow, aren't you, Wyatt?"

Though only one side of his mouth lifted, what he offered his companion was most definitely a grin. "I never thought about it."

"Well, I'm telling you, you are. I've known you, what? Five years?"

"Something like that."

She simply shook her head. "Peculiar." Before she could elaborate, she saw Rachel Bailey step out of the telegraph office. "Oh, there she is."

"Mmm."

"Looks like her packages came."

"Looks like."

"She's juggling an armful. Might be she could use an extra pair of hands."

"Might be she should have taken Artie up on his offer to help her."

"Now, how do you know he offered to tote those home for her?"

"He always offers. She always refuses."

Rose gave him another sideways glance. "You been askin' after her."

Wyatt didn't confirm or deny her claim.

Sighing softly, Rose changed the subject. "I hope she's got the peacock-blue sateen in one of those. That's for me."

"I thought it might be."

"Adele's been waiting for the Belgian lace. She's been

pining for that trim on a nightgown since Miss Bailey showed her a sample."

"She sews for your girls, too?"

"Sure she does. Pays to have them lookin' real nice. Like I said, if you dropped in more than once in a blue moon, you probably would have realized it. Where have you been anyway?"

"Around."

"Not in town, not so folks have seen you much. You leave that no-account Beatty boy in charge. What do you suppose he'd do if there was trouble?"

"Same as me. And you shouldn't call him that."

Rose rolled her eyes at his rebuke. "Why not? You do. Everyone does."

"Everyone else doesn't say it with the same mean edge that you do."

"I'm sure you misheard. Is it all right with you if I call him a boy?"

Wyatt drew back and regarded Rose with interest. "Are you sweet on him?"

"Sweet on him? Didn't I just say he was a boy?"

"He's twenty-seven. Seems about the right age for a man."

"No man as far as I can tell, and my girls have been wonderin' the same. We're thinkin' he's sweet on you, Wyatt Cooper, and that explains why he never visits us."

Wyatt considered all the responses he could make to the particulars of that statement. "Well," he said slowly, "I suppose that's a compliment. Will's a real fine-looking young man."

"You've only got five years on him, Wyatt."

"But a lot more time in the saddle."

"That's what I mean. No one doubted you were a man at twenty-seven. Will's still got pink in his cheeks and green behind his ears."

Wyatt settled his hip against the rail and folded his arms

across his chest. "Will does all right for himself, Rose. He likes Denver women just fine."

"Denver women?" Her dark eyebrows arched dramatically. "Whores, you mean. What's he doin', goin' to Denver? What's wrong with my girls?"

"Did I say he was bedding whores?"

"There's no respectable women in Denver that aren't married. Is he seeing a married woman?"

"No."

"Ha! Then he's bedding down in the tenderloin."

Wyatt laughed. "Is it losing his business that bothers you or something else? Maybe I was wrong about you not having a jealous bone."

Rose's mouth flattened. "As if I'd give him the time of day."

"Maybe not, but you'd wind his clock."

Pushing away from the rail, Rose spun around and jerked her chin in the direction of the departing Rachel Bailey. "Shouldn't you be trailing after her skirts?"

Having riled her sufficiently to make his point, he merely gave her his laziest half grin. "I know where she's going."

Rose fingered Wyatt's suspender from his waist to his shoulder. In case the gesture wasn't obvious to him, she offered a coy come-on. "What about me? Do you know where I'm going?"

"I have a pretty good idea."

She abandoned the suspender strap in favor of taking a fistful of his shirttail. "Why don't we see if you're right?"

Offering no resistance, Wyatt allowed Rose to lead him back inside her fancy house and into her fancier bed. They were satisfied, as they always were, to make good use of each other.

Rachel Bailey dropped one of her parcels. Even as she stooped to retrieve it, young Johnny Winslow was bending to scoop it up.

"Here you are, Miss Bailey." He held it out to her before he noticed she was having difficulty with her remaining load. As more packages bobbled in her arms, he made another offer. "Better yet, let me take some of these from you. No trouble, I promise you."

"That's kind of you," she said, "but Mrs. Longabach likely has need of you elsewhere. I can hear her calling for you. Just help me rearrange these, and I'll be all right."

Johnny regarded her with a mixture of skepticism and disappointment. He glanced at the broom he'd set against the restaurant's window so he could help her. Sometimes he wished Mrs. Longabach would just hop on and ride it out of Reidsville. "Course, miss. I'll get them settled in your arms just the way you want them."

Rachel allowed her arms to relax as Johnny took the weight of the parcels from her. She knew she shouldn't have tried to carry everything herself, but she'd stubbornly insisted that she could do it even though Mr. Showalter offered one of his boys to share the load. It wasn't that she didn't appreciate the kindness; she simply didn't want the company. She never wanted the company.

The sudden appearance of Mrs. Longabach made Rachel jump and lose the two parcels that Johnny had already put in her outstretched hands.

"Heavens! I didn't mean to startle you, Miss Bailey. I came out to learn why Johnny was ignoring me." Mrs. Longabach's thin face lost its pinched, disapproving expression as she took account of the scene in front of her. "Well, I can surely see that he's up to good this time, and I can tell you, it's a nice change. Go on, Johnny, finish helping Miss Bailey. You take some of her packages and see that she gets home without another mishap."

"No, really—" Rachel's protest fell on deaf ears. Mrs. Longabach had her own reasons for making certain that the parcels arrived undamaged.

"My batiste came today, didn't it?" As if she could divine the contents, Mrs. Longabach looked over the plainly wrapped parcels with an eager and eagle eye. "The moss green? Oh, I dearly hope it was the moss green."

"The moss green *and* the shell pink."

Mrs. Longabach's eyes brightened. "Well, isn't that just grand? I swear, Miss Bailey, you have the greatest good fortune when it comes to getting what you want."

Rachel's smooth brow creased. "I do?"

"Your material, dearie. Seems to me like the train from Denver runs to Reidsville just for you. There's always something waiting for you when it reaches our end of the line."

Rachel considered that. "I suppose you're right. I hadn't realized."

"Course the train runs for all of us, doesn't it just? I'm not the first one to say that we don't know what would become of Reidsville if Clinton Maddox hadn't decided we were worth the cost of rails and ties." Mrs. Longabach tucked a frazzled tendril of nut-brown hair behind her ear. "None of that's neither here nor there, is it? I don't imagine you ever give it any thought, what with you being so new to our town and all."

"I've been here more than a year now," Rachel reminded her. Out of the corner of her eye she saw that Johnny Winslow's arms were beginning to sag under the weight of her parcels. She snatched two from the top of the pile and shored up the others. "But you're right, Mrs. Longabach, I never gave it a thought. That doesn't speak well of me, I'm afraid."

"I didn't mean it as a criticism, Miss Bailey." Her hands fiddled in the folds of her calico apron. "You shouldn't think I meant it like that."

Rachel hardly knew what to say. Rather than be caught in an endless circle of apologies where not even one was required or desired, she pointed to the armload that Johnny was barely balancing. "I should see to these, Mrs. Longabach. I'll call on you when I've sorted through the material and schedule a fitting."

"Oh, yes. Yes, of course. I'll look forward to that. Go on with you, Johnny. Miss Bailey doesn't need you dawdling, and I certainly need you back here. There's pots, pans, and a kitchen floor that needs scrubbing. Now scat."

Rachel noticed that Mrs. Longabach was primarily speaking to Johnny's back, because as soon as she'd said "go," the boy made a dash for it. "Good day, Mrs. Longabach." She offered a brisk wave and took off after Johnny, lengthening her stride until she caught up with him in front of Wickham's Leather Goods. "Whoa, Johnny. There's no point in making a race of it."

Johnny slowed his step so Rachel could fall in beside him. "Sorry, miss. Mrs. Longabach, well, sometimes I don't know if I'm comin' or goin' when she's around. Mister says that he just circles her and that seems to work most times."

That no-account Beatty boy stepped out of Wickham's. "Hey, Johnny. Miss Bailey. You need some help with what you got there?"

Johnny Winslow thrust out his chin, immediately defensive. "I got it."

For Johnny's benefit, Rachel was careful to temper her smile, but her response was no less firm. "We can manage, Deputy Beatty. Thank you."

"But you don't mind if I tag along, do you?"

Rachel did mind. Very much. The trouble was she couldn't think of a single credible reason to keep the deputy from joining her. She hoped Johnny would be inspired to offer an objection, but he'd just struck a resigned, sullen pose. "If that's your pleasure," she said. She was polite but unenthusiastic, and judging by Will Beatty's quick grin he didn't fail to notice. Nevertheless, he was undeterred and loped along beside them, his long and lanky arms swinging at his sides.

"Shall we cross the street here, gentlemen?" she asked.

"Unless I am mistaken, that's Mr. Dishman taking a stretch from his checkers game and he looks set to join our parade." She didn't need to mention that Abe Dishman, a widower of some ten years and at least thirty years her senior, was one of her most ardent, persistent admirers. Everyone in Reidsville knew that Abe made a marriage proposal to her on or around the seventh of every month. Today was the fifth, too close to Abe's chosen date for Rachel to risk a public declaration. She'd been setting herself to the problem of how to turn him down this time, and since she hadn't quite worked it out in her mind, she judged it was better to avoid him.

"Too bad for Abe that checkers is his game," Beatty said, looking up and down the street before they made the diagonal crossing.

"Hmm?" Rachel was unhappily aware that the deputy had placed his palm under her elbow to assist her from the sidewalk to the street. Distracted, she realized she hadn't heard him. "I'm sorry. What did you say?"

Standing just behind them, Johnny stared hard at where Will Beatty's hand rested on Rachel's arm. "He said, 'too bad for Abe that checkers is his game.' Ain't that right, Will? That's what you said."

Will nodded amiably. "I did."

Rachel accepted the deputy's help until she had firm footing on the dusty street, then gently disengaged herself from his fingers. "Why is that too bad?"

"Why, Miss Bailey, if he was a chess man, he'd have captured you long ago."

"Is that so, Deputy?" She didn't look at him but concentrated on keeping a step ahead so that when they reached the opposite sidewalk she could take the step up without his help. "Is that your notion alone or the prevailing thought?"

"Can't take credit for it. Seems like I heard it somewhere else first. I guess that makes it the prevailing thought. It's a good one, though, don't you think?"

"I don't suppose the person who observed it was moved to wonder if I play chess."

Will Beatty chuckled. His grin spread easily, taking up most of the lower half of his face. Cradling that wide smile and lending it a mischievous, boyish charm were two deep, crescent-shaped dimples. He gave Rachel a nod and what passed for an appreciative salute by tipping his hat back with his forefinger. A shock of hair as light and feathery as corn silk was revealed in the gesture.

"I reckon you do play chess, Miss Bailey," he said. "Probably good at it, too, ain't you?"

"Do you play?"

"No, ma'am."

"Then let me just say I'm good enough to make the game interesting for my opponent."

Beatty tugged at the brim of his hat so it settled securely on his head. "I'll pass that along."

She looked at him sharply. There was a decided lack of warmth in her coffee-colored eyes. "Pass that along?" she asked. "To whom? I'm sure I don't like being the subject of anyone else's conversation."

"Now ye're in for it," Johnny told Will, clearly relishing the notion.

"I don't need a Greek chorus tellin' me what's what," Beatty said.

"Uh? That don't make no kind of sense. I ain't Greek."

Rachel's expression lost some of its chill. "Enough," she said, sounding more than a little like a schoolmarm charged with settling two unruly boys. "Both of you. Look, here we are." She stopped on the short flagstone walk leading up to her porch and spared a glance at her home. The sight of it warmed her and helped her draw deeper on her well of patience.

The small, whitewashed frame house beckoned as a sanctuary. The window boxes held a variety of herbs: dill, mint, thyme, and chive. Around the side was a modest vegetable garden that she'd already harvested and cleared in anticipation that a cold snap would be upon them soon. The greenery of morning glories covered the lattice that she'd painstakingly repaired and painted. She'd forgotten that she'd left the windows open at the front of the house. A breeze had drawn out both pairs of lace panels and they fluttered against the shutters as flirtatiously as a dewy-eyed coquette.

There was some talk in town when she painted her front door red, but folks had gotten used to it—more or less—and put it down to one of her many eccentricities. Come spring, she would paint the shutters.

"I'll take my parcels now," she said, turning to Johnny.

Johnny looked a bit longingly past her shoulder to the front porch and the intriguing red door. "It's no problem, Miss Bailey. I'd be pleased to—"

"No, truly," Rachel said, interrupting him. "I'll see myself inside." She held her ground, effectively blocking the path for both of her escorts, then held out her arms. "Pile them on."

Johnny's eyes darted to Will Beatty. "Ain't there some law that says a fellow oughta help a lady?"

"Suppose we could pass an ordinance or some such fool thing, but that'd take time, and Miss Bailey's lookin' fit to be tied. Give her the parcels, Johnny, because neither one of us is goin' to get on the other side of that red door today."

Johnny Winslow's expression was so perfectly hangdog that Rachel was moved to laugh. "I'm telling you, Mr. Winslow, that your imagination is far superior to anything you'd discover inside my home. Let's leave it at that, shall we?"

Will Beatty didn't wait for Johnny to object. He began taking the plainly wrapped packages from Johnny's arms and placing them carefully in Rachel's. "You don't mind if we wait here to make sure you're safely inside?"

"I don't mind at all," she said. She used her chin to secure the pyramid of parcels in her arms and gave them a smile that was at once warm and firm in its dismissal. "Thank you, gentlemen." She turned away then, but not so quickly that she missed their preening, wanting to look every inch the gentlemen she'd named them.

Once inside the house, Rachel dropped her packages on the large dining table that she used for spreading material and cutting patterns but never once for eating or entertaining. She shook out her arms to remove the sensation of still carrying the parcels. Once the ghost weight was gone, she approached one of the windows at the front of the house but never went so close to it that she could be seen from the street. She was in time to see the deputy and Johnny Winslow turning away from her flagstone walk and heading to their respective destinations.

She nodded, satisfied that they weren't going to loiter in front of her house until one of them arrived at an excuse to call on her. Stepping back from the window, she set her hands on her hips and looked around, trying to see her home with the fresh eyes of someone who'd never been in it. Since that accounted for almost all of the fine citizens of Reidsville, it wasn't difficult to imagine how someone like young Johnny Winslow would be curious.

As homes in the mining town went, this one stood as something apart from the others. It was one of only a baker's dozen of houses built on the north side of the main street. The south side was home to the majority of the town's early settlers, mostly miners and their families, and a good many people still lived above their businesses, took rooms in the hotel or the boardinghouse, bunked near the livery, or, like Miss Rose LaRosa and her girls, lived and worked in the same place. There'd been talk that Ezra Reilly and Miss Virginia Moody were going to put up a house when they married, but that seemed to hinge on whether Miss Moody was going to give up whoring.

It made Rachel smile to think her closest neighbor could be a whore. There was a plot of land next to her that was perfect for a home about the size of her own. She'd considered buying it herself, even gone so far as to inquire about it at the land office, but since her only purpose in making the purchase would have been to further secure her privacy, she fought the inclination and made no move to claim it.

There was no point in worrying that she'd ever have neighbors on the other side of her. A pine woodland rose sharply up the mountainside on her left. No one in Reidsville wanted to build a house on a hillside when there was better land to be had east and south of the town proper.

Rachel knew the interior of her home was finer in its appointments than any of the homes she'd had occasion to visit. The denizens of Reidsville only suspected it was true as she did not issue invitations in response to the ones she received. It was certainly not because she thought they would be uncomfortable surrounded by imported porcelain vases, gold-plated music boxes, and rococo-styled parlor chairs, or that she was worried that these objects would be stolen or become the subject of envy. The nature of her reluctance to share the museum-like quality of her appointments was that so very few of the pieces bespoke of her own tastes that she was certain she'd be identified for the fraud she was.

Still, she could not help but feel a peculiar kinship with the objects that appointed her home. They evoked memories that were at times pleasant, at others, painful, but needed to be recalled to sustain her resolve.

Rachel wandered through the parlor with its gold-toned damask-covered side chairs and emerald brushed-velvet bench seat, dragging her fingers lightly across the elaborate scrollwork that framed the back of the bench. Her eyes fell on the Italian gold-leaf clock on one of the walnut end tables, and she made a detour toward it, pausing long enough to give the key a few turns.

The kitchen was a practical affair, dominated by a temperamental wood stove and a square oak worktable. She prepared meals for herself when she could engage the stove's cooperation, although she didn't necessarily have to. The Longabachs served hearty fare in their restaurant and better desserts than she had been able to master. The boardinghouse, too, offered three squares, and the Commodore Hotel provided fine food and as elegant a dining room as existed anywhere in Denver or even St. Louis. Fighting with the stove, though, was worth it most days, just because she generally preferred to keep to herself in spite of not always enjoying the company.

Rachel poked at the small fire in the stove, then added another log. She picked up the kettle, felt the weight of the water inside, and judged it sufficient for a cup of tea. She set the kettle in place and took a daintily hand-painted cup and saucer from the china cupboard. She carefully spooned tea from her store in the stoneware jar and placed it in the silver brewing ball; then she set a jar of honey beside the cup.

Having better things to do than wait for the water to boil, Rachel returned to what was now her workroom and began unwrapping packages, inspecting bolts of material, and examining the lace for unfinished edges or snagged imperfections. Fabric was not the only thing she received. She fingered the precious replacement gear that she'd ordered for her sewing machine. After Mr. Kennedy, the town's blacksmith and wheelwright, had not been able to make so fine and exact a replica, she'd sent to Chicago for the part. She'd made do with Mr. Kennedy's piece, but the machine jammed too often to make it practical to use for the long term.

In truth, she liked creating her gowns with the industry of

her own hands. The delicacy of the stitching could not be duplicated by Singer's machine, but it had its place, and when one of the men in town needed durable work clothes or a shirt in short order, the Singer was more blessing than curse.

By the time Rachel heard the rumblings of the kettle, the polished surface of the dark walnut dining table was no longer visible for the spread of satin, velvet, damask, linen, and lace. The corners of her mouth lifted as she examined the conflict of colors. The bright peacock-blue sateen did not work in concert with the muted, subtle shades of the sage damask and shell-pink batiste. Rather, the colors seemed to be engaged in an argument, not unlike the one that erupted from time to time between the town's madam and Estella Longabach. Not that there was any real heat or malice between the pair. They seemed to scratch at each other simply because they could, and Rachel had noticed early on that every observer of their little skirmishes not only expected there would be an exchange of words, but found it entertaining, especially Mr. Longabach, who was frequently the subject of their tiffs.

Rachel poured the heated water into the pot and allowed the tea to steep while she took one of the wooden buckets resting near the back door and went outside to get water from the spring. Depending on how much piecework she had to do, she sometimes hired Mr. Showalter's oldest daughter to help her with chores, but it was only recently that she'd lowered her guard enough to make this exception for visitors, and then only after Mr. Showalter had assured her most emphatically that his Molly was in no way a gossip like her mother. Thus far, it had proved to be true.

Rachel held the bucket away from her as she walked back to the house, careful not to let the water slosh over the sides and splatter her dress. It wasn't that the black-and-white pinstriped poplin would have suffered any permanent damage, but rather that she was naturally fastidious—Molly would have said prissy—and that she was more comfortable when she didn't have to apologize for hair that was out of place or a stain on her skirt. It was easier to stay clean than make excuses for her appearance.

After setting the bucket in the tub, Rachel attended to her tea. She drizzled honey into her cup and gave the tea a gentle stir, then leaned back against the table, wrapped both hands around the cup, and enjoyed her first sip.

It caught her unaware, this fresh wave of loneliness. It came upon her sometimes, but rarely so out of the blue. Perhaps it was because she'd wound the ornately sculpted gold-leaf clock, or run her finger across the scrollwork along the back of the bench, or perhaps it was that Johnny Winslow had made such a gallant offer to carry her packages, but whatever the trigger, she'd felt as if it had been pulled.

Gut-shot.

She'd heard people talk about it, understood it was a hard way to die. Slow. Painful. She thought she knew something about what it must feel like, though not from any buckshot or bullet. Loneliness could do that to a body, she thought. Longing, too. When the mood was on her, as it was now, she knew both, mostly in equal, intimate measure, and she bled a little. Always just a little.

She was assured of living a long life dying.

"Find your backbone, Rachel." She saw the surface of her tea ripple in response, proof, she supposed, that there was breath left in her. "Else you're liable to be mistaken for a"—she paused, considering her options for spineless creatures, and settled on—"a mealworm." Sufficiently disgusted by that comparison, she drew herself up, finished her tea, then set herself to the task of replacing the gear in her sewing machine.

She was studying the fit of the parts that she'd removed, frowning in concentration over the gears spread out before her, when the front door rattled hard in its frame. The sound of it was loud and insistent enough to alarm her. She jerked her head upright and sat poised on the edge of her chair waiting to hear it again before she acted. The next time it came, she rose calmly, walked in the opposite direction, and lifted an empty bucket by the back door. Stepping out, she circled the rear of the house and came around the side.

Her visitor had a distinct height advantage over her even when he wasn't standing on her porch. Just now he looked more than a little imposing, standing three-quarters turned toward her door and one-quarter in her direction. Not that he'd noticed her yet. He seemed every bit of him intent upon splitting her door from its hinges.

"You break it, Sheriff, you'll have to pay for it. I like my red door."

Wyatt Cooper pivoted on his boot heels and stared past the end of the porch at Rachel Bailey. At the angle she presented herself, she looked kind of smallish, trapped behind the vertical porch rails as if they were his jail's iron bars. He managed to stop his fist from hitting the door again, thus saving the wood and his bare knuckles.

He nodded once. "Miss Bailey."

"Sheriff Cooper."

This exchange was what generally passed for conversation between them, so they were on familiar ground. The silence that followed stretched long enough to give rise to discomfort, but neither was inclined to give in. Rachel felt she had offered the gambit when she commented on her door. It was incumbent upon the sheriff to make the next move. For Wyatt's part, he thought it fell to her to extend an invitation instead of standing there as though she hadn't just sneaked around the house to avoid opening the door.

He couldn't very well tell her that he knew that's what she'd done. She'd realize before he finished accusing her that he must have looked in the window before he knocked—which he had—and that was certain to get her back up. She guarded her privacy closely, obsessively, and he mostly respected that, understood it better than he wished he did, and still he had to stand in opposition to it when it got in the way of what he had to do.

Wyatt reached inside his vest and removed a neatly creased piece of paper. "Artie Showalter hunted me down to hand this to me a little while ago. I thought you'd want to see it."

Rachel didn't move. "If it's for me, I should have seen it first, don't you think? Mr. Showalter knows where I live."

"It came to my attention."

"Then why—"

"Can we go inside, Miss Bailey? I think you'll want to read this where you can be comfortable."

Rachel lifted her bucket. "I was going to get water when I heard you pounding. I came back, but I still have to get water. You can go with me if you like and read it to me on the way."

Wyatt allowed that it was the best he could do. They were far from ideal circumstances, but she couldn't know that. He wasn't certain how she would accept the news anyway. He'd imagined her fainting or being moved to hysterics, but seeing her now, holding that damn bucket so tightly he feared she meant to clobber him with it, he supposed he could have exaggerated her reaction. While he didn't relish the idea of ducking the bucket and restraining her, it was preferable to applying smelling salts or sacrificing his freshly laundered handkerchief.

Not putting it past Rachel not to wait for him, Wyatt ignored the front steps and strode to the side of the porch instead. He'd anticipated that she would be surprised when he vaulted the rail and landed softly beside her, but he had not anticipated that she would be so afraid that she'd use the bucket against him right then and there. He was barely able to sidestep her swing before she rounded on him. The weight of the bucket spun her, and he moved quickly to catch her, throwing out his arms and stopping her just before she came full circle. He released her as soon as he halted her momentum. The bucket still swung like a pendulum at the end of her arm. They both stared at it.

"I think I'll take that," he said.

She nodded slowly and stiffly opened her clenched fingers, releasing the rope handle. The bucket dropped into his hands.

"Thank you," he said, drawing it to his side. He lifted his chin in the direction of the spring. "Why don't you show me where you get your water?"

Rachel realized he was just filling her appalled silence. He knew very well where she got her water. She simply averted her eyes and stepped slightly ahead of him to lead the way.

Apologizing should not be so difficult, she thought. She went over what she'd done and couldn't find a single moment where she conceived the plan to injure him. There was no premeditation, only reaction. Should she apologize for that? Didn't he bear some responsibility for provoking her?

"I didn't mean to scare you," Wyatt said.

"You didn't scare me."

"Oh," he said. "I thought I might have."

Rachel stopped in her tracks so sharply that Wyatt bumped her from behind with the bucket. She turned just enough to catch his eye and set her gaze stubbornly on him. "We both know I lied. And you lied by pretending to believe me. I don't think you meant to frighten me, but you saw what happens when you do. That should serve as warning enough, and if it doesn't, you'll have to be quicker on your feet because the next time I *will* replace your head with my bucket."

Wyatt considered that. After a moment, he said, "It's my bucket now, but it still seems fair enough."

"Good." She gave him her back and continued along the

flagstone path. It bothered her to have him a step behind her where his view would be the rigid brace of her shoulders and the steely set of her spine. There was no chance that she could relax with him so close. He wasn't always physically imposing, but he held himself in a way that others took notice of him, even when he was slouched in a chair outside his office with his long legs stretched lazily against the porch post. People actually walked around him, sometimes stepping into ankle-deep mud on the street rather than disturb his contemplative posing, or—and this was far more likely in Rachel's opinion—his nap.

She couldn't believe that he was unaware of people cautiously trooping around him. She thought it was possible that he was secretly amused by it, and in truth, so was she—a little. It was her practice to take the opposite side of the street as soon as she saw him tilted back in his chair. There was no point in surreptitious skulking when she could give him a wide berth.

She couldn't do that now without giving herself away. It was one thing for him to know his unexpected leap had alarmed her, another thing entirely to let him see how his continued presence disturbed her. She slowed her step and gave him the opportunity to fall in beside her. They were almost upon the spring, and she still didn't know the precise reason for his visit. In fifteen months, he'd never called on her. It seemed extraordinary that he would ever choose to do so.

Rachel held out her hand, expecting to receive the bucket. Instead, Wyatt Cooper placed the folded paper in her hand.

"I'll get the water," he said.

Rachel watched him step onto the wooden platform that had been built to make the spring more accessible. He walked to the edge, bent, and placed the bucket under the wooden tap that had been carefully fitted into the hillside to direct the spring. It only took moments for the bucket to fill. Rachel had not yet begun to open the letter.

She was aware that he was waiting patiently, and somehow

that made it more difficult, not easier. She kept her head down, made a delaying gesture of tucking a wind-whipped strand of hair behind her ear, then took a steadying breath and unfolded the paper.

Rachel recognized Mr. Showalter's handwriting. She'd only ever received a few messages via the telegraph, but it was enough to be familiar with his careful block lettering. It was his job to translate the electric pulses that he heard as dots and dashes into words that could be understood by everyone.

CLINTON MADDOX DEAD STOP C & C CONTROL TO FOSTER STOP

Not many words. Only the first three mattered to Rachel. She carefully refolded the paper but didn't surrender it. She couldn't think what she should do or why it should matter. Her arms felt as heavy as they had earlier when they were filled with packages. She didn't bend, although her legs felt as if they might. Weight didn't settle on her shoulders; it tugged on her heart.

"How did you know to bring this to me?"

Wyatt had to strain to hear her above the rushing spring water. "I can explain better if we go inside, Miss Bailey. I imagine you're going to have more questions once you hear the answer."

Rachel glanced back at the house and then again at the note in her hand. She said nothing.

Wyatt observed Rachel's indecision. She had never struck him before as someone who could not be moved to act. It was a fact that he didn't know her well. No one did. But that was because she wanted it that way, and on the whole everyone respected her wishes. He included himself, restraining his curiosity to keep from asking too many questions or joining the speculative discussions that sometimes arose when she came gliding down the street. If anything, he was the one who discouraged others from making assumptions about her. Not that he had to say anything outright. His presence alone was sufficient to quell the beginnings of a rumor.

"You look as if you could use something to settle your nerves." His remark had the desired effect. She was looking at him now.

"There's nothing wrong with my nerves."

Wyatt's cool blue eyes dropped to where Rachel's fingers were closing convulsively around the note. He said nothing, merely let the direction of his gaze speak for him.

Rachel's fist opened and the note dropped to the platform. Before she could retrieve it, an eddy of wind lifted and spun it toward the icy stream. She made a grab for it, missed, then almost toppled into the stream on her second attempt. Her arms circled like sails on a windmill to keep from falling forward, but it was the handful of skirt that Wyatt grabbed that did the trick.

Wyatt pulled her back from the edge, set the bucket down, and waded into the stream to retrieve the telegram. The stream was running swiftly, but he was fortunate that the paper bobbled on the surface and got caught between two rocks shortly after it entered the water. He managed to get it out before the ink ran and the message was no longer legible.

Wading against the current, Wyatt returned to the platform and stamped his feet hard, squishing water out of his boots. He couldn't help the shiver that went through him. Inside his damp woolen socks, he clenched and unclenched his toes.

"I could stand to get out of these boots," he said, holding out the note to her. "It wouldn't hurt to dry my socks, either."

Rachel regarded him a long moment. She couldn't very well accuse him of planning this, not when she was the one who dropped the note. It made her wonder if perhaps she had planned it. Could a mind be so devious as to keep its secrets from the one who was supposed to command it?

"All right," she said. "You can come in."

It was, at best, a reluctant invitation, but Wyatt didn't let that bother him. He knew better than to comment on it. Giving her a single opportunity to think better of it could not possibly work in his favor. He picked up the bucket and jerked his chin toward the house, indicating she could lead the way on the narrow path.

The first thing he noticed in her kitchen was the bucket of water sitting in the washtub. He raised an eyebrow at her but said nothing. She didn't apologize for her lie about going out for water, but she did have the grace to blush. Wyatt set his bucket beside hers and picked up a towel to dry his hands.

"You can sit right there," Rachel said, pointing to the chair closest to the stove. "Let me add some wood first and—" She stopped as he began to balance himself on one foot and raise the other. "What are you doing?"

"I'm taking off my boot."

"No, you're not."

"I believe I am." He bounced a little in place as he yanked at the heel.

"I mean, I don't want you to remove your boots."

Wyatt used the edge of the oak table to steady himself and continued working the boot free. He asked conversationally, "How am I supposed to dry my feet?"

Rachel shoved a log in the firebox and closed the loading door hard. Her movements had more heat than the meager fire. "If you sit down, you can prop your feet against the stove and dry everything at once. You are familiar with the position. It's the same one you affect so frequently on the sidewalk outside your office."

Wyatt continued to shuck his boots. The brim of his hat created a shadow that safely hid the half curl of his mouth. He couldn't imagine that she'd be calmed by knowing she'd amused him. More likely, she'd try stuffing him and his boots in the firebox.

Rachel jerked a little as Wyatt dropped his second boot on the floor, then turned away, grabbed the kettle, and busied herself filling it while he removed his socks. When she was ready to return the kettle, she saw it had to share space with his boots and socks. She also observed that Wyatt occupied the chair she'd suggested, and that now his long legs were stretched out and angled toward the stove.

And completely blocking her way.

Chapter Two

Rachel determined right then that she would set herself apart from the general populace of Reidsville. She knocked his legs out of her path with enough force to almost unseat him.

"You could have asked me to move," he said, righting himself. "I would have, you know."

"No, I didn't know." She set the kettle down hard. The stove flue rattled. She turned on him and held out her hand. "You may as well give me your hat. Your coat, too, if you're warm enough."

Wyatt handed them both over. When her back was turned, he raked a hand through his hair, belatedly remembering how many times Rose had twirled and curled it with her fingertips. It occurred to him that he might still have the scent of sweat and sex on him, or at least the cloying fragrance of Rose's perfume. She favored attar of rose petals these days. Until he got used to it, it was like bedding down in his mother's hothouse, and there was nothing at all that appealed to him about that.

Wyatt waited to see where Rachel would sit before he stretched his legs again. She was liable to knock him off his chair the next go around and take unholy pleasure in doing it. She must have been working up to it for a long time, he decided, which was kind of interesting since he'd never been sure that she was paying him any mind. It made him wish he'd come on some other business. He couldn't take advantage of the fact that she'd tipped her hand. She probably didn't even know what she'd revealed to him. She was just plain mad.

And scared.

Rachel took a chair at a right angle to his. She'd taken a tartan shawl from the peg rack where she'd put his coat and hat, and now she threw it over her shoulders and loosely tied the ends to secure it. She tugged at the cuff of her long sleeve and removed the crinkled telegram from where she'd tucked it.

Wyatt turned his head just enough to study her without giving the appearance of doing so. He watched her unfold the paper and smooth the creases with the flat edge of her hand. She seemed to read it again, although he was almost certain she'd memorized the words from the first moment they were revealed. How could she not?

"Why did you bring this to me?" she asked.

"That's not the question you asked me outside. I don't suppose you thought I'd recognize the difference." When she said nothing, he went on. "The first time you asked how I knew to bring it to you. That's far and away different from you pretending ignorance now."

Rachel wished he had simply shown her the message and gone. She wanted to grieve in private, not show her open wounds to this man. His remote glance saw too much to be as impersonal as it seemed. He was sizing her up without benefit of a tape measure.

Wyatt waited her out. He was in no hurry, and he knew from his experience in the darkroom that it took nothing so much as time to see a picture clearly.

"What do you think you know about this?" Rachel said finally.

It was a beginning, Wyatt decided. He could give her

something that would help her be less wary of his intentions. "Mr. Maddox was no stranger in these parts. He visited a few times before he approved the spur that brings the railroad to Reidsville. There's no one in town that doesn't fully appreciate the impact of the rails on us. Towns like Reidsville can simply disappear; folks pack up and move on when they can't get what they need or get where they're going."

"It's only a sidetrack," Rachel pointed out. "It doesn't go through to anywhere."

"It doesn't have to. Back and forth to Denver is enough. The link to Denver gives Reidsville a rail link to the rest of the country, but I think that's something you know as well as anyone."

When Rachel did not confirm it, Wyatt elaborated. "You order sewing machine parts from Chicago, fabric from New York and San Francisco, lace from Europe. Your threads come from Denver, and you've never had to leave Reidsville. It's the same for everyone here. What people can't grow or raise or make for themselves comes to them by rail."

Now that his toes were nicely warm, Wyatt shifted and angled his chair a little toward Rachel. "Clinton Maddox never pretended he was a philanthropist, at least not when he was still making his money. He didn't approve the spur because Reidsville needed it. There were plenty of boomtowns around that could have lasted longer if they'd had his rails. He recognized there was something here for him, and that's how the partnership was formed."

"Partnership," Rachel said softly, more to herself than to her guest. She rose gracefully as water began to rumble in the kettle. "Tea, Sheriff? I have coffee if you prefer."

"Tea's fine, though I wouldn't mind a spot of whiskey. I don't suppose that you—"

"I have a bottle, but I'm surprised that you didn't know that. You seem to know a great deal about my business."

"Whiskey isn't your business now, is it? I don't ask myself

what you buy from Rudy Martin when he takes delivery of liquor for his saloon."

"It's a wonder," she said, turning her back on him. She found the routine of making the tea to be helpful in regaining her calm. Each tidbit he revealed set her teeth on edge, and she couldn't say that she'd been very effective in hiding it from him. He must have wondered at the muscle jumping in her cheek as she clamped down hard on her jaw.

Wyatt watched Rachel's efficiency as she made the tea. After the first few moments, she seemed to have forgotten him, and her slender, long-fingered hands moved briskly, not a motion wasted as she set out cups and saucers, measured, and poured. His eyes followed her as she made to leave the kitchen to get the whiskey bottle, and he was waiting for her when she returned from the dining room with it. She didn't look at him until she was ready to pour the whiskey into his teacup, then she simply raised a questioning eyebrow.

He let her pour what his eyes told him was a full shot before he put out his hand to stop her; then she gave him pause by pouring an equal measure in her own cup.

"I don't know why you're looking at me like that," she said. "If I buy the whiskey, I must intend to drink it, don't you think? I imagine you know I don't keep it around for visitors I don't have."

He knew it. Everyone did. "Molly Showalter comes by."

"To work when I need her, not drink my liquor." She sat down as he turned his chair completely around so that he faced the table instead of the stove. "She hasn't said differently, has she?"

"Molly? No. She's a quiet, serious girl. If she knows you sometimes drink alone, she's not saying."

Rachel's mouth flattened. Wyatt Cooper made drinking alone sound pitiable, and she cringed from the notion that she was the object of anyone's pity. "Go on with your story," she said coolly. "You were going to tell me what the town had to offer Mr. Maddox."

Wyatt lifted the delicate cup she'd given him in his palms and took a sip. Over the rim, he watched her drizzle honey into her tea, and when she put it aside, he drew it toward him and added some to his own cup. "Sweet tooth," he said by way of explanation.

Rachel was not impervious to the half grin that changed the shape of his mouth and appeared briefly in his eyes. It made his simple admission a bit more like a confession, and therefore, made it intimate. She imagined he was used to drawing women in with that unaffected smile.

"Your story," she repeated.

Wyatt was fairly certain that butter wouldn't melt in her mouth. She'd regained her considerable composure through the simple act of preparing tea, and she was full steam ahead now. "Maddox met with the miners."

"That seems extraordinary, even for him."

"Perhaps. I can only say that what he heard from the Reidsville miners made him decide to build a spur here."

"What did they tell him?"

Wyatt shrugged. "That was better than twenty years ago, before the war, before the Union Pacific and the Central Pacific pounded their last spike in Utah. Benton and Frémont and others were still exploring and surveying the territory. The pathway west was trails, not rails, and I wasn't there to hear what the early miners had to tell him. Very few people could envision the Atlantic and Pacific ever connected by a railroad."

"Are you saying Mr. Maddox was one of the few?"

"Could be." He took another swallow of tea. "Could be the miners were the visionaries." Wyatt allowed Rachel to consider that. She appeared poised once more, unruffled. She held herself carefully, but not rigidly. The slender stem of her neck was no longer bowed under the weight of what troubled her. Her lips were parted a fraction, and the bottom one was slightly swollen where she had worried it. Her cheeks retained some of the pink that had infused them at her first blush, but her deep, coffee-colored eyes had not lost their veil of hurt, no matter how direct she kept her gaze. He wasn't certain she was aware that tears washed her eyes from time to time, or that she blinked them back with a sweep of her long, sable lashes, seemingly without effort.

There was no hint of tears now. Curiosity had cleared them.

"When Maddox was ready to build his railroad in the West, he brought his line from California to Colorado by way of an alternate trail through the Rockies," Wyatt told her. "He wasn't beholding to the Central Pacific, and he used their same tactics to achieve his ends. Government grants, tracts of land at prices he couldn't afford to pass on, and a cheap, mostly Chinese labor force, helped him become Central's chief competitor, and once he reached Denver he hooked up with his own system of rails to the East. One standard gauge for all of his tracks and spurs. Only John MacKenzie Worth could boast of that back then."

Rachel followed what he was telling her to its logical end. "So he built the spur to Reidsville to thank the miners."

"You're confusing Clinton Maddox with a generous man. He built the spur to secure the mining operation."

Rachel blinked slowly, and her eyes were marginally wider when they opened. "He owns the mine?"

Wyatt wondered if he could believe that her astonishment was real. He would have bet dollars to doughnuts that she'd known it all along. "He's a partner in it, or he was," he amended. "He brought in the machinery needed to mine the deeper veins of ore after the placer gold and silver were gone."

"I never knew," she said quietly.

"Then maybe I was wrong to tell you, but I figured we needed to get past this pretense that you didn't know Clinton Maddox."

Rachel let that settle a moment before she spoke; then she asked the question that had been uppermost in her mind. "How is that you imagine I know him?"

"If I can speak plainly, until he sent you packing, you were his mistress."

That revelation effectively knocked the wind out of her. She expelled a breath that whistled softly between her teeth. "Well, that's something, isn't it? Does everyone in town know?"

"If they do, they didn't hear it from me. I've never heard it discussed."

"Small mercies, I suppose. How do you know?"

"Mr. Maddox told me."

"Told you?"

"Wrote to me. I was the one who arranged the purchase of this property and supervised the construction of your house."

"So you knew I was coming as long ago as that?"

"I'd been led to believe it, yes."

Rachel's brow puckered. It was vaguely unsettling to realize that Clinton Maddox had known well in advance what her decision would be. "The house is really mine, isn't it?"

"It always has been. He made sure of it."

Her eyes reflected some of her anxiety. "And it wouldn't be too easy for others to discover, would it?"

"No, I don't suppose that it would."

She relaxed the white-tipped grip on her teacup and took a sip. "It's odd that he told me so little about the town when it seems as if he must have known it fairly well. I suppose he meant for it to be a secret all the way around. We agreed that when the time came for me to leave I would use the Central line to ship the furniture and all of my trunks."

"I think that might properly be what's called an irony."

The line of Rachel's slight smile was bittersweet. "And I think you might be right, Sheriff." She collected herself, took a breath, and let it out slowly. "How did you know he sent me packing?"

"That was in his letter. Not those exact words, of course, but to that effect."

"I see."

Wyatt rubbed the underside of his chin with his knuckles, felt the rough stubble of a three-day growth. "He was considerably older than you."

"He was? I hadn't noticed."

"Sorry. It's not my place to comment on your arrangement with him."

"No, it's not."

"There's one thing I'd like to know, if you don't mind."

Rachel was quite sure she didn't want to hear his question, but she heard herself answer him differently. "I won't know if I mind until I hear what's on yours."

Wyatt wondered how often Rachel Bailey actually drank. There was a hint of provocation in her tone and in the tilt of her head that seemed as if it might be whiskey-proof. "Fair enough," he said. "I was wondering—since it seems he didn't want to hear from you again—why you think he made it part of our agreement that I'm supposed to look after you?"

Rachel's head snapped up. "Look after me? He said that?"

"Drew up an entire document." Wyatt watched Rachel's lips part. Whatever she was going to say, she reconsidered it, and her mouth snapped shut. He was disappointed that she wasn't going to tell him what she knew. He said, "I suppose Maddox thought he had his reasons."

"I suppose he did." Her dark eyes wavered, then fell away from Wyatt's flinty pair. She began to reach for the teapot, stopped, and reached for the bottle of whiskey instead. She poured a generous shot for herself, then nudged the bottle toward Wyatt.

Wyatt just pushed it aside. He imagined one of them

should remain clearheaded. He tried again to prompt her to talk, wondering if the whiskey would work in his favor. "So what do you think his reasons were, Miss Bailey? If you had to make a guess."

"Do I?"

"Do you what?"

"Do I have to make a guess?" She bit off every word as if it were its own sentence. "Really, Sheriff, try to follow your own lead."

One corner of his mouth kicked up a fraction. "You're a regular termagant, aren't you?"

She took a deep swallow. There was considerably more whiskey than tea in her cup, and she felt the liquor's heat all the way to the pit of her stomach. "Termagant. There's a word I don't hear every day."

"It means shrew."

"I know what it means. I didn't expect you would."

"I've been studying up on words. Passes the time. There's not a lot of criminal activity in Reidsville in case you hadn't noticed."

"I noticed you don't wear a gun."

"Most days it seems like a bother."

"Your deputy wears a gun."

"It must not bother him."

A small vertical crease appeared between Rachel's eyebrows as she considered this. She couldn't possibly be having this conversation, and yet she was certain that she was.

"Are you all right, Miss Bailey? You're looking a little peaked."

"Pike's Peaked?"

"Uh-huh," he said slowly, watching her carefully. "When did you last eat?" The fact that she had to think about it did not give him confidence. "Did you have breakfast?"

"I did." Her frown deepened. "Coffee. I burned the eggs."

She cast a sour glance at the stove, then brightened a little. "Your socks are done."

Wyatt looked over his shoulder. Not simply done; his woolen socks were smoking. He jumped up from his chair and plucked them off the stove top. He held one between the fingertips of each hand and gave them a frenetic wave, hoping he did not cause them to burst into flame.

Watching him, Rachel was put in mind of a coquette energetically waving her handkerchief as she bid farewell to a parade of departing soldiers. Even if she were sober, the image would have amused her. The warm spread of whiskey in her blood guaranteed that she would laugh out loud.

Pausing, Wyatt explained expressionlessly, "They're my favorite socks."

"Oh." Rachel placed three fingers over her mouth to quell her laughter and hide her smile. "Then, by all means, continue."

He dropped them on the seat of his chair. "I've lost my enthusiasm for it." He retrieved his boots, examined them, then let them thump to the floor.

Rachel leaned over and whisked his socks from the chair before he sat on them. She quickly thrust them in his hands.

"Thank you," he said. He regarded her a moment before he sat, wondering if her action was made clumsy by the alcohol or her natural reluctance to be close to him. Most likely, it wasn't one or the other, but both. He drew up his left leg, settled it crosswise over his knee, and put on one sock. When he reversed position, he caught her staring at him. "You must have seen a man put on his socks before."

"I must have," she agreed.

Wyatt was aware that she was parroting him rather than offering a direct response. There was also a faint singsong quality to her voice that he recognized as the whiskey's influence. She apparently heard it, too, but decided that the cure was more of the same. He didn't try to stop her when she reached for the bottle and poured two thick fingers of liquor into her empty teacup. Shaking his head, he slipped on his other sock. "You might want to take your time with that."

Rachel's defiance of his suggestion made her gasp and brought tears to her eyes.

"Or," he said with complete equanimity, "you can knock it back like a sailor." He set his foot down, shifted in his chair, and slid his legs under the table. Each movement was deliberate and communicated his intent to stick around for a while longer.

Frowning, Rachel cast a sideways look at his boots. "Aren't you going to put those on?"

"Don't see the point." He folded his arms across his chest. "About what you had to eat today. All I heard was coffee."

"Burned the eggs," she said.

"That's been established. What else?"

She thought back. "There was a plate of cookies at the telegraph office. Mrs. Showalter made them for her husband. He offered me some."

"But did you eat any?"

"I don't remember. We got to talking, and I—" Rachel chewed on her lower lip as she reviewed her exchange of pleasantries with Mr. Showalter. "No, I don't think I did."

"Lunch?"

Rachel shook her head, then wished she hadn't. She set her cup in its saucer and placed her fingers at her temples. Closing her eyes, she massaged the twin aches in her head. "I never got around to it," she whispered.

Wyatt took the opportunity presented by her closed eyes to sweep aside her cup and the bottle, putting both of them outside of her easy reach. "Sore head?"

"No. A little dizzy."

"Makes sense. The sore head'll be there for you in the morning." He smiled when she groaned softly. "It's not too early for supper. Day's giving way to night. Why don't I poke around your kitchen and see what I can rustle up?"

Rachel held her head very still and risked darting the narrowest glance at him. "I'm not hungry."

"I am."

"Help yourself, then. There's some ham in the larder and—"

"I'll find it," he said, interrupting her. Wyatt pushed away from the table, kicked his boots under it, and stood. He'd glimpsed the larder when he came in the back door. Now he had a chance to inspect it and see for himself how she was set for winter. From the number and variety of jars filling the shelves, he could tell that she had been busy over the summer and taken advantage of the bounty of her own garden. She'd pickled cabbage, onions, beets, and cucumbers, and made two different kinds of relishes. She had also canned stewed and whole tomatoes, rhubarb, green beans, and huckleberries, and she had three small jars of venison jelly made with wild grapes and several more of grape marmalade. There was a dry store of potatoes, onions, beans, and apples. Fruits and vegetables that she had canned or preserved were all labeled in her neat, flowing script. Items that she'd bought or traded for carried the labels of Estella Longabach, Mrs. Showalter, Ann Marie Easter, and a few he didn't recognize.

He found the ham, chose a couple of potatoes and an onion, picked up a jar of applesauce, and carried it cradled in one arm into the kitchen. Rachel hadn't moved from her position. Even better, she hadn't moved either her cup or the bottle. "Still dizzy?"

"Less than I was."

He nodded, set his things down. "Looks like you have enough in the pantry to see you through."

"I'm more prepared anyway. Last winter was . . . well, it was—" She sighed. "I didn't know what I was doing." Her regard of him suddenly turned accusing. "It was you. You were the one."

"I was?" Wyatt began looking around for the skillet. He found it hanging on a hook above the washtub and took it down. "The one what?"

"The one who made certain I didn't go hungry. Or are you going to tell me you weren't responsible for those baskets that showed up on my front porch just before three feet of snow blew in?"

"Wasn't me," he said. "Maybe one of your hopeful suitors didn't want to see you waste away, but it wasn't me."

"But you knew about it."

"Sure. That's part of looking after you. Folks around here don't need me to tell them to help a newcomer out. If they hadn't done it, I would have stepped in. There was just no need."

"But you know who I should thank."

"Could be that I do, but none of them are asking for it, and most of them would be embarrassed to receive it, so I don't figure I'll be telling you." He washed the potatoes, sliced them thin, and tossed them in a pan of cold water to soak. Next, he peeled and chopped the onion and threw it into the skillet with some lard. He set the skillet on a trivet on the stove to keep it from getting hot too quickly. He rinsed his hands and dried them on a towel he'd tucked into the waistband of his trousers. "You're low on wood. I'll get some from the shed."

"I'll do it." Rachel actually started to rise, but a combination of his quelling look and her wobbly knees set her right back.

Satisfied that she saw the error of her ways, Wyatt sat down long enough to pull on his boots. He didn't bother with his coat or hat; it was a short walk to the shed. He looked over her stacks of wood and kindling, loaded a canvas bag with six logs that looked like they could fit into her firebox, and hauled it back to the house. He scraped his boots on the mat in the mudroom. "You're going to need more wood cut," he called to her. "There's not—"

He stopped, some sixth sense telling him he was wasting his breath. He stepped into the kitchen and saw his senses hadn't failed him. Rachel Bailey was no longer sitting at the table. "Rachel?" There was no answer, and no sound to indicate where she'd gone. He dropped the canvas bag, selected one log for the firebox, and pitched it inside; then he went in search of his reluctant, and moderately drunk, hostess.

He passed through what should have been a dining room but was now clearly Rachel's work area. Bolts of fabric covered the table and more material was draped over the chairs. The sideboard was stacked with remnants of every conceivable print and plaid. A cabinet filled with spools of thread hung on the wall between a pair of windows. Pins, needles, and more thread filled one basket. Dress patterns were neatly folded in several others. A dressmaker's doll stood in the corner, the torso of its plain muslin form covered with the beginnings of a cherry-and-white-striped shirtwaist dress.

He recognized the shape of the form as Rachel's own. There was no mistaking that long slender line of her back, the narrow waist, and the curve of breasts that was at once high and full. He didn't have to work hard to imagine what she'd look like come spring when she glided past him—and every other man in town.

"Pure pleasure," he said softly.

The foyer and parlor were also empty. He had more than a passing familiarity with fine pieces of furniture and cabinetry and recognized the work of Chippendale and Alexander Roux. He took a moment to examine the ornate gold-leaf clock, lifting it just above his eye level to check for the name of the Italian craftsman. The porcelain vases, he thought, were probably from Europe, but the decorative glass bowls and pitchers were likely the products of New England

and Pittsburgh. It was a curious collection, little of which seemed to suit her in line and form.

Wyatt wended his way through the parlor, entered the hallway again, and came upon the door to Rachel's bedroom. It was ajar, so he stepped up to it and cocked his head. He jerked back when the door opened suddenly, but he didn't know which of them was more surprised. Rachel's doelike eyes could have been only marginally wider than his own. His small advantage was that he collected himself more quickly.

"I didn't know where you'd gone," he said.

Still getting her bearings from having almost barreled over him, Rachel merely blinked.

"Are you all right?"

"Do you mind stepping away?" He did so, and she swept past. Leading the way back to the kitchen, she said, "Mr. Maddox is dead. Your obligation is at an end, Sheriff. I'm not your responsibility, and you don't have to look after me."

He ignored that. "Are you all right?"

Rachel wanted to whirl on him, but he was just a half step off her heels, too close to deliver a dressing-down, especially when he had the benefit of height. She returned to her chair at the head of the table instead. "Did you hear me? It doesn't matter. I'm not your responsibility."

Wyatt rounded the table to stand at the stove. "We'll get to that in a moment." He used the towel at his waist to carefully remove the trivet from under the skillet, then found a wooden spoon to move the onions around in the hot grease. "Were you sick?"

Rachel's heavy, exasperated sigh preceded her surrender. "Yes, I was sick. And yes, I'm all right now."

"You only had to say so. It didn't need to be painful."

"I was trying to make the point that it needn't matter to you."

He glanced over his shoulder at her. "See, that's where you're wrong. My agreement with Maddox didn't end when he died. The contract specifies that I look out for you even after his death. In fact, *especially* after his death."

"That cannot be true."

"Sure it can. Contract's in the safe at the bank, if you care to look at it."

"I do care."

Wyatt gave the onions another stir. "Why do you suppose he did that, Miss Bailey? Make sure you were looked after even when he was gone?"

So they were back to that, she thought. "I don't even know that he did do that. You're asking me to accept your word."

"It was good enough for Mr. Maddox."

Rachel had no reply for that.

Wyatt found plates, silverware, and napkins and set them out. "I've been giving it some thought," he said, "and it occurs to me that he considered you might be a danger to yourself. Maybe someone else. I don't know that I would have put much stock in it if I hadn't seen how you wielded that bucket."

"Oh, but that I would have found my target."

The drama she made of her disappointment brought his wry grin to the surface. "Were you an actress back in California?"

"An actress? No. Never."

"Might be that you have the talent for it."

"I'll keep that in mind, Sheriff, in the event someone in Reidsville opens a real theater."

"Good." He rinsed the potato slices, patted them dry with a clean towel, then spooned them into the skillet with the onions and covered them. He leaned back against the dish cupboard and folded his arms. "So, which is it? A danger to yourself or someone else?"

"Your mind is a single track, very narrow gauge."

"Could be you're right." He fell silent, waiting her out.

"For pity's sake," she said, feeling those predatory eyes boring into her. "Perhaps he thought I was both those things."

Wyatt considered that, nodded. "Did you know him long?"

"Long enough."

"Sorry," he said, retreating a bit. "Curiosity's my worst fault."

"Who told you that? And how did they ever choose?"

"Yep," he said after a moment, "I'd say you're feeling all right. You always been a fighter?"

"When I've had to be."

"I don't know how it worked for you in Sacramento, but it'll serve you here."

"How it worked for me in Sacramento *is* the reason I'm here."

Wyatt didn't miss the trace of bitter sadness in her voice. He had no doubt she hadn't meant to say what she had, nor to lay bare her feelings about it. He deliberately changed the subject. "You never asked how Mr. Maddox died."

Rachel leaned forward at the table and reached for the teapot. "Could I have another cup, please? Mine still has liquor in it."

Wyatt got her a cup and placed it on the table. He resumed his position, waiting for her answer.

"I think you mean well, Sheriff," she said, pouring her tea. "But from my perspective your interest feels a bit like an interrogation, or worse, an inquest."

"Point taken."

It wasn't precisely an apology or an assurance that the conversation wouldn't go on as it had begun, so Rachel accepted it for what it was: an acknowledgment that he'd heard her. "I'll tell you this much," she said, rising from the table. "I didn't ask how he died because I know. It doesn't matter to me what the newspapers report or what anyone present at his deathbed says to the contrary, I know the truth."

Wyatt thought she would say more, give him what passed for the truth in her mind. She didn't, though. She disappeared into her workroom and came back a few minutes later with a large glass globe oil lamp that she lighted and placed on the kitchen table. "It was getting too dark in here. The lantern's fine when I'm alone."

"That helps," he said, unwrapping the cured ham. He lifted the lid on the skillet, stirred, and added the meat to warm it. "Let me hang the lantern over here."

She passed it to him. "It smells good," she said, sidling up to the stove. She put her hand out for the lid, but he knocked it away.

"Careful. That's hot." He pulled his towel free and handed it to her. "Use this."

She did, inhaling deeply. The fragrance of sweet, browning onions and the moist aroma of the potatoes tickled her nose. "I didn't think I could eat anything, but I'm hungry now."

"Good." He took the towel and lid from her and replaced it.

Rachel returned to the table and opened the jar of applesauce. She spooned some onto each of their plates, then sat and waited for him to finish at the stove. "Do you cook often?"

"Just often enough to hold my own. Mostly I eat at the hotel or Longabach's."

She'd seen him there sometimes. "How did you learn?"

"Necessity. How did you learn?"

"My mother taught me. Mrs. Farmer, also. She was our cook when I was growing up."

"Well, my mother definitely did not teach me. I'm not sure she knew where the kitchen was, and Monsieur Gounod suffered no one to enter that he could not abuse with a wooden spoon and a tirade."

That caught Rachel's attention and confirmed a suspicion she'd been harboring since she first met him. "New England," she said. "I keep hearing something in your speech. Massachusetts. Boston? A Brahmin, I imagine. Oh, but that's a good one." She smiled when she saw him flush. It might have been the steam coming from the skillet that turned his sharply defined features ruddy, but she didn't think so. She'd embarrassed him. "I'm right, aren't I?"

"You have a good ear."

"You do a credible job of disguising it, but Mrs. Maddox was from Boston. I was around her for a lot of years." She stopped him when he looked expectantly at her, as if she might comment further. "That wasn't an invitation to talk about me or that family. We were talking about you and yours."

Wyatt lifted the lid, turned the meat over, then put the lid to one side altogether. He gave the skillet a shake, flipping the potato slices. "My mother's family could properly be called Brahmins. A couple of brothers and my sister, also. As for me, it's generally held by the family that I take after my father."

"But that's a compliment, isn't it?"

"Not if you heard my grandparents say it." He removed the skillet from the stove and divided the contents evenly between them, ignoring Rachel's protests that he should take the lion's share. "You could stand to eat my portion as well," he told her. "Colorado winter's not kind if you have no meat on your bones."

"I'll sit closer to the stove," she said dryly.

Wyatt tossed the skillet and spoon in the dishpan and sat. He motioned to her to pick up her fork and waited until she'd had her first bite before he did the same. "All right?" he asked.

She swallowed. "Better than that. Delicious." She intercepted his skeptical look. "No, really. It is."

"This is pretty standard fare. You must burn a lot of eggs."

She ducked her head a shade guiltily. "Seems like."

"You should try soft-boiling them."

Rachel quickly took another forkful of potato and onion and avoided looking at him.

"Oh," he said, drawing out the single syllable. "You *were* soft-boiling them this morning. What did you do? Forget about them?"

"I was putting the hem in a dress for Mrs. Morrison." She

winced at her defensive tone and tacked on a more agreeable admission. "Yes, I forgot about them."

Wyatt glanced around the kitchen, most particularly behind him around the stove. "Looks like you got the mess scraped off the walls." He looked up at the ceiling and pointed with his fork. "I'll get that for you after."

"You don't have to."

"Didn't think I did, but I'll do it just the same." He tucked back into his food. "Maybe scrambled is the way to go for you. Even if they burn, they don't explode."

Rachel knew he was amusing himself and decided it would serve him right if he choked on his next mouthful. She waited, hopeful that she'd have an excuse to pound him on the back. He was mannerly, though, and chewed his food thoroughly before swallowing. She blamed his Boston Brahmin mother for that.

"I looked around your woodshed when I was out there," he told her. "There's more wood that needs splitting."

"I know."

"Who are you going to hire to do it for you?"

"However that contract between you and Mr. Maddox reads, I don't believe the intent was for you to insert yourself into every aspect of my life." She paused to give him an opportunity to argue the point, but he merely continued eating. She sighed. "I haven't asked around yet."

"Ned Beaumont could use the work."

Rachel was unsuccessful at masking her surprise. She'd been so certain that he meant to foist himself upon her.

Wyatt correctly interpreted the reason her mouth was now slightly agape. "I have a job, Miss Bailey." He pointed to the star on his vest. "Plenty to do."

Her lip curled. She fed his earlier words to her back to him. "There's not a lot of criminal activity in Reidsville in case you hadn't noticed."

"I'm sure you mean that as a compliment to law enforcement, and I thank you for it. I'll pass it along to my deputy."

She stared at him a long moment, then simply shook her head and returned her attention to her meal.

"So you'll give Ned a try?" he asked. "He injured his leg in the mines a couple of years back. That's why he mostly plays checkers with Abe and picks up the odd job now and again. You won't be sorry for giving him a chance."

Rachel didn't answer right away. It went against her grain to be pressed into a corner. "All right," she said finally. "I'll speak to him. Does he have any influence with Mr. Dishman?"

"Couldn't say. They're both stubborn cusses. Why?"

"It's nothing important. Just a wayward thought."

"I don't think he can convince Abe to stop proposing, if that's what you were wondering."

Rachel beat an impatient tattoo against her plate with the tines of her fork. "Is there *anything* you don't know?"

He shrugged. "Plenty, I expect."

She didn't believe him, not about what went on in Reidsville at any rate. She stabbed a triangle of ham and brought it to her mouth. "I gather that most folks know about Abe."

"Mmm." He finished cleaning his plate and pushed it aside. "How're you going to turn him down this time?"

"Maybe I'm not."

Wyatt showed no reaction, just waited for her to come to her senses.

"I haven't decided yet," she admitted. "You don't think he's really serious, do you?"

"All you have to do to find out is say yes."

"I've thought of that, but I'm a little afraid."

His mouth took on a wry twist. "Trust that feeling."

Rachel smiled a little herself. "Thank you. I'll do that." She stood, gathered their plates, and carried them to the washtub;

and she filled the kettle with water from one of the buckets and set it on the stove to heat. Setting her hip against the oaken washstand, she addressed Wyatt. "I appreciate what you've done, Sheriff, bringing me word about Mr. Maddox. I didn't make it easy for you. I didn't kill the messenger, but it wasn't for lack of trying." She spoke carefully, no trace of humor in her tone. She meant for him to understand how much she wanted him gone. "I tolerated your presence and to a point, your inquiry. Dinner was excellent, and I thank you for that, but I want to have my home back and that means you can't continue to occupy a chair in my kitchen—or anywhere else."

It was a firm dismissal. Wyatt considered his options and decided that ignoring her wishes was not the better course. He made a halfhearted attempt to see if he could turn her by pointing at the ceiling. She didn't bite. Her dark eyes remained unwavering on his. The remnants of eggshell, albumen, and yolk would be there for a while, he supposed.

His chair scraped the floor as he pushed away from the table. He swept his napkin off his lap and dropped it on the seat of his chair when he stood. "I'm sorry about your loss, Miss Bailey, but you should know you won't be the only person in Reidsville grieving the passing of Clinton Maddox." He saw her eyes widen marginally, so he knew she'd heard him; then he nodded once in her direction and showed himself out the same way he came in.

Rachel resisted the urge to go to the window after she heard the back door close. With the lamplight behind her, he would have only had to glance up to see that she was watching him. She had to trust that he was leaving. The thought of him lingering nearby made her more uncomfortable than entertaining him in her kitchen. She didn't need him to know that.

She collected the items remaining on the table. Before she wiped it off, she used one of the chairs to comfortably and safely reach the tabletop; then she applied herself to removing every vestige of the morning egg mishap from the ceiling. If Wyatt Cooper thought she was going to supply him with an excuse to wriggle his way back into her house, he was mistaken. The mealworm.

That image, which had curdled her stomach when she'd applied it to herself, had the opposite effect when she used it to describe him. This time, she smiled. The fact that it was a wildly inappropriate comparison appealed to her. It wasn't as easy to know what he would think of it.

Rachel could admit that she found him surprising in that regard. She hadn't anticipated his rather sly sense of humor or the lengths he'd go to make his point. He could be self-deprecating as well, when it served him. He impressed her now as the kind of man who saw advantage in taking a few steps back to gain a better view of the end game.

He was a chess player.

Rachel's legs were a little wobbly when she climbed down from the table. She realized that Wyatt Cooper was likely the source of his deputy's earlier observation about checkers, chess, and Abe Dishman's proposals. The lingering doubts she still harbored about the contract he'd signed vanished. Little that she'd done seemed to have escaped his notice.

"You never breathed a word about that, Clinton Maddox. Canny old bastard." In her mind's eye, she imagined him smiling. Like Reidsville's sheriff, he knew how to turn an epithet into a compliment.

Rachel slept fitfully. Once she woke to discover she'd been crying. It didn't seem possible she could have tears left, not when she'd begun mourning Clinton Maddox's passing fifteen months earlier. His insistence that she could have no contact with him meant that for all intents and purposes he was dead to her, if not dead in fact. Only when she wanted to punish herself did she seek out any information about him, and it was hard to know if it was more blessing than curse that there was so precious little news to be had.

Clinton Maddox had outlived her expectations and his own. Neither of them gave him as long as fifteen months once she left. He must have played the game like a master to hold on so long. She regretted that she couldn't have seen it for herself, but that had always been their conundrum. If she'd stayed he couldn't have maneuvered his pieces nearly so well.

He'd been correct. Sacrificing her was the right strategy.

Turning on her side, Rachel saw a needle's width of light slipping between the curtains. It wasn't dawn, just the precursor to it, when the margin of the ink-blue sky began to fade in narrow increments.

She knew a certain reluctance to get out of bed. On any other morning, it would have been because the floor was cold, but today it was the thought of going through her routine knowing as an absolute truth that Clinton Maddox was dead.

Did her mother know? she wondered. Rachel couldn't imagine that she didn't. There wasn't much that Edith Bailey didn't know about the Maddox family. It was because she had that breadth of knowledge that she sanctioned, even encouraged, Rachel's departure. This morning Rachel felt the separation from her mother even more acutely than she usually did.

She found her thoughts drifting to her sister, Sarah. Sarah and her husband, John, had been every bit as adamant as Edith that Rachel should leave. Rachel could hardly blame them for their firmness on the matter. They had their twins to consider, and Sarah hoped to have another child someday. There would never be peace if Rachel stayed.

But it was also a fact that her mother and sister had each other to turn to. She was the one on her own. She didn't doubt they missed her with an ache that left a lasting impression on their hearts, because she felt it in the very same way. Yet it didn't mean she could easily put aside the envy she experienced, knowing they were still a family and she was gone to them.

It hardly mattered that leaving had been the right decision. She was safe. And to the best of her knowledge, so were they. As long as they never traded a single card, letter, package, or telegram, it would remain that way.

Rachel realized she had to turn away from that thinking if she was ever going to get out of bed. Her head was beginning to pound and knowing she was facing a cold floor didn't help, either. What did give her the impetus to throw back the covers and jump to her feet was the sound of wood being split in her own backyard.

Ignoring her slippers, Rachel yanked her robe over her shoulders on her way to the window. She threw back the curtains and stared through the murky blue-gray light at the two figures standing in front of her woodshed. One of them cast a shadowed profile exactly like Wyatt Cooper's and was raising a maul over his shoulder, while the other one wore his coat collar turned up to protect his jug ears just like Ned Beaumont and was sitting on a short stack of wood with his feet resting comfortably on a stump.

Rachel opened her mouth to yell at them, then thought better of it. "It would serve him right if he amputated something," she muttered. She didn't weigh much, but she managed to make every pound of her thunder on the way to the back door. Grinding her teeth, she stuffed her feet into a pair of work boots, then flung the door open and continued her punishing march to the woodshed, bootlaces dragging.

Ned Beaumont sat up straighter, but Wyatt Cooper didn't miss a beat. He brought the maul down in a graceful arc on the log and split it cleanly in two. Satisfied, he threw them one at a time at Ned, who stood to catch them, turned to set them neatly on the stack, and then sat right back down again.

Wyatt hefted the maul so the handle rested on his shoulder and turned to Rachel. He looked her over and liked what he saw. "It's easy to see why Adele's been pining for some of that Belgian lace."

Chapter Three

Rachel heard herself actually stutter and realized her brain was doing the same thing as her sewing machine: slipping a gear. Her tongue tripped over itself as she tried to make sense of what he'd just said to her.

"What in—? Did you just—? Belgian lace?" She followed the direction of his gaze to look down at herself. Her robe, which she'd no time to close securely, was gaping open, and the delicate ecru lace border of her nightgown's neckline was what had provoked his comment. She was hardly immodestly covered, but Rachel closed her robe and belted it anyway. Wyatt, she noted, had already turned his attention to her face. It was Ned sitting a few feet back that was having a difficult time putting his eyes back in his head. In spite of both those things, she managed to collect herself.

"It's at least ten minutes before daybreak. You're standing in my yard, splitting wood. Mr. Beaumont's . . . well, I'm not certain what Mr. Beaumont's doing, but I—"

"I'm stackin'," Ned said helpfully.

"He's stacking," Wyatt said. "You were going to hire him, weren't you?"

"Yes, but—"

"Well, he can't split wood, now, can he? I told you about his injured leg."

"Yes, you did, but—"

"Can't split wood," Ned interjected. "Can't plant my feet proper and throw my shoulder into it."

"Thought I could help him," Wyatt said. "You don't have to pay me, just him."

Rachel looked at the throne Ned had made for himself out of Wyatt's labor. "Pay him for sitting."

Wyatt and Ned objected with one voice. "And stacking."

Rachel was certain her brain slipped another gear. She took a steadying breath. "Why are you here now?"

"Sorry about waking you," Wyatt said, setting up another log. "Ned's got a second job to do this morning, so we thought we'd come early and get a decent start on this one."

"Actually," Ned said, sliding off the stack, "I need to be goin'. Joe Morrison's got some shelves that need repairin' at the emporium. Told him I'd be there before he's set to open." He tipped his hat at Rachel. "Don't worry about paying me now, Miss Bailey. I'll come back round for it later."

Rachel stared after him, her lower jaw a tad slack with disbelief as Ned loped off, favoring his injured leg. When she looked back at Wyatt, she saw his features were so seriously set that he could only be suppressing a howl of laughter. "I su-p-pose you think you're f-funny," she said, thrusting her hands deep in her pockets to keep them warm.

"Go on back inside. You're cold." He swung the maul, driving the wedge cleanly into the wood and splitting it in three pieces this time. "I'll be in when I'm finished here and you can make me breakfast. That'll even things out between us." He set another foot-long length of wood on its end and took aim. Just before he swung, he spared a glance for her. "Scrambled eggs, if you don't mind."

Rachel decided the best response was not to make one. She

pivoted smartly and marched back to the house. If she owned a shotgun she'd use it to point out the direction of Longabach's restaurant, then shoot him with it if he didn't take the hint. She liked the idea so much that she entertained herself with plans to buy a shotgun. That kept her occupied while she washed up, pinned back her hair, and dressed for the day, but when she went to put a pot of coffee on, she saw he was still cutting and splitting wood. In spite of the briskness of the morning, there was a fine sheen of perspiration on his face and throat. She watched him pause once, lift his hat, and wipe his brow with a kerchief, then go right back to work.

It shouldn't have softened her toward him. Rachel reminded herself that she hadn't asked him to do anything for her and, in truth, had made several attempts to direct him elsewhere. She sincerely doubted this was what Clinton Maddox had in mind when he arranged for Wyatt Cooper to look after her.

Rachel wondered if she could find a way to better explain her opinion on the matter over breakfast.

Wyatt stomped his feet as he came in the door, alerting Rachel to his presence. The combined hearty aromas of bacon and coffee made him hope that she intended to feed him. He hung his coat and hat by the door and stepped into the kitchen. It was a consequence of the appetite he'd worked up that the first thing he noticed was that there were plenty of eggs and bacon in the skillet. She'd even made some biscuits that were now staying warm on top of the stove. Evidently she'd elicited the great black beast's cooperation this morning.

"Smells good." He came up beside her at the stove and warmed his hands several inches above the basket of biscuits.

"Wash up. I *know* your mother taught you manners." Rachel glimpsed his half smile before he went to the tub and lathered his hands. She placed the biscuits on the table and served up the bacon and eggs, then took up the chair she'd occupied the night before. She was uncomfortably aware that she usually sat in the chair she was giving over to Wyatt. He'd only spent one evening in it and somehow she'd allowed him to claim it.

She'd have to be careful she didn't let him wander around the house, marking territory.

"Did you say something?" asked Wyatt. He slathered butter on a warm biscuit.

"Hmm? No. No, at least I didn't mean to. I was just thinking."

"A penny, then."

"It's not worth that much."

Wyatt let it go. "Ned and I made a pretty good start on the wood you'll be needing."

"About that, Sheriff Cooper, I—"

"Wyatt." When she just looked at him, he added, "Wyatt. Most folks call me that."

"Not that I've heard."

Biting into the biscuit, Wyatt let it melt over his tongue. As the first taste slowly made its way to all of his senses, he was tempted to simply close his eyes for the sheer fine pleasure of it. "Well, they do," he said around a mouthful. "Lord, but this is good. Why did you let me think you were all thumbs in the kitchen?"

"Please don't make me responsible for what you think. I had problems yesterday with the eggs. I never said I couldn't make a biscuit."

"No, you didn't, did you?" He nudged the honey jar toward him and drizzled a curlicue on what was left of the biscuit in his palm. The sweetness made the last two bites just about sinful. "I promise not to tell anyone you can cook like this as long as you fix them for me from time to time."

"Now, why would I care if you told anyone?"

"First off, because they'd know you were entertaining me and that's bound to make for speculation, and second, Abe Dishman will take it as a sign that you're wavering in your old maid ways and is likely to lead the charge to your front door. There's no hope I can beat back all your suitors."

"Old maid, Sheriff?"

Wyatt didn't answer. He picked up a forkful of eggs instead.

"Old maid, Wyatt?"

He lifted an eyebrow as he gave her a sideways look. "You're just about the oldest unmarried woman in Reidsville. That pretty much defines old maid here."

"I was only twenty-four my last birthday."

"When was that?"

"March."

"Twenty-four and one-half. You're making my point for me." He used his fork to indicate her plate. "You better eat. You're going to need your strength to fight off Abe and everyone else who wants their name on your dance card."

Rachel rolled her eyes, but she picked up her fork and tucked in. "Where did you get the wood that you were splitting?"

"Ned has a lot of it behind his place. He gathers it up, hauls it in from all around, and delivers it to most of the businesses. He'll give you a good price."

"All right," she conceded, though not graciously. "I knew I needed it. I just wish you'd talked to me first."

"I thought I did."

Her mouth flattened briefly to communicate that her own thinking was at odds with his. "We have to settle this matter of your agreement with Mr. Maddox."

"Mr. Maddox and I settled that. I don't see that you have any say in it, but the offer's still there to read over the contract. Come by my office today if you have a mind to. I'll take you over to the bank."

"Or I could go to the bank by myself." She bit into a biscuit. They *were* good. "I do know where it is."

"Jake Reston won't allow you to see my private papers without me being there."

Knowing that he was right, Rachel surrendered. "Very well. I'll come by around two, if that's not inconvenient. I promised Mrs. Longabach I'd schedule a fitting with her. I can see her afterward."

"Around two's fine." He gave her a narrow smile. "Feel better now that that's settled?"

It was uncomfortable to realize she had such an expressive face. There was no other explanation for how he was able to read her mind. "A little, yes."

"Good, but don't expect to feel much relieved when you read the contract. I'd have brought it around for you to see even if you hadn't asked, but I'm fairly confident that you're not going to like it."

Her slight smile held no humor. "I'm fairly confident that you're right."

Silence settled between them. It wasn't precisely uncomfortable, so neither of them was moved to fill it. For Rachel's part she found it confusing that she'd managed to keep people like the sheriff, most particularly the sheriff, at arm's length for fifteen months. Now, with Clinton Maddox's death, she'd entertained him twice in her kitchen, had him fetching water and cutting wood, and had arranged to see him again this afternoon. If he really thought she was a danger to someone else, he surely was putting himself in harm's way.

Watching her, Wyatt was struck again by the stillness she could affect. It suited her, this quiet. Not that he didn't enjoy sparring with her, but that had been the surprise. He was used to seeing her in town, engaging, but not engaged. She was unfailingly polite, always pleasant, but those qualities were also a product of good manners and breeding, not necessarily fundamental to her character. The stillness was.

It was easy to imagine her with needle and thread, enjoying the solitary pursuit of creating something by her own hand, realizing a vision that was in her mind. He was moved by that.

He wondered if he'd ever tell her so.

"I don't suppose that it matters much that I was someone's mistress," she said quietly.

The abrupt resumption of conversation startled Wyatt as much as what was said. "In Reidsville? No, not much. Maybe it did in Sacramento. It sure as hell would in Boston. But here?" He shook his head. "I like to think we're the better for it. There must be lots of reasons why a woman agrees to become a man's mistress."

"Most people assume it's money."

"That's probably the most popular."

She nodded absently. "Probably is."

"Have you thought any more about the biscuits?" When she merely stared at him blankly, he said, "Remember? You fix them for me and I keep your secret?"

"Oh, that. I can't say that I like being blackmailed."

"Imagine how I feel resorting to it. People around here expect me to be above such things."

"But you're not."

"Sadly, no. Your biscuits prove that."

Rachel shook her head, mildly exasperated. "Do you have any idea how ridiculous that sounds?"

"Some."

Her eyebrows knit as she gave him the skeptic's eye. What he gave her in return was the uncomplicated expression of innocence. Convinced now that he was cunning beyond easy comprehension, Rachel acknowledged that the best she could likely do was make the game interesting.

"Once a month," she said. "Once a month I'll make biscuits for you."

He chewed on a strip of bacon while he pretended to consider that offer. "No," he said finally. "Once a week on Thursdays and every other Sunday."

"I don't think so. But I'm curious, why Thursdays?"

"That's when I ride out, make a sweep through the passes to make certain no gangs have moved. There are a lot of hideouts in these parts. I also check on the folks that live farther up or out, take them mail if they have any and supplies if they've told me what they need."

"Doesn't your deputy ever go in your place?"

"That no-account Beatty boy strikes out on Mondays."

"Oh." She turned this over in her mind. "Well, I imagine I can make biscuits for you every other Thursday and one Sunday a month."

"Two Sundays. Two Thursdays. Alternating. And on Sundays I get to eat them here."

"Absolutely not. Two Sundays. Two Thursdays. And I'll see that you get them."

"All right," he agreed. "Just so you know, I strike out pretty early on Thursdays."

"I'll keep that in mind." She went to take another bite of food and realized she'd finished off her plate. She set her fork down. "I didn't know I had such an appetite."

"You want another biscuit? Here. I'll split this one with you and call it my sacrifice for the day."

That made her smile. "Thank you. I will."

Wyatt sliced the biscuit, buttered both halves, then held them in his open palms and let her choose top or bottom.

Rachel chose the bottom. She settled back in her chair as she ate. "How long before I arrived was my house built?"

"About six months."

That meant Mr. Maddox was making arrangements for her

departure long before she'd decided to leave, perhaps before they had first discussed it together. She shouldn't have been surprised that he saw the handwriting on the wall before she did. He'd made his fortune anticipating the mood of the country and the strategies of his peers. She considered herself prescient if she could guess what soup would be served at luncheon.

"How did you explain that you were building a house?" she asked.

"Told everyone it was for me." He shrugged. "That didn't cause stir, though some folks were surprised when I didn't move in."

"Did you want to?"

"I didn't let myself think too much about it. I knew Maddox was pretty confident that you'd come here, so it seemed better just to wait and see how things turned out."

"He maneuvered me about without the slightest indication that he was doing so. I had a lot to consider last night. In hindsight, I know this is where he wanted me to be. There were subtle pressures that I never understood until now." She brushed her hands together over her plate, ridding herself of biscuit crumbs. "I doubt he would have been so adamant about me leaving if I'd pressed to go anywhere else."

"Where else did you consider going?"

"San Francisco. Chicago."

"Big cities. Never Denver? St. Louis? Somewhere back East?"

"No. I never gave them any real consideration, and there's no 'back East' for me. I was born in California. I guess he knew me better than I knew myself. San Francisco was too close. Chicago was too far. And a small town was a better choice than a city. He realized I'd need help that would be hard to come by for a woman alone in places like Denver. Reidsville's just about perfect."

"Folks here think so," he said. "Tell me about 'too close' and 'too far.'"

Rachel knew what he meant, but she declined to answer. "I better see to these dishes. I have plenty of work to do today before I can leave to look at that contract." She started to rise, but he caught her wrist. It was a light grip, just firm enough to let her know that he could insist that she sit. She set her jaw, unhappy with this turn, but she sat.

Wyatt let her go immediately. "Just one other thing," he said. "Did you know about the Calico spur before you came here?"

"Not until I began making arrangements to leave and realized I'd have to use the spur to make the very last leg of the journey. I wasn't certain I'd come here after all."

"What decided you?"

"The need to be connected, even if that connection is by steel rails and spikes." Rachel saw Wyatt nod slowly, as if he understood better than she did. "You know, Sheriff, Mr. Maddox tolerated people using C & C when they talked about his western railroad, but he disliked it immensely when they referred to the great California and Colorado as Calico."

Wyatt raked back his sunshine-threaded hair with his fingertips and shared a slip of a smile with her. "I know."

Rachel slowed her steps as she passed the bank. She entertained the notion that she could ask Mr. Reston to show her the contract without Wyatt Cooper's permission or presence, but what reasons she could offer did not occur to her, especially since Wyatt was reclining in front of his office in his familiar, sublimely restful pose.

Sighing, Rachel moved on. She'd chosen her dress with some particular attention today, wanting to appear as a woman who was both careful in her deliberations and confident in her decisions. With that in mind, she'd picked out a brightly colored batiste handkerchief dress, vaguely masculine in its tailoring with its double-breasted jacket and deep pleats. When she had critically regarded herself in the mirror, she was satisfied to see that she looked striking and not alluring. It was the first order of business for a woman who wanted to be taken seriously.

She nodded or spoke to everyone who greeted her, and even risked a proposal from Abe Dishman by acknowledging him first. Ned tipped his hat at her, laughed gleefully, then jumped two of Abe's red checkers and palmed them. Johnny Winslow offered a cheery hello when she passed him coming out of Morrison's on an errand for Mrs. Longabach. Rudy Martin stopped sweeping the sidewalk in front of his saloon when she passed, and Mr. Caldwell wandered outside his apothecary shop just as she was going by and bid her good day.

By the time she reached the sheriff's office she estimated that she'd acknowledged the compliments of some fourteen men and one from that no-account Beatty boy. She stopped at the gate that Wyatt had erected with his long legs and waited for him to move aside or in some other way indicate that he knew she was there.

After a moment he nudged the brim of his hat back and looked her over—slowly—from her ribbon-adorned bonnet to her soft kid boots. "Are you planning to dress every woman in town in that fashion?"

"Why? What's wrong with it?"

"Nothing, as far as I can tell, but you were accosted upwards of a dozen times once you turned the corner from Aspen Street until you got here. I can't say that I see Gracie Showalter or Ann Marie Easter putting up with that sort of attention."

"I was hardly accosted," she said. "People are friendly here. At least most of them. And this dress wouldn't suit Mrs. Showalter or Mrs. Easter, so I won't be suggesting the design to either of them."

"There's a relief." He dropped his legs so that his chair fell hard on all fours, and rose easily to his feet. "Let's go. Jake's expecting us."

"I could have met you at the bank."

"Sure you could've." He didn't add what he was thinking, namely that he'd have missed her gliding toward him if she had. The mannish cut of the dress she was wearing shouldn't have lent itself to her floating walk, but somehow it was emphasized, not diminished.

Wyatt stepped to the outside of the sidewalk, giving Rachel the inside track, and gestured toward the bank. "Are you anxious?"

"A little," she admitted as they began walking.

"Do you think I've been lying to you about it?"

"No. It was just unexpected, that's all."

He nodded. "When we get to the bank, you'll have to read it with me there. I only have the one contract. I can't risk something happening to it."

"You hardly have to be concerned that I'll destroy it. What would be the point? You seem dead set on living up to the terms of the agreement whether or not there's a paper that says you have to."

"Glad you see it that way, Miss Bailey."

They fell quiet until they reached the bank; then Wyatt opened the door for her and ushered her inside. "Here we go," he said softly, a bit resignedly, and Rachel was moved to wonder if he was speaking to her or himself.

Jacob Reston was the sort of man that *medium* was meant to describe. He came in at average for height, weight, and the length of his sideburns. He spoke in carefully modulated tones and was never passionate on any subject. He was genial, unaffected, and comfortable to be around. In matters of finance, he was the agreed-upon expert, and he managed the bank efficiently and with integrity because it was not in his nature to manage it in any other manner.

Mr. Reston engaged in precisely one minute of small talk, then showed them to the back room where the bank's safe was located. The words HAMMER & SCHINDLER were set in bold gold-leaf typeface on the door and sides. The brass lock was as big as Rachel's fist. Mr. Reston stepped in front of the safe and used his body to conceal the combination. It took him mere seconds to find what he was looking for; then he closed the safe and spun the dial.

He handed an envelope to Wyatt. "You'll have privacy here," he said. "Take your time."

Wyatt waited until Reston closed the door upon exiting before he gave the envelope over. "Would you like to sit?" he asked, pointing to the ladder-back chair closest to the oil lamp.

"Yes, I think I would." She put herself at the corner of the small table and leaned forward so her elbows were resting on the edge. She was peripherally aware that Wyatt had chosen not to join her but was leaning back against one wall, his hands behind him. "I guess I'm a little nervous. Did he write it in his own hand, do you know?"

"I believe so. I remember thinking the script matched his signature. You'll know better, but I never doubted it was from him."

Rachel nodded once, then slipped her finger carefully under the envelope's flap where the seal had been broken once and then reset lightly by the pressure of the things placed on top of it. She eased out the contract, set the envelope aside, then carefully unfolded the paper.

She read.

Her vision did not blur immediately. She'd prepared herself for that first shock by asking if she'd find Clinton Maddox's handwriting, so she was able to beat back tears for a while. The content was straightforward, outlining the terms, expressing that she was to have land, a house, and such assistance as she required from time to time to make certain that she would stay in Reidsville. That assistance, he was careful to specify, would have to be offered in a way that did not arouse suspicion. He did not put it to paper in plain words, but it was there between the lines that he thought she was too proud or too stubborn—perhaps both—to accept too many kindnesses, thereby ensuring that she would cut off her nose to spite her face and guarantee that she would decide to leave. The final implication was that she would decide to move back to him, and that was the very last place she was welcome. It was little wonder that Wyatt thought she'd been sent packing, albeit with much consideration and a great many possessions in her trunk.

Halfway through, she fumbled for her handkerchief and dabbed at her eyes. Without looking up, she addressed Wyatt. "I understand why you think you're required to look after me, but that's an interpretation, not a condition."

"Read on," was all he said.

She set down the first page and continued until her breath caught sharply. She stared at the page. "He wasn't serious." At first it was all she could think to say. "If you knew him better, you'd know he had a wicked sense of humor. This is clearly a joke or proof of an addled mind."

"You knew him very well. Was his mind addled?"

It occurred to her to lie, but this was Clinton Maddox she was talking about, and she couldn't bring herself to tarnish his memory. "No," she said softly. "Anything but."

"Which makes it a joke."

Relieved, Rachel nodded. "Then you do see it. I'm glad. For a moment I was concerned that—" She bit down on her next words when she glanced up and saw that Wyatt Cooper wasn't smiling. Not even a little bit. "You certainly don't have to be worried that I'll hold you to it. This sort of thing isn't done any longer. I'm not even sure that it was done in Mr. Maddox's youth."

"A marriage arranged for property and protection?" he asked. "It's done all the time."

"I'm sure you're wrong."

"I don't think so. I signed the contract, didn't I?"

"Well, yes, but it's not binding. It can't be, not with such a ridiculous clause. You agreed it was a joke."

"I didn't say that exactly. You should know I put my name to it with a sense of the consequences." He shrugged. "And now I have myself a mail-order bride."

Rachel's mouth opened. Closed. Opened again.

"You'll catch flies that way but not much else."

Her mouth snapped shut. She glared at him, rattled the paper in her hand, and continued to read. Clinton Maddox was clear that there could be no marriage while he lived, but at his death, her need to be protected was paramount. He did not outline his reasons, which Rachel knew was quite deliberate. She understood them well enough, though it was clear from her earlier conversations with Wyatt Cooper that he did not. Mr. Maddox had cared deeply for her, enough so that he arranged for her safety, but in the end blood will out. He could not bring himself to leave a record of why she'd been compelled to go in the first place.

"He must have thought that marriage was the only sure way to . . ." She let her thought trail away.

Wyatt picked it up. "To keep you from doing injury to someone?"

"If you like."

"That's what he implies."

"Yes, I read that."

He waited to see if she would say more, but on this subject she was obstinately quiet. "Will I have to spend our married life sleeping with one eye open?"

"Don't suggest that, even in jest."

"What? That you'll murder me in my sleep?"

"That I'll marry you."

Wyatt released a pained sigh as he pushed away from the wall. He spun around one of the chairs at the table and straddled it. Placing his forearms across the uppermost rail, he jerked his chin at the contract she still held in her hands. "Finish reading it; then we'll talk."

His expression did not invite argument, although Rachel was sorely tempted. She did as he suggested but only after she made certain he understood it was because she wanted to. Her lips moved slightly as she read, not because she was quietly sounding out the words, but because she was cursing Clinton Maddox.

When she finished reading, but not cursing, she refolded the contract and slid it and the envelope in Wyatt's direction. "He mentions the mine," she said. "And reminds you that I'm to have a half interest in it."

"That's right."

"That was his share?"

"Yes."

"Who has the other half?"

"I have a quarter. The town has the other." He watched her try to take that in, work out what it meant. "That's not the important part," he said before she began to raise objections that would make no difference in the end. "Did you read the paragraph about the spur?"

"Yes. He means to give me sole ownership of it."

"If you marry me."

"Yes, I saw that. And since I don't want the Calico spur, there's absolutely no motivation for me to marry you." She tucked her handkerchief out of sight, then raised her eyes to regard him with frank satisfaction. "That ends it, doesn't it? I believe a wedding contract requires the approval of both parties."

Wyatt gave her a moment to enjoy what she thought was

checkmate before he said the words that proved she had only checked him. "I told you how important that spur is to the town. Do you recall the second half of the message I showed you yesterday?"

She did. It was etched in her mind as deeply as the first, but it didn't concern her. Then. "C & C control to Foster," she said. "That's to be expected, isn't it? Foster is Mr. Maddox's only grandson and therefore, his heir."

"That's right. Heir to everything but half of the Reidsville Mine and the Calico Spur." He paused, watching Rachel's cheeks lose color and her eyes darken until the black centers were nearly all that he could see. "How well do you know Foster Maddox?" She didn't answer, but it was there in her expressive face. "That well," he said. "Then you must suspect as I do, as most of the town will when they all learn of Clinton Maddox's passing, that Foster Maddox isn't likely to keep the spur open. He won't have an interest in the mine, so you see, that pretty much eliminates *his* motivation."

Rachel felt her shoulders compress as she drew in on herself. "I can't—that is, I don't know if—" She shook her head, trying to clear it. "How did Mr. Maddox arrange for me to inherit his half share of the mine? I mean, is it in his will? Will I have to go to Sacramento?"

"You don't have to leave Reidsville, which, if you noticed, he was particular about. His right to name an heir was settled when he entered into the partnership. The town's share can never be reassigned, but he and the other shareholder retained the right to pass their portion along."

"I thought you were the other shareholder."

"I am. Now."

"And you received it from your . . ." She paused, considering the likely candidates. "Your mother's family?"

"From my father. Matthew Cooper. Do you know the name?"

"No. I never heard Mr. Maddox speak of him."

"Probably just as well. He followed his own mind about most things and didn't take kindly to reasoned debate. He was stubborn to a fault and prided himself on being ornery." He held up one hand, palm out. "And before you say the apple doesn't fall far, you should know I heard it so often growing up that I thought it was our family's motto." He caught the glimmer of her smile, slightly wobbly, but a good sign that she wasn't digging in. If he could keep her listening, and more importantly, thinking, there was a chance she would come around.

"I still don't understand how Mr. Maddox could have named me his heir to the mine. Those partnership papers must have been drawn up years ago, maybe even before I was born. It couldn't have occurred to him then."

"No, you're right. Like my father, he named his son."

"Benson."

"Yes, but both of them understood that they might outlive their children. There was war talk even then. Neither of them knew what would happen. They wrote out a proviso that in the event of their heirs predeceasing them, they could name another at a later time. The intent was not to pass it to a third generation without forethought. Clinton Maddox named you six and one-half years ago."

Rachel was properly astounded. "On my eighteenth birthday?"

"So it seems."

"But I—"

"I can't speak for the workings of that man's mind, but that's what he did. He made sure I knew about it right away. Of course, I didn't know what was coming down the pike. I don't think he did, either, though from where I'm sitting it's hard to put anything past him."

That had occurred to Rachel also. "Do you think Foster actually knows about the mine?"

"I don't know what his grandfather would've told him. Probably very little."

But Rachel didn't want to talk about Foster Maddox, and she regretted asking the question. "It doesn't matter," she said, and quickly changed the subject. "Can I refuse to accept my share?"

"No. You can do whatever you like with it, but you can't refuse to have it put in your name first."

"And that's not dependent on me marrying you?"

"No, not at all. But if we lose the spur, the mine won't help the town much. We still need to bring machinery in and out, and the rails transport gold and silver. If you're thinking someone else will step in to lay track, think again. There's no other right-of-way as direct or safe."

Rachel rolled her neck, then her shoulders. The beginning of a headache was forming behind her eyes. "I need time," she said. "I can't possibly think this through now."

"I didn't expect that you could."

"Do you have the partnership papers?"

"Yes. They're here, but Jake will have to get them for us."

She shook her head. "No, I don't want to see them now. But later . . . later I'd like to look them over."

"Of course."

Rachel lifted her head to look at him. He appeared damnably untroubled, but then she knew he'd had considerably longer to get used to the idea. "I haven't asked if you're prepared to do it," she said.

"I think you know the answer to that. I wouldn't have delivered the message, allowed you to see the contract, or made an attempt to explain how it all will work if I wasn't willing."

"It's a lot of money," she said softly. "I can hardly imagine it. Do you need a lot of money?"

"Not a lot. The mine takes investing in to keep it operational. What about you?"

"Mr. Maddox gave me more than enough to start out. You know I don't owe anything on my home or the land. I've been careful with what I have, so I get by nicely. The women here, they like my dresses." She frowned, regarding him with suspicion. "That's not your doing, is it? Another way you've been looking out for me?"

"No. I swear that accomplishment's your own. I just learned yesterday that you've been sewing for Miss LaRosa and her girls. She's particular about her clothes, so if she's patronizing you instead of the fancy dressmakers in Denver, I'd say you earned your success."

She nodded slowly, still uncertain if she could believe him, but the turn in the conversation reminded her of her other commitment. She placed her palms firmly on the edge of the table, prepared to push herself up. "I have to go. I want to see Mrs. Longabach, and I'm already later than I meant to be. I don't like showing up and interfering with her routine. She'll be starting to prepare for dinner soon."

Rachel narrowly avoided the restraining hand that Wyatt put out for her. "No, really. I have to go." She stood and easily stepped around the chair, putting some distance between them. "You know I wasn't going to make a decision now, so there's no reason for me to stay."

Wyatt leaned back in his chair and crossed his legs at the ankle under the table. He tapped the center of one palm with a corner of the envelope. "Very well. Go on. See Estella. You'll have your work cut out for you if she wants her dress to outshine Miss LaRosa's."

That observation dampened some of Rachel's enthusiasm, but she resolutely headed for the door. At the last moment, she turned. "I've never inquired before, but does Reidsville have a lawyer, or at least someone well versed enough to go over the contract and the partnership papers with me?"

"We have a lawyer. There's not much for him to do these

days as it regards contracts and such, but if you want him to look over the papers with you, I'd be happy to arrange it. I imagine he'll be pleased to do it."

"You don't mind?"

Wyatt shook his head. "Consider it a leg up on an extra plate of biscuits."

He had a one-track mind, Rachel decided, and it followed the most direct route to his stomach. "All right," she agreed. She offered him a brief, tentative smile, then let herself out.

Wyatt gave her what he thought was sufficient time to leave the bank; then he poked his head out the door and called to the manager. "Hey, Jake, I'll be needing you to get in the safe again. Miss Bailey wants to see the incorporation papers for the mine."

Rachel sat in a green-velvet-upholstered side chair in Estella Longabach's parlor and sipped tea from a fluted, gold-rimmed cup. "I brought my tape measure," she said. "Just to be certain that what I have in my records at home is still accurate."

Estella held out her cup a fraction so she could stare down at herself. "I'm certain I haven't gained any weight."

"As hard as you work, Mrs. Longabach, it's more likely you've lost some, and a fraction of an inch here or there, well, you can understand that it makes a difference in the fit of the dress."

Nodding, Estella made another study of Rachel's dress. "I sure like what you're wearing today. I don't remember seeing that in the pattern book you lent me. I'm sure it would have caught my eye."

"It's my own design, but there are dresses similar to it in the book."

"Well, I like yours. It looks, hmm, I don't know, like maybe you could lead a charge in it. What's the name of the French girl that fought the English?"

"Do you mean St. Joan? Joan of Arc?"

"That's her. Your dress puts me in mind of her. Not sure why because you couldn't really ride a horse in it, now, could you?"

Laughter parted Rachel's lips. She smiled warmly. "No, it's not practical for horse riding or swinging a sword. I think you're noticing the double-breasted cuirass. It feels a bit like I'm wearing armor, I can tell you, but then I wanted to dress for battle today."

"Well, it sure is pretty, that's what I know. Must've made every man in town sit up and take notice."

"It's a friendly town," said Rachel, realizing she'd spoken those same words to Wyatt earlier.

Estella snorted. "Friendlier to some than others, I've seen."

"I'm sorry. Did I—"

"I'm not talkin' about you." She waved one hand dismissively. "I'm talkin' about that LaRosa woman. I swear she thinks she can get her painted claws into my Henry."

Rachel wasn't certain that there was a correct response to this statement. She hurriedly took a shortbread cookie from the tray Mrs. Longabach had set between them and bit into it. Her hostess didn't seem to notice that she hadn't replied or even made sympathetic noises.

"Course, if I was wearin' a dress like yours, Miss LaRosa would know I was serious about wantin' her to take a step back. I like the idea of dressing for battle."

The dress was something Rachel felt that she *could* talk about. "Why don't we look in the pattern book and see what would suit you best?"

Estella pointed to Rachel's tailored cuirass. "That's what I want. What about that shell-pink batiste I ordered? Couldn't you use that?"

"It's a beautiful piece of fabric. I looked it over yesterday and wished I'd ordered more, but it doesn't really work for this dress. I'll tell you what, I'll stand up and you take a few moments to study my dress, concentrate on the particulars you like, and then I want you to close your eyes and try to imagine your lovely piece of shell-pink fabric cut and styled and detailed in exactly the same way."

Estella set her cup aside and laid her hands flat on her lap, prepared to concentrate. "This is a new one on me," she said. "Is this how they do it in those Paris salons?"

"I don't know," Rachel said, rising to her feet. "I've never been to Paris. What made you think I had?"

Estella shrugged. "Just my imaginings, I suppose. You don't really talk much about yourself, so I fill in the gaps on my own."

"But Paris?" asked Rachel. "That gap's the Atlantic Ocean."

Estella twirled her finger, indicating that Rachel could start turning. "I saw paintings of Paris when Henry and I still lived back East. Oh, that was years ago now, but I never forgot them. Seemed like a place I'd like to visit someday, though it was always hard to picture myself there exactly. You, though, I could see you real easy in those paintings. Think of it every time you come glidin' down the street in one of your pretty dresses, standin' out of the background like you were movin' through the painting, strolling on one of those boulevards with the little shops and cafés. Sophisticated, like. Just a bit separate from the crowd, you know. But real nice, too, 'cause you always make a point of smilin' or givin' folks a nod."

Rachel finished turning to face Estella once again. Her eyes were troubled and the small smile she forced was uncertain. "Thank you," she said softly. "You're kind to say so."

Estella's eyebrows rose halfway to her dark widow's peak. "Lookin' at you now, I'm wonderin' if I should have said a thing. I don't think you know how to hear a compliment, 'cause that's what it was. Meant what I said in the kindest way, and that's the truth."

"Well, thank you, then," Rachel said with more conviction this time.

"That's better. Now I'm going to shut my eyes and think about a shell-pink batiste, and if I can get Paris proper in my mind again, I'll be draggin' Henry into one of those cafés with me."

"Yes, ma'am." Rachel waited. The clock on the wall ticked off the seconds, and she counted fifty-two before Mrs. Longabach opened her eyes.

"Well," Estella said firmly, "the shell pink isn't going to do at all, is it?"

"No."

"No sense putting brass buttons on confectionery. But then, you knew that."

"It was important to me that you realize it," Rachel said. "Now, if you'd like me to show you some fabrics in other colors, like indigo blue or burgundy, or some plaids similar to what I'm wearing, I'd be happy to bring them by."

"What about the moss-green material that I ordered?"

"It will work, of course, but the dress you picked out for it is really the perfect choice."

"Are we talkin' about three dresses now or two?"

"We're talking about as many as you'd like, Mrs. Longabach."

Estella's gaze was both shrewd and appreciative. "Let's see. I'm hearin' the burgundy and brass for stopping Miss LaRosa in her tracks, the moss green for every day, and the shell pink for . . . Now, what do I need the shell pink for?"

"It'd make a lovely nightgown."

Chuckling, Estella picked up her cup. "Aren't you the quick one, Miss Bailey, but I'm forty-two years old with about as many curves as a string bean, and in a Colorado winter I prefer flannel."

"Does Mr. Longabach?"

Estella's laughter was strangled by the fact that she was trying to swallow a mouthful of tea. She recovered before Rachel could lend assistance. "I'm fine," she said. "That was unexpected, is all. But I trust your instincts and your needlework. I'll find that pattern book for us." Standing, she sighed. "Don't know that anyone else could have made me think I needed three new pieces. You have a gift, Miss Bailey." Then, just to make certain Rachel understood, she added, "That's a compliment."

"I know. Thank you." And this time there was no doubt that she meant it.

Rachel paused, looking up from the fabric she was cutting as Molly Showalter entered through the back door. "Put a kettle on, Molly," she called, going back to work. "We'll have tea when you want to take a break."

"Yes, ma'am. Do you have a list of chores for me?"

"It's on the kitchen table. Come here first. I want your opinion."

Molly only poked her head into the workroom. "My opinion, Miss Bailey?"

Rachel glanced over her shoulder and smiled. "Of course. You have them, don't you?"

"I guess so."

"Come on. Over by the table. You can't see anything from where you're hiding."

Molly made a slow, cautious approach and stopped when she was still a few feet from the table. "My hem's been a magnet for dust today, Miss Bailey, and I have ink on my hands. I was cleaning my father's office, and I knocked over an inkpot. I don't want to touch anything in this room."

"Hold them up. Let me see." Rachel set down her shears and regarded Molly's hands. "Oh, yes. You look as if you've been picking blueberries. I have something on my vanity that might remove that. I'll get it for you in a little while. First, tell me what you think of this." She reached for the leather portfolio lying on one of the side chairs and unwound the grosgrain ribbon that secured the flap. Her fingers moved quickly over the contents, separating the sketches she'd made until she found the one she wanted. She pulled it out and laid it on the table for Molly to see.

Molly sidled closer and bent at the waist to peer over the table, her hands set in a fist behind her back. The woman in the sketch had no features to speak of, and her hair was merely a suggestion made by a few bold spiral strokes of a pencil, but what she lacked in detail of face, she was compensated for in detail of form.

She was a lithe figure, with young curves that promised a full blossom in time, and she held herself with confidence, shoulders back, head erect. She wore a party dress with a square-cut neckline and long, tight-fitting sleeves that tapered to points that lay softly against the back of her wrists. The stiff ruffle that defined the neck was repeated in a tiered cascade that began twelve inches above the hemline. The bodice was flat and plain so the woman's figure was seen to its advantage rather than disappearing in flounces and an abundance of lace.

"What do you think?" Rachel asked.

Molly and Rachel both gave a violent start when a masculine voice behind them answered the question. "Johnny Winslow won't be able to keep his eyes where God intended."

Chapter Four

Rachel spun around, hand raised, clutching her shears.

"Whoa!" Wyatt jumped back and thrust his palms out defensively. "I knocked, ladies."

"Did you hear him, Molly?" Out of the corner of her eye, she saw Molly flinch and realized that the girl had misinterpreted her snappish tone as an accusation directed at her. That forced Rachel to calm herself as nothing else would have. "I didn't hear him," she said with a credible lack of inflection. "Did you?"

Molly stuttered something that might have been yes *or* no.

"It's all right, Molly," Wyatt said. "Miss Bailey has her shears pointed at me, not you."

Rachel dropped her hand to her side. "You shouldn't sneak up on people."

"I didn't know I was. I thought I heard you tell me to come in."

"Now, that's just a lie, plain and simple."

"Oh, he doesn't lie, Miss Bailey. He's the sheriff."

Wyatt nodded once at Molly. "Thank you for that stout defense." He then regarded Rachel with a slip of a smile. "See? I don't lie. I'm the sheriff."

Seeing no merit in carrying the argument further and risking disillusioning Molly, Rachel asked, "Why are you here?"

"Tomorrow's Thursday."

"And?" she asked, drawing out the single word.

He shrugged. "Just reminding you."

"Well, thank you. I'll make a note of—" She stopped, remembering her promise. "Oh. Thursday."

Wyatt saw she finally understood. "I leave real early."

"Crack-of-dawn early or chopping-wood early?"

He chuckled. "Crack-of-dawn early."

"All right." She turned, intent on dismissing him, but he somehow managed to insinuate himself between her and Molly.

"Can I get a better look at that sketch?"

She agreed, albeit reluctantly, and made more room for him at the table. "I still want to know what Molly thinks." She leaned forward, looking around Wyatt to catch Molly's eye, and nudged the sketch toward the girl. "Be honest, Molly. Like the sheriff." She set her shoe on the toe of Wyatt's boot and ground down gently. She heard him suck in a breath, but to his credit, he didn't move. "You won't hurt my feelings."

Molly stared raptly at the sketch for a few moments longer, her sigh speaking for her before she offered any words. "It's beautiful, Miss Bailey, and that's a fact."

"Would you change anything?"

"No, ma'am. I especially like the sleeves. They taper so daintylike." Her voice changed, some of her initial enthusiasm diminishing as she said, "Sheriff Cooper's right. You'll strike Johnny Winslow blind wearing it."

Wyatt made a small choking sound. "I don't think I said it quite like that. Besides, Molly, can't you see this dress isn't for Miss Bailey? That's you she sketched wearing it."

"Me?" She stared at it again. "Is that true, ma'am?"

"Mm-hmm."

"Does my mother know? She might not . . . well, this is a grown-up dress, and she thinks I'm . . ."

"Not so grown up?"

Molly nodded. She pulled the tail of her long honey-color braid over her shoulder and began chewing absently on the end of it.

Rachel reached over and gently removed the braid from Molly's nervous hands and mouth. "You're seventeen, aren't you?"

She nodded again. "Almost eighteen."

"I'll speak to your mother, Molly."

"She'll want flounces. She always does."

"That's because they suit her. They'll swallow you."

Wyatt raised a fist to his mouth and coughed gently. "If I could offer a suggestion?"

Rachel regarded him with annoyance, but she noticed that Molly looked at him as if he were bringing the Ten Commandments down from the mount. "What is it?"

"You might want to consider getting Artie's approval first."

"My *father*?" asked Molly.

Rachel smiled. It was as if Wyatt had just shattered the stone tablets, Molly was that appalled. It went against her grain to agree with him, especially in front of a witness, but she had to admit his idea had merit. "You're the apple of his eye," Rachel told Molly. "He could lend some support if your mama balks."

"I don't know. What if he doesn't like it?"

"He will," said Wyatt. "You'll just have to trust me. Now, whether he'll like Johnny trailing after you like a love-struck pup, I can't say."

Molly's green eyes went a little vague and dreamy. "Johnny's so stuck on Miss Bailey, I don't know if he . . ." She looked at Wyatt hopefully. "Do you really think he would notice . . . ?" Her voice trailed off again.

"Yes, indeed." Wyatt and Rachel exchanged glances that Molly missed in her rapt attention to the drawing.

It was Rachel who breached Molly's wistful silence. "Go start on that list I left you in the kitchen," she said. "And don't forget about putting the kettle on."

Molly nodded absently, turned, and wandered off in the direction of the kitchen with a little sashay in her step.

"She's already the belle of the ball," Wyatt whispered.

Rachel smiled, pleased. "And so she should be. She's a lovely girl." She picked up the sketch and slipped it back inside her portfolio, then handed it to Wyatt to put aside. Keeping her voice low, she asked, "How did you know that she was sweet on Johnny?"

"When I'm not studying up on new words, I watch people." He ignored her mocking smile. "Did you think I was napping?"

"It certainly occurred to me." She pointed to the chair beside him as she turned her attention back to cutting the peacock-blue sateen. "You can put the portfolio there. I'll have your biscuits in the morning."

Ignoring her dismissive tone, Wyatt sat down and opened the portfolio. "May I?"

She didn't bother looking at him. "Could I stop you?"

In answer, he drew out a third of her sketches. Molly's humming reached him from the kitchen. "She can carry a tune."

Rachel nodded absently and moved around the table to give her a better position to make the next cut. She smoothed the muslin pattern that she'd pinned to the sateen carefully, then began cutting. "If she's no good to me this afternoon because you've got her mooning over Johnny Winslow, I'll expect you to finish her chores."

"What's she have to do?"

"Sweeping, mopping, dusting. That sort of thing. Carrying wood and water. There's a load of bed linens that go to Mrs.

Ritchie's for laundering. Molly takes the basket when she leaves, so you better hope she doesn't forget it."

"I'll see that she doesn't." Wyatt tipped his chair so that it rested on the two back legs and balanced himself while he began looking through Rachel's sketches. "I thought you were going to stab me with those shears," he said conversationally.

Rachel didn't look up from cutting. "I thought I was, too. What's the penalty for killing a lawman?"

"Hanging, most likely. Of course, if there're mitigating circumstances—"

"Oh, there are, since you sneaked up on me."

"A jury would have to decide that, but let's say they're sympathetic to the defense's explanation, then you might only have to spend the rest of your days in jail. Folks around here are partial to me, so I think you'd hang."

"I'll try to keep that in mind."

Wyatt held up one of the drawings. "I like this one a lot. You ever put fabric to it?"

Rachel glanced at the sketch. "That's a walking dress for occasions when young ladies of fashion and means are taking an idle stroll."

"There's nothing idle about a stroll when a young lady's wearing this. There's a clear purpose here, and it's that she wants to be noticed. She's telling all of the gentlemen in her social circle that she's available."

"Available?" Rachel asked carefully. "I surely hope you aren't saying she looks like a strumpet. And will you please put that chair down? You're making me nervous."

"Sorry." Wyatt let the chair thud to the floor. "I was thinking she's letting her gentlemen friends know she's available for marriage. This dress is part of a much larger strategy to snare a husband. Spiders aren't the only creatures who know what to do with silk." He slipped the sketch back into place and began leafing through the rest. "So, did you ever make the dress or did it remain a sketch?"

"I made the dress five years ago. Miss Charlotte Petersen wore it to attend Meriwether race day in Sacramento."

"Was it a success? Did you do more work for Miss Petersen?"

Rachel didn't look at him. She could see where this was going. "Very successful. She hired me to make her traveling clothes."

"Her traveling clothes." He pondered that for a moment; then one corner of his mouth quirked. "I think that's a euphemism for trousseau." Wyatt saw Rachel's mouth purse disagreeably, and he was certain he was right. "Interesting. So she married."

"Mmm."

"Don't suppose she married someone who saw her in that walking dress on race day."

"What if she did?"

Wyatt's half grin lifted a fraction higher. "Oh, that's rich. Who did she marry?"

"Charles Meriwether, if you must know."

"Of the Meriwethers of race day. Even better."

"And spiders don't make silk," she said tartly. "Silk comes from the caterpillar of the moth *Bombix mori*."

Afraid she might have good aim with the shears, Wyatt managed to keep his laughter in check. "Guess you told me."

Rachel made a derisive sound at the back of her throat and did a credible job of ignoring him until Molly appeared with a tea tray. "We can't drink in here," she said. "I'm not risking staining any fabric. We'll take it in the parlor. Molly, where's your cup?"

"In the kitchen. I'll drink my tea while I'm workin'."

"I promised you a break."

"It's all right. Really. You and Sheriff Cooper don't want

me around, and if it's all the same, I'd rather be by myself right now."

"If you're sure," Rachel said with more generosity than she felt. Her preference would have been to take her tea with Molly in the parlor and point Wyatt Cooper to the kitchen. "Thank you, Molly." She took the tray and gestured for the sheriff to precede her.

Wyatt chose to sit on the upholstered bench where he could comfortably angle himself into one corner and set his arm along the scrolled back. He knew there was almost no chance that Rachel would join him on the bench, but until she set the tray down and picked a nearby velvet side chair to sit in, he didn't give up hope.

Rachel leaned forward to pour. She remembered he liked honey and added some from the little pot that Molly had provided. She passed him his cup, he thanked her, and then they sat in unexpected and awkward silence for the better part of a minute, alternately sipping their tea and staring at it.

Rachel broke first, good manners dictating that she offer something up for discussion. The problem was that there were so many subjects she simply wanted to avoid. Weather seemed a safe choice.

"Do you anticipate rain for your ride out tomorrow?"

"No. Sid Walker—do you know who he is?" When Rachel looked as if she was trying to put a face to the name, he explained. "Well, Sid's been mining since the discovery of placer silver, and his wife, his children, and his grandchildren can't get him to give it up, even though his rheumatism about cripples him when the weather turns. I saw him this morning as he was heading out, and he was walking tall. No hint of a limp. That's as good a guarantee of fair weather as you're likely to get."

"I see. Does he know he's the town barometer?"

"Sure he does. He enjoys some notoriety for his aches and pains; it probably helps make them a bit more tolerable."

Wyatt regarded Rachel more closely. "You were feeling a little sorry for him, weren't you?"

She nodded faintly, surprised he'd noticed. "A little," she said. "I didn't look at it in the same light you did, that the notoriety might help him tolerate his pain, it just seemed that people might be taking unfair advantage."

"That bothers you?"

"Of course it does."

Behind the rim of his cup, Wyatt smiled. "Good."

Rachel bristled. "I'm so pleased that you approve."

"You're touchy this afternoon," he observed mildly. "I was only thinking that it's a fine quality in a lawman's wife." This last comment found its mark, just as he knew it would. He watched, fascinated, as a tide of pink rose from beneath the collar of her dress and flushed her face all the way to her scalp. "You look like you've got something to say."

Rachel caught herself before she let her temper fly. It was the gleam of amusement in his eyes that penetrated her red haze. If she was touchy, it was because he was deliberately provoking her and enjoying himself a mite too much at her expense.

"I'm sure you have a very good idea what I want to say," she told him. "So there's no point in repeating it, is there?"

"Never knew a woman to spare a lecture, especially one she could deliver to a man. You must be as close to perfect as your sex comes." He set his teacup down and leaned forward, his cool blue eyes intent. "So, about that marriage . . ."

She stared right back at him. "No."

Wyatt accepted her refusal with perfect equanimity. He picked up his cup, sat back again, and regarded Rachel with an easy smile. "It was worth broaching the subject since you seem hell-bent on avoiding it."

"Molly's in the other room. I don't want her to overhear."

"Molly can't hear a thing over the waltz she's playing in her head. She's probably got Johnny Winslow spinning in circles about now."

"Well, you put the idea there."

Wyatt took a breath and let it out slowly. "My point is," he said with deliberation, "that she isn't paying us any attention and that we can talk about anything. Now, you haven't asked me a word about that appointment with the lawyer. I promised to arrange it for you, and so I have."

"That was days ago. I expected to hear from you before now." She waited to see if he would offer an explanation for his tardiness, but he didn't appear to think one was necessary. "When is the appointment?" she asked.

"Friday."

"I thought you said he wasn't busy."

"I didn't say he wasn't busy. I said he didn't have a lot of lawyering to do. And I'm not available to go with you tomorrow because I make my rounds. Biscuits, remember?" She gave him a sharp look, so he imagined she hadn't forgotten again. "Do you want to keep the appointment or not?"

She nodded shortly. "What time should I be there, and where am I going?"

"You know where the land office is?" When she indicated that she did, he went on. "He has space above it. Stairs are on the outside of the building. I'll meet you there—around eleven—if that's all right."

"I'd prefer it. There's no point in raising speculation by being seen going in together."

"That's what I figured you'd say. Lucky for us that Molly's so closemouthed."

"Yes, indeed."

Wyatt finished his tea and set his cup aside, then got to his feet. "Don't go accepting Abe's proposal before you talk to the lawyer."

"Already asked and answered," she said. It struck her as

odd that he hadn't heard about it since Abe Dishman caught her unawares in Caldwell's Apothecary yesterday morning. He'd made Mr. Caldwell stop explaining the digestive and regulatory benefits of cod liver oil just long enough to ask for her hand, then waved to the druggist to continue when she politely turned him down. "He wasn't feeling well," she told Wyatt. "So it wasn't his finest proposal. I think he was relieved to have it done and out of the way for this month."

"That's all right, then."

"I didn't turn him down because of an agreement *you* signed, so don't fool yourself into thinking it had anything to do with you."

"It never entered my mind." He gave her a nod. "Friday at eleven. Crack of dawn tomorrow. And I'll set your basket of linens at the back door so Molly takes them when she leaves or trips over them on her way out."

Rachel waited until she heard him go to return the tray to the kitchen. Molly was folding dish towels at the table when she walked in. The girl was still so lost in her own thoughts that she started when Rachel addressed her.

"You gave me a fright," she said, clutching a towel to her breast. She smiled and added, teasing, "Good thing I don't have a pair of shears."

"Yes, well, the less said about that the better."

"Oh, you don't have to worry that I'll mention it," said Molly. "Folks wouldn't believe me anyway."

"Why wouldn't they? You're trustworthy."

"Sure I am, but it'd be hard for them to imagine you takin' on the sheriff. He's got a reputation, you know, way outside Reidsville."

"I didn't know. What sort of reputation?"

Molly shrugged her narrow shoulders. "He's a fast draw, for one thing."

"Molly," Rachel chided, "he doesn't even wear a gun."

"Not so much around here, no, but when he has to go out he does. He's a member of the Rocky Mountain Detective Association, so he makes use of it."

Though she was certain it wasn't Molly's intention, Rachel was mortified by her own ignorance. "What's the Rocky Mountain Detectives?"

"Detective Association," Molly corrected. "Mr. Cook out of Denver thought it up a whole lot of years ago. I guess you gotta be from around here to know about it." She thought about that a moment and added, "Or come around here and break the law. That'd make you take notice of them real quick."

"What do they do exactly?"

Molly began to fold towels again. "Well, they're not vigilantes, I know that for sure. Every one of them's a lawman somewhere here in Colorado. They started out goin' after rustlers. There's still some of that, you might be surprised to hear, but on account of Reidsville not being a cattle town, it's never been much of a problem. Still, Sheriff Cooper and that no-account Beatty boy do their fare share to help out. That's the idea of the detectives' association, you see. The lawmen work together to catch criminals and bring them around."

"Around to what?"

"Justice, I suppose. Wouldn't you think that'd be the right thing to do?"

"Yes," said Rachel. "I think it would." She sat at the table and began helping Molly fold. "How long has Sheriff Cooper been a member of the association?"

"I couldn't say exactly. You'd have to ask him. He can tell you all about it. In fact, he just got back from riding with them. Would have thought you knew that. He's been gone a couple or three days."

Rachel wasn't certain why she felt compelled to offer an excuse. "I've hardly left the house," she said, and because it sounded so inadequate, she added, "I went out once, yesterday, to Caldwell's for headache powders." That was perfectly true. She'd suffered a headache off and on since Wyatt had shown her the contract. If Molly thought it was odd that she explained herself, the girl was kind enough not to mention it.

"Why did he have to leave?" she asked.

"My father says it was a robbery out Georgetown way. That's in Clear Creek County, not so far from here. There's a mining operation, but the town's not wild the way Denver gets. Seems some folks thought it needed a little excitement and decided to hold up the bank. They got silver and cash for their effort and went straight out of town."

"I imagine your father was one of the first to learn about it."

"Yes, indeed," Molly said proudly. "He got the message over the wire and took it directly to the sheriff. I don't suppose it was more than a couple of flicks of a dog's tail later that Sheriff Cooper was riding out of town."

"He went alone?"

She nodded. "He and his deputy don't usually ride together. Besides, that was Monday, now that I think on it, and Will Beatty was taking his turn scoutin' around the town. He wasn't even here when the message came."

"Do you know what happened?"

Molly looked up from folding. "You saw him for the first time since he's been back, the same as I did. I think he must've cleaned up before he came by because his duster was the only thing that showed he'd been out on the trails. It was so covered with bits of the mountains and brush that I took the liberty of shaking it out while he was talkin' to you. Maybe I shouldn't have, but—"

Rachel put one hand over Molly's, reassuring her. "You did fine, Molly. I'm sure he appreciated it."

"I wish I'd thought to give him some of those sand tarts you have with his tea. He probably would've liked those. He was most likely hungry."

"I should have thought of it. I'm not used to having guests." She withdrew her hand and squared off a stack of folded towels. "So what does it mean that he's back?"

"Oh, that's a sure sign that he and the others caught the thieves. I've never known him to come back until he does. Usually takes longer, though, so these fellows must have been just about as stupid as they come."

"You're probably right."

"That's not to take anything away from the sheriff," Molly said quickly. "He's smart as a whip. Knows somethin' about nearly everything."

"Mmm."

Molly gathered the towels and put them away. "I need to scrub the floor now," she said. She picked up one of the chairs and turned it over to place the seat on the tabletop, then paused as she came to stand behind another. "I was a little surprised to see him come by today." She didn't meet Rachel's eye, but let her fingers run back and forth over the uppermost chair rail. "Knowin' how you don't much like people droppin' by, and what with him keepin' what my father calls *his own counsel*, it seemed something out of the ordinary."

"It was."

"Yes, indeed," said Molly.

Rachel had no difficulty reading the turn that Molly's mind was taking. It was there in her shy and secretive smile and definitely needed to be nipped. She rose from her chair and put it on the tabletop. "You take care of the floor, Molly, I'll take care of the rest."

Rachel was ready with four flaky, golden-brown biscuits bundled in a blue kerchief when Wyatt rode up. She stepped out the back door onto the stoop and held it out to him.

"They're still warm," he said, feeling the heat of them through his gloves.

"Of course they are, I just made them."

"I would have been pleased to have day-old biscuits."

"Then hand them back and come by for them tomorrow."

His eyes narrowed. "Not a chance." Cradling the biscuits as carefully as he would a bundle of a baby, Wyatt slipped them into his saddlebag.

"Aren't you going to eat one now, while it's warm?"

"Do you have an extra?"

Sighing, Rachel did an about-face and returned to the house. She emerged a few moments later with a biscuit resting in her open palm. "Did you hear me say you're impossible?"

"No, did you?" He plucked the biscuit out of her hand and bit into it. "Oh, Lord," he mumbled as it melted in his mouth. "You have to marry me."

In answer, Rachel went back inside the house and didn't come out again.

Rachel worked on Miss Roseanne LaRosa's gown up until the moment she had to leave to meet Wyatt at the lawyer's office. She was satisfied with her progress and almost certain she could have it done by Sunday, which meant she'd receive an extra commission for finishing it early. The madam was willing to pay for fine work, and she was willing to pay even more to have the first opportunity to display it.

Giving the mannequin a last critical look, Rachel made a few adjustments to the gown's pleated panels, then forced herself to abandon it. She hurried through the house, grabbing her bonnet and jacket, and finished putting them on as she was walking across the flagstones.

The land office was directly opposite Morrison's Emporium. Rachel was just turning the corner when she recognized the approaching whistle of the No. 473 engine. The depot was situated beyond the edge of the last buildings in town, but the lumbering engine, with its boiler pushed to maximum pressure to complete the climb, made its presence felt through a low vibration that rolled down the sidewalk. Rachel knew that if the No. 473 was on time, and she had no reason to suspect that it wasn't, then she was already late for her meeting.

She merely waved to Abe and Ned when they called out to her and increased her pace across the street. The stairs took a turn to the second floor, and she only paused once to take a breath and collect herself before she finished the final part of her climb with her dignity and her bonnet intact.

She hesitated outside the door marked LAW OFFICE in bold black lettering and wondered if she should knock or simply walk in. The decision was taken away from her when she recognized Wyatt Cooper's voice telling her to come in, and she belatedly realized her silhouette must have been visible through the frosted glass that was fitted in the upper half of the door.

Prepared to apologize for her tardiness, Rachel stepped into the office. The words never made it as far as her lips when she saw that not only was Wyatt alone in the room, but he was sitting behind the desk looking very much at ease there, which, of course, he was. If his supremely relaxed posture and the mere suggestion of a smile hadn't tipped her to the truth, his clothes did. Gone was the softly scarred brown leather vest, the pale blue chambray shirt, and the buff-colored denim trousers that he generally combined for everyday wear. He'd even removed his scuffed leather boots. In place of what was familiar to her, he was now wearing a black brushed wool jacket, a dark emerald, single-breasted vest with a top pocket, and a starched white shirt with an equally stiff collar. She couldn't see his trousers or his shoes, but she'd seen enough lawyers in her years with the Maddoxes to know that they would be black and black.

She shut the door. Hard. "You're the lawyer I'm meeting?"

"Mmm."

"I don't believe this." She looked around. There were all the accoutrements that one expected to find in a lawyer's place of business: law books, file cabinets, several chairs for clients, a table for spreading out documents, a large desk, and a framed diploma. Rachel walked straight to the diploma. "Harvard Law? You graduated from Harvard Law?"

She slowly lowered herself into one of the round-armed chairs and stared at him. "Isn't it illegal?"

He frowned. "To graduate from law school?"

"No, to forge a diploma. Shouldn't you arrest yourself?"

Wyatt took pity on her and gave her time to acclimate while he tidied up his desk. He gathered some papers he'd been reviewing while waiting for her and stacked them to one side; then he opened the folder that held the documents she wanted to see and laid them flat in front of him.

"It's real, isn't it?" she said finally.

"Yes."

"Why didn't you tell me you were the lawyer I'd be meeting when we were at the bank?"

He regarded her frankly, seriously. "Because it was one too many pieces of information. You had a lot to consider already, and you'd only learned about Maddox's death the day before."

"So you were being kind."

"I thought I was. Perhaps I misjudged."

"And what was your excuse yesterday?"

Wyatt didn't flinch from her accusing stare. "I don't have one."

Rachel wondered if he knew that his admission was what kept her in her seat. "Are you any good?"

"Pardon?"

"Are you any good?" she repeated. "As a lawyer?"

"Third in my class."

"That only means you were a good student."

"A sound distinction. The truth is I don't practice much, so it's open to debate whether I'm fair or middlin'. I know the law, though, and I can answer your questions about the incorporation of the mine. If you don't trust me—and from your expression, I'm guessing that's a distinct possibility—I'll get someone from Denver to come up and meet with you. In the meantime, you can also talk to Henry Longabach or Sidney Walker. They represent the town's interests in matters of the mine."

Rachel didn't say anything immediately. In her mind, she leaned both for and against him and wasn't satisfied with any position that put her so off balance. "Why did you go to law school?" she asked finally.

Wyatt picked up a pencil and sat back in his chair. He rolled the pencil between his fingertips as he continued to look at her steadily. "Fair enough," he said quietly. "My grandfather wanted me to go. My mother, also. For a lot of reasons I believed I owed it to them. It didn't take, though. I'm more my father's son, and I've made peace with that, even if I still have family back in Boston who hasn't."

Rachel realized he had given her his confession, so she was careful not to throw it back at him. "You wanted to be a good son."

Wyatt said nothing.

"Well," Rachel said before the silence became overlong and painfully uncomfortable, "I'd be obliged if you'd show me the papers."

His gaze narrowed. "You're certain?"

"Oddly, I am."

Wyatt used the pencil to point to the table. "It will be easier to review things over there."

Once they were seated, he passed the articles of incorporation to Rachel as well as the substantiating documentation. She looked it all over, recognizing Clinton Maddox's initials scrawled in the corner of every page and his bold signature on the final one. She also read the names Matthew Cooper, Sidney Walker, and Henry Longabach. Matthew's name had been succeeded by Wyatt's on the attached addendum.

Everything was outlined as Wyatt had explained to her. There were provisions for dissolution and perpetuation and the articles clearly delineated the process by which the single partners could name their heirs but still retain the right to rename them if the heirs predeceased them. If no one was named prior to their death, then their shares became part of their estate.

"Wouldn't it have been better if the shares went to the town when either Mr. Maddox or your father died?"

"Henry and Sid, speaking for the miners, wanted that, but back when this was signed they weren't in a position to keep the mine going without Mr. Maddox's backing. If he had died early on, they would have owned shares that were essentially worthless because the placer silver would have played out. They needed the railroad, so they were willing to bet that Maddox's heirs would bring it to Reidsville if Maddox didn't live long enough to do it."

"What about your father? It says here that his heir was Nicholas Cooper, not you."

"There were a whole lot of reasons he wanted to keep his share for the family. He intended for my oldest brother to have it, but Nick died at Chickamauga in sixty-three, and my older brothers—Jonas and Andrew—well, it didn't suit my father to pass it on to them. That's how it became mine."

Rachel searched through the documents until she found the paper that passed Matthew Cooper's share to his son Wyatt. "So Mr. Maddox was just following procedure when he wrote up the separate document naming me his heir."

"Yes. He added the paragraphs about the spur because he wanted you to have it to protect the town's interests." He paused. "And your own, of course."

"And yours?"

"I imagine he gave me a thought. In spite of their differences, Maddox and my father respected each other, and Maddox was fair in his dealings with all of us. He didn't want to see any of us lose out because his grandson was now in a position to inherit. Things would have been different if Benson had lived. With Foster . . ." He let the idea lie there and watched Rachel's dark eyes cloud and her mouth slowly reshape itself into a tight, worried line.

Not unsympathetic, he said, "It's a lot to think about."

Uneasy laughter bubbled to her lips at the understatement. It was difficult to form a coherent thought. She couldn't imagine herself taking the step that the terms of the contract outlined. "How long?" she asked.

"How long?"

Rachel nodded. "Until I have to make a decision? I didn't read anything about how much time I had. Did I miss it?"

"You didn't miss it," Wyatt told her. "It's implied. The half share of the mine is already yours. I need to draw up some new papers, amend the articles, and get your signature on them. Henry and Sid will witness everything, of course, but all of that is more or less a formality. You own half of the mine whether I get the papers done today or three months from now."

"Yes," she said. "Thank you. I think I'm clear on that." She absently raised one hand and laid her fingers just below the hollow of her throat. Unaware of the gesture, she began to massage the area gently.

"Are you all right?" asked Wyatt. "Should I open a window?"

"What? Oh." She realized what she was doing. "Yes, please, if it's no bother, some fresh air would be good."

Wyatt rose and went to the window. He drew the curtains aside and lifted the sash. "Do you think you should come over here where you can take advantage of it?"

She wasn't sure she would be steady on her feet. As a compromise, she shifted in her chair so she was angled toward the open window. "I'll be fine sitting here."

Wyatt didn't argue the point, but he made another offer. "I can't make you anything to drink here, but I can go downstairs and get you coffee. Sam Walker—that's one of Sid's boys—always has some brewing in the land office."

"No, really, I'm fine. I don't need anything."

Wyatt wasn't convinced, but then his view of her pale features was not the one she had. He returned to his seat. "I haven't yet explained about the timing of all of this," he said. "Are you certain you want to hear it now?"

"I'm quite certain I don't," she said, "but I can't imagine that changing, so you might as well tell me while I'm sitting down."

Honesty and a thread of humor ran through her words. Wyatt appreciated both. "As I mentioned," he said. "The timeline is implied. Once control of the C & C passes to Foster, the spur to Reidsville—that includes the land, the depot in town, and the two main engines, six helper units, and twelve freight cars that regularly make the run—will become part of his holdings. That takes more time than you think. There's upwards of three weeks before all of that's finalized and made public."

"Three weeks?" A breath hitched in Rachel's throat. "That's no time at all."

"I understand that's true from your perspective. To Foster, though, it will seem like an eternity. That's the way his grandfather wanted it. He placed certain conditions in his will that will slow the process of Foster taking actual ownership. For instance, Foster has to demonstrate that he has the support of three of the five largest financial institutions in California by securing loans to expand C & C to the Northwest."

"He'll hate that."

"No doubt, but if he wants full control, he'll have to answer to Maddox's lawyers or risk having to share control with a board of directors."

"He'll waste time, digging in his heels."

"That's why I said there's upwards of three weeks."

Rachel considered that; then her regard turned suspicious. "You had a hand in drafting Mr. Maddox's will, didn't you? You couldn't know some of this without having seen it."

"Not a whole hand," he said. "A couple of fingers. When he knew what he wanted to do about the mine and the spur, that's when he requested some assistance from me. His lawyers did the lion's share, and I wasn't privy to the final document."

"Then you can't be sure it was written up the way you suggested."

"You knew him. Did he ever back away from his word?"

Rachel didn't have to think about it. "No," she said quietly. "He never did."

"There you go."

"That doesn't mean he didn't mislead me. He promised me that I would be cared for, and you and I are talking now because this is his crazy quilt way of keeping his word. Admit it, Sheriff, this is just about the most peculiar and preposterous thing that's ever been proposed."

"Wyatt," he said mildly. "And you sure have a gift for alliteration."

Rachel sighed. She had to admit he had a knack for settling her nerves. It was proving to be a good thing, since he was also the one who jangled them. She stared down at her hands in her lap and finished collecting herself. "I don't know what to do."

"Understandable."

"I don't want the town to suffer."

"I never imagined that you would."

She nodded almost imperceptibly. "I like the people I've met here. I know I haven't gone out of my way to be sociable, but no one's held it against me. Whenever I've stepped out, I've been welcomed."

"Live and let live. That'd be what passes for common sense around here."

Rachel turned her head and glanced at him. "Maybe. And maybe that's your influence."

"Nope. That'd be my father's legacy."

And he was his father's son. She didn't want to cite the commonalities. Instead, she said, "I've noticed that not many strangers arrive to settle here. They pay a visit to the hotel, test the card play, see what recommends the town to its inhabitants, but they don't stay. I may well be the last new person to come to Reidsville and put down roots. And that was fifteen, almost sixteen, months ago."

"Could be you're right. I'd have to think about it."

She knew very well that he didn't have to give it any thought at all. He was aware of everything that happened in the town—sooner or later. "Reidsville is a bit of a secret, isn't it?"

"I don't know what you mean. We're on all the maps drawn up in the last twenty-five years. We have a regular train run, a telegraph line, and a first-rate hotel with hot and cold running water that advertises in the Denver papers. People come and go all the time."

"But they go. I don't think staying is encouraged." She didn't expect him to answer, and he didn't. "It's all right. I think it has something to do with the mine, so I'll just leave it at that."

"All right," Wyatt said agreeably. "Suit yourself."

Rachel gathered the documents into an orderly stack and took her time reviewing them yet again. She was aware of Wyatt's extraordinary patience with her; then she forgot about him entirely as she delved through the partnership agreement.

When she finished, she passed the papers to him and rested

her folded hands on the table. "If I marry you, does it mean that my share of the mine becomes your share?"

"No. At least it doesn't have to. You can choose anyone you like to draw up the papers so you can trust that your interests are protected."

"What about my other property? You told me I owned the house outright. Does it become yours?"

"I don't want it."

"That isn't what I asked. Does marriage in this state make it yours?"

"It doesn't have to. You can make provisions to see that it doesn't. The laws here allow for it."

"You know that for a fact?"

"I looked it up." He shrugged. "In your place, it's something I would want to know. You might not realize it, but Colorado only entered the union six years ago. The general assembly was a bit more forward thinking when it drafted its constitution and started setting its laws."

"Can I vote?"

"No."

She snorted delicately. "Then you're not as progressive as Wyoming, and it's still a territory."

Careful to reveal none of the humor he found in her chastisement, he said, "I stand corrected."

Rachel waved that aside as unimportant. "I have some money in the bank, almost all of it from Mr. Maddox, and I want to be sure it remains in my control."

"Of course. It's part of your holdings. Drawing this up won't be hard to do, since I won't be arguing any point of it."

She considered that. "So, if I understand what you're telling me, what belongs to me now will still belong to me after marriage."

"With the proper documents in place, yes."

"And, by the same token, you can retain what is yours."

Wyatt didn't answer immediately. He had a feeling she was about to make a move that he hadn't anticipated. Wariness made the skin at the back of his neck tingle. "Yes," he said slowly. "I suppose I could arrange to keep what belongs to me now."

"Just like with the mine," she said, "we wouldn't be compelled to combine our property."

"Well, yes, but—" He stopped because she was shaking her head sharply and had leaned toward him a fraction to lend emphasis to her appeal.

"Hear me out," she said quickly. "It could be a partnership. A marriage in name, but a partnership in fact. There's no reason we couldn't live entirely separately. It meets the requirements set forth by Mr. Maddox, and—"

"But not the intent," said Wyatt.

"Perhaps not," she conceded, "but it follows to the letter the terms he laid out, and right now that's about as much control over my life as I'm willing to surrender."

Wyatt heard her voice tremble at the end with the passion she felt for her argument. He saw that she must have heard it, too, because she took a slow, deep breath and took pains to let it out in measured beats. Her eyes were made suddenly luminous by a wash of tears that only her hard resolve kept at bay.

"You seem like you're a good man, Sher—" She caught herself. "Wyatt," she amended. "I don't know anyone who doesn't think you do right by them. Your willingness to enter into that agreement with Mr. Maddox proves it. You'd sacrifice your own chance to meet someone in a more traditional manner, court her properly, and settle down to—"

"I was married before," he said quietly, cutting her off. He held her surprised, slightly wounded gaze and was reminded that for all her sharp wit and determination, this business had left her fragile. "I wouldn't have let you sign anything without knowing. I just didn't figure I would be telling you now."

Rachel pressed her fingertips together and offered up an apologetic, mildly embarrassed smile. "I should have known."

"I don't know why you think that."

"I'm not going to place a dozen compliments in easy reach of you."

One corner of his mouth lifted a fraction. "Fair enough."

"Thank you for telling me, though. It doesn't really change anything, but it's nice to know something about you since you seem to know so much about me."

"I didn't choose to tell you now because you needed to know on general principle. I told you because it *does* change things."

"I don't see how."

"I'm not making a sacrifice," he said. "I met my wife in the traditional way. I fell in love, courted her, proposed, married, and . . ." He paused, surprised that he could still be moved off center by the sudden, powerful tug of memories. "And settled down."

Rachel continued to regard him expectantly, but after a few moments, she realized he'd said all he intended to on the matter. "But you're not married any longer."

"No. She died. It was seven years ago first of the month."

"I'm sorry."

He nodded curtly. "It's the past."

Not from where Rachel was sitting. She'd glimpsed a hollowness in his eyes, and although he recovered quickly, banishing it thoroughly, she knew what she had seen. There was still emptiness there. It was not lost on her that he'd signed Mr. Maddox's proposal not long after his wife died. He couldn't have been thinking clearly—and perhaps he still wasn't—all his opinions to the contrary. "So you're telling me that you don't need—or want—another opportunity to find a wife of your own choosing."

"That's what I'm saying. Maddox's contract was acceptable

to me, and his intent that we should have a conventional marriage didn't cause me to hesitate."

"Can you appreciate it's somewhat different for me?"

"I can. I do. But it's not my place to apologize for something I didn't set into motion."

Rachel stood abruptly, placed the flat of her hands hard on the table, and stared at Wyatt from the advantage of height. In carefully measured tones, she said, "If you expect a marriage that is generally defined by the usual practices of sharing a common dwelling, coital relations, and raising children together, then I must tell you that I won't agree to it, but if you're willing to accept marriage as the partnership I described earlier, I can give you my answer."

Wyatt's blue eyes narrowed in a glance that would have pinned lesser opponents to the wall. Rachel held fast, and he was forced to judge that what she'd just delivered was no threat but a serious statement of intent. He'd be a fool to test her now.

Wyatt recognized he was faced with making his first real sacrifice since signing the agreement with Clinton Maddox. He couldn't blame Maddox for it, because even that crafty robber baron hadn't foreseen this end. Who could have predicted that his journeyman opponent Rachel Bailey would so cleverly maneuver him into checkmate?

There was no point in standing up, not when she'd effectively cut him off at the knees. Wyatt simply extended his hand toward her and offered a shake. "I'll take your terms, Rachel, and God help us both."

Chapter Five

The papers were drawn up four days later. Rachel and Wyatt were married the following evening, just about the time the first stars were appearing in the eastern sky. It was a private ceremony, conducted in Wyatt's law office by a judge he brought in from Denver because Reidsville didn't have its own, and two witnesses, Henry Longabach and Sid Walker. Sid needed help to negotiate the stairs because a storm was brewing somewhere distant, he warned them, and accordingly, his rheumatism made him as stiff as the stays in his wife's corset. He'd thought up that comparison just for Rachel, he told her, because what with her being a seamstress and all, she knew about corsets. Usually, he went on to explain before anyone realized where he was going with his story, he just told the fellers he was as stiff as their wakin'-up peckers.

Rachel managed a weak smile while blushing to the roots of her hair. It was the only reason there was color in her face when she and Wyatt exchanged vows.

She wore a simply cut gown with a modest train that she had fashioned several years earlier. The fabric was a pale, creamy satin printed with clusters of pink poppies. The long sleeves were close-fitting except at the shoulder, where she had introduced and gathered more fabric to create a puffed look. Wyatt had admired her gown. She'd said nothing about his pin-striped lawyer suit.

Although their reasons were different, they were in agreement that the fewer people who knew about the wedding, the better. For Rachel, the decision was a practical one. Since they were going to live separately, and go about their business in the same manner, announcing they were married would only muddy the waters, not clear them. For Wyatt, the decision was more personal. He didn't like the vision of himself as an object of pity because his wife did not want him in her bed.

Henry and Sid were literally sworn to secrecy by the judge, and the judge, being from out of town, had no reason to talk about it to anyone. That left Wyatt and Rachel to hold their own, and neither of them could imagine the circumstances that would persuade them to reveal their marriage.

What Henry and Sid passed along at the town meeting scheduled to follow the ceremony, was that Rachel Bailey had inherited Clinton Maddox's share of the mine and the Calico Spur to boot. Sid, in particular, liked the "Calico Spur to boot" part of his speech, and found several ways to fit it in. Henry was more stolid imparting the news to the miners and business owners. He acknowledged all the speculation about the fate of the town since Clinton Maddox's passing and knew that calling for a town meeting had raised hope and anxiety in equal measure. Now he was free to tell them what had taken place in the shareholders' meeting in Wyatt Cooper's office.

And then he solemnly introduced Rachel Bailey, just as if everyone in Reidsville didn't already know who she was.

The applause was thunderous and prolonged. Rachel was embarrassed to accept this greeting and approval when she'd done nothing but put her signature to some papers. And marry Wyatt, of course.

When Henry and Sid gestured to her to join them on the

dais, she shook her head. No one had breathed a word that she would be expected to speak. Wyatt, standing just behind her, put his hands on the small of her back and gave her a gentle, but firm, push.

"Reassure them," he whispered. "That's all they want."

Having no idea what she might say, but certain she didn't want Wyatt to nudge her again with his fingertips, Rachel accepted Henry and Sid's outstretched hands to assist her on the step up to the platform. This gesture was seen by the crowd as largely symbolic of the new partnership, and when Wyatt joined them a moment later, the Commodore Hotel, which always hosted the town meetings, actually shook with the clapping and foot stomping that was a demonstration of the town's approbation.

Henry called for order before the timbers collapsed on them, and when it was quiet enough to begin, he motioned Rachel forward. She stood flanked by Henry and Sid with Wyatt just off to one side, but he was the one she looked to when her confidence flagged. He made a small nudging motion with his hand and oddly enough, it was just the encouragement she needed.

"Good day, everyone," she began. "I'm Rachel Bailey." There were some hoots of approval, especially from the miners who had taken leave of their shift at last minute and crowded in the back. "Mr. Clinton Maddox was a dear friend to my family, and a person of great influence in my life. I know your genuine mourning of his passing has been mixed with considerable personal concerns. It seems to me to be a perfectly natural response when the fortunes of all of us, and therefore the town, are irrevocably linked to the fortunes of the California and Colorado Railroad."

This engendered a low hum of agreement throughout the crowd, and Rachel continued. "I hope you are heartened to learn that Mr. Maddox shared your concerns and made plans years before his death to see that Reidsville could continue to operate its mine and its businesses and provide a decent livelihood for its hardworking citizens."

There was another round of generous applause, and for the first time, Rachel believed she could see this through. "You all know that Clinton Maddox was a man of vision who knew how to seize an opportunity, or create one. He was, first and foremost, a financier who took the stake his father gave him and increased it a hundredfold in his own lifetime. He didn't do this by being a generous man in his business interests or by making financial decisions based on putting money in the public's pockets. Yet, through his self-interest, he invested in all of you and continues to do so by passing ownership of the Calico Spur to me. It is now also in my interest, as a member of your community, to see that the spur survives, that the No. 473 and the Admiral engines continue to make their runs, and that goods and services and gold and silver are transported to Denver and from there to all points east and west. I promise you that Mr. Maddox did not misjudge my resolve to honor his legacy and profit equally from the gift and the responsibility he's given me."

Rachel looked over the crowd, picking out faces that she knew better than others. She saw Mrs. Longabach regarding her with a fulsome smile, and Ann Marie Easter nodding her head at just the right moments. Ed Kennedy had his thick arms folded across his chest and his head cocked to one side, consideration in his posture. Abe Dishman and Ned Beaumont traded elbow jabs now and again when they liked what she had to say. Mr. Caldwell and Jacob Reston regarded her with rapt attention, and sometime during her speech Artie Showalter began making notes for the weekly paper he published.

"I can assure you," Rachel concluded, "that when I profit from Clinton Maddox's trust, so will you."

The applause went from thunderous to deafening. People

who were not already on their feet, jumped to them. Having no clear idea how she was supposed to remove herself, Rachel glanced back at Wyatt a bit uneasily. He stopped clapping long enough to discreetly wave her over. She eased from between the bookends that were Henry and Sid and sidled up to Wyatt.

Out of sight of the crowd, Wyatt found Rachel's fingers and gave them a squeeze. He half expected her to yank her hand away, but whether it was the chance of being observed or the fact that she truly needed the support, she left her fingers in his until he released her.

Henry and Sid were looking at him expectantly. "Just reassure them," Rachel whispered, lightly mocking him with the same encouragement he'd given her. He took his place front and center and the crowd settled almost immediately.

"You folks who remember my father know that he was a cynic and a contrarian, but if Matthew Cooper were here this evening, he'd tell you that he never made a mistake trusting Clinton Maddox's instincts. And Maddox? Now, he would tell you that it was never instinct that guided him, but experience and study and knowing what he wanted to achieve.

"The other day I overheard Estella Longabach telling Gracie Showalter that Miss Rachel Bailey has a gift. And if Estella doesn't mind, I'd like to tell you what she meant by that." He looked directly at Estella, received her firm nod of approval, and then addressed the town. "Everyone here knows that Mrs. Longabach operates her restaurant with a firm hand on the till. Isn't that right, Henry?"

Henry nodded hard, rousing laughter from his friends and neighbors.

"And she's not generally of a temperament that allows her to spend money on what she considers frivolous things."

"That's right," Henry said. "She's real practical that way." There were murmurs of agreement and approval in the audience, and even Estella was nodding her head.

"That's why," Wyatt continued, "when Rachel Bailey was able to sell her, not one, not two, but *three* new gowns at a single sitting, all of them to be cut from the finest fabrics, Mrs. Longabach was moved to tell her friend Gracie that Miss Bailey surely has a gift."

"*Three* gowns, Estella?" Henry called from the dais. "Good God, wife, did you take leave of your senses?"

Estella pursed her lips, gave him a dismissive wave, and otherwise ignored him.

When the crowd had finished having their laugh at Henry's expense, literally, Wyatt concluded making his point. "It seems to me that when Estella was speaking of Miss Bailey's gift she was remarking in the same way my father did about Mr. Maddox's instincts. We all know that like finds like. It's the nature of things. So is it any wonder that Mr. Maddox saw in Rachel Bailey the very things that made him a successful entrepreneur? Experience. Study. And knowledge of what she wants to achieve. Time will prove he was right to name her to succeed him as our partner in the mine and as owner of the Calico Spur."

It was going on ten o'clock before Rachel and Wyatt were able to make their exit from the hotel. The crowd was slow to disperse, partly because people wanted to seek Rachel out and voice their confidence, and partly because they were waiting for Nigel Pennyworth, the English émigré who owned the Commodore and liked to be called Sir Nigel, to open his wine cellar and stores of fine brandy to further their celebration. Sir Nigel held out as long as he could but surrendered to the inevitable when the miners began making noises about blasting a tunnel to the cellar.

Wyatt saw Rachel shiver when she stepped out of the hotel. "Here," he said, removing his pin-striped jacket. "Take this. It was considerably warmer when we were at my office." She didn't object, so he fit it across her shoulders like a cape. He moved protectively to the outside of the sidewalk and waited for her to fall into step. "You did well this evening."

"I don't know," she said honestly. "There was a moment there when I felt as if I were running for office."

"Maybe you should. Ted Easter's coming up for reelection soon. Could be Reidsville could use a new mayor."

"Could be I want to be sheriff." Rachel gave him a sideways glance, but away from the hotel lamps, it was too dark to make out his features except in shadowed profile. "What? You don't think I could?"

"Actually, I was thinking what a tough opponent you'd be." She laughed. "That's kind of you."

"Not kind. Truthful."

For reasons she didn't entirely understand or care to consider at length, Rachel was warmed more thoroughly by his response than by the jacket he'd flung across her shoulders. "Did you know we would have to speak tonight?"

"I thought it might be expected, yes."

"I wished you'd warned me."

"Are you certain? I thought it would have been cruel."

She considered that and nodded slowly. "You're right. It would have been." It was too easy to imagine herself collapsing under the weight of the anticipation. "Do you remember exchanging vows?" she asked. "I've been trying to, but I don't think I was there."

He chuckled. "You were. And you said your part beautifully."

"Did I? I've been wondering. How did you do?"

"I was very definite, I think you'd say. Firm."

"That's good." They walked in silence for a while, the celebratory noises from the hotel fading behind them with each step. "It was a little bit like a wedding reception, wasn't it? Back at the Commodore, I mean, with everyone offering their congratulations. I found myself thinking it a couple of times, which surprised me since I can barely recall the wedding."

"We could go back and tell everyone," he said. "Make it a reception in fact."

There was a hint of sadness in her answering smile. "No, we couldn't."

"All right," Wyatt said. "But I feel certain that Sir Nigel was holding back his finest liquor right up until the end. Could be a marriage announcement would get him to bring it out."

The edge of sad regret vanished from her smile as laughter lifted the corners of her mouth. "Perish the thought," she said in a fair imitation of Nigel Pennyworth's clipped West End accents. "There is no doubt that you would spend the rest of the night rounding up inebriates and putting a period to the worst sort of licentious behavior."

"In other words," Wyatt said dryly, "picking up drunks and stopping orgies."

"Precisely."

"Well, then, I suppose that walking out and moving on was the right choice."

Rachel found herself wishing, perversely, that he'd offer more argument. She disgusted herself with that thinking, so she didn't dare share the drift of her thoughts with Wyatt. She said instead, "How did you come to overhear Mrs. Longabach talking about me to Gracie Showalter?"

He shrugged. "The same as I overhear most things. In passing."

"Meaning they were passing you."

"That's right."

"Do you sit outside your office in the dead of winter?"

"Lord, no. There's not much in the way of traffic. I get around, though, checking on people, listening to what they find interesting." Wyatt took Rachel's elbow as they came upon the end of the sidewalk at Aspen Street, and she teetered on the edge. "Whoa. Careful." He helped her down, and they turned the corner together. "Do you feel the storm in the air?"

She held her step and breathed deeply. An icy undercurrent almost stole the breath back. She pulled Wyatt's jacket more closely around her and wondered that he seemed impervious to the cold. "Is it snow coming, do you think?"

"Between eight and fourteen inches, according to Sid's shoulder and his left knee."

"Goodness. What if his right knee joins the band?"

"Blizzard."

Rachel laughed at Wyatt's wry tone. "I suppose we'd better hope that he doesn't cripple up any more."

Wyatt thrust his hands into his trousers. "That's a fact." Since they'd turned the corner, the wind had been whipping the sleeves of his shirt and beating against his vest. He put his head into the wind to keep his hat on as they approached Rachel's flagstone walk. Aware that her steps were slowing and that she was preparing to bid him good night, Wyatt interceded on his own behalf.

"I'll walk you to your door," he said.

"It's not—" She stopped because she was already talking to his back, and she had to hurry to keep up with him. He wasn't so much escorting her as leading the advance. She caught up to him just as they reached the porch.

"I wouldn't mind a cup of coffee." He insinuated himself between Rachel and the door and managed to get his hand on the knob first. "And maybe a bite to eat. I didn't have dinner this evening."

She was prepared to argue the lateness of the hour when her own empty stomach betrayed her by rumbling loudly. Sighing heavily, she offered a reluctant invitation. "I have some chicken soup I could heat, and there's three-quarters of a loaf of Mrs. Easter's brown bread in the larder."

"That sounds just about perfect," he said, and began opening the door.

Rachel couldn't resist asking, "What would make it perfect?"

"Hot water gingerbread."

That stopped Rachel in her tracks. She turned on him, hands on her hips. "How could you possibly know that I have—"

Wyatt didn't give himself a moment to think about it, or a moment to think better of it. He simply reacted to the wide doelike eyes and generously shaped mouth tilted in his direction and backed her up against the wall in her foyer, where he kissed her until survival dictated he come up for air.

Rachel's hands were no longer on her hips; her palms lay flat against the wall behind her. Beneath her fingertips she could feel the velvet flocking of the paper. She stared at Wyatt, more wide-eyed than she had been before. Her lips felt vaguely swollen, and her breath came through their narrow parting.

"You won't do that again," she said, though she wasn't clear if she was asking or telling him.

Wyatt removed his hat and laid it on the entry table. "We'll see." He looked over her flushed features, gauged the likelihood that she was going to slap him as small, then wandered off to the kitchen in search of sustenance for the other part of him that needed it.

Rachel followed at a slower pace and gave him a wide berth in her own kitchen. She let him fire up the stove while she retrieved the crock of soup and the bread from the larder. She also set out squares of gingerbread and topped them with a dollop of applesauce.

"You're not spending the night," she said.

"Can't. I have to ride out tomorrow." He glanced over at her, lifting an eyebrow. "Thursday," he reminded her.

"You're not invited anyway."

"I understand."

"Good." She nodded once for emphasis and pushed the

crock across the table so it was within his reach. She wrapped the bread in a moist towel and set it down for him to place in the warming pan. With studied casualness, she asked, "Should you be going anywhere if there's a storm coming?"

"It's my job."

"But you could be riding into it."

"Oh, I expect it'll be here by morning. It could hold me up from getting an early start, so you shouldn't worry if I'm late coming to collect my biscuits."

"I won't be worrying. I'll be sleeping. It's every *other* Thursday, remember? I gave them to you last week."

"So I'll have to wait until Sunday?"

"That's right."

"You're a hard woman, Rachel Bailey," he said, stirring the soup. "But I'll be damned if you don't have the softest lips."

Rachel almost dropped the bowls that she was carrying to the table. "Don't do that," she said softly, recovering her composure. "It's not fair. Not fair to either one of us."

He turned away from the stove and saw that Rachel's expressive features were set gravely, the line of her mouth no longer curved but grim. "I don't necessarily share your opinion."

"It's not what we agreed to," she said.

"I don't remember that we discussed it." He tapped the large wooden spoon he was holding against the pot, then set it down in the spoon stand. He folded his arms across his chest and mirrored her humorless mien. "Sharing the same dwelling. Coital relations. Raising children together. Those were what you said defined a marriage. We never talked about what defined our partnership."

"Do you push your tongue in Sid Walker's mouth?"

For a moment, Wyatt could only stare at her. "That's a hell of a thing to say, Rachel." He absently rubbed his chest where it felt as if she'd been jabbing him with her fingertip.

She didn't back down. "It was a question, and you haven't answered it."

"For God's sake, let it be."

"Because it's uncomfortable for you?"

He turned back to the stove and checked the bread in the warming pan. "What do you really want, Rachel? An apology?"

"An explanation."

He shut the door on the oven again and glanced at her over his shoulder. "An explanation for what exactly? The kiss? The comment about your lips?"

"For the way you're acting toward me. You never kissed me before, never hinted that you wanted to, and now you—"

"Never hinted?" His eyebrows lifted. "You didn't want to see it." Shaking his head, he stepped away from the stove and without a word left the kitchen entirely. When he returned a few minutes later, it was with a bottle of whiskey from the sideboard. He took out a glass from the cupboard, raised it slightly in Rachel's direction to ask her if she wanted to join him. When she shook her head, he shrugged, and set the glass on the table.

Rachel watched him uncork the bottle and pour himself enough for a swallow. He let it sit there on the table while he gave the soup another stir and sip and judged it hot enough to serve. That's when she realized it wasn't his intent to get drunk. "I'll get the bread," she said as he began to ladle soup into their bowls.

He paused and tossed her a towel to keep her from burning her hands. "It looks good," he said. "Is this Mrs. Longabach's or did you make it yourself?"

"Mine, more or less. Molly helped. I was . . . well, I had a lot on my mind. I think she was afraid I was going to slice a finger when I was cutting the carrots, so she took over." She set the warm bread on a small cutting board and carried it to the table. Wyatt had already pushed her bowl of soup in place, so she sat down and spread a napkin on her lap.

She waited for Wyatt to sit before she picked up her spoon and dipped it for her first taste. When she gasped and began waving a hand in front of her open mouth, he was on his feet immediately.

Rachel sucked in a breath and accepted the glass that Wyatt thrust in her hand. "Thank you," she said when she could speak again. "I wasn't expecting that. Not at all. It didn't seem to have bothered you in the least." It was exactly what she might have said about the kiss they'd shared. Realizing it, Rachel felt her cheeks grow warm, but she didn't turn away from Wyatt's frank study of her reaction.

"I want you to respect me," she said quietly.

"And you don't think I do?" He shook his head. "It was a kiss, Rachel. You were standing there with your hands on your hips, exasperated certainly, but amused, too, or at least I thought so, and I gave in to an impulse. It doesn't mean I don't respect you. It means I find you attractive."

"Now," she said.

"What?" He frowned and reached for his glass of whiskey. He held it in his hand, fingers curled around it, but he didn't drink.

"Now," she repeated. "You find me attractive now, but nothing's changed except that we signed some documents. I've been living in Reidsville for almost a year and a half, and you barely said a hundred words to me until you brought me the message that Mr. Maddox had died. You never tried to kiss me before or thought you needed to offer a comment about my mouth. What am I supposed to believe except that you've decided I'm convenient?"

Wyatt was glad he hadn't taken a drink because sputtering it across the table would have been a waste of good whiskey. "Convenient? I'd be hard pressed to name a single thing about you that makes you convenient, and if there was such a single thing, it definitely wouldn't be your mouth." He knew a moment's satisfaction watching Rachel snap that particular body part closed. "I've been watching you glide up and down the sidewalk since you came to town, so I guess I know better than you how long I've found you a pleasure to look at. As for not talking to you much, it seemed to me it was mutual. You didn't exactly go out of your way to be friendly to me, and I had to wonder why, when you sure as hell were friendly to Abe and Ned and Henry and Johnny and even that no-account Beatty boy."

When Rachel looked as if she wanted to speak, Wyatt set her back in her chair with a stony, no-quarter-given glance. "Besides that, there was the matter of my contract with Maddox. He was pretty clear that there could be no marriage until he was dead, so what would have been the point of putting myself in your path any more than I did? Hell, Rachel, you crossed the street two blocks before you ever got to my office. What was I supposed to make of that?"

Wyatt gave her a moment to digest all that he'd just fed her and then pointed to her soup, her spoon, and her mouth, which was slightly agape once more. "Your food's getting cold. Eat up."

He didn't know which one of them was more surprised when she did.

The following day, Rachel alternated working on Mrs. Longabach's moss-green skirt and jacket and cutting out a muslin pattern for Molly's party dress. Several times she discovered herself standing at the window in her workroom, looking out at the curtain of falling snow, with no clear memory of having abandoned her needle and thread. She knew what had caused her mind to wander, but it was a new experience, and somewhat disconcerting, to find that the rest of her could follow so easily.

Rachel wished she'd sent Wyatt off with biscuits this morning. Really, what was the point that she'd been trying to make? That she could be firm? Not taken advantage of? It made her feel petty now that he'd ridden out without something warm from her kitchen. She was well aware that he'd been managing his regular Thursday rides for years with no assistance from her, but that knowledge didn't particularly soothe her.

Sid Walker's aching shoulder and swollen left knee had accurately predicted the accumulation. When Rachel woke, there were already four inches of snow on the ground and a drift upwards of a foot at her back door. She swept the path to the spring and brought another load of wood to the mudroom. She kept the kitchen stove fired up and started a fire in the parlor. The house was tolerably warm, but she was aware that outside the wind was becoming increasingly more forceful.

No doubt Wyatt would be startled to learn that she'd spent any part of her day worrying about him. She certainly hadn't left him with the impression that she cared what happened when they parted company the night before. Not that she'd wished him ill, but without a word crossing her lips, she had communicated that she most definitely wished him gone.

He overwhelmed her. And frightened her.

Neither settled well. She'd spent years neatly sidestepping confrontation when she could, standing firm when she had to, and pushing back when she was pushed, but the lessons learned weren't so easily applied when her opponent was Wyatt Cooper.

Rachel pressed her forehead to the window and closed her eyes. It occurred to her that it was her own thinking that she needed to challenge. How would things be different if she stopped thinking of Wyatt as an opponent? Life experience didn't allow for her to treat him as other than an adversary from the moment of their introduction, but the view from where she stood now made her question if it had ever been truly necessary.

She liked him. Admitting that didn't make her easy, and she forced herself to consider why that should be. She had no difficulty saying the same thing about Johnny Winslow or Mr. Showalter or even the persistent Abe Dishman, so what made it seem uncomfortably like a revelation when she applied those words to Wyatt Cooper?

Rachel's insides twisted and a certain wariness for the direction of her thoughts made her turn away from the window. She told herself there was nothing she could do for him either through worry or reflection, and yet, some niggling voice at the back of her mind would not be quieted and called her coward.

It was Saturday afternoon before Rachel left her house for anything but water or wood. The cloud cover had vanished by daybreak and the sun was bright in a cerulean sky. There was eight inches of snow on the ground, but that was the least amount Sid had predicted and merely a minor accumulation compared to what she'd witnessed the year before. With clear skies overhead, it seemed possible that this first round of snow would disappear before they were visited by what she understood was real winter in the Rockies.

Shopkeepers had cleared the sidewalks in front of their businesses, which made walking easy once she reached the main street. The first thing she noticed was that Ned and Abe had moved their checkers game from the sidewalk to somewhere indoors. The second thing was the empty chair in front of the sheriff's office.

She went straight to the telegraph office to check on the delivery of packages that she'd ordered weeks earlier and to show Artie Showalter the sketch of the dress she intended for

Molly. She didn't mention to him that she'd already measured Molly and cut the pattern.

"I'll be honest with you, Miss Bailey," Artie said. "I like it just fine, but my wife is the one who generally makes these decisions. She's in the back right now. Why don't I get her? She'll be real pleased to see this."

Rachel's heart sank, not so much for herself, but for Molly. "Of course," she said, revealing none of her trepidation. "How wonderful that she's here."

Artie glanced at the sketch again, nodded thoughtfully, then pushed his spectacles up the bridge of his nose and called for his wife. "Gracie, come out of there. Miss Bailey's got something to show you that I think you're going to fancy."

A musical, vaguely girlish giggle came from the backroom. Rachel tried not to show her surprise when she realized the source of it was Grace Showalter. A moment later, Gracie emerged, barely suppressing her coquettish laughter, her round face flushed and happily set.

Rachel's own welcoming smile faded ever so slightly when she saw what had brought about Mrs. Showalter's remarkably cheerful mood. As Wyatt Cooper appeared from behind Gracie, Rachel offered him a polite nod. "Sheriff."

"Miss Bailey." His nod matched hers for reserve.

Artie Showalter observed the exchange and said, "Could be that folks seeing you trade nods like you have a rusty hinge in your neck might get to thinking all those friendly words Wednesday night were only for show. Just something to keep in mind when you cross paths out and about. People are liable to get a little nervous if the mine's two biggest shareholders are already at odds."

Gracie's keen eyes darted from Rachel to Wyatt, but she was a moment too late to see what her husband had. Rachel's warm smile remained welcoming, and Wyatt's glance was appreciative. She looked back at her husband and simply shook her head. "Where do you get these notions, Arthur? It's a constant mystery to me that a man who can make sense of dits and dots coming across a wire can't make sense of the starts and stops of the human heart. Wyatt was just telling me about the gown Miss Bailey wants to make for Molly. And I can tell you that he was nothing but complimentary of her talents, same as Estella was when she spoke to me."

Grace reached out a hand toward Rachel and patted her forearm. "Wyatt couldn't say enough good things about you, Miss Bailey. I don't think I recall that he's ever been so admiring in his comments."

Wyatt stepped up to Artie's desk and hitched his hip on one corner. He offered Gracie a wry smile. "You're confusing what I said about that slice of red velvet cake you gave me with my remarks about Miss Bailey's work."

"Go on with you," she said, though she flushed prettily at this mention of her prize-winning cake. "I know what I heard."

Wyatt shrugged. When Gracie's attention strayed momentarily to her mildly bewildered husband, Wyatt surreptitiously gestured to the sketch in Rachel's hand, urging her to seize the opportunity to discuss Molly's dress.

Rachel laid her hand over Gracie's, which was still resting on her forearm. "Mrs. Showalter? I'd like to show you my idea for—"

"What? Oh, yes. Your drawing." She gave Rachel's arm a gentle squeeze. "Of course I want to see it." She began tugging gently, maneuvering Rachel to the rear of her husband's office. "Let's go in the back, shall we? There's really no point in talking about it with the men around. Wyatt's seen it and approved, and Arthur's seen it and immediately called for me." By the time she finished speaking, she was ushering Rachel through the door. "Don't mind the look of the place," she said. "I came in to bring Arthur his lunch and help him with . . ."

Wyatt and Artie exchanged knowing glances as Gracie's voice trailed off after she firmly shut the door behind her.

"Looks like Gracie's got Rachel in her grip," said Wyatt. "How long do you suppose they'll be?"

"She had you back there upwards of half an hour. Could be about that long again."

"Enough time, then, for me to get to the depot and meet the Admiral. It's running on schedule, right?"

"I haven't heard differently," Artie said. "Some special reason you want to meet the train?"

"I think it's time for the crew to meet Miss Bailey. They work for her now." He stood and got his coat and hat from the rack by the door. "You sent word to them like I asked, didn't you?"

"Wednesday night. Right after the town meeting."

"Any word back?"

Artie chuckled. "You know, Wyatt, if you hadn't let my wife tempt you away with the promise of food, you'd already have that answer." He held up a finger. "Wait. I have the reply right here somewhere." He moved things around on his desk, opened a couple of drawers, then found what he wanted among a stack of notes that were under a pyrite rock he kept around as a paperweight. "Here you go," he said. "This is what I sent."

Wyatt took it and read: SPUR INDEPENDENT PER C MADDOX INSTRUCTIONS STOP FOSTER OUT STOP. "You have a way for getting to the heart of the matter."

He sighed and poked at his spectacles again. "Not according to my wife." He gave Wyatt a second piece of paper. "Here's the reply."

Wyatt read: HURRAH. He glanced at Artie and grinned. "Pithy."

"That's John Clay for you," he said. "The man just wants to drive his train and be left alone. He's got no use for Foster Maddox, so I'm thinking that when he meets Miss Bailey the least of his concerns is going to be that she's a woman."

"We'll see," Wyatt said, less certain. "I better be going. It can't hurt to clear the track, so to speak."

"You should have warned me," Rachel said, looking sharply at Wyatt. They were seated at a relatively private table in the Commodore Hotel's dining room. There were only a few other diners and two large potted ferns shielded them from being immediately noticed. Still, Rachel kept her voice low. It was her color that remained high.

After getting Grace Showalter's blessing for Molly's dress and assuring her that she'd come by with the latest fashion book and her sketch pad, Rachel walked back into the telegraph office and was dismayed to find it crowded with the Admiral's solemn-faced and silent crew. She'd swallowed her discomfort and pressed forward after Wyatt made the introductions, assuring the men that she meant to learn about the operation and make certain it remained as efficient and profitable as it had under Clinton Maddox's direction.

Immediately following that meeting, Wyatt had whisked her away from the Showalters and taken advantage of the first sanctuary offered—in this case, the Commodore—and escorted her inside before she'd built up a full head of steam.

"To waylay me like that." Her jaw tightened just thinking about it. "That was unconscionable. Did it occur to you that I had given the matter of an introduction some thought, and had determined that I would greet the 473 and the Admiral this very week? Can you imagine why I hadn't already done so?"

Wyatt knew the value of silence in response to a rhetorical question, so he simply waited for her to continue.

"It will shock you, I believe, but I wanted to speak to you first." She touched three fingers delicately to the side of her head. "Whatever was I thinking? Oh, yes, apparently I thought you might be helpful in facilitating the introduction, rather like you did this afternoon, except it would have been with my full knowledge!" She'd heard her voice rising steadily but was unable to rein it in. The urge was there to look around and see if she'd drawn the attention of any of the other diners or the wait staff. She managed to resist it for herself, but asked quietly, "Are people looking at us?"

Wyatt's eyes shifted from Rachel to points elsewhere in the room. He paused several times and nodded politely in the direction of the other tables.

"You're pretending," she said under her breath. "There's not a person looking at you."

Lifting one eyebrow, Wyatt asked, "Are you sure?" He watched a muscle jump in her jaw, but she didn't take the bait he dangled. "Do you want an explanation, or do you want to continue your harangue?" In the event it was going to be the second choice, Wyatt picked up the menu card and began reading.

"What are you doing?" she said, teeth clenched.

He regarded her over the top of the card, his expression perfectly bland. "I'm trying to decide between the potato soup with the boiled fowl or the Irish stew with dumplings."

"I want your explanation."

Wyatt placed the menu at the corner of the table and motioned to the waiter. "You only had to say so," he said pleasantly. "Do you know what you want?"

Because she hadn't glanced at the menu since they'd been seated, Rachel shook her head.

"I'll have the vegetable soup," Wyatt told the waiter. "The veal cutlets. Mashed potatoes and the creamed limas. Coffee."

Rachel stared at him. "I thought you were trying to decide between . . . oh, never mind." She gave her menu to the waiter. "Tea, please. Honey, not sugar." When the waiter was gone, she turned back to Wyatt and found him looking at her as if she were completely unfathomable. "I had red velvet cake with Mrs. Showalter," she said. "And a sandwich before I left home. Tea will suit me fine, thank you. But, please, you go ahead and eat like a bear coming out of hibernation."

"I wasn't going to order dessert," he said.

It was his mildly defensive tone that almost roused Rachel's smile. She caught herself, certain nothing good could come of giving him an inch. "The explanation?" she said.

"I've been out of town since I left Thursday to make my rounds. I only got back a couple of hours ago." He saw her sit back in her chair as if pressed there by invisible hands. Her chin came up a notch and her brow puckered. Her expression suggested to him that, as he suspected, she hadn't known he'd been gone so long. "I wondered if you asked after me," he said. "I guess I know the answer."

"Today is the first I've been out of the house."

"And today's the first I've been inside one."

She took in a sharp breath, steadied herself, and said evenly, "I'm not going to feel sorry for you."

"I should hope not."

She would not tell him how many times she'd stood at the window looking out for him. It was a gesture with no meaning. She hadn't left home to inquire after him. Concern that her questions would bring unwanted attention from others or be misinterpreted by him had kept her silent—and alone. "Are you all right?"

"I will be once I get something in my belly besides Gracie's cake."

Rachel flushed a little. "What happened that you were gone so long?"

"I was tracking and got stranded above the tree line. It took me a while to work my way back to where I could make a shelter and hunker down."

"What were you tracking?"

"Two men on horseback without a brain between them.

Their mule had enough sense to stay down on the mountain."
His smile was self-mocking. "Of course, I don't like to think
what it says about me that I went after them."

Rachel had been thinking the same thing. "And?" she
asked.

"And . . ." His voice softened; then he collected himself
and shrugged. "I found them. I thought they might have been
up to something, but it turned out they were just stupid."

It was then that Rachel understood *how* he'd found them.
Knowing they'd died on the mountain, she let it be. The waiter's
arrival was timely. He set vegetable soup in front of Wyatt and
served her tea from a silver teapot that he left on the table.

Wyatt spooned a few mouthfuls to remove the sharp edge
of hunger; then he offered the explanation that Rachel had
asked for. "I never set out to overstep, but I'm not denying
that's what I did. When I got back into town, I took just enough
time to clean up before I went to see Artie. I needed him to
send a message off to the Denver marshal about the bodies. I
had some information about the men that might help someone
identify them. While I was there I mentioned the dress you
wanted to make for Molly and asked Artie if he'd seen the
sketch. Since he hadn't, I took it on myself to tell him about it.
He liked the idea just fine, but he knows his wife, and since
Gracie was making a mess reorganizing his back room, he
sent me in to give her something else to think about. I sure as
hell didn't expect you to show up, and you looked like I was
the last person you wanted to see, so I figured it was just a
chance meeting. When you went back with Gracie, I noticed
the time, realized the Admiral would be arriving soon, and
seized an opportunity for you to meet John Clay and his crew
since Artie assured me you hadn't gotten around to it yet."

Rachel felt as if Wyatt had pulled the stopper on her anger.
By the time he was finished, she was drained. Shaking her
head, she sighed deeply. "I don't know how you do it, but you

make it sound almost reasonable." She gestured to him to start eating again. "I can acquit you of making plans to take over my life, but that's only because you don't make plans. You just seize the moment. I don't very much like surprises, Wyatt. I hope you'll remember and respect that."

He acknowledged this with a short nod. "That doesn't mean it won't happen again."

"I'm fairly certain the same can be said of my temper."

Wyatt paused with his spoon halfway to his mouth. "That's not exactly a deterrent," he said. "I like your temper."

Rachel frowned at him. "I find that vaguely insulting."

"Maybe I should say, 'I like your passion.'"

"I'm sure you shouldn't."

Wyatt's meal arrived. He protected his soup bowl from being whisked away by shielding it with his arm and permitted the waiter to arrange the rest of his meal around it.

Watching him, Rachel was moved to smile. She wished she could take back her comment about him eating like a bear coming out of hibernation. "Tomorrow's Sunday," she said. When this didn't elicit the response she'd hoped for, she added, "I was wondering if you'd join me after church? I could make chicken and gravy over biscuits."

"Are you bribing me? I'm an officer of the law, remember."

"I'm not certain it can properly be called a bribe when you blackmailed me in the first place."

"Oh, that's right."

Although he said it as if he'd forgotten about their deal, she was certain that just the opposite was true. "I'd like to talk to you about the Calico Spur. We're both aware I don't know the first thing about its operation or what I should be doing. I don't mind saying that I need your help."

"Then you probably want to invite John Clay. Sam Kirby, too. He's the engineer for the 473."

"If you think that would be best," she said evenly, careful not to show her disappointment. "Will you arrange it?"

"I have to go back to see Artie, so I'll take care of it. About one o'clock?"

"That should be fine."

"You're frowning," Wyatt said as she poured herself some more tea. "What's wrong?"

She waved aside his concern. "I was just thinking that we can't eat comfortably in my kitchen. I'll have to rearrange my workroom so we can use the dining table."

"Then let's not meet there. We can get together right here at the Commodore. Sir Nigel has a private dining room. It won't be a problem." He cut into his veal. "In fact, it will be better if we meet here. We'll be observed coming together, and that's good for people to see. They'll know you're serious about operating the spur."

"Do you think so?" she asked, doubtful.

"I'll talk to Nigel on my way out. It shouldn't be—" He stopped because Rachel was shaking her head. "We're not talking about the same thing, are we?"

"You said that people will know I'm serious about operating the spur."

"Well, aren't you?"

"How do I know?" She pushed her teacup out of the way and set her folded hands on the tabletop. "I admitted to you that I don't know the first thing about it. What if I hear things at the meeting that assure me that I'm unsuited for this responsibility?"

"You don't have to drive the trains yourself, you know."

Rachel gave him a sour look. "I know that."

"I didn't mean it in the literal sense."

"You have to speak more plainly. I didn't go to Harvard."

Wyatt finished chewing, swallowed, and set his fork down. "I'm ignoring that snipe because I figure you're pretty damn scared, and I notice when you get scared you tend to go after me with whatever's handy."

Rachel had the grace to flush. "You're right. I'm sorry. But I *am* scared. I make *dresses*, Wyatt."

"So you do. And if I needed one, I wouldn't try making it myself. I'd hire you to do it from start to finish. Is that plain enough?"

It was. "You're suggesting I hire someone to manage the operation."

"That's right. That's what Clinton Maddox did."

"Well, why aren't we inviting that person to the meeting?"

"Because Ben Cromwell manages more than just the spur. He's in charge of operations from Denver north to Cheyenne and east to Omaha. The popular thought is that he's going to remain Foster's man."

Rachel felt her insides clench. "How long before Foster Maddox realizes that I own the spur?"

"Not long, I expect. Not now. Cromwell's likely going to send him word by telegraph before the formal documents reach him in Sacramento."

"But that means he's going to learn I'm here."

Wyatt's eyes narrowed sharply on Rachel's pale features. "What is it that I still don't know?"

She took a deep breath and forced herself to release it slowly. "Foster Maddox is the reason I left California."

Chapter Six

Rachel pushed her chair back from the table and stood. Her movement was so abrupt that upon standing she teetered. Uncertain suddenly, she looked around, trying to think of what had become of her coat and bonnet. Her fingers worked nervously at her sides, curling and uncurling, pulsing to the same frantic beat of her heart.

"Rachel?" Wyatt put down his fork and tossed his napkin on the table. He started to rise. "Rachel. You need to breathe. You're going to—" He watched her suck in a deep draught of air. It was enough to keep her standing until he was at her side.

"What is it?" he asked, cupping her elbow. He took a step forward to shield her from the other diners. They were now attracting the attention she wanted to avoid.

"I want to go," she said, her voice low and urgent. "I want to go home."

"All right."

She tried to step around him, but he gripped her elbow more firmly and moved to completely block her path. "What are you doing?" she asked.

Wyatt held his ground. "What are *you* doing? You're hardly steady on your feet, Rachel, and you're pale as death." With his free hand, he grasped one of hers. "Your fingers are like ice. You're so close to fainting that I don't think you can go five steps without dropping to your knees."

The truth of that was forced on her as she was overcome by deep, abiding cold. Unable to help herself, she began to shiver. A wave of dread washed over her, and she felt as if the ground were shifting under her feet. She tilted her face in Wyatt's direction and made a silent appeal.

Wyatt eased Rachel into her chair just as her eyes rolled back in her head. Still shielding her, he got the waiter's attention and motioned him over. "Miss Bailey's not feeling well," he said quietly. "Do you have some smelling salts?"

"No. Nothing like that here. Is it something she ate? Sir Nigel will—"

"Jim. She drank tea, remember? She probably *should* have eaten. Listen, the last thing she wants is to bring about anyone's notice. Can you get me some horseradish sauce?"

"Horseradish?" The concern etched in his sharply drawn features eased as he realized what Wyatt intended. "Sure. That should do the trick."

Wyatt managed to keep Rachel from slumping down so far in the chair that she slid out of it. He glanced behind him a couple of times and saw that the interest that Rachel had attracted when she'd jumped up from the table was gone now. He believed that if anyone realized she had fainted, there would have been at least one offer of assistance.

When Jim Moody arrived with a salt dish piled high with horseradish sauce, Wyatt thanked him, reminded him to be discreet, then sent him away. Wyatt gently raised Rachel's head and held the dish directly under her nose. It required less time than he'd imagined. Her head jerked, her nose crinkled, and her eyes opened wide in alarm.

"Better," Wyatt said, removing the dish and setting it on the table well away from her. "It goes straight to your head, doesn't it?" He watched Rachel try to make sense of what had happened. "Just sit there. Don't move." He made certain she was firmly planted in her chair before he returned to his own.

"Rachel. Look at me." When she did, he gave her an encouraging nod. "I'm going to get our things and bring them here. Once we have our coats on, I'll escort you out and home. I can get a buggy, if you don't think you can walk."

She hesitated a moment, testing the idea in her mind. "I can walk," she said. "I *can*."

He remained skeptical but gave in. "Very well. It's probably better that you do."

"I really fainted?"

Wyatt could tell she found the idea distasteful. It wasn't so much that she was embarrassed by it, but that she was disappointed. "You did. Your first time?"

She nodded. "Did anyone . . . that is, um, did I . . ." Her eyes darted to the right where the other diners sat.

"No one noticed, Rachel. You didn't make a sound."

"Then you must have stopped me from hitting the floor."

"I did. Put you directly in your chair. Jim knows, naturally."

"Jim?"

"Jim Moody, our waiter. He helped me out. The next time we eat here together, one of us will have to order the braised beef. It's served with horseradish sauce."

Rachel managed a weak smile. "Moody? Is he Virginia Moody's brother?"

"Cousin." He leaned forward. "If you're able to ask about those kinds of connections, I'd say you have your feet under you again. Give me a moment. I'll be right back." He excused himself and went for their coats.

Rachel drank a little bit of tea while she waited. It was still warm enough to make an impression on her deeply cold insides. When Wyatt returned, she stood on her own to prove to both of them that she could do it. She let him help her into her cashmere-lined pelisse but managed her bonnet by herself. She found her leather gloves in her pocket and pulled them on. "What about our bill?"

"Jim knows to put it on my room charge."

"Your room charge?"

He regarded her oddly for a moment. "I live here, Rachel."

"You have a room at the Commodore?"

"A suite, actually. Where did you think I lived?"

She didn't know that she'd ever thought about it. "Behind your office."

"That would be the jail."

"Oh. Of course."

"My deputy lives above the office, so you're not far off supposing I might have lived there." He took her arm and noticed that she didn't try to pull away. As they left the dining room, he asked, "Have you ever seen the rooms here?"

"No."

"Well, Clinton Maddox told me they compare favorably to what's available in places like New York and Chicago, though naturally Sir Nigel's inspiration was London. The beds in every room are solid walnut. The chairs and chaises in my suite are just about the quality of what you have in your own home, and the washstands all have marble tops. No one could believe it when he said he was putting in hot and cold taps, but that's just what he did. He brought in Irish linen and Wedgwood china to promote his idea that refinement wasn't beyond the reach of a little mining town. Just in case anyone didn't get the idea, he put up elaborately framed paintings of London landmarks in the upstairs hallways. Cambridge. Parliament. Westminster Abbey. That wasn't too bad, but then he decided to add the portraits." Wyatt rolled his eyes, prompting Rachel to smile as they reached the sidewalk.

"Are they family portraits?" she asked, falling in with him. He had dropped his hand away from her elbow, and the realization that she missed him being so close almost made her stumble. She caught herself quickly, and the hesitation in her step was corrected easily. "His family, I mean."

"To hear him talk, they are. But I think he might be stretching the truth. I can't find a resemblance, and I've looked them all over."

"You've lived at the Commodore a long time?"

He nodded. "I was the second tenant. Nigel being the first. He finished construction on it in seventy-five. It came at the right time for me."

Rachel remembered that his wife had died seven years ago. She understood his reference to the timeliness of his move. She didn't comment on it, though. Instead, she asked, "Where did you live before that?"

"Two streets over on Miller. It was my father's house; then it became mine—and Sylvie's, of course."

"Sylvie. That was your wife's name?"

"Sylvianna, really. Even she thought it was pretentious. She preferred Sylvia, but she didn't mind Sylvie." Wyatt's steps slowed in front of Longabach's as movement inside the restaurant caught his attention. "Just a moment," he told Rachel. He poked his head in the door and looked inquiringly at Henry, who was standing behind the counter at the cash register. "You all right, Henry? You better not let Estella catch you with your hand in the till."

"Ain't that the truth?" said Henry. His hand remained precisely where it was.

Wyatt glanced around the restaurant. Ned and Abe were sitting at a corner table hunched over their checker play. They returned his greeting but didn't offer conversation as they made several moves in quick succession. Jacob Reston and his senior teller occupied another table. Jake lifted his hand in acknowledgment, while Andy Miller didn't look up from spooning split pea soup. Adele Brownlee smiled coyly at him when his glance came her way. She was sitting alone at her table.

"I've got Miss Bailey with me," Wyatt said. "She took a little sick while she was out, so I'm walking her home. I don't expect I'll be more than half an hour or so. Tell Estella that I got a good whiff of her shortcake while I was by, and I'll be back for some directly. Good day, folks." He ducked back out of the restaurant and shut the door. "We can go," he told her.

"I can't believe you're going back for shortcake," she said.

He shrugged. "Have you tasted Estella's shortcake?"

"No."

"Then you have no idea."

Rachel started to say something, but Wyatt suddenly took hold of her arm and hustled her into the sheltered entrance of Caldwell's Apothecary. The only time he'd ever been that forceful or urgent was when he'd pressed her against the wall in her own home and kissed her so hard her knees folded. It was incomprehensible to her that he meant to do the same thing now, but her knees went a little weak in anticipation of it.

"Listen to me, Rachel." Wyatt took hold of both of her arms above the elbow and squeezed. If she had any thought of struggling, his narrow-eyed glance ensured that she didn't. "I want you to do exactly what I say. Nothing more or less. Do you understand?"

Heart hammering, she offered a faint nod.

"Tell Chet I need him to go to my office and get Will. He should not run past Longabach's, but walk normally, then get to Will as quickly as he can. He's to tell Will that the bank's about to be robbed, and that the thief is in Longabach's moving things along. Will needs to strap on, bring my gun and my rifle, and meet me in the alley. Do you have that?"

"Yes."

"All of it?"

"Yes."

He looked hard into her eyes and saw it was true. "You stay in Caldwell's. Don't you leave until I come for you, and stay away from the windows. Do you hear me?"

She nodded.

He did kiss her then. Once. Hard. Then he opened the door to Caldwell's for her and urged her inside. He took a shortcut between Caldwell's and the emporium to get to the alley. Everyone had heard him say he'd be gone about half an hour, so that gave the thief a window for making his move. Wyatt didn't expect anyone to come out the back, but he couldn't loiter on the sidewalk waiting for the thief, or thieves, to come out the front. Depending on whether the would-be robber was one of the locals—which Wyatt sincerely doubted—it was likely that he wouldn't be recognized on sight as the sheriff. The problem was, Wyatt couldn't count on Jake Reston or Andy Miller not to do something that would give him away, and Wyatt fully expected Jake and Andy to be accompanying the thief to the bank.

On a Saturday afternoon, having the bank manager and one of the tellers around was about the only way a person was going to get into the bank without causing a ruckus. The citizens of Reidsville didn't much care for a ruckus. Their sheriff, Wyatt reminded himself as he waited for his deputy, liked it even less.

Will came loping up the alley within the five minutes that Wyatt had allotted him. Chester Caldwell followed about twenty paces back, puffing heavily as he tried to keep pace with a man who was half his age, and more telling, half his weight.

"You go back in your store, Chet," Wyatt told him. "Take care of your customers."

"Miss Bailey's all alone in there."

"Then look out for her." He strapped on the gun belt Will brought for him. "She'll likely get to thinking there's something she can do. If you can't talk her out of it, drug her. I mean it, Chet. If she shows up anywhere near the trouble, I swear I'll hunt you down and shoot you."

Caldwell nodded, his fleshy second chin wobbling under his first.

"Good. Go on. Get out of here." As Chet lumbered off, Wyatt addressed Will Beatty. "I think we have to assume there are at least two of them. One was hiding behind the counter by the register when I poked my head in the restaurant. I'm fairly certain there was someone else in the kitchen because neither Johnny nor Estella was out front, and it was Henry at the till."

"Damn," Will said. He handed Wyatt the Henry rifle. "Cleaned and ready."

Wyatt nodded. "Thanks." He jerked his chin in the direction of the bank. "There're too many people in Longabach's to take them there. I want us to set up in the bank and wait for them to come. That sound good to you?"

"Sure does."

They turned simultaneously and began striding down the alley toward the bank.

"How are they getting in?" asked Will.

"Jake and Andy were in the restaurant. I think the plan is to force them to open the doors."

"All right. And how are we getting in?"

"I've got the key to the back."

Will's stride shortened, then paused a beat. He caught himself and hurried to catch up. "You do? Have you always?"

"Yes. And yes."

"How come I never knew that? It's because I'm that no-account Beatty boy, isn't it?"

"It's because there was never any reason that you should know. Until now."

"Does Mr. Reston know?"

"Yes, he knows. Of course he knows."

"I was just asking."

"Well, if you tell anyone, don't be surprised if I shoot you."

Will glanced over at Wyatt's starkly set profile. In spite of that hard look, Will couldn't help grinning. "You sure seem like you're fixin' to shoot somebody today."

"Could be that I am. Make certain it's not you."

When they reached the rear of the bank, Wyatt tipped his hat forward so it fell upside down in his palm. He ran his index finger under the hatband until he found the key. "You didn't see that," he said.

"No, sir."

Wyatt carefully inserted it into the lock and turned. He opened the door quietly and stepped inside, motioning Will to follow. They paused on the threshold and listened. Except for their breathing, there was no sound.

Satisfied, Wyatt nodded once. He replaced the key and his hat, then hefted his rifle. "Shut the door," he whispered. "No noise."

"You're certain they're coming?" asked Will, following closely on Wyatt's heels as they started up a short set of stairs.

"About as certain as I can be. You understand, they didn't exactly confide their plans to me." Wyatt was fairly certain his deputy caught the edge of sarcasm because Will refrained from more questions. The lobby was empty when they reached it. Wyatt motioned Will toward the room at the rear. "There will be nothing in the tellers' drawers now. Everything's been moved to the safe. If all their concentration is on getting to it, as I believe it will be, then we'll wait for them back there." He pointed to the tellers' cages. "We'll let them move toward the safe and come at them from behind."

Will nodded and moved into position, ducking down just as voices could be heard approaching from the street. Wyatt followed. They exchanged glances, indicating they were each prepared, and held their crouch, sheltered by the polished oak cabinetry that separated the tellers from their customers.

Unable to benefit from sight, they cocked their heads in the direction of the front of the bank and listened.

The front door rattled as it was tried first without benefit of the key. There was a pause, then the twist of the knob and the grating sound of hinges that required a bead of oil. Footsteps followed.

It was difficult to separate them at first, but as they moved across the floor, Wyatt counted three distinct patterns. Had someone remained behind at the door? Until Wyatt put his head up, or some words were exchanged, there was no way to be sure. He hoped for words. Raising his head above the cage had definite risks.

"The safe is behind that door," Jacob Reston said. His voice was reedy, with a slight tremor.

"Then what are you stopping for? You haven't forgotten the way, have you?"

Behind the cage, Wyatt held up his index finger so Will could see it, indicating this would designate the first thief if there was more than one.

"I n-need to get the key," he said. "I don't have it on me. I keep it in my desk. That's over there."

"At the window? I bet you like to be seen there, don't you?"

"I never thought about it."

"Go on. Get the key if you don't want me to shoot the lock."

Jacob crossed to his desk, unlocked the middle drawer with a key that he did carry, and opened it. He removed the key he needed, then responded to the urging of the pearl-handled Colt that was aimed in his direction and started to cross the floor. The 7½-inch barrel of the Colt followed his progress.

"He's moving like molasses. Shove your gun in his back."

It was a different voice, deep and clipped with impatience. Wyatt held up a second finger. Two questions remained in his mind: was there still a thief standing at the door, and where was Andy Miller?

"The gun won't be necessary," Jacob said with quiet dignity. "From either of you."

Wyatt glanced at Will to see if his deputy understood the significance of what Jake had just said. Will was now holding up two fingers and nodding, confirming that he knew, as Wyatt did, that there were only two thieves.

From their position they could see one of the bank manager's legs and the hand he used to turn the key in the door. The thieves were not yet visible. They didn't come into view until Jacob Reston moved beyond the threshold; then they followed behind him, single file.

Wyatt waited until all three men disappeared into the room; then he gave Will the signal to move.

They came up quickly, and every element of surprise favored them. Jacob was kneeling in front of the safe, his right hand trembling on the brass dial as he turned it slowly. His shoulders were hunched protectively on either side of his head, an instinctive gesture in response to the Colt pointed at his temple.

Thief number two had holstered his weapon in anticipation of the stacks of bills he would have to handle. This man was Will Beatty's target, and Will clubbed him with the ivory butt of his six-shooter in the same moment Wyatt raised his Henry rifle.

"Put it down," Wyatt said, holding the rifle steady. "Don't flinch. Don't feint. Be smarter than I think you are, and just set it on top of the safe."

Will's quarry dropped hard, knees first, then the rest of him. His nose shattered when his face hit the floor and blood pooled to the side.

It had the desired effect on his partner. The Colt was slowly, carefully, raised and placed on the safe. That cooperative gesture was followed by two hands being lifted in surrender.

Wyatt nodded. "Seems like you have some experience with this. I like it that you know what to do without direction. It makes things simpler." Keeping his rifle pointed where he meant to shoot, Wyatt spoke to Will. "Help Jacob up. Careful that you stay clear of—" He paused. "What's your name?"

"Morrisey," he said. "Miles Morrisey."

"Good name. Hear that, Will? Stay clear of Miles Morrisey. He knows what's ahead for him."

Will stepped around Morrisey's felled partner and helped Jacob to his feet, then pulled the banker out of arm's reach and harm's way.

"Who is your partner?" asked Wyatt. "Kin or friend?"

Morrisey shrugged. "Hardly know him. Told me his name was Jack Spinnaker."

"Morrisey and Spinnaker. Okay. Not everyone can be a James or a Younger." He nodded at Will. "Take the gun. Jake? Is everyone all right back at the restaurant? No injuries?"

"Andy Miller hit his head on the corner of a table when Mr. Spinnaker tripped him up. That's why he was left behind."

"Estella and Johnny?"

"I don't know. They didn't come out of the kitchen when Spinnaker did."

Wyatt gave Morrisey a sharp look. "You better hope they're fine. I don't know that I can vouch for your safety in my jail if they're not." He shook his head, disgusted. "Let's get them out of here, Will. I've had about enough of chasing down half-wits."

Chester Caldwell did not attempt to hide his relief when Wyatt finally returned for Rachel. "Thank God," he muttered, wiping his hands on his apron. "She's a handful, isn't she?"

"I have no idea what that means," said Wyatt, straight-faced. He looked around. "Where is she?"

"I let her lie down in the back. I keep a cot there for folks who come in so sick sometimes that they need to rest a spell."

Wyatt paused as he was rounding the counter. "Did she take ill? Should I get Doc Diggins to come by?"

"Doc? No. She doesn't need him. I gave her something, like you said, when she got all up in arms and determined she was going to leave."

"Oh." Wyatt felt a twinge of guilt. "What did you give her?"

"Laudanum. Slipped it in her tea. Two cups of tea, actually, and lots of honey. She would have tasted it otherwise. And if she figures out what happened, you better tell her I was following your orders, because I surely will."

"Is she going to be able to walk? Maybe I should get a buggy after all."

"She'll need some help, I imagine. She had a time of it trying to stay on the stool here, which is why I suggested she lie down. She's not in a stupor, just drowsy. Pleasant, like."

"Pleasant? Is that right?" Wyatt's head angled to one side as he considered this. "How long do you suppose that lasts?" Not expecting an answer, he let the question hang and went in search of Rachel.

Wyatt stepped behind shelves of ointments, liniments, tinctures, and pills to find that Rachel was not lying down at all. She was sitting curled at the foot of the cot, her head and shoulder resting against the wall. Her heavy lashes were at half-mast, and watching her, he could see she was fighting sleep.

"Rachel?" He had to step around a stack of boxes to reach the cot. "I've come to take you home."

She tipped her head back and stared up at him through the dark sweep of her lashes. "Have you? That's good, then." Her smile had no real consciousness behind it. It merely existed as the result of facial muscles being tugged upward by the tilt of her head. "You're all right?"

"I'm fine." Wyatt watched her attempt to nod, but when her chin dropped, it just stayed there. "You appear to be doing rather fine yourself. Can I help you up?"

"Sleepy."

"Yes, I know you are." He slipped one hand behind

her back and urged her to move closer to the edge of the cot. She inched far enough forward that he was able to ease her legs over the side and finally pull her to her feet. It was no surprise that she wasn't steady. When she began to sway, he put one arm around her shoulders and the other in front of her at the level of her waist. "Where's your coat and bonnet?"

"Mr. Caldwell."

Wyatt supposed that meant that Chet had put them somewhere. "Let's find them."

It required considerable maneuvering and some assistance from the druggist, but Wyatt finally got Rachel into her pelisse, bonnet, and gloves and to the front door. On the point of leaving, he asked Chet, "Are you certain I don't need to get Doc?"

"If it will make you feel better, sure, but he's just going to tell you to let her sleep. The fresh air will clear her head. You want me to help you get her home? I can close up shop for that long."

"No. Thanks. We'll be fine."

"Fine," Rachel repeated. Her voice was pitched unnaturally high. Even to her own ears it sounded as if she was chirping. "Goodness." Then, having said all she cared to, she smiled vaguely and closed her eyes.

Wyatt resolutely turned her in the direction of the street while Mr. Caldwell held the door open for them. "We'll see you, Chet."

The cold air hit Rachel like a slap in the face. Her head came up sharply, and she blinked several times in quick succession. The first deep breath she took sent a shiver through her.

"Come on," Wyatt said, keeping a hand at the small of her back. "You can do this."

She could, and did, although it was unclear to her how she was managing it. Certainly, Wyatt's support accounted for her progress in the beginning, but by the time they reached her flagstone walk, she was navigating largely on her own.

Her sense of well-being held right up until the moment he helped her out of her coat; then she felt the uncomfortable heaviness return.

She leaned back against the wall while Wyatt removed her bonnet. When he finished she held out her hands for him to take off her gloves. "This is where you kissed me."

"So it is."

"You shouldn't have."

Wyatt worked her gloves off and set them on the foyer table. "You've been clear on that."

"I think I'd like to sleep now."

"Good idea."

She pushed away from the wall as he stepped back. For a moment, her eyes focused, and her regard of him was steady and clear. "You're really all right?"

He nodded. "I'll tell you about it later." When that seemed to be enough to satisfy her, he stood to one side so she could pass. He remained where he was, watching her closely as she walked on her own down the hall toward her bedroom.

When he heard the door close, Wyatt took off his own coat and hat and went to the kitchen to make a pot of coffee. He checked on Rachel's wood supply at the back door and saw it was adequate to see her through another day. While the water was heating, Wyatt wandered into the parlor and began to examine the shelf of books he'd seen when he was taking tea with her.

Interspersed among the illustrated fashion books from London and Paris were the novels of Twain, Austen, Alcott, and James. He thumbed through several of them, noticing that the bookplates indicated they were hers and that they had been read more than once. *Little Women*, in particular, seemed to be a favorite, followed closely by *The Adventures of Tom Sawyer*. He found the presence of Jules Verne intriguing and the absence of a single volume of poetry somewhat startling.

It seemed that Rachel Bailey's romantic streak was of a more practical nature than the poets allowed for.

He carried *Around the World in 80 Days* with him into the kitchen and set it on the table while he made coffee. He read with his feet up on the rung of another chair, sipping coffee, and enjoying the molasses cookies he found in a tin in the larder, and when he judged that twenty minutes had passed, he put the book aside and went to Rachel's bedroom to check on her.

She was sleeping on her side, facing the door, her cheek resting on the cradle of her own palm. By the time she reached her bed, she'd been too tired to bother with more than unpinning her hair. The pins lay scattered on the bedside table, while her hair lay in a thick, dark wave over her shoulder. She was still wearing her dress, though she slept so deeply it didn't appear she'd wrinkled it at all. He'd never known anyone who could sleep neatly.

Shaking his head, Wyatt hunkered at the side of the bed and undid the laces on Rachel's ankle-high boots. He gingerly removed the boots and set them on a nearby chair; then he lifted the quilt that was folded at the foot of the bed and spread it over her. She didn't stir.

He couldn't imagine that there wouldn't be hell to pay when she woke. Once she got her bearings, she'd realize something had been done to her, and while she might give Chester Caldwell a piece of her mind, she was going to do much worse to him. Wyatt couldn't even say that he wasn't looking forward to it. She had something to answer for as well.

"Foster Maddox is the reason I left California."

She probably would like to forget that she'd said it. He remembered how pale she'd become, how icy her hands had felt. He would swear that she never meant to answer his question, yet the words came out in spite of that, and it was in their wake that she had fainted.

Wyatt still didn't know what it meant. As an explanation,

it didn't amount to much. Foster Maddox was known to him only by reputation, much of it complimentary of his business acumen, if one agreed that words like *cold-blooded* and *hard-nosed* were complimentary. He was acknowledged to be keenly intelligent and fiercely competitive, traits that should have made his grandfather proud, yet for Wyatt, the most serious indictment of Foster's character was that Clinton Maddox didn't entirely trust him.

Wyatt understood that this last fact was not widely known. He was privy to it because of the contract. The document would hardly have been necessary if Foster had had the full confidence of his grandfather.

What had Rachel had to do with it? Looking at her now, her beautifully realized features set serenely in rest, it was hard to imagine what part she might have played, but if Foster Maddox had given her reason to leave California, then it seemed that there had been a role for her.

All things in time, Wyatt decided. He left Rachel's door open a crack so he could hear her in the event she needed him; then he returned to the kitchen, set his feet up, and lost himself in the adventures of Phileas Fogg and Passpartout.

Will Beatty had never been inside Rose LaRosa's fancy house. He allowed Adele to go upstairs and get Rose while he waited in the parlor. A couple of girls he recognized from seeing them about town wandered in and inquired after him. News of the foiled bank robbery had already reached them, and they were insatiably curious about the details.

They scattered like dandelion fluff when Miss Rose breezed into the room. Her ebony hair was dressed high on her head and held in place by combs encrusted with seed pearls. She was wearing a scarlet gown with a scandalously low, square-cut neckline, a waterfall of lace trim at the front from waist to hem, and a train so long she had to reach behind her to yank it forward. Seed pearl earrings in a shape that suggested roses lay delicately against her fair skin and made a striking contrast to her dark hair. Her throat was bare, but that merely called attention to the strong line of her collarbones and the hollow between them.

"So Adele didn't lie," she said, looking Will over. "That no-account Beatty boy has actually come calling."

Will removed his hat, raked his fingers through his tousled corn silk hair, and offered a polite, but cool smile. His dimples hardly made an appearance. "It's business, ma'am. Official."

Rose responded with a measured smile of her own. "Is there any other kind?"

"I don't suppose so," said Will. He glanced around. "Do you have somewhere private that we can talk?"

"Do you see anyone else around?"

He shook his head. "I guess this will do." He shifted his weight slightly from one foot to the other. "You heard about the attempt to rob the bank, I imagine. Two of your girls knew something about it."

"Yes. I heard, the same as them."

"Did you know Miss Adele was gone during that time?"

"Of course I knew. She left with one of her—" Rose stopped and put a hand to her head. "Don't tell me that he was one of the bank robbers."

"Afraid so, leastways that's what Miss Adele's telling me. She says he asked her to take a walk with him, promised her lunch, but when they were out, his friend shows up and joins them. Not long after, she says, they're draggin' her behind Wickham's Leather Goods and makin' it real clear that she needs to get the bank manager for them."

"What are you saying? She helped them?"

"I don't think they gave her any choice. I thought you should know. She's real upset about it, and I had to ask her a

lot of questions on account of there being two men in jail.
Hard for her to settle her nerves. Mr. Caldwell gave her something he swore would calm her down since it worked fine on
Miss Bailey. Mr. Reston's not blaming her—Adele, I mean,
not Miss Bailey—no one else is, either, for that matter, but I
figure you know her best, and if she was really part of it—the
planning and all—well, I figure you'd know."

Rose decided she needed to sit. She jerked on the train of
her gown, lifted it so she could drape it over her forearm, and
perched on the arm of an overstuffed chair. "How does Miss
Bailey figure into your story?"

"She doesn't really," Will said. "She was just passing
Longabach's with the sheriff when he noticed somethin' was
wrong inside."

"Oh." She supposed he thought that explained it all because
he didn't seem inclined to tell her more. She decided not to
pursue it. "Deputy, if you're asking me if Adele Brownlee is
capable of planning a robbery, then the answer is no. That
girl's idea of a plan is laying out her Sunday clothes on Saturday night. She's got a good soul, too, not just a good heart, and
her worst fault is that she's too trusting. There's probably not
another girl here that would have accepted an invitation out
with a man she'd just met, no matter how flush he seemed."

"No one tried to stop her?"

"Doesn't seem like, does it? I didn't see her go. I only
heard about it afterward." Gold and silver flashed as Rose
pressed her long-fingered hands together. "Is that all you
needed, Deputy?"

"It is, ma'am."

"God, but you make me feel like an old whore."

Will blinked. His cheeks went bright red. "Ma'am?"

"Stop calling me that. I'm your age, maybe younger. Call
me Rose, or Miss LaRosa, but stop tiptoeing around me like
I was your maiden aunt."

"Sorry, ma'—Miss LaRosa."

Rose rolled her eyes. "Is there something wrong with you, Will Beatty?"

"Wrong?"

"Never mind. I don't suppose you'd admit it anyway." She gave him a dismissive wave. "Go on. I need to look after Adele. If she's in a bad way, then I should be with her." She stood up and turned to go, only to be brought up short by that no-account Beatty boy's hand on her arm. She looked down at his hand, then at him. Her expression could not have been more disdainful.

Before she drew another breath, his mouth was on hers. The kiss was deep and fiery and went on just about as long as two people could make it last and still stay on their feet. When he drew back, he gave her a look that was as penetrating as his kiss. He returned his hat to his head, tipped it slightly.

"Just in case you were wonderin', Miss LaRosa." Then he left her, damn sure he'd answered her question.

Rachel felt as if someone had stuffed her head with cotton batting. She rolled slowly onto her back and lay very still, aware of nothing so much as her breathing and an odd tightness in her chest. She ran fingertips over her midriff and identified the problem. She was still wearing her corset.

In fact, she was still wearing her dress. She tried to recall if she'd ever fallen asleep wearing anything but a nightgown and nothing came to mind. In her present position, with the steel stays pressing tightly against her, even her ability to heave a deep and satisfying sigh was restricted.

Rachel opened one eye, then the other. Her bedroom was dark. A slim strip of light coming from another room defined the opening between her door and the frame. She turned her head to the window and saw the curtains had not been drawn.

It was darker outside her room than in it, and she was alert enough now to realize she'd slept for hours.

From somewhere beyond her room, the low hum of voices was carried back to her. Curious, rather than concerned, especially as she recognized one of them immediately as Wyatt Cooper's, Rachel sat up, pushed aside the quilt, and eased her legs over the side of the bed, careful to make as little noise as possible.

Her feet touched the floor. She congratulated herself for at least having the good sense to remove her boots before she climbed into bed; then the sliver of light revealed the pair she'd been wearing were resting on the seat of a caned chair—a place she would *never* have put them—and she had reason to wonder if she had any sense at all.

Rachel's footfalls were cushioned by her stockings. She put her ear to the opening in the doorway, listening for the direction of the voices before she nudged it enough to allow her to slip through.

She couldn't see into the kitchen from her place in the hallway, but it was no longer so difficult to make out the conversation or identify the owner of the other voice. Her immediate sense was that they hadn't been talking long. There still seemed to be some settling in to do, and she thought it was even likely that Will Beatty's arrival at her home was what had awakened her.

Rachel didn't dwell on why she wasn't announcing her presence to them, but if she had she would have concluded that she wasn't the intruder here. They were. Justified or not, she listened without a qualm.

"Careful, Will, that coffee's hot. You saw me just pull it off the stove." Wyatt handed his deputy a towel to wipe up the table where he'd just sloshed some over the rim of his cup and saucer.

"Doesn't she have any mugs?" asked Will. "Why do ladies

like these little cups? I'm always afraid I'll break one. They hardly hold more than a mouthful anyway."

Wyatt scowled. "Here, give me that towel. You're making a mess."

"When did you get so fussy? Ow!" He rubbed the red welt on his wrist where Wyatt had expertly snapped him with the towel. "What did you do that for?"

"For calling me fussy." Wyatt unwound the towel and tossed it behind him at the sink. "And keep your voice down, Will. I told you that Miss Bailey's sleeping."

"And that's another thing," said Will. "If she's sleeping, what are you still doing here?"

"Waiting for her to wake up."

"You know that doesn't make no sense."

"It does if you'd seen her at Caldwell's. He must have used a ladle to measure the laudanum. Someone has to be here to make sure she's all right."

Will tried his coffee again. "Hey, this is good. How come you don't make it like this at the office?"

Wyatt ignored the question. "Since you're here, who's minding the store?"

"Ed Kennedy agreed to spell me. Sam Walker stopped in and said he'd keep Ed company. Our prisoners aren't going anywhere."

"Good." Wyatt warmed up his coffee and took a swallow. "What about Adele? Did you get her back to Rose's?"

"Sure did. Just about the last thing I got done. I had to wait for Doc Diggins to show up and look her over. She was still jumpy and weepy, and Mrs. Longabach looked about ready to give her a mercy slap, so Doc sent me next door for a bottle of laudanum. Of course, the doc just spooned it in her mouth. Miss Adele calmed right down, and I took her home before it wore off."

"Good thinking. What did Rose say?"

"Just what you thought she would, that Adele could have easily fallen in with Morrisey and Spinnaker but couldn't have been part of the planning." Will shook his head at Adele's naiveté. "What I can't figure out is why those two wanted to make it seem like it was all her idea."

"Maybe to avoid an abduction charge. Who knows? Maybe they think the jury will go easier on them if they say they were struck stupid by a woman."

Will was quiet a moment considering this. "Do you think that can happen?"

"No, the jury's going to be—" Wyatt stopped because Will was shaking his head. He regarded his deputy with a growing sense of disbelief. "What? You're wondering if a woman can strike a man stupid?"

Will nodded. "You think that's possible?"

"Possible? I'm wondering how you got to be twenty-seven and not know it for a fact."

"I guess I never thought about it. Women . . ." He dragged his fingers through his hair and shrugged a bit sheepishly. "Women, they just seem real fine to me. It's like . . ."

Wyatt waited, but Will seemed to be stuck for a metaphor and finally just shrugged again, ending his speculation.

"Are those cookies in that tin?" he asked.

Amused by Will's wandering attention, Wyatt pushed the tin closer to his deputy. "Molasses. Don't eat them all." He watched Will embrace the tin before he opened it, and when his deputy lifted the lid and the aroma was released, his eyes just about rolled back in his head. That no-account Beatty boy had been struck stupid, all right, but apparently it was cookies that did the trick. "I may as well be hanged for a sheep as a lamb," Wyatt said, holding out his hand. "Give me another one of those."

Will chose one from the tin and put it in Wyatt's palm; then he took one for himself. He continued to embrace the tin as he took a big bite of his cookie. "So tell me again how you knew something was wrong at Longabach's. People are going to be talkin' about that for a while, and I want to be able to set them straight."

"People need to find better things to talk about." When Wyatt saw that Will wouldn't be moved from this subject and now had the food he needed to sustain him, he reluctantly gave in. "Henry was at the till, and Estella wasn't around. Johnny, either. I told you all that."

"You did, but there's more. I've been your deputy long enough to know there's more."

"Well, Abe had a string of jumps set up on the board, and he ignored them in favor of making a nonsensical move that gave Ned the advantage. Not only didn't Ned bite, but he moved a double stack right where Abe could take it."

"So they were rattled?"

"Rattled? I don't know. More likely they were trying to tell me that something was wrong." Wyatt dunked his cookie and quickly took a bite. "Have you ever seen Jake Reston or Andy Miller taking a meal together on a Saturday afternoon?"

"Never seen them sharing a table any day of the week."

"Exactly. On Saturdays, Jake goes directly home as soon as the bank closes at noon. He didn't speak to me when I poked my head in, which is hardly his usual greeting. Andy never looked up, and his face was about as green as his soup. Most telling, though, was Adele. She was sitting alone at her table."

Will whistled softly. "That would have gotten my attention. She's never by herself."

"That's what struck me first; then she gave me a coy look, and that confirmed everything I'd just seen."

"Why? Adele flirts with everyone. She can hardly help herself."

"Now, there you're wrong. Adele *never* gives me a look like that. Rose says she's scared of me."

"Well, ain't that something?"

Wyatt ignored that. "Did you go see Artie like I asked?"

"Sure I did. I got your reply right here." He started to reach inside his vest for it, but Wyatt told him to just tell him what it said. "Mr. Clay and Mr. Kirby will be at the Commodore tomorrow."

"Good."

"That have something to do with the spur?"

"It does. Miss Bailey wants to learn as much as she can about the operation."

"She's takin' it real serious, ain't she?" Will plucked another cookie from the tin. "I have to say I admire that."

"That cookie or her determination?"

Will grinned. "Both." He took a sizable bite and chewed thoughtfully. "Seems to me that one complements the other."

"How's that?"

"Well, I expect her cookies are just that good because she's determined that they should be."

Wyatt stared at that no-account Beatty boy.

"What?" asked Will. "What did I do?"

"Nothing." Wyatt rubbed the underside of his chin with his knuckles. "Sometimes you just surprise me, is all." He eased the tin away from Will's territorial hug and pushed it to the far side of the table. "Do you want me to bunk down at the jail tonight?"

"No reason for you to do that. I don't expect they'll get rowdy. They weren't even talkin' to each other when I left. Ed said he'd stick around if I need him." He hesitated. "Ah, are you goin' to be . . . that is, um, are you . . ."

"Say what's on your mind, Will."

"Since I don't need you at the jail, does that mean you're bunkin' here tonight?" When Wyatt just stared hard at him, Will's hands came up defensively. "You said I should—"

Wyatt interrupted him. "I'm trying to decide what I regret

more: encouraging you to speak up or leaving my rifle at the back door."

"I can see how that'd be a . . . what's that word you were tellin' me about . . . means a puzzle?"

"Conundrum."

"That's it. You have yourself a regular conundrum."

"I'm leaning hard toward getting my rifle."

Rachel stepped out of the hallway and presented herself in the alcove to the kitchen. Her glance darted from Wyatt to Will, then back again. "I think that's a very good idea, Sheriff."

Chapter Seven

Startled, Will leapt to his feet. His chair tipped on its back legs and would have crashed to the floor if Wyatt hadn't reached around the table and caught it.

"Easy there, Will. I think she means to aim that rifle at me."

Will Beatty studied Wyatt's face for some sign that he was kidding and couldn't find a twitch or a twinkle. It was more of the same when he looked at Rachel. "Well, all right, then. I'll just be goin' and leave you two to sort it out. I'll talk to the one that's still alive in the mornin'."

Judging that the most direct route out of the kitchen was to squeeze behind Wyatt's chair, that's what Will did. He nodded at Rachel. "Excellent cookies, Miss Bailey. Good day."

"I'll be talking to you tomorrow, Deputy."

That assurance made Will glance back at Wyatt and offer a sympathetic smile; then he slipped into the mudroom and took up his coat, gloves, gun belt, and hat. He was still putting them on as he stepped outside.

From where she was standing, Rachel could see Will leave. When the door closed behind him, she turned her attention to Wyatt. "That no-account Beatty boy must want your job, Sheriff. He didn't trouble himself to take your rifle."

"I imagine getting out of your way was his first priority. It's hard to fault his sense of self-preservation."

Rachel nodded, approaching the table. "Is there coffee left?"

"Mm-hmm." Wyatt reached behind him and took the pot off the stove while Rachel got a cup and saucer. He poured when she held the cup out across the table.

"I've always favored a dainty cup," she said. "I suppose because it lends itself to grace and good manners."

Wyatt paused in the act of returning the pot to the stove. "Well, that answers my question about how much you heard."

She smiled, the placement of her lips both sweet and insincere. "I thought it might."

Wyatt set the pot down and swiveled back around. He pointed to the chair she usually sat in when they were together. "Will you consider joining me?"

It went through her mind to tell him he was in her chair, but she caught herself before she challenged him in such a petty way. He would move, of course, even be gracious about it, and she would be the one diminished by her spite. "Yes," she said. "I will."

Wyatt waited until she was settled. "Are you warm enough? You don't have your shoes." She hadn't taken the time to pin up her hair again, either, but he didn't mention that for fear she'd do something about it. He liked the way it fell in waves all the way to the small of her back, though he didn't mind at all when she drew it over her right shoulder and began to loosely plait it. She had beautiful hands, long, slender fingers and buffed, elegantly tapered nails. They didn't look as if they ever chopped wood or hauled water or did any of the score of other tasks that made up the routine of her day. They were the hands of a woman who was flanked by servants, not one who occasionally employed a seventeen-year-old girl.

Rachel's fingers lost their deftness when she became aware

of Wyatt's curious interest in her hands. She stopped plaiting but kept her fingers in place on the braid. "Is there something wrong?"

"No."

"You're staring."

He resisted the temptation to continue and lifted his eyes to hers. "Am I?"

Rachel simply arched an eyebrow, observed that Wyatt was utterly shameless in his denial, and sighed. She quickly finished with her hair and brushed the braid behind her back. Taking up her coffee, she asked, "Can I assume there's no laudanum in this?"

Wyatt's response was a grimace.

Rachel smiled, lifting the cup to her lips. "Why would Mr. Caldwell put laudanum in my tea?"

"Because I told him to make certain you stayed put. I might have suggested the method of ensuring it as well."

"Might have?"

"All right. I did suggest it. I didn't know he'd be so liberal with the dose." He pointed a finger at her. "You agreed that you wouldn't leave the drugstore."

"I don't remember it quite like that, but I know you were trying to live up to the letter of your contract."

Wyatt swore softly and made no apology for it. "I never thought once about that damn contract. I needed you to stay off the street and out of the way, and I told you that I'd come for you when it was over."

"I'm sorry."

"You're not the only person I had to—" He stopped, finally hearing her apology, and regarded her suspiciously.

"I *am* sorry. I meant to do exactly what you said. The waiting . . . well, the waiting was interminable. I was unprepared for how . . . how *intense* it was. I didn't know what to do with myself, so I began insisting that I needed to leave. I will apologize to Mr. Caldwell tomorrow for placing him in such an unenviable position."

Wyatt realized he was having some difficulty regaining his footing. "I imagine he'd appreciate that," he said carefully.

"Still," she said, "you took an absurd liberty when you advised him as you did."

His predator's gaze narrowed. "You don't expect an act of contrition from me, do you?"

"No," she said softly, an amused smile playing about her lips. "I don't expect that."

"You're a hard person to figure out, Rachel Bailey."

"A conundrum?"

Taking stock of her slightly hopeful expression, Wyatt realized she wanted to be that much of a puzzle to him. It made him wonder about all the things she had yet to reveal. "You're exactly like that."

She thought she probably should not be so pleased, but his answer made her feel safe, as if she still might have secrets, and that, in turn, warmed her. She pointed to the cookie tin. "Did you and your deputy leave any for me?"

Wyatt nodded and pushed the tin toward her. "Not as many as I meant to."

Simultaneously, they said, "That no-account Beatty boy."

Rachel laughed. "Poor Will. Why does everyone call him that?"

Wyatt didn't bother to conceal his surprise. "No one's told you?"

"I never asked."

"You know the Beattys?"

"Some of them. There must be at least four or five families with that name in town."

"And they're all related. Two brothers begat eleven children; they begat upwards of thirty offspring. There's a lot of begetting with the Beattys. The boys are mostly miners. The girls generally marry miners. Mrs. Easter was a Beatty. So was Sid Walker's wife. Once you become familiar with the family, it's easy to see the commonalities."

"There are a lot of redheads, aren't there?"

"That's right. Widely spaced eyes, most of them green, and they're all on the wrong side of tall. I don't know as there's ever been a Beatty that stood as high as my chin."

Rachel frowned. "Will's as tall as you are."

"And his eyes are blue, he's got hair like silk on a corncob, and a pair of dimples that no one can figure out where they came from. What everyone agrees to is that on no account is he a Beatty boy."

"That's it?" she asked, incredulous. "He's carrying around that name because he *isn't* one of them?"

"Oh, he's one of them, just not one of them by blood. His mother was one of the town's early working girls, and when she died of childbed fever, it was Janet Beatty that agreed to suckle him. No man ever stepped forward and claimed to be the father, so John and Janet raised him with their own."

Rachel realized she was reaching for a second cookie and pulled her hand out of the tin. "What a curious town this is," she said, pensive. "Unexpectedly rich." She waved a hand airily. "I don't mean wealthy, though that seems to be true, but abundant in character."

"And characters."

"Certainly."

"You like it here, don't you?" said Wyatt. "I think that surprises you."

"I do," she admitted. "And, yes, it surprises."

Wyatt tipped his chair to rest on the back legs and watched Rachel wince as he found his balance. He crossed his arms. "Why?" he asked, continuing to study her.

"I suppose because when one has no expectations everything surprises."

He considered that. "And doesn't disappoint."

"Yes. That's true also."

"Why did you come here, Rachel? You didn't know that you'd be inheriting a mine. You certainly hadn't anticipated that you'd own a spur, and I imagine if you'd had a hint that marriage was waiting for you, you'd have run for the hills."

Rachel smiled at the expression. "At the risk of diminishing the majesty of these mountains, I thought that's what I did."

Amusement lifted one corner of Wyatt's mouth. "Point taken."

Gathering up their cups, Rachel rose and padded softly to the washtub. She set them gently inside, then turned back to Wyatt, resting her hip lightly against the washstand. "Do you play cards, Wyatt? Perhaps know a few tricks with them?"

"Yes to both," he said.

"Then you probably know how to force a card on someone. That's what Clinton Maddox did to me. The card I chose was the one he wanted me to have, the only one he really offered. I understand why he did it, but that doesn't mean that I've made peace with it. I don't know anyone who appreciates being manipulated, even when it's deftly done."

"What about Foster Maddox?"

"What about him? He certainly doesn't like being manipulated."

Wyatt chided her with a look. "I think you know that's not what I meant. You told me that Foster Maddox is the reason you left Sacramento, yet you're saying that it was his grandfather who manipulated you."

Rachel frowned deeply. "I told you that Foster Maddox is the reason I left? When did you hear me say that?"

"Before you fainted in the Commodore's dining room."

"Under those circumstances, you probably shouldn't give much credence to whatever you may have heard."

He gave her a long, considering look. "You think that's clever, don't you?"

"What is?"

"Casting doubt on my hearing rather than flatly deny what we both know you said."

"I don't think it's that clever," she said. "But you're kind to say so."

"Tell me about Foster Maddox."

Rachel stifled a yawn. "Pardon me. I suppose I'm still trying to shake the effects of the laudanum, unless it's the lateness of the hour. What time is it?"

Wyatt set his chair on all fours and consulted his pocket watch. "A quarter after eight."

"Then I did sleep a long time. I wondered." She covered her mouth again when a yawn split her jaw so wide that it cracked. "Forgive me. I can't seem to help myself."

"I'll just bet you can't," Wyatt said. "Maybe what you need is a turn outside in the cold, or I could pour a bucket of spring water over your head."

"Neither sounds appealing."

"They're not meant to, but one or the other is in your future." He made a steeple of his fingers and looked at her over the peak. "Once more, tell me about Foster Maddox."

Rachel stood away from the washstand, rounded the table, and kept on going. She heard Wyatt's chair scrape the floor as he stood up. "I'm not running from you," she snapped when she heard his footfalls behind her. "I can't be idle any longer. I was getting something to occupy my hands."

Wyatt leaned in the doorway to her workroom. "You might have said as much."

Not turning around or sparing a glance for him, she said, "I can't think of a single reason why I should be accountable to you." She surveyed the table, looking over the patterns and fabric pieces for something suitable. After she examined several gowns in different stages of completion, she chose Adele Brownlee's nightgown. Attaching the lace to the neckline was precisely the sort of mindless, almost effortless task she liked to do to keep her fingers busy. "I can do this right here," she said. "Sit anywhere except beside the lamp. I need that close by so I can see what I'm doing."

Wyatt recognized the agitation that defined her movements as well as her need to move. He remembered she was also capable of almost unnatural stillness, although there was nothing about her now to suggest it. He waited for her to collect what she required from various baskets and drawers before he joined her at the table.

"We're partners, Rachel," Wyatt said. "That's the single reason you're accountable to me. And the single reason I'm accountable to you." He watched her expertly thread her needle. "Back at the hotel you asked me for help with the spur. If that's changed, if you want to go it alone because it's yours and it's your right, then I won't ask again about Foster Maddox, but if you haven't changed your mind, I need to know what you know."

Rachel set the lace against the neckline and began basting. She didn't look up as she spoke. "Perhaps you need to know something about him, but not everything. There's no one alive who needs to know everything."

"All right," he said. "Let's begin with that. With *something*."

"You make it sound as if it should be simple."

"Do I? I don't mean to. I can see you find it troubling."

Troubling? she thought. She found it painful. "He disliked my association with his grandfather. He said it was because I influenced him, which was ridiculous of course, because no one held sway over Clinton Maddox. I simply spent more time in his company than Foster did."

"Did Foster live with his grandfather?"

"For years, yes. His mother is Cordelia Rice. When she married Benson Maddox, she moved into the mansion with him. I've always been given to understand that Benson and his father got along exceedingly well, but when Benson was killed in the war, Mrs. Maddox moved out and naturally took Foster with her. He would have been twelve or thirteen then. I've been told that Mrs. Maddox blamed her father-in-law for Benson's death. She believed he could have done more to stop Benson from going. For whatever reason, she held her husband harmless for his decision and placed the responsibility squarely on Mr. Maddox's shoulders."

"So she punished him by removing Foster from his influence?"

Rachel looked up from her needlework. "I can't speak for her motivation. Mr. Maddox's wife died shortly after Benson and Cordelia were married, so Cordelia had taken over the reins of managing the home. She was the hostess for all the important functions held at the mansion and looked upon by her society as the arbiter of fashion and manners. She was extraordinarily well regarded."

Wyatt stretched his long legs under the table as he leaned back in his chair. "Where did she go?"

"Back to her parents' home. Her father's a merchant who made his fortune supplying goods to the miners during the rush. Mr. Rice and Mr. Maddox were never competitors in any business venture, but neither were they partners. I think there was a time that Mr. Rice wanted to invest in the C & C, but Mr. Maddox wanted to keep it private. I don't know any of the details."

Rachel bent her head and returned to her stitching. "I do know that there was no love lost between the two men. Cordelia's presence in the Maddox home formed a bridge of sorts between the two families, and Benson's death changed that. I think Cordelia was strongly encouraged to return home, but that is only my opinion. Mr. Maddox certainly never said as much. In fact, he rarely mentioned Cordelia."

"Did Mrs. Maddox try to keep Foster away from his grandfather?"

"I don't know. I'm not certain that Mr. Maddox was very curious about Foster when he was young. I don't think he knew what to make of children. It was his view that they were the responsibility of women until they were of school age; then they became the charges of tutors and teachers. He once said that Benson was not particularly interesting until the summer he took a laborer's job on the railroad. I know he wished Foster had done something like that. He thought Foster dismissed certain types of work as being beneath him, and Mr. Maddox believed that a man who places himself above work—any work—has already lost his soul."

"Do you believe that?" asked Wyatt.

Rachel did not answer immediately. Her fingers stilled as she considered her answer. "I must believe it," she said finally. "Foster Maddox is the most soulless man I know."

Wyatt watched her hands begin to move again. "You mentioned Cordelia's father was a merchant. Was there ever a plan for Foster to be involved in the Rice family business?"

"Cordelia Maddox has two sisters and a brother. Two of her nephews were groomed to take over. Mrs. Maddox was firm that the railroad was Foster's birthright and her father championed that."

"Perhaps as a way of becoming a partner in the line?"

"That certainly occurred to Mr. Maddox," Rachel said. "He didn't want to see the industry of his life turned over to Charles Rice."

"Is there a possibility that Foster will do that?"

"Not if Mr. Maddox addressed it properly in his will. He led me to believe that he had." Her lips twisted in a humorless smile. "Foster Maddox is also extraordinarily selfish. It might be that the provisions in Mr. Maddox's will were unnecessary."

"When did Mr. Maddox start to include Foster in the rail operations?"

"Sometime after Foster finished his studies at William and Mary."

"William and Mary? Really?"

"Mr. Rice came to California from Virginia. He paid for Foster's education, not Mr. Maddox. It came to that when Foster didn't go to Yale."

"That damn war will never be over."

Rachel's eyes darted sideways and saw Wyatt's gravely set features. "No," she said quietly, "it won't."

Wyatt didn't feel the need to say anything for a time. He contented himself watching Rachel, finding the repetitive movements of her hands vaguely hypnotic. "How do you fit in, Rachel?"

"Surely you already know. I thought you decided that I was Mr. Maddox's mistress."

"I did. You read the agreement. You know why I came to that conclusion. Maddox led me down that path."

Rachel paused long enough to sweep back the thick plait of hair that had fallen over her shoulder. "I'm not sure what you're saying."

Wyatt reached over the corner of the table and lifted Rachel's chin with his fingertips. She didn't flinch, but her dark eyes mocked him. "I'm saying that I changed my mind a while back about you ever being Clinton Maddox's mistress."

"All right." She tilted her chin away from him and sat back in her chair, putting herself just outside his easy reach.

"Is that it?" he asked. "You don't want to say more?"

She shrugged. "I asked you once if it mattered around here that a woman was a man's mistress. You told me it didn't. I can't imagine why you're pursuing the question now. It has nothing at all to do with our partnership."

It was a new experience for Wyatt Cooper to find himself cornered. He was very sure he didn't like it. He had expected she would leap at the opportunity to tell him what a thick-headed idiot he'd been for believing she was Maddox's mistress in the first place. Instead, she'd decided to simply allow him to think whatever he liked. Again.

"Don't you ever defend yourself?" he asked.

The question raised a flickering smile. "How quickly you've forgotten the bucket I swung at your head."

"You know what I mean."

"If that answer doesn't satisfy you, then clearly, I don't."

Wyatt's glance darted sideways to where Rachel kept her small store of liquor. It was tempting to think she would make more sense to him if he was pouring a third or a fourth shot just now.

Rachel caught the direction of his wandering attention. "Would you like a drink?"

"God, no," he said feelingly. "If you're offering, it couldn't possibly help."

Choosing not to be offended, Rachel chuckled. "You have a suspicious nature, Sheriff, though perhaps it's not a failing given the position you hold in this town. I imagine that every-one in Longabach's today is very glad for your suspicions."

Wyatt shrugged. "Perhaps."

"You don't want to discuss it?"

"You heard everything I had to say when you were eaves-dropping."

There wasn't a direct response Rachel thought she could make that wouldn't sound defensive. She said, "I'm grateful that you're good at what you do."

"Are you?"

"Of course." She caught his skeptical look. "Perhaps I

should be clearer. I'm grateful for what you do for the town. Your persistent suspicion is not at all comforting when I'm the subject of it."

"Did Foster Maddox believe you were his grandfather's mistress?"

Rachel sighed deeply. "Not at all comforting," she said softly, addressing herself more than Wyatt. "Yes, that's precisely what he believed. When Mr. Maddox had his stroke, Foster understood the nature of our relationship to be changed in certain fundamental ways, and he decided he wanted what his grandfather had."

"You."

"Yes."

"You weren't interested?"

She looked up. "Not in the least."

Wyatt could not mistake the resolve in her expressive eyes. "Foster Maddox has a reputation for ruthlessness."

"It's not unfounded."

"So I imagine he made your situation difficult."

Rachel pushed her needle into a pincushion and removed her silver thimble. She carefully examined the lace she'd basted onto the nightgown's neckline. When she was satisfied, she neatly folded the gown and placed it on the table, then turned to Wyatt and regarded him openly.

"Foster Maddox made my situation intolerable. Difficult was when he asked me to accompany him to the theater or the races or some other social event where a woman with my reputation was not only welcomed but desired, and the invitations continued in spite of every one of my firm refusals. It was difficult when he told lies about me to his grandfather, and his grandfather was still so crippled in his speech that all he could do was listen. Hearing him tell Clinton that I enjoyed the attentions of a man who knew what to do in bed was difficult. Standing accused of stealing heirloom jewelry and taking money from the household funds was difficult."

Rachel resisted pressing a hand to her heart even though it was fluttering wildly against her breast. Her cheeks felt hot, and her mouth was dry. She could feel her throat constricting and an uncomfortable ache forming behind her eyes. Her insides twisted.

And still her gaze remained steady and stubborn.

"Arguments were difficult. Attempts to humiliate me were difficult. Avoiding him was difficult. I could not be alone anywhere in the house. If I was, he cornered me. No servants in the house dared to interfere for fear of losing their position. Clinton Maddox was the only one who could have stopped it, and for months he lay helpless in his bed. But even that, the groping, the insinuations, the suggestions that I whore for Foster's friends, all of that was merely difficult.

"It was when he made threats against my mother, my sister and her family, and his own grandfather that my situation was made intolerable." Rachel didn't look away, but her voice fell to a husky whisper. "I'm not proud of this, but I began to think that killing Foster Maddox was the answer. Not idle thoughts, either. I considered all the reasons that justified it. I became the one who did the watching. I knew his schedule and the route he took between work, his home, and Mr. Maddox's house. I thought about all the different ways he might die. Poison. Hanging. A fall. Gunshot. A blow to the head. An accident on the street. I wanted to—"

"Rachel." Wyatt spoke her name quietly, firmly. "I understand. You don't have to—"

"No," she said sharply. "You wanted to know. That means you have to listen, no matter how uncomfortable it is to hear. You said I'm accountable to you, and this is my accounting."

"I wasn't trying to spare myself. I was trying to spare—" He stopped because it was a partial truth at best, at worst, a lie. If he had wanted to spare her, her eyes seemed to say, then he should never have pressed for answers. "Very well," he said. "Say it all."

"I wanted to kill him," she said. "I dreamed about it. I imagined how I would do it. I thought about how I would live with myself if I were never caught, and I considered what it would be like to hear a judge pronounce my own death sentence. I decided I could accept either eventuality."

Rachel set her hands on top of the table and folded them into a single fist. "Mr. Maddox's recovery was slow, but everyone responsible for his care observed the changes. As he improved, he began to find ways to communicate. Blinking. Finger movements. Squeezing my hand. He was surprisingly talkative using these methods, and I came to realize that he knew what I was contemplating. During that time when he couldn't find a way to say anything to us, he became an extraordinary observer and an even better listener.

"It shouldn't surprise you that he began encouraging me to leave."

"No," Wyatt said carefully. "It doesn't surprise."

"There were a number of things to consider," Rachel said. "Foster's threats were predicated on the fact that I refused to share a bed with him, but at the same time, my presence in the house kept him from acting on his threats toward Mr. Maddox. I rarely left Mr. Maddox's side, but that gave Foster the opportunity to direct threats toward my mother and sister."

"He said he would hurt them?"

"His threats to do harm were mostly financial in nature. He would have made it impossible for my mother to find another position. My sister's husband would have been dismissed from his job. These things would have happened at great cost to their pride. The same sort of accusations he'd leveled at me would have been turned on them. On those occasions when he talked about unfortunate accidents, his accounts were always about children. I have a niece and a nephew. Twins. Just six years old. It required no imagination on my part to know he was speaking about them."

"Jesus," Wyatt said under his breath.

"Besides killing Foster, there really was no other choice than to remove myself from Sacramento. I suppose that it can be argued that by encouraging me to go, Clinton Maddox was trying to save me from myself. For reasons that are entirely understandable, my mother and Sarah also wanted me to leave. I still felt certain that Mr. Maddox's full recovery would be compromised if I left, making him supremely vulnerable to Foster. We talked about it. He knew and accepted the risk to himself. I was the one who kept balking."

"What tipped the scales?"

Rachel closed her eyes and pinched the bridge of her nose. After a long moment, she let her hand fall to her lap and looked at Wyatt, her gaze weary now. "Foster came upon me in my sewing room. Until he walked in, I hadn't known he was in the house. While no one on the staff stepped forward when Foster and I were arguing, it was typical that someone would warn me of his arrival. No matter where I was in the house, I usually managed to get to Mr. Maddox's room first.

"There was no chance of that this time. The details of the argument are unimportant. There was little variation on the theme. We exchanged words, but there was no conversation. We each had lines and delivered them by rote. On this occasion, Foster was suffering with one of his migraines. He was all but lost to reason, and there was little hope that he'd recover it. He was louder, more forceful, and ultimately more physical. It was as if he'd decided that bombast would make his argument convincing."

The memory caused Rachel to visibly draw into herself. "He knocked over a chair and caused a small table to skid across the floor in one of his clumsier efforts to reach me.

I'd been forced to grapple with him before to defend myself from his blows, so I was prepared for something like that to happen again. Before he came within arm's reach of me, I yanked up the hem of my gown so I could move quickly in any direction. Foster must have interpreted it as an indication that I'd changed my mind and was issuing an invitation. It's the only reason I can imagine that he stopped in his tracks."

Wyatt kept his own counsel, afraid that saying anything would damn him for being a man like Foster Maddox. The hard truth was that he was having a difficult time not letting his eyes stray to the slim ankles and calves that could stop any man cold. "And?" he asked.

"And I charged him. I've never seen a bull do it, but I think it must have been something like that. I put my head down and ran at him. I drove into his midsection and heard the breath leave his body."

"I've seen a bull charge," said Wyatt. "That sounds about right. What happened?"

"He stumbled backward, tripped over his own feet, and landed hard on his back. He didn't get up. I thought he'd passed out, but when I collected myself enough to look more closely, I saw that he'd hit his head on the marble apron of the fireplace. There was blood, quite a bit of it, but he was still breathing. I stared at him for a long time, knowing that it would probably never be easier to kill him. And when I didn't, when I realized that I never could, I knew the time had come for me to leave."

Wyatt let the words lie, absorbing them, appreciating that this was as much a confession of what she hadn't done as of what she had. He could not tell which troubled her more. "You left everyone behind?" he asked.

She nodded. "I've had no contact since I left the station in Sacramento. I wrote to my mother and sister and gave the letters to Mr. Maddox to pass to them. I didn't dare risk seeing them in person. A visit to them would have been out of the ordinary at that time, and I was afraid that Foster would suspect my intent. I told them nothing that would reveal where I was going. My silence was in consideration of their safety and I depended on Mr. Maddox not to reveal anything to them. I'm sure he didn't."

"So you thought you were well out of Foster's reach."

"Of course I did. I used another name to purchase my tickets. I even used a rival rail line to make most of the journey. I was confident that no one I left behind would be able to give me away. I worried what Foster would do when he realized I was gone, but I had to hope that by sending no letters, no packages, not even a single telegram, he would come to accept that my family were all telling him the truth when they said they didn't know where I was. I depended on Foster understanding that he'd finally gotten what he wanted."

Wyatt frowned as he considered this. "What did you think he wanted?"

"For me to be away from his grandfather. He thought I was influencing Mr. Maddox's decisions, remember? I explained this already."

"You explained it, but I didn't realize you actually believed it." He shook his head, his mouth grim. "Rachel, if only half of what you told me is true, it's still clear as Pittsburgh glass that he wanted you. Not wanted you out of the way, just wanted you. I don't think he's much accustomed to being refused. The one strategy you didn't try was bedding him."

Her chin came up. "Not because I didn't think of it. I could more easily have killed him."

"It wasn't meant as a criticism," said Wyatt. "It's just an observation."

"You can keep your observations, then." She rubbed her hands over her face, agitated. "God, but I wish I hadn't told you anything. You can't know what it was like. What he was like. You can never understand." She placed her palms flat on the table and stood. "What purpose did telling you serve except to satisfy your prurient curiosity?" She could feel herself shaking. Her eyes were dry and gritty. "You asked me to be accountable, and I let you dig at my wounds with a stick. Shame on me for that." She stared at her hands. "Shame on me." And although her lips moved around the words, they were largely without sound.

Rachel didn't see him leave his chair, didn't know he was standing just beside her until she turned to go and blindly walked into his embrace. She fought it at first, struggling hard, pushing at him in earnest. Her nails scrabbled at his shirt. She twisted and turned and would have clamped down on his shoulder with her teeth if he hadn't managed to jerk away in time.

He held her fast, his arms so tight around her that she thought she might not be able to draw another breath, and yet she heard herself sobbing deeply, and felt the keening cries like a razor at the back of her throat. Her fingers curled into fists around the fabric of his shirt.

She heard his voice in her ear, his hot breath against her skin. She couldn't make out what he was saying, couldn't hear him above her own weeping, but it wasn't comfort that he was offering. The tenor of his voice was not calculated to soothe or placate her. This was a low growl that was intended to urge her on, as if he knew instinctively that trying to quiet her would have been not merely infuriating, but at the core, disrespectful as well.

His embrace simultaneously confined and shielded her. She was pressed against him intimately, yet the contact felt impersonal. He didn't try to rub her back or massage her shoulder. He didn't press his lips to her forehead or finger her braid. He simply took the brunt of her anger and absorbed her self-loathing.

She felt the cadence of her sobs change as they quieted.

The pause between shuddering breaths lengthened as she drew air deeper into her lungs. She wept, but almost silently now, turning her cheek against his shoulder and finding the warm curve of his neck. He didn't try to press a handkerchief into her hands or avoid the discomfort of having his shirt made salty and wet by her tears.

His arms tightened once, briefly, when she could no longer suppress a shiver, but he didn't belabor the moment by coddling her. His restraint was a revelation to her. He demanded nothing, expected nothing, and when she let herself slump against him, he stood firm.

Rachel found her own handkerchief and pressed it against her eyes and then her nose. When she began to ease away, he let her go. "I think I'd like to lie down now."

"Of course. I'll let myself out."

She nodded. When he didn't move, but merely regarded her patiently, Rachel glanced down and saw she was gripping his forearm. Some part of her was astonished that she didn't release him immediately. "Tomorrow," she said. "Nothing's changed about that. For me, that is. I'd still like you to be there when I meet with Mr. Clay and Mr. Kirby."

"I'll be there."

"Good." Her fingers unfolded slowly and she watched as his arm settled against his side. Her smile was a bit watery and uneven. "I'll still owe you biscuits."

"I know. I like being owed."

"Maybe I could—"

"Don't worry about it. I'll tell you when I want to collect them."

She hesitated, then finally said, "All right."

Wyatt nodded and started for the kitchen. "Do you have any trousers?"

"Trousers?" She stared at his back, her eyebrows fiercely knit. "Me? Why would I have—"

He held up one hand, staving off her questions as he lifted his coat from the peg rack with the other. "You'll need them tomorrow. I figure we'll only be in the meeting an hour or so, and there'll be plenty of daylight left for what I have in mind." He looked her over with a critical eye. "I expect Ted Easter's oldest boy is about your size. I'll see if he won't lend me a pair of dungarees."

"I'm not wearing Theo's dungarees."

Wyatt chuckled at her affronted expression. "We need to do some hiking. Not far, just to get beyond the town limits. There's a law on the books that makes it a crime to throw lead in town."

"Throw lead?"

"Shoot."

"You're going to take me into the hills and shoot me?"

"Mountains, remember? And I thought I'd teach you to shoot first before I aimed my weapon at you. It's more sporting that way."

Rachel knew her jaw was slack, but closing it seemed inappropriate in light of what she was hearing. "You're serious?"

"About teaching you to shoot, yes. As for shooting you, I sure as hell wish you hadn't put the idea in my head." He tipped his hat. "I'll see you in church, Rachel."

Rachel kept her eyes on the minister and her thoughts on everything but what he was saying. Reidsville's population numbered 782. There were only two places of worship: the Lutheran church and the meeting hall on Pine Street for the practice of the religions that weren't Lutheran or Catholic. The Lutherans had services at eight thirty and ten. The meeting hall was used by the Presbyterians at nine, the Methodists at ten thirty, and about thirty-eight citizens who liked to read and interpret the scriptures for themselves at noon.

The slate-gray roof of the Lutheran church boasted the year it was built with white-painted tiles embedded into each of the steeply pitched sides. The fact that it was located on Tent Church Road spoke to its humble beginnings when miners slogged in the mud to stand under a tarp and listen to Pastor Duun. The Norwegian immigrant, late of Minnesota, delivered a rather dour message that appealed to them after a week of hard labor and a night of harder drinking.

Pastor Duun, well into his sixties now, could still be relied on to offer a grim sermon come Sunday morning. Rachel surmised that it was this reliability that remained a comfort to his congregation.

When the offering plate was passed, Rachel came out of her reverie long enough to place a few coins on it, then stood with the rest of the congregants to participate in prayer. With her head bowed, she surreptitiously glanced sideways to where Wyatt Cooper stood flanked by Ned Beaumont on one side and three members of Will Beatty's family on the other. He was leaning forward just enough that she could make out the line of his cleanly defined profile, and the tilt at the corner of his mouth that made her think he knew she was watching him.

Rachel lowered her gaze immediately and prayed that she'd be forgiven for thinking about that mouth and not doubly damned for thinking about it pressed against hers. As far as she was concerned, the benediction could not come quickly enough.

When the service was over, Rachel stood in line to shake Pastor Duun's hand and compliment him on his message. She purposely set herself behind Sir Nigel Pennyworth and in front of Grace and Artie Showalter and made a point to engage them in conversation as they shuffled toward the door. She would never be able to say how Wyatt managed to put himself directly at her back before she reached Pastor Duun, and she held out no hope that he'd tell her how he did it. She suspected the Showalters of being actively complicit, while she thought Sir Nigel's habit of long-winded discourse merely provided a convenient diversion.

Wyatt didn't speak to her at all, but she was aware of his presence at her back all the while she moved closer to the door. She spoke sincerely of her appreciation for the sermon when Pastor Duun took her hand in both of his and expressed his best wishes for her success with the mining operation. As soon as she could gracefully extricate herself from his firm grasp, she hurried down the steps and across the flat, open yard.

"Liar," Wyatt whispered when he caught up to her.

Rachel glanced at him, her expression openly perturbed. "Why are you following me? And I'm not a liar."

His lips twisted wryly. "Tell me what part of Duun's sermon spoke to your heart. That's what you told him, isn't it?"

"You were right there. You know what I told him."

"I rest my case." His voice fell to a whisper again, and he bent his head slightly toward hers. "Liar." He chuckled when she shifted her elbow as if she meant to poke him only to catch herself and draw it back.

Rachel slowed her steps so it would not appear as if she was running from him, which was precisely what she was doing. "I don't need an escort home."

"Good, because I'm going the other way."

"When?"

"Just. About. Now." Wyatt took a deliberate step sideways as they came upon the hitching post. "Come here. I have something for you."

She glanced around, then spoke to him with urgency. "Don't crook your finger at me. There are people here who will surely notice."

"Then don't act so furtive. I can guarantee they'll notice that." He opened the flap on his saddlebag and drew out a pair of tightly rolled dungarees. "Here. Mrs. Easter says they're clean, and you shouldn't worry about giving them back. Theo's just about grown out of them and the younger boys are nowhere near ready to fill them out."

Rachel made no attempt to reach for the roll of denim he was holding out to her. She stared at it instead. "I'm not taking that."

"Now, that's downright churlish, Rachel. Ann Marie's a Methodist, but you can be sure she's going to hear about this. Someone will mention that they saw me try handing a thing to you, someone else will say it looked like denim bolster, and a third person will say you shied away from it like it was a copperhead. Mrs. Easter will figure it all out when the story reaches her." Wyatt consulted his pocket watch. "I'd say that would be at about one thirty, halfway through our meeting with the Calico engineers. That could be just the thing that would distract you."

Exasperated, Rachel snatched it out of his hand and tucked it under her arm. "I'm only taking it so you'll stop talking."

He shrugged. "That works, too, I guess."

"I don't know where people in this town come by the idea that you don't have much to say."

"Could be on account of I don't have to explain everything to them. You're a little slow-witted that way, aren't you?"

She must be, she decided, because Wyatt didn't rush to un-hitch his horse and mount, and she still didn't have a blistering retort by the time he was riding away.

John Clay and Samuel Kirby had been hired by the California and Colorado Railroad when the track was still being laid. Rachel didn't hide the fact that she was fascinated by their stories of the earliest days. Coming through the mountains, they told her, was slow going. Sometimes only a few miles of track could be put down in a day. There were tunnel

failures and landslides. Bridges made for a long week, even
month, in one place.

While they knew a great deal about the line in general, they
understood everything about the Calico Spur. They told her
about the schedule, the shifts, the routine maintenance. They
explained where problems with the track were most likely to
occur. Over the main dinner course of stuffed leg of lamb
with currant jelly and sauce, Anna potatoes and lima beans,
and raised hominy muffins, Rachel listened to these men
speak so affectionately of the No. 473 and the Admiral that
they might well have been speaking of the great loves of their
life. They knew the temperament of the engines, the exact
point to which the boilers could be pushed, the speed for a
safe descent to the plateau where Denver stood, and the speed
that disregarded every kind of caution but brought the train in
on time in spite of an unexpected delay. They knew the location of the water towers and what was required to keep them
in good repair. Ready water for the boilers was a necessity if
the engines were going to make the climb to Reidsville. A
tower lost to disrepair could stop their beloved locomotives.

Rachel was aware that Wyatt acted as the meeting's con-
ductor. He knew how to raise a point that enabled her to ask
just the right question. Her ability to put matters before them
plainly seemed to impress Clay and Kirby, but she understood
that she was merely accepting Wyatt's direction or following
his lead.

"If it's all right with you, Miss Bailey," Sam Kirby said,
"I'll just speak my mind here about somethin' that's been
weighin' on us for a time now."

"Please," Rachel said. "It would be disagreeable if you
didn't."

Sam set down his dessert fork and reluctantly pushed away
what was left of his slice of cranberry pie. He patted his

slightly distended stomach. "My wife doesn't mind a little extra weight here, but it gets crowded in No. 473's cab."

Rachel smiled politely while John Clay, who was as thin as one of the rails he rode, cast a quick look at Sam's belly and nodded heavily.

"After you were kind enough to invite us to a splendid meal and listen to our tired stories, it's a rudeness to tell you that John and I weren't certain we could work for another one of Clinton Maddox's handpicked successors. We've seen what Foster Maddox accomplished in the short time since his grandfather took sick. I don't know what you know about that, but he fired a lot of good operators up and down the line and replaced them with men answerable to him. There might have been some sense in it from where he was sitting, but for John and me, sitting in the cabs, we couldn't find the sense of it with a map and a compass."

"I see," Rachel said carefully. "And you're concerned it will be the same with me."

"That's the thing, Miss Bailey. We were real pleased to learn that Foster Maddox wasn't going to control the spur, but we cooled a little to the idea after we considered what that might mean."

Rachel looked from Sam to John and back again. "Better the devil you know, gentlemen. Is that it?"

"That occurred to us, yes."

"And you still feel that way?"

"No, ma'am. No, we don't. Leastways, I don't, and John's been kickin' me under the table, so I expect he doesn't feel that way, either. We're real pleased to be working for you, and if it's not too forward of us, we'd like to suggest a name to you of someone who can manage the operation day to day and report to you."

Relieved, but recognizing that she couldn't show it, Rachel

simply nodded. "That certainly was on my agenda. Who did you have in mind for the position?"

"Well, I don't know that he'll suit since we learned from the sheriff that he's a little taken with you, but Abe Dishman's your man."

Chapter Eight

"That's a hell of a thing you're wearing, Rachel." Wyatt lifted his hat and raked back his sun-streaked hair as he looked her over. "Damn me if it's not."

"Apparently you weren't listening to Pastor Duun's sermon, either. He always has a thing or two to say about cursing." She closed the back door behind her and stepped up to the edge of the small porch. Her stance was stoic as Wyatt continued to examine her from the height advantage of his horse. The fact that his expression was what Miss LaRosa would call squinty-eyed did not dispose Rachel to think kindly toward him. She looked down at herself. "What's wrong with what I'm wearing? I put on the trousers, didn't I?"

Wyatt replaced his hat and patted his gelding to steady it. "It's hard to tell. Lift up the hem of that gingham sack you've got on."

"It's a smock."

"Well, I'm telling you, it's a fancy sack. Go on, run it up the pole. I promise not to salute." He quieted his mount again. "Shh, Raider, that look's aimed at me, not you." He continued to regard Rachel. "You're scaring my horse."

"Will he throw you?"

"Probably not."

Her mouth flattened, disappointment explicit in the line of it. She raised the red-and-white-checked gingham smock halfway to her knees. The denim trousers, cuffed twice at the ankles, were there for Wyatt to inspect. "See?"

"I do. How are you keeping them up? I forgot about suspenders."

"I tied some scraps of fabric together and made a belt."

"I bet that's pretty."

Certain that he was making fun of her again, Rachel ignored him and released the hem of her smock. "Can we go?"

Wyatt shook his head, pointing to the article of clothing she had thrown across her shoulders. "Now, what do you call that?"

"It's a mantle." She fastened the red silk frog at her throat so the short cape fell over her shoulders and closed. The brocade trim hung just below her waist.

"Uh-huh. It looks as if it might be velvet."

"It is. It will keep me warm."

"And the lining. That flash of scarlet I saw when you were closing it, I think that might be satin."

Rachel's nostrils flared slightly as she heaved an impatient sigh. "Is it important?"

"Don't know, but it sure is interesting. Do you have a pair of gloves?" When Rachel produced a pair of butter-soft, red kid gloves from the pocket of her smock, Wyatt quickly put the back of his hand to his mouth and coughed to cover his roar of laughter. "You don't chop wood in those. Where are your work gloves?"

"They're too thick. They'll make me clumsy with the gun. I might shoot you."

Wyatt thought her eyes gleamed a bit too brightly. He grunted softly. "You won't be wearing them when you're handling the gun, but you'll need them for warmth until then."

He called her back when she started to go. "Wait. Do you have another pair of boots? And maybe a less extravagant bonnet? Something without strawberries on it."

She clapped a hand on her head. "There's nothing wrong with my boots or my bonnet."

"The boots can stay," he conceded after a second glance at them. They looked dainty because her feet were small, but he recognized they were a sturdy pair from Wickham's Leather Goods. "Wear the bonnet only if you don't mind giving up those strawberries to target practice."

Rachel gave him her back and stomped into the house.

Wyatt stroked his black gelding's even blacker mane. "You saw her, didn't you? Was I wrong?" Raider shook his head and snuffled loudly. "That's right. And if you still had your balls, you would have stood up to her."

Turning Raider toward the spring, Wyatt followed the path and collected a canteen of cold water while he was waiting for Rachel to reappear. He allowed Raider to take a little water and drank some himself; then he leaned negligently against his horse while he examined his gun.

He was holstering it when he heard Rachel approaching from behind. "I didn't know it would take so long to choose another bonnet," he said, taking his time to turn around. "I should have picked one out for—"

Wyatt fell silent for a long moment, incapable of more than a single thought. Rachel was no longer wearing any of the ridiculously unsuitable clothing she'd had on earlier. She'd replaced the bonnet with a black, wide-brimmed felt hat. She wore a sheepskin-lined leather jacket with the collar turned up at the back. He had a glimpse of a white shirt and a dove-gray vest before she finished buttoning her jacket. The black wool trousers she was wearing fit her better than the kid gloves she'd had on earlier. They sure as hell weren't Theo Easter's hand-me-down denims, and they sure as hell weren't cuffed at the ankle. This pair was neatly hemmed and fit closely over her boots, the only items she hadn't exchanged. He continued to stare at her as she pulled a pair of black leather riding gloves out of her jacket pocket and slipped them on her elegantly turned hands.

"Holy Mother of God."

"That's not flattering, Sheriff."

"Wyatt," he said absently. "What's not flattering?"

Rachel's lip curled derisively as his coolly colored eyes completed a second pass over her. "Do you even know you spoke?"

He blinked. "Mmm?"

"Oh, for goodness' sake. You should be thinking twice about letting me near a gun."

He was, but that was because he was thinking about taking her to bed. "Where did you get those clothes?"

"Is that what you really want to know? Be glad I've already spent a winter here and that I learned something about what I need." She pointed to his horse. "I don't ride, though, so I hope you meant it when you said we're not going far."

"I meant it," he said, dragging his eyes away from her so she could mount. He held out a hand to her. "C'mon. Put your foot in the stirrup and I'll pull you up behind me."

"What about hiking?"

"I might have lied about that."

Huffing once, Rachel extended her hand. She watched the horse warily while she lifted one foot to the stirrup.

"Don't watch Raider," Wyatt told her. "Look at me."

She did, making a little jump at the same time. He pulled her onto Raider's back in a single, fluid motion. A small breath escaped her as she came to rest directly behind him. The gelding shuffled back and forth until Wyatt steadied him with some pressure from his knees.

"Hold on to me," he said over his shoulder.

Rachel stared at his back and wondered what she was supposed to grab. His jacket fit him tautly across the shoulders, and there was almost no give at the waist. Her dilemma was answered when Wyatt reached behind him and brought her hands forward until they practically rested inside his pockets. This had the effect of pressing her hard against his back.

"Ready?" he asked.

"I'd really rather be walking."

He pretended he hadn't heard. "Good."

Behind him, Rachel rolled her eyes before she squeezed them shut and put herself completely in his hands.

Riding with him was not so very different, she discovered, than being held fast in his embrace: he made it safe for her to surrender control.

The epiphany startled her into opening her eyes.

"Are you all right back there?" asked Wyatt.

"Fine."

"You're looking around, aren't you? There's nowhere else like it."

Rachel's cheek brushed against his coat as she nodded. "It's beautiful. Are we riding toward the mine? I've never been there."

"No, not to the mine. I don't imagine you're going to much like it when you do get there. They've been blasting and using hydraulic cannons for years now. It scars the land, but that's what it takes to mine the gold and silver. I'll take you there, but not today."

Rachel held on tighter as they began to climb. "Is this where you go when you ride out on Thursdays?"

"It's one of the trails I take."

She found herself lulled by the quiet, husky timbre of his voice as he pointed out the variety of pines that filled the mountainside. Looking around, she saw that sometimes they stood shoulder to shoulder, like a phalanx of giants set protectively around the mountain, and sometimes, one stood alone in the shadow of a more majestic figure. The ponderosas were particularly impressive, rising as much as one hundred eighty feet above the slopes, with bark like dragon scales. In the far distance, and at a much higher elevation, Rachel could make out the timberline trees, most of them limber pine that found purchase in the rocky soil but grew twisted from exposure to the wind and weather.

As Wyatt told her about the firs and the junipers, the infinite, and yet subtle, diversity of their cones, needles, and seeds, Rachel recalled what Molly had told her about Wyatt: *He's smart as a whip. He knows something about nearly everything.*

"You've spent a lot of time out here, haven't you?" she said.

"Every Thursday for the past eight years."

"More than that, I think. Molly told me about the Rocky Mountain Detective Association. You must be familiar with just about all of these mountains."

He chuckled. "You're seriously underestimating the length and breadth of this range, even the part of it that rests here in Colorado, but I know some parts better than others. I've taken a lot of photographs out here."

"Photographs? Really?"

"Hundreds, I imagine, though I never made a count of them."

Rachel found it easier to move with the horse when she wasn't thinking too hard about it. She turned her head and rested her chin comfortably against his shoulder, lifting it just a bit when she spoke so she didn't sound as if she had a stutter. "Where did you learn about photography?"

"I took it up during the war."

Of all the things he might have said, this answer was the least expected. She did some calculating in her head. "You couldn't have been more than thirteen or fourteen."

"Twelve, but there were plenty of others like me, and most of them were fighting. I ended up attaching myself to Mathew Brady and carried tripods and glass plates, drove the wagon when I had to, and learned whatever he was willing to teach me."

Rachel had some understanding of what he wasn't telling her. Following Mathew Brady's lead would have meant that Wyatt had traipsed over battlefields *after* they were littered with bodies. He would have sat in the camps in the morning, perhaps listening to men trade stories and watching them write letters home, and even at twelve, he would have known that for some of them it would be the last time they'd do those particular things. At the end of the day, he would have been at the side of the photographers, making a visual record of the fallen.

Wyatt pulled up on the reins as they came upon a clearing beside a fast-running mountain stream. "This'll do." He glanced over his shoulder. "You first. I'll help you down." He gripped her hand and forearm and took his foot out of the stirrup so she could put a toe in. She levered herself up a bit awkwardly, then swung one leg over Raider and managed to jump to the ground without mishap. "Not too bad. Are you steady?" When she nodded, he moved Raider a few feet away and dismounted. He gave his horse a friendly pat and fastened the reins to a fallen branch. "Do you want a drink?" He held out his canteen to show her that he did not mean liquor.

"No, I'm fine."

He nodded and replaced the canteen. "I brought a few things to use for target shooting. Why don't you look over the gun, make yourself comfortable with it, while I set the targets out?" He removed his Colt from the holster and held it out to her. He expected that she might be reluctant, but she walked right up to him and took it out of his hand. "It's not loaded," he told her. "Just in case you have any notion about using it before I teach you how."

"What kind of gun is it?" she asked, turning it over in her hands. "It's heavy."

"Some call it a 'Peacemaker,' but there's a variety of those. This one's a forty-four-caliber Henry rimfire." He placed an empty coffee tin and three smaller cans on rocks at different heights and distances, then walked back to Rachel, who was removing her gloves. He did the same, stuffing them into his pocket. "I thought this one would be better for you. It has a four-and-three-quarter-inch barrel. I left the seven-and-one-half-inch barrel behind because it just didn't seem like it would suit."

"The grip is ivory."

"That's right. Some are pearl." He set the grip in her palm and closed her fingers around it. "You'll need your thumb for the hammer and your index finger for the trigger." Easing around her, he stood at her back and supported her arm as she lifted and extended it. "Go ahead. Try pulling the trigger."

She did. "It doesn't work." She tried several more times and the trigger always caught before it was fully depressed.

"That's because you need to cock the hammer first."

"Seems as if it might be too much to remember when you need it."

"In the beginning it does, but practice makes it second nature. The hammer rotates the cylinder so the next cartridge lines up with the barrel. The trigger guard is there for your safety." He brushed her thumb aside, replaced it with his own, then demonstrated how to pull the hammer back. "Every once in a while a man that thinks he needs an advantage will saw off the trigger guard. The trouble with that is he usually shoots off a body part just holstering his weapon." He removed his thumb and nudged hers back on the hammer. "Go on."

Rachel did and found the motion of cocking the hammer required more effort than she'd anticipated. She did it half a dozen times before Wyatt was satisfied.

"I'll show you how to load the weapon." He left her to get the cartridges from the saddlebag.

Rachel continued to examine the gun, turning it over, testing the weight, wondering if she'd ever truly feel it was an extension of her own hand. She doubted it. "Why are you doing this?" she asked.

He glanced up from looking over the cartridges. "You know."

"It's part of your protection plan, is that right?"

"That's right." He took the Colt from her hand, pushed open the cylinder, and set the hammer at the half-cock position, then loaded the cartridges "I don't think there's a woman in Reidsville who doesn't know how to load, aim, and fire a weapon. Some are better than others at hitting things, but everyone learns sooner or later how to scare someone off."

"Is that what you're hoping I'll be able to do? Scare Foster Maddox off?"

"I'm hoping you'll be able to hit him if it comes to that." He emptied the cylinder, then handed the revolver and the cartridges to her. "You load it now."

Rachel's first effort was clumsy, but she got it done. "Neither one of us can be certain that Foster will follow me here."

"Are you willing to say that he won't?" asked Wyatt. "I'm not. It's not unreasonable to expect him to send someone in his place. You're the last house on a street that doesn't have many families living on it. You'd only be more isolated if you lived up the mountain." He stepped a little to the side and back of her. "Of course, you could always let me move in with you. That would go a ways to easing my mind."

"I'm sure it would," she said dryly. "Oddly enough, it would give me more incentive to learn to hit my target."

Wyatt grinned. "That's why I'm standing back here." He slipped his hand under her right elbow and encouraged her to raise her arm. "What do you want to try to hit?"

"The coffee tin." It had the advantage of being bigger,

although Rachel thought her best chance for hitting something depended on whether Wyatt had the proverbial broad side of a barn in his saddlebag. She levered her arm where she thought it should go.

"You're going to send the slug into that big rock. The one that looks like Ned Beaumont's head."

She had to admit that it did look a little like Ned Beaumont's head. The rock had unusual protrusions on either side that resembled Ned's jug ears. "Well, I don't want to hit Ned." She lowered her arm a fraction.

"Use the sight."

"I will when you tell me what it is."

"The raised bit near the end of the barrel. Line it up with your target."

"Oh, I see. Well, yes, that's better."

He lowered her arm a little more. "This weapon has a kick. They all do. It's going to make your arm jerk when you fire. You need to aim lower than where you want to hit. If you want to hit a man in the chest—and usually you do—then you need to aim at his privates."

"And if I want to hit him in his privates?"

"You're a whole bucket of sass, aren't you?" He leaned around her shoulder and got a good look at her face. There was enough heat in her cheeks to warm his hands. He just shook his head. "All right. How's your arm holding up?"

"It's fine."

He dropped his hand and stood back. "When you think you're ready, cock the hammer and squeeze the trigger."

Afraid she would lose her position, Rachel didn't dare nod. She caught the hammer with her thumb and cocked it. Her finger twitched on the trigger. She squeezed her eyes shut and pulled.

Ned Beaumont's rocky replica lost an earlobe, and Rachel lost her balance. Wyatt used one hand at the small of her back to catch her and the other to grab her wrist and keep her from dropping the gun.

"You closed your eyes."

Since he couldn't have possibly seen, Rachel realized he had expected it. "Poor Ned. You might have warned me."

"It generally doesn't do any good. You have to experience it. Now that you know, you'll do better. Did you feel the kick?"

"All the way to my shoulder."

He nodded, gave her shoulder a light squeeze, and indicated she should try again. "Whenever you're ready."

Rachel finished off the cartridges in the cylinder without ever hitting the tin. Five more shots. Five more misses. Disappointed, she handed the Colt back to Wyatt. "Show me. I need to be reminded that it can be done."

"All right, but you load it for me."

She did, deftly handling the revolver this time. "Six rounds."

He took the gun and holstered it carefully. "What's my target? You choose."

"The tin's fine."

"Which letter? There're six of them."

She frowned. "What are you—" Then she realized he was referring to the bold black letters on the side of the green tin. COFFEE. "Are you trying to impress me?"

"Can I?"

Rachel hated to admit it to herself, let alone to him, but the answer was most definitely *yes*. "The *F*," she said. "The *second F*."

"You're a hard woman."

Smiling as if she'd been complimented, Rachel watched Wyatt eye his target. The very air around him seemed to still, and she realized she was the one holding her breath while he was slowly exhaling. She actually flinched when he drew and fired.

Rachel barely shifted her attention from Wyatt to the target in time to see the coffee tin jump, wobble, and then disappear behind the rock it had been perched on. It was no good pretending that she wasn't awed by what he'd done, not when she knew it was plainly etched in her features.

"Wait right here," she told him, then hurried off to find and examine the tin.

Wyatt lowered his weapon and waited for Rachel's return. He had a renewed appreciation for the fit of her trousers as she bent over the anvil-sized rock to make her retrieval. He carefully composed himself before she turned around, although there were adjustments he would have liked to make to the fit of his own trousers.

Rachel poked the tip of her finger through the hole made squarely in the medial crossbar of the second F. Even with the evidence before her eyes, she couldn't quite accept it. "That's impossible."

"Actually, it is," Wyatt told her. "That was just plain luck. I'm not that accurate."

She set the tin back on its perch and turned on him. "Now, why would you tell me that? Don't you want me to be impressed?"

"Are you saying that telling the truth doesn't do the trick?"

"You're right," she said, coming to stand beside him. "That's impressive." She pointed to the tin. "Do it again."

"Think you can stand there without jumping out of your skin this time?" He didn't wait for her answer. He raised and fired his weapon in a single fluid motion. The coffee tin spun; then so did the other cans, one right after the other.

Rachel managed to hold her ground, but now she found herself staring slightly openmouthed in the direction of Wyatt's shots and unable to hold back her admiration. "I want to do that," she said, laying out her palm for the gun. "Did you bring a lot of cartridges?"

"Enough."

As it turned out, he brought half again as many as she could use. After emptying the Colt four times, Rachel discovered she could barely lift it. Loading it for the fifth round of shots was difficult, as her fingers had begun to tremble with the exertion of her previous efforts.

Watching her, Wyatt could see discouragement warring with determination. She'd come close to hitting the coffee tin a few times, but there was no satisfaction for her in that. He pushed away from the trunk he'd been leaning against and stepped out from under the broad pine canopy.

"Will you let me help you?"

Until he asked the question, Rachel hadn't realized how much she wanted to do this on her own, and still, she was able to recognize the conceit of taking that position. Coming here hadn't even been her idea, and in fact, she couldn't have conceived of it. Refusing his offer was both impolite and arrogant.

"Please," she said. "I'd like that."

His fingers brushed hers as he took the Colt from her open palms. "Your hands are like ice."

"Mmm."

Wyatt holstered the gun and pocketed the cartridges. "Here, give them to me."

She decided it was the cold that made her so slow to respond because for a long moment she simply regarded him blankly. It was only when he reached for her that she understood what he wanted. She didn't so much give him her hands as not withdraw them. He pressed them together in an attitude of prayer and clapped his much larger hands around them. Watching her closely, he began to rub briskly. Rachel felt her knees sag a little as the first wave of warmth surged through her. She pressed her lips together and closed her eyes, reveling in the heat he pressed into her.

"Good?" he asked.

"Mmm." She forced herself to open her eyes and saw he

wasn't looking at her hands at all. His cool blue predator eyes were studying her face, and the hint of a smile curling his lips might have been amusement . . . or something else. "That's fine," she said, and as soon as she began to ease her hands out of his grasp, he let her go.

Wyatt nodded. "Put your hands in your pockets while I load the gun." What he did, though, was take the gun out of the holster and empty the chamber of all but one of the cartridges.

"Why did you take them out?" she asked as he slipped them in his pocket with the others.

"Because you're only going to need one."

He said it so confidently that Rachel didn't challenge him. Moreover, it struck her that she *wanted* to believe him. "What do you want me to do?"

"Exactly what I tell you." He stepped behind her and edged his body right up to hers; then he reached around with his gun hand and encouraged her to take it. While she was doing that, he used his free arm to set her shoulders and hips. He nudged her feet a few more inches apart, broadening her stance. "All right. Position the gun."

It already felt too heavy in her hand, but when she began to raise it, Wyatt's arm supported her just as he had in the beginning of her instruction. She felt his warm breath near her ear as he adjusted his own height and stance to duplicate her view.

"The coffee tin, right?" he asked.

"Yes."

He pulled her arm down a fraction of an inch; his hand cupped hers. "Put your thumb on the hammer." When she did, his thumb moved to rest lightly on top of hers. "Pull it back." He let her do the work. "Good. Is your finger on the trigger?"

She answered in a whisper. "Yes."

"Don't close your eyes," he said, his voice not much louder

than hers. "Don't hold your breath." When he felt her begin to exhale, he gave his final instruction. "Squeeze."

Rachel didn't know the precise sequence of events. It seemed the tin jumped before she heard the Colt's report. She barely felt the weapon's kick. Wyatt absorbed the recoil and cushioned her tremor. She knew she gave up a cry that was all joy and excitement, but she hardly heard it. Twisting in Wyatt's embrace, she threw her arms around his neck and made a mad little leap that forced him to take a step backward to regain his balance.

Laughing, full of the thrill of her accomplishment, Rachel held on and turned her head. Her lips lightly grazed his cheek.

It might have ended there, except that Wyatt also turned his head and it was then that their mouths met. The kick made her shudder. Her hat fell to the ground as Wyatt's palm lifted to cradle the back of her head. His mouth moved over hers, slanting first one way, then the other, pressing the advantage she had given him with the first tentative caress of her lips.

She held on tightly because it seemed that nothing else was possible. Her mouth opened under his, a mere fraction at first, then wider as the tip of his tongue traced her upper lip. She wanted this, but that admission, as fleeting and private as it was, also had the power to alarm her.

"Don't close your eyes," he whispered.

Rachel looked at him. He was so close that she imagined it was her own reflection in his darkening eyes. This was Wyatt. Wyatt. And she had put herself in his arms. Her eyes opened wider.

Watching her, he smiled a little crookedly. He nudged her nose with his. "Don't hold your breath."

The light brush of his mouth against hers tickled. She leaned into the kiss.

One of his hands solidly cupped her bottom, and her legs were wrapped around his thighs, but in spite of both those things she began to slip. Rachel responded to the instruction as he whispered it.

"Squeeze."

She breathed in the scent of pine and leather and man and did exactly what he said. Tightening her knees brought her flush against his groin. The whimper at the back of her throat gave sound to her need, and the soft feline growl that followed was the voice of her own predator instincts.

She matched his kiss, openmouthed and wanting. She pressed her lips to the corner of his mouth, his cheek, the line of his jaw. One of his hands remained at the back of her head, fingers sifting her hair to loosen the simple plait that confined it. The sensation of his fingertips against her scalp caused a spark to skip all the way down her spine and ignite a charge that she didn't know was buried there. Heat simply exploded. She felt it deeply at first as her womb contracted; then it rippled through her, rising to the surface of her skin, making her toes curl and her heart stammer.

Wyatt drew back slightly. His fingers closed more tightly over her braid of hair, and he positioned her face so it was tilted toward him. Her lips were swollen and wet and cherry red. When they parted, her breath mingled with his. The centers of her eyes were black and wide, yet she did not have the vague look of a sleepy lover. She was alert and just a little guarded. It seemed to Wyatt that she was waiting for him.

He turned her head and found the sensitive hollow just below her ear. His mouth moved to her neck, where he sipped on her skin. Feasting on her mouth, he covered ground quickly, stopping when he could press her against the wide tree trunk of a ponderosa pine. The back of his hand scraped the broad, scaly bark, but protected her head. Supported by the trunk, she eased her tight hold around his neck and shoulders. He could still feel the gun at his back.

"You want to holster that Colt?" he asked, nudging her lips with his.

Nodding, she eased her gun hand away.

"Wrong hand. The holster's on *my* right."

"Too much to remember," she whispered.

"You're doing fine." He could feel her transferring the revolver to her other hand and lowering it toward his holster. There was some awkwardness as she tried to find it. The fact that she was still clinging to him like ivy meant she had to reach beneath her own hip to locate it. She didn't ask to be released, though, and Wyatt had already decided he'd let her drop the empty gun before he'd let her go.

Rachel slipped the Colt into Wyatt's holster. "You're going to have to put me down sometime."

"Probably." He nibbled on her upper lip. "Not now."

It struck her as extraordinary that she could smile. "No," she said. "Not now."

His tongue darted into her mouth. She pressed hers against it, circled, suckled. She swallowed his soft groan; his hips drove into her. Her hands were finally free, and they fisted in his hair. His hat fell to the ground, and the shadow that had been cast across his features disappeared.

Rachel saw him clearly, saw the taut line of his jaw, the features that were slightly drawn as he held himself carefully away from her. She cupped his face, brushed her thumb across his lower lip. He sucked in a breath and the tip of her thumb. He bit down gently.

She began to slip away in that moment. Her legs slowly unwound until she was standing, though not without help from him. Her hands remained on his face, her heels dug into a bed of pine straw between his feet. She felt his fingers twisting the buttons on her coat; then his hands were inside, trapped between the lamb's wool and the linen of her shirt, warming themselves, but warming her, too.

She hardly dared breathe. He seemed to know it because he bent his head and touched his lips to hers, a kiss so light that it was hardly more than a puff of air. She took it greedily, gratefully.

He tugged at the tails of her shirt, pulling it free; then his fingers slipped beneath the linen. Swearing softly, he laid his forehead against hers.

Rachel knew what had frustrated him. She reached under her shirt and caught each of his wrists in her hands. When she tugged, he let her pull him away. Her slightly ragged breathing matched his own.

"That's a hell of a thing you're wearing, Rachel."

"It's a corset."

"It's a cage."

She smiled a little ruefully. He wasn't far wrong. "Steel ribs."

Wyatt lifted his head and studied her face. Her skin was still flushed, but he could see that something had changed. Regret edged the line of her mouth, softened the look in her eyes. It didn't stop him from saying what was on his mind. "I want to touch you."

"I know."

"I think you want me to."

"It could be that you're right," she said quietly. "In fact, I think you are."

"But . . . ?"

She dropped his wrists and tucked in her shirt. She pulled her jacket closed. "But it's not going to happen."

"Jesus, Rachel." He plowed through his hair with his fingers. "I didn't start this. You were the one throwing yourself at me."

Rachel glanced up from buttoning her coat. Her right eyebrow rose in a perfect arch. "Is that really the position you want to take?"

The fact that she was right to call him on it didn't exactly go down well. He bent, scooped up his hat, and jammed it on his head. Turning away, he stalked off in the direction of his horse.

Rachel leaned back against the tree trunk and watched him go. His shoulders looked bunched, and his hands were thrust deeply in his pockets. "I'm sorry," she called after him. She saw him shrug, so she knew he'd heard her. Her voice fell to a whisper that was well outside his hearing. "I'm sorry."

Monday morning, Rachel met with Abe Dishman. She found him at Longabach's, eating breakfast alone, and learned that Ned was out and about doing odd jobs. As he lacked an opponent for his favorite game, she joined him at the table and outlined her proposal over the checkerboard.

"If you accept," she told him, "it means you'll have to stop asking me to marry you."

Abe's mouth screwed up to one side, and he scratched his lantern jaw as he thought about that. "I don't know, Miss Bailey. Could be it's a deal breaker. There's folks that might say you offered me the job on account of me courtin' you ever since you came to town. Maybe they'll say that you're a little sweet on me, too. Wouldn't look right for me to stop all of a sudden. Strains the balance. This way you can keep turning me down and all's right with the world."

"Mr. Dishman, if there is logic in that argument it escapes me, but rather than ask you to elaborate, I'll agree to your terms. Mr. Clay and Mr. Kirby warned me that you wouldn't give up easily."

Abe smiled so broadly that his eyes almost disappeared. "That's a fact. John and Sam know me that well."

"They said you helped build the spur."

"They told you right, then. I guess I know about every inch of that track. I managed the depot for a time." He lowered his head and made a study of the board. "Maddox hired a new manager a couple of years back. I imagine John probably told you about that."

"Not the details."

Abe shrugged and made his move. "Ben Cromwell—that's the man Maddox hired—he didn't much care for my suggestions."

"Your suggestions? I think you'll find that I'm reasonable in that regard."

"Don't know about that, Miss Bailey, but then I don't expect I'll be tellin' you what you can do with your foot after you finish stompin' on my . . ." Abe flushed. "See? I don't think I'll be sayin' that to you."

"Oh. I do see. Well, I suppose if you need to say something like that . . ." Rachel pressed her lips together to keep her smile in check. Even the tips of Abe's ears were red. She countered Abe's last jump with one of her own, pulling his attention back to the board. "So there was no love lost between you and Mr. Cromwell."

"No. None at all. He didn't appreciate that the spur was special. Didn't understand why it required more attention than other parts of the line."

"Well, it's only a small section," she said. "Sixty miles?"

"Seventy-three and a quarter. It's got one bridge, three tunnels, and two water towers. It's a lifeline to these folks, and it's sure been good to the Maddox family, so there ought to be some respect for it."

"Mr. *Foster* Maddox hired Ben Cromwell, is that right?"

"Sure is. Wasn't no time at all until there was changes."

Out of the corner of her eye, Rachel saw the door to the restaurant open. She didn't turn her head as Wyatt Cooper walked in, although Abe lifted his hand to acknowledge the sheriff. "What changes will you want to make?" she asked.

"Mostly put things back the way they ought to be. Schedule regular inspections of the bridge, shore up the tunnels.

Things like that. Come winter, we'll have to send out crews to clear the passes. Always an avalanche or two. Sometimes it makes sense to start one ourselves so the trains don't do it accidentally. Nothin' upsets John Clay like having his precious engine buried in the snow." Abe shifted in his chair as Wyatt came to stand at the table. "Howdy, Sheriff. How're your guests doin'?"

"Morning, Abe." He nodded at Rachel. "Miss Bailey."

"Good morning."

Wyatt addressed Abe's question. "They don't like my jail much, but that doesn't begin to compare with how much they don't like each other. They pick and peck at each other like Estella and Miss LaRosa. Draw blood, too."

"I heard that," Estella called from behind the counter.

Wyatt and Abe chuckled. Rachel forced a smile.

"You want to join us?" Abe asked.

"No. Don't want to interrupt. I just stopped here to find out if you accepted Miss Bailey's offer."

"So you know about that." Abe's eyes darted to Rachel for confirmation.

She nodded. "The sheriff introduced me to Mr. Clay and Mr. Kirby."

"Well, how about that? You takin' a special interest in the spur, Wyatt, or are you a rival for the affections of Miss Bailey here?"

Wyatt chuckled. "It's the spur, Abe. I'm no rival."

"Good to hear." He pointed to the checkerboard. "Looks like I won't have much time for this, 'cept evenings and Saturdays. You're talkin' to the new operations manager."

Wyatt clapped Abe on the back. "Congratulations." He looked at Rachel. "You found a good man, Miss Bailey."

"I think so."

Giving Abe's shoulder a squeeze, Wyatt moved on to the register to pay his bill.

Abe turned in his chair to face Rachel. "Is what I heard true?" he asked, knuckling his chin again. "The sheriff took you out shootin' yesterday?"

"How did you hear that?"

"So it's true."

"I didn't say that."

"So it's not true."

She sighed. "I didn't say that, either."

"I heard it from Ned first thing this morning. That's just about as good as reading it in Artie Showalter's paper."

"Then I won't dispute it."

Abe's broad forehead became deeply furrowed as he considered her response. "Now, that doesn't quite answer my question, does it?"

Rachel smiled as she came to her feet. "I'm appreciative of your willingness to return to work, Mr. Dishman. Once you've settled into your office at the depot and have looked things over, I'd like a report. Friday?"

"Friday'll be fine," he said, standing. He accepted the hand she extended, and they shook firmly. It wasn't until she was gone that Abe realized she'd beaten him soundly at his own game.

That no-account Beatty boy was sitting behind a rolltop desk with his feet up when Rachel walked into the sheriff's office. He was not quite as skilled as Wyatt in supporting himself on the two back legs of a chair and nearly went ass over teakettle when he saw Rachel. The chair rocked unsteadily as he jumped up.

"Miss Bailey. Somethin' wrong? You need the sheriff? He's not here right now. Went up to Longabach's to get breakfast for the prisoners."

Rachel began removing her gloves. "I know. I just saw him

there. I'll wait." She walked over to the wood stove and held out her hands to warm them. "I thought you ride out on Mondays."

"I do." While Rachel's back was turned, Will tucked in his shirt, smoothed it over his chest. "Judge Wentworth's coming today, taking the Admiral. We got the news from Artie this morning, so the sheriff told me to stick. I'll probably head out tomorrow."

Rachel looked back over her shoulder. "Does the judge's arrival mean there will be a trial?"

"Yep. You think you'll want to watch? Most people do. I can make sure you get a seat."

"It's a kind offer, but no." She rubbed her hands to infuse them with more heat, then stepped away from the stove. "I suppose a trial is something of an entertainment here."

"Oh, it sure is. Better than the travelin' shows that Rudy sometimes hires to entertain at the saloon, though I don't like to miss those, either."

Rachel smiled. "I liked the illusionist. The Astonishing Arturo. Did you see his performance?"

"Twice. I still can't figure how he—" He stopped, cocking his head toward the back where the sounds of a scuffle could be heard. "Excuse me, Miss Bailey. Got to settle the boys. They know the judge is on his way." He took his gun out of a drawer in the desk. "They're a mite twitchy."

Nodding, Rachel watched him disappear through the connecting door to the jail cell. She thought it was just as likely that his prisoners were hungry as anxious about Judge Wentworth's arrival. Wondering what was keeping Wyatt when she'd seen him such a short time ago, Rachel made a circle of his office. There were notices tacked on the wall, rough sketches and grainy photographs of men wanted for robbery, cattle thieving, and murder. Interspersed among them were bills of sale for a saddle from Wickham's Leather Goods and a Colt .45 with a pearl grip. She recognized the latter as the revolver that Will Beatty had taken from the desk.

She listened with half an ear to the deputy trying to reason with Morrisey and Spinnaker. The scuffling continued. Shaking her head, thinking again that food was a more likely peacemaker than the gun, Rachel turned her attention to one of the maps on the wall that detailed the local area. She followed trails that were marked in Wyatt's own hand, and she imagined these were the routes he and Will Beatty took when they did their regular surveys.

The map detailed the last leg of the Calico Spur, and she followed the track as it wound up the mountain, closely following a trail blazed years earlier by men sent west to learn the lay of the land. She glanced at a map that showed a larger area of the state, and one that took account of the neighboring states and territories. She traced the spur and then the C & C line all the way to Salt Lake. It was just as well the map didn't show Sacramento. She had no interest in going there, even in her mind.

It wasn't until Rachel sat behind the desk in the same seat that the deputy had occupied that she realized that the scuffling had stopped. She imagined that Will had finally used his gun to reason with his prisoners, since they hadn't seemed to care what he had to say. Smiling to herself, she began an idle examination of the papers lying on top of the desk. There were several complaints, a few telegraph messages from Artie, and some records related to the arrest of Morrisey and Spinnaker. Curious about these last accounts, Rachel picked them up and began to read.

She heard the door open behind her, but she didn't have time to glance back and acknowledge Will's return before an unfamiliar voice took the choice away from her.

"Stay where you are, ma'am. Just keep reading and there's no harm that'll come to you."

Rachel didn't look up. The words she'd been reading clearly moments before blurred on the page. She would never know where she found the temerity to ask, "Are you Mr. Morrisey or Mr. Spinnaker?"

"Morrisey, ma'am."

"Is Deputy Beatty all right?"

"Just a sore head. One to match the one he give ol' Spinnaker here t'other day."

"That seems fair."

Morrisey cackled. "Ain't it just?" He stepped more fully into the room and motioned to Spinnaker to follow. "Now, who are you, ma'am?"

"Miss Rachel Bailey."

"Schoolmarm?"

"No. Seamstress."

"Is that no-account Beatty boy your fella?"

"No. May I put this paper down?"

"Yeah. That's all right." He spoke to his partner. "See if you can find a gun. I know the sheriff's got a Henry rifle around here somewheres."

Rachel looked up. She blinked, her breath catching slightly when she saw Morrisey had Will's Colt aimed at her. "The sheriff's Henry rifle is being repaired. Something about the firing mechanism. I'm sure I don't understand it, but there's a receipt here. I just saw it."

"That right?"

She nodded. "May I?" When he gave his approval, she riffled through the notes in one of the rolltop's compartments. "Here it is. It's dated Saturday. He must have taken the rifle to Kennedy's shortly after arresting you."

Morrisey sidled close enough to glance at the piece of paper she waved at him. "Now, that's something. Did you hear that, Jack? The sheriff was holdin' a Henry on me that wasn't any good."

"I heard. C'mon. Let's go."

"Now, we can't leave by the front, Jack. I told you that. Just came this way for a gun and some insurance. Since you ain't found a gun, guess that leaves the insurance." He jerked his weapon at Rachel. "You go on and stand up now, ma'am. You're leavin' with us. Get her coat, Jack. She's no good if she freezes before we get into the passes."

Jack Spinnaker took coats, hats, and gloves from the rack at the door. He decided he preferred Will's coat to his own and simply rolled up the sleeves when they fell below his own wrists. Morrisey gave the Colt to Jack so he could put on his coat; then he gestured to Rachel to lead the way through the back.

She saw Wyatt first. He was coming through the jail's rear entrance carrying the prisoners' breakfast. It didn't matter that he was wearing his gun belt because both of his hands were occupied with the wooden tray. His hesitation was hardly that at all, just a missed beat in his step; then she saw his eyes follow her glance to the open cell and Will's body sprawled on the floor.

He was dropping the tray even as Morrisey was pushing her ahead of him. Jack Spinnaker was on their heels, taking aim between Morrisey's shoulder and the wall. Rachel tried to press herself against the iron bars of the cell, but Morrisey grabbed her by the waist, dragged her back, and used her as a shield.

Jack fired. So did Wyatt. Rachel jabbed Morrisey with her elbow. He grunted, staggered, then loosened his grip on her waist. There was another exchange of fire. Jack grunted. Rachel felt a sharp back blow, and she dropped to her knees. The gunshots were deafening in the small space. She could only feel herself gasping for breath, not hear any sound of it. Wyatt lost his footing on the scattered contents of the breakfast tray. He was spun sideways as Spinnaker charged forward, firing.

Rachel kept her eyes open until the moment unconsciousness gave her respite.

Chapter Nine

Rachel stirred from her light sleep when she heard the sound of Wyatt's breathing change. She rose from her chair beside the window and went to his bedside. Pressing the back of her hand against his forehead, she felt for a break in his fever. He was still too warm to the touch. She prepared a damp cloth at the basin on the nightstand and used it to gently wash his face.

The lamp revealed the glow of perspiration on his upper lip and the unnatural flush to his complexion. She wiped his brow, his temples, and used it on either side of his throat. After she dampened the cloth again, she rolled it and placed it at the back of his neck.

His eyelids flickered, then opened. He stared at her. "Don't go."

She had only intended to move to the chair, but now she lowered herself back to the mattress. "I won't."

"What day is it?"

"Thursday."

One of his eyebrows slowly lifted. "Morning or night?"

"It's night before morning."

Using his elbows, Wyatt started to push himself up. Pain in

his left shoulder pushed him right back. He grimaced. "I imagine getting kicked by a mule hurts about this much."

Rachel saw beads of sweat reappear on his upper lip and brow. "Dr. Diggins is against you getting on your feet just yet."

"I heard him. It doesn't mean there aren't things to be done."

Rachel's expression was plainly skeptical. "Do you want me to talk you out of it?"

His short laugh made him remember how painfully tight his chest was. He grimaced again. "You already have."

That made her smile. She removed the cloth from under his neck and placed it in the basin. When it had soaked up the cool water, she wrung it out and wiped down his face and throat once more.

Wyatt closed his eyes. A vertical crease appeared between his eyebrows as he tried to draw on vague memories. "Doc took a bullet out of my shoulder, didn't he?"

"That's right. And another out of your chest. He thought he was going to lose you looking around for that one. He said if he hadn't had the ether, he would have left it in. He didn't hold out much hope that you'd live long with it inside you."

"Men do."

"So I learned, but it didn't seem the same would be true for you."

He made a scoffing noise at the back of his throat. It turned into a hard, racking cough that made him regret taking offense of Doc's pessimistic prognosis. "I remember bits," he said after he took a sip of the water she gave him.

"You've been talking now and again."

"Did I make any sense?"

"About as much as always."

Coming from Rachel, Wyatt took it to mean that he'd been talking out of his head. "How's Will?"

"You've asked before," she told him. She saw his distress

when he couldn't remember. "Never mind, it doesn't matter. You're still fevered. Will's fine. The doctor said his scalp's as tender as a schoolboy's heart, but his skull's as thick as a two-by-four. I think the latter's a reference to a lumber plank."

The edges of Wyatt's mouth turned up a fraction. He closed his eyes again. "It is."

Rachel realized she was rolling Wyatt's empty water glass between her palms. She set it aside and laid her hands lightly on her lap. She waited to see if he would ask another question, but the even rise and fall of his chest seemed to indicate he was drifting back to sleep. Leaning over him, she turned her cheek to feel the gentle exhalation of his breath against her skin. "Get well," she whispered. She eased off the bed and returned to her chair at the window.

Wyatt's fever broke some ten hours later. Rachel was in the adjoining sitting room bent over the round dining table while she pinned a muslin pattern to Estella Longabach's moss-green sateen. Her head came right up when she heard swearing and thrashing coming from the bedroom.

"Don't you move!" she called to him, dropping her shears. "Don't you dare move. You'll split your stitches." He was propping himself on his good arm when she got to the threshold and kicking the covers off his bed by the time she reached his side. "I swear, Wyatt Cooper, if you—"

"You don't."

Hands planted on her hips, Rachel stared hard at him. "I don't what?"

"You don't swear. I've never heard you swear."

"Well, it's not because I don't know how. Lie down. Let me look at you before you start pacing the floor. Dr. Diggins might still be in the hotel. I can get him."

It was improbably comforting to know she was as bossy as

he remembered. He rolled onto his back. "Don't take too long." Rather than elaborating, he looked significantly in the direction of the bathing room.

Rachel blinked but didn't blush. "I'll help you there in a moment."

Wyatt wasn't certain he'd let her, but he didn't argue about it now. He smelled the stink of sickness on him and didn't know how she stood by without turning up her nose. Her movements were efficient, just as they were when she was cutting a pattern or placing her stitches. She briskly unbuttoned his nightshirt and laid it open so that she could tend to the bandage on his shoulder. Lifting it, she examined the wound and gave him a sour look.

"You're bleeding." She washed away the blood and saw that he'd only cracked the scab, not torn the stitches.

"You don't look very happy that I'm going to live."

"Happy that you didn't rip my best work."

"Your best work?" He winced as she pressed a clean bandage to his shoulder. "What does that mean?"

Ignoring him, Rachel tugged carefully on the bandages that covered his chest wound. Her small, neat stitches still closed his skin. There was no foul-smelling pus or weeping around the injury, and his skin was warm, not hot. She replaced the bandages, then closed his shirt. "The fever's left your body."

"Good riddance, I say."

She nodded. "Let me help you up." Rachel slipped an arm under his shoulders and lifted. He'd lost considerable strength, but he still assisted her effort. "Put your legs over the side. Would you like your robe and slippers?"

Now that he was sitting up the urgency was upon him. "If it's all the same to you, I'll go as I am."

Rachel understood. She placed his uninjured arm around her shoulders and supported him as they came to their feet together. He was about as wobbly legged as a foal for the first few steps; then he managed to find his balance. Rachel stayed with him until he got to the bathing room door. "I'm going to find Doc Diggins," she said. "I won't be gone long."

Wyatt nodded and waved her off, shutting the door at the same time.

Rachel stood staring at the door for a few moments before she rushed off in search of the doctor. He wasn't in the hotel any longer, but after a few inquiries she was able to trace him to the Miner Key Saloon where he was playing cards with Ned Beaumont and two of Sid Walker's boys. She had to shame him before he would leave his winning hand, and by the time she brought him back to the hotel, Wyatt had managed to get himself into his bathing tub and was soaking in hot water just below the level of his chest wound.

When Doc Diggins backed out of the bathing room and told her what Wyatt was doing, Rachel was so astonished that she had to see for herself. She poked her head in the room, observed Wyatt resting comfortably in the tub with his head tipped back and his eyes closed, and made certain right then that he knew she could swear. Even Doc Diggins, who knew a thing or two about peppering his speech with blasphemies, was impressed with the deep blue color of her vocabulary.

It was the doctor who sat with Wyatt until he was prepared to get out of the tub, and the doctor who helped him into a clean shirt and drawers and put him back to bed, and it was the doctor who finally convinced Rachel that Wyatt could benefit from some light fare and that she should arrange it.

Rachel regretted that she had gone to get Doc in the first place.

Diggins left instructions with her when she returned with Wyatt's food. She was aware he didn't share them with his patient because Wyatt would have argued his way out of them. The good doctor was expecting her to cage the wild beast and wanted no part of it himself.

Rachel saw him out, picked up the tray, and carried it to Wyatt's bedroom. He was sitting up in bed, not looking nearly as comfortable as he had in the tub. He'd exhausted himself already and was never going to admit it to her.

Rachel set the tray on his lap. "Do you require help?"

"I'm not an infant."

She resisted the obvious retort and uncovered the dishes, revealing milky rice soup with a sprinkling of brown sugar, two triangles of dry toast, and a baked apple.

Wyatt stared at the plates. "I still have my teeth, don't I?"

"Very nice ones. Dr. Diggins suggested light fare. I would have chosen a thick steak, a little on the rare side, I think, and perhaps some stuffed potatoes, spinach, and warm apple cobbler." Her smile was rueful. "But this is what you get, I'm afraid."

He didn't for a moment believe she wasn't enjoying herself. Curling his lip to let her know what he thought of her performance, he picked up the soup spoon and began eating.

"Doc said you were the one who stitched my wounds. He said you stood by during the operation, helping him. I don't remember that."

"That's as it should be. The ether made you sleep. In fact, it made all of us a little light-headed until Will thought to prop open a window."

"Will was there?"

She nodded. "Dr. Diggins examined him and turned him over to Gracie Showalter to clean up. He wouldn't leave Doc's office while Doc was working on you. He held a compress to his head and kept a bucket on his lap."

"Hard head. Weak stomach."

"Indeed."

Wyatt bit off a corner of toast. "Maybe I should ask who *wasn't* in Doc's office."

She chuckled. "It was only Will, Doc, Gracie, and me with

you. The front room of Doc's place was full, but I couldn't begin to tell you who all was there. A lot of people were frightened for you. You were as pale as Morrisey and Spinnaker when you were carried out of the jail, and they were dead."

"Doc said something like that."

"Did you know you'd killed them?"

Wyatt shook his head. "I knew I hit Morrisey. I thought I winged Spinnaker. I saw you go down, and I just kept firing." His gaze narrowed on her. "Were you hit?"

"A ricochet. Will explained it to me. A shot from Mr. Spinnaker's gun hit the bars, glanced off, and I was far enough ahead of him that it caught me in the back." She saw Wyatt's face drain of color so that it looked very much like it had after the gunfight. Speaking quickly, she said, "I'm fine. Truly. The bullet hit one of the steel ribs in my corset. I have a lovely yellow and purple flower of a bruise on my back, but other than that I'm fine. It would be a good story if I hadn't lost consciousness, and a better one if I'd shot someone myself, but I'd probably never tell it all that well anyway."

Wyatt sympathized with Will's need to hold a bucket in his lap. His own stomach was feeling a little weak. He bit off another bite of toast to settle it. "I find that I have a new appreciation for corsets."

"That's as it should be," she said. She set her mouth primly to mock him, quite content now to have the opportunity. "Go on. Eat up."

Taking up his spoon again, Wyatt tried some of the baked apple. He alternated between soup and dessert, occasionally dunking his toast into the warm, sweet milk of the soup. Rachel watched him for a while, offering no conversation; then she left his bedside and disappeared into the sitting room. While Wyatt didn't particularly care for her hovering, he liked her absence even less. This perversity annoyed him, especially when he recalled his mother remarking on it when she nursed him through a bout of the influenza when he was eight.

Rachel swept back into the bedroom, her arms filled with material and a sewing basket, and stopped abruptly when she glimpsed Wyatt's face. "Do you want me to leave? You're scowling."

He realized she was right. "Not intended for you."

She made a point of looking over her shoulder. "There's someone else?"

His scowl firmly in place now, he grunted softly and jabbed the spoon toward his chest. "Me."

"Would you like a mirror? Because I can positively say that I don't like being on the receiving end of that look." Ignoring him, she set the basket and fabric on the narrow window seat and positioned her chair so she had the best light. She sat, chose a needle and thread from the basket, and drew a portion of the moss-green sateen toward her. Bending her head, she applied herself to her work.

"Can you talk while you do that?" he asked.

"If you like."

Wyatt looked down at his tray. He'd finished half of the soup, a quarter of the baked apple, all but a few bites of toast, and he knew he was done. "Does Doc Diggins know you have experience caring for invalids?"

"I'm surprised you're admitting that you are one."

"It's a temporary concession, and you didn't answer my question."

"I have no idea what the doctor knows. He didn't question my competency, and as far as I know, until I left you alone in order to find him, I never gave him a reason to."

"Are you still mad at me because I drew a bath?"

Rachel glanced up. "I'm mad at myself for leaving because there was no opportunity to stop you. It was a foolish risk you took. You might have fallen. You were hardly steady on your feet. And you risked getting the stitches wet and causing the wounds to open."

A glimmer of a smile played across Wyatt's mouth. "I think I liked it better when you just swore at me."

She scowled at him, a near perfect imitation of his own, and returned to setting the sleeve of Estella's gown.

Wyatt chuckled, finding that humor was sometimes worth the wince. "So, how many invalids have you cared for?" he asked as he moved his tray to the nightstand. "Not counting me."

"Two."

"Clinton Maddox was one, wasn't he?"

"He was, and he had as little liking for being an invalid as you." Because she knew he would press the question, she went on. "The other was my father."

"Tell me about him."

Rachel hesitated. Wyatt's tone wasn't demanding, merely conversational, curious. For Rachel it didn't make it any less intrusive. Just thinking of what she might say brought the sting of tears to her eyes, and that was as unexpected as it was unwanted. She kept her head down and pressed her lips together.

"Rachel?"

She made a few blind stabs with her needle, knowing full well that she'd have to pull them out. Abandoning her work, Rachel fumbled under the fabric to find her handkerchief. She pressed it to her eyes, then blinked rapidly. Her smile was a trifle watery as she collected herself. "Forgive me. I didn't anticipate that rush of feeling." And because she felt she had to offer him something, she said, "What would you like to know?"

"I'm sorry, Rachel. I didn't—"

"I know." She put her handkerchief away and began removing the ill-placed stitches. "My father was an officer in the Union army. He and Benson Maddox enlisted together, and both of them were quickly promoted. Neither had fighting experience or an inclination for battle, but they were leaders and that's what was recognized."

"They knew each other before enlistment?"

"I suppose I didn't say, did I? They were friends. Good friends. My father worked for Clinton Maddox. He kept the financial records for all of Mr. Maddox's rail lines. When Mr. Maddox expressed interest in a western line, my father and Benson moved to Sacramento. Mr. Maddox came later. I think my father had it in his mind that he could protect Benson if they enlisted together, and perhaps that was even true for a while, but eventually their individual responsibilities separated them. Benson moved with the infantry. My father's special financial skills kept him at the side of generals, figuring the costs of war, not only of supplies, but of men. Mr. Maddox was laying track all over the East, especially in the mid-Atlantic, so Union troops would have food and weapons. My father had a lot to do with helping to determine the routes. He would tell me later that he was Mr. Maddox's government man, and he never said it as if it pleased him."

"No, I don't imagine that it did." Wyatt had been resting the back of his head against the Gothic-styled walnut headboard that Sir Nigel Pennyworth swore was reminiscent of European cathedrals. Now he tucked a pillow behind his back, because cathedral spires be damned, he wasn't comfortable. "But he survived the war."

"A truth in the literal sense," Rachel said quietly. "He was different afterward, at least that was what I understood. I was seven when he returned to us, so I'm sure that my view was colored by the perspectives of my mother and my sister, but I noticed things as well. He was quieter, more introspective. It was not uncommon to find him sitting alone in his study. He could appear deeply contemplative, but what he was studying was a wall, a window, or the tips of his own fingers. Melancholia was his companion unless he was trying very hard not to allow us to see it. That took its toll."

Wyatt realized he'd never been certain if her father was dead or alive. Now he knew. "How long ago?"

"Ten years. It was just after my fourteenth birthday."

Offering his regrets seemed inadequate in the face of grief that was still so easily tapped. Rachel took the opportunity for unsolicited condolences away from him by quickly going on.

"My father and I were very close. My mother and Sarah are the proverbial peas in the pod. I suppose that's why I was the one who looked after him. I had the temperament for it, and they didn't." She laughed a little when she saw Wyatt's skeptical look when she mentioned her temperament. "Caring for someone doesn't mean giving in to their whims. There is a place for compassion and an equally important place for—"

"A complete lack of feeling?" Wyatt interjected. "A cold heart?"

"Common sense, I was going to say, but if you prefer either of the others, I don't mind."

"You know I was teasing, don't you?"

She flashed her most slyly contented smile. "So was I."

Wyatt held his chest as he laughed this time, finding it hurt a great deal less. When he settled back again, he asked her if her father had worked for Clinton Maddox until his death.

"He died in his office," she told him. "His heart just gave out. Mr. Maddox was distraught. I didn't understand it at the time, but I think that for Mr. Maddox it was like losing his son. He never held it against my father that he came back and Benson didn't. My father's feelings toward Mr. Maddox were more complicated, I think. He respected him, was more than a little in awe of him, but he was disappointed, too. That Mr. Maddox's wealth increased tenfold during the war was difficult for him to reconcile. His own role troubled him. He urged

Mr. Maddox to make gifts, contributions, set up trusts, but that didn't happen until years later."

"When you were living with Clinton Maddox."

"When Mr. Maddox decided he'd had enough of acquiring wealth," she corrected. "Do not mistake his gestures for atonement. He never thought he had anything to atone for."

"Didn't he? What about you?"

"I don't know what you mean."

"You came to live with him. How did that happen?"

"My mother was his housekeeper, Wyatt. She took the position to support us after my father died. I lived in the mansion with my sister and mother. When my sister married, my mother left with her."

"But you stayed."

"Yes. I performed valuable functions for him, acting as his hostess from time to time, scheduling his appointments, and making certain he was available for them. Later, after his stroke, I took care of him."

Wyatt did not miss that her explanations were rendered defensively, but she didn't seem to notice. He let it go. Her own feelings toward Clinton Maddox were as complicated as her father's.

"You're tiring," Rachel said, watching him rub his jaw. "Perhaps you should lie down."

It was an indication of how well she'd read his face that Wyatt didn't argue. He lowered himself onto the mattress, taking the pillow with him, and drew the covers up to his chest. He didn't remember falling asleep. It just happened.

Over the course of the next ten days, a steady stream of visitors came to the Commodore to evaluate Wyatt's progress for themselves. Rachel referred to it as a pilgrimage, a description that Wyatt had to admit had crossed his mind also. He appreciated Rachel's common sense when she turned it on the pilgrims, insisting that they wait until after lunch to visit and leave before dinner. The only visitors she made exceptions for were Doc Diggins and that no-account Beatty boy.

Molly took care of Rachel's house in her absence and brought her whatever she needed, but Wyatt had always known it wasn't a practical arrangement for her. More interesting, at least to him, was that everyone seemed to accept it without raising an eyebrow or posing a single question. He remembered telling Rachel that Reidsville embraced "live and let live," but this was extraordinary even for them. Gracie Showalter couldn't be moved to explain it. He pressed Estella and Molly and Ann Marie Easter, and they gave him nothing in return. Pastor Duun's wife wouldn't hint that there was any sort of impropriety in Rachel's presence. Rose LaRosa and Adele dropped in and neither made suggestive remarks. The women had nothing but praise for her, and even the men were unsympathetic of his objections. When he complained that she wouldn't allow him to drink whiskey, not one of them offered to bring him a flask. He organized a poker game, and his friends left the first time she hinted that he was getting tired.

He supposed it was a natural consequence of her owning half of the town's mine and all of the spur. The Calico Spur. That name had always seemed a little disparaging when Clinton Maddox had control of it, but now that it was Rachel's it was an exact fit, perfectly tailored to suit.

It was late. He'd heard the clock in the sitting room strike ten, and he thought it was probably closer to eleven now. She was still working at the dining table. He could hear the shears clicking as she cut fabric. Sometimes he could hear her moving around the table, humming softly to herself. He didn't recognize the tune, but that was probably because she couldn't carry one with a pack mule.

He tried to remember if Sylvie had ever hummed. The

problem was that he couldn't recall that she'd ever worked. Sylvianna Hammond planned parties, attended parties, and invented reasons for parties. She loved choosing her gowns, her jewelry, her shoes, and the combs and feathers for her hair. She married him believing they would remain in Boston, that he would be successful in her father's law offices or part of his own family's banking business.

He hadn't been fair to her, he'd always known that. She thought he'd lied to her, but he hadn't. It was truer that he'd lied to himself, convinced himself that he could live in Boston, a city he found too narrow, and work for his family, which he also found too narrow. He was dying there, and in the end, he'd made the same choice his father had—to save himself.

Wyatt set the book he'd been reading on the nightstand and turned back the lamp. When he looked up, he saw Rachel was standing in the doorway.

"Am I keeping you awake?" she asked.

He shook his head.

"Is something wrong?"

"No."

She studied him a moment longer, her head angled to one side. "All right," she said quietly. "I'll just shut the door."

"No. Don't." He spoke just as her fingers closed around the crystal knob. "I like it open."

"Well, I'm almost done." She started to back away, but she paused when she saw his hand come up. "What is it?"

"I'm not tired," he said. "Just the opposite. Would you mind if I sat out there while you work?"

"Of course not." His question was curious because he'd sat with her on other evenings, although never as late as this. She wondered why he asked now when he had never asked before. "Would you like something? Perhaps some warm milk?"

He came close to growling at her, and he had to be satisfied that his look was enough to send her into full retreat. Throwing back the covers, he sat up and reached for his robe. He shrugged into it, belted it loosely, then padded barefoot into the sitting room. There was a comfortable damask-covered chair next to the stove. He sat there and rested his feet near the firebox to keep them warm.

Rachel was poised over her open sketchbook. The tip of her pencil tapped lightly against the paper. There was a vertical crease between her dark eyebrows and a pink sliver of her tongue peeping out from the corner of her mouth.

Wyatt's gaze shifted from Rachel to the couch. She'd already covered it with a couple of sheets, blankets, and the quilt from her own bed. The pillow had a lace sham over it. It still didn't look very inviting, but it was where she had been sleeping since she'd moved into his suite. Every morning since he'd started to improve she cleared away the linens, removed the lace sham, and stored all of it in the bottom of his armoire. He couldn't remember what she'd done in those early days of her stay, but he didn't think she'd attended to those details. It seemed to him that the maids had been in and out more frequently than they were now.

It was almost as if she didn't want people to know they weren't sharing—

The footstool tipped and thudded on its side as Wyatt bolted upright. Rachel jerked at the suddenness of his move and straightened herself. She flinched when she met his reproachful stare.

"What?" She dropped her pencil and took a step back. "Why are you looking at me like that?"

"You told them. That's why no one's saying anything. You told them the truth."

Rachel started to skirt the table as he approached, keeping distance and a barrier between them. "You're accusing me of telling the truth? About what?" She thrust out her hand as if it would stay his advance. "And why is that a problem?"

Wyatt was unconvinced by the questions she lobbed at him. He was learning something about how she mounted her defenses, and they were entirely made of question marks. "We discussed it, Rachel. We both agreed that we weren't going to tell anyone. You were the one who insisted on it, and now you've gone back on your word without even consulting me. You know what this means, don't you?"

She continued to circle the table. "Did you hit your head? Has something happened that—" She felt a little jolt akin to alarm, but not alarm exactly. Wyatt's smile matched the cool and cunning of his eyes. He was watching her so carefully that she couldn't move. It was easy to imagine that he would stop circling, forget his injuries, and leap across the table at her.

"All right," she said, lowering her hand a fraction. "They know."

"Say it all," he said.

"They know we're married."

He dropped back on his heels, relaxing his ready-to-pounce posture. "Well, how about that?"

"But I didn't tell them," she said, folding her arms under her breasts and giving him the steely end of her sharpest stare. "You did."

"What?"

"You told them, Wyatt. You were half out of your head with pain when the ether began to wear off. You started talking about your wife. Where was your wife? You wanted your wife. Gracie, Will, Dr. Diggins—even I—thought you were talking about Sylvianna. That's why Gracie was so sure you were going to die. Will was holding on to the bucket, whispering about Sylvia being dead and how you shouldn't think about joining her, and Doc was trying to spoon laudanum down your throat to ease the pain. He was repeating some of what Will was saying and some of Gracie's prayers. His hands were shaking, and he still hadn't finished sewing you up. That's when I decided that he could attend to the laudanum and I would attend to your stitches. As soon as you saw me, you started to quiet. I was your wife now. That's what you said, and when I tried to make light of it, humor you so no one would take what you were saying seriously, you just wouldn't let it rest."

Rachel sighed deeply. "You convinced them I was your wife because you also convinced them that you knew Sylvie was dead. You told them they were fools if they couldn't see that I was nothing like Sylvie, and then you told them the truth—or at least a version of it—about our marriage.

"I stopped trying to deny it. I knew I wasn't going to allow anyone else to look after you, so what would have been the purpose of pretending you were lying? No one's said a thing to you because I asked them not to."

"Didn't anyone think that was strange?"

"I explained you meant to keep our marriage a secret for a while, just until people got used to the idea that I was half owner of the mine and you had a chance to court me properly. I don't know why that made sense to them. I can only suppose they're used to your lawyer way of making things compli-cated so they accepted it. I imagine, too, that no one wants to remind you that you blurted it all out while you were under the doctor's knife."

"But I wasn't."

Rachel bit the inside of her lip and said carefully, "Some people think you were. There's no accounting for how a story changes with each telling."

Wyatt was fairly sure he knew how the story changed, and he was itching to get his hands on her. "And what do you mean about my 'lawyer way of making things complicated'? It was your idea to keep our marriage secret."

"Well, yes, it was, but I wasn't going to tell them that. I couldn't think of how to say it that wouldn't make me seem foolish."

Wyatt plowed through his hair with his fingers, his look almost a caricature of incredulity. "Make you seem foolish?" he repeated slowly. "Didn't it tug on your conscience just a tad to put me in that position?"

Rachel had the grace to blush, but she was also quick to point out that no one would ever think he was a fool. "People think you walk on water."

"Well, I damn well don't."

She blinked at the sharpness in his tone. "I'm sorry. I didn't mean to be—"

He dismissed her apology with an abrupt, impatient gesture. "Don't." He stared at her for a long moment, his eyes narrow and remote and unexpressive; then he turned away and retraced his steps to the bedroom.

Watching him go, Rachel couldn't fathom why she was suddenly fighting the urge to cry. She hardly knew what she'd said that had shuttered his expression. Until that moment, there had been an undercurrent of humor, of tolerance. He didn't necessarily like everything she told him, but she could tell that he was calculating how to use it to favor him. His retribution would have been swift and fierce, but not frightening.

It was his retreat that frightened her, not his advance.

She pressed one hand to her temple and massaged lightly. Her vision blurred. The bold colors of the tartan fabric in front of her bled at the edges. She sat down, closed her eyes, and determinedly began to compose herself.

In bed, Wyatt lay with his head cradled in his palms and stared up at the ceiling. His posture was too rigid for relaxation or sleep. He had to consciously unlock his jaw to keep his cheek from twitching. There was still a tightness in his chest, and it had nothing at all to do with his injury.

He was weary of being cooped up like a damn chicken. The farthest he'd managed to stray in the last week was Sir Nigel's suite on the floor above him, and he'd done that when Rachel had gone to the depot. It wasn't that she was against him moving around, taking in several walks each day up and down the corridor, but that she wanted to hold the reins. He'd had just about as much of that as he could stand. He needed to get outside, fill his lungs with fresh air and his vision with a view that was mountains and sky, and she was barring the way.

The fact of it was, Rachel Bailey was a better jailer than his deputy.

Wyatt considered going back in the sitting room and telling her that. He'd make certain she understood it was no compliment. There were any number of things he wanted her to know, all of them guaranteed to relieve her of the notion that he was some sort of paragon.

"People think you walk on water."

He grimaced as he turned over the phrase in his mind, grimaced more deeply as he considered how easy she made it for him to be annoyed with her. She certainly was a clear target, setting herself in his path no matter which one he chose. She knew his aim was true, yet she never wavered, never stood aside.

It finally occurred to him to wonder why she would do that. Self-preservation should have ensured that occasionally she would duck or dodge. Instead, she faced him down. It was true that she possessed an uncanny ability to deflect his shots, parting or otherwise, with a logic that defied his own sense of reason, but it was also true that he was able to wound her.

What made her stay when she knew she was vulnerable to that?

The clock in the sitting room struck the half hour. Eleven thirty. Wyatt realized he'd been lying awake for better than forty minutes and that Rachel hadn't stirred in all that time.

It was her habit to slip into his room when she thought he was sleeping, make use of the bathing room to prepare for that bed of nails she slept on, then slip out again, this time like a wraith in a white linen nightgown and red kid slippers.

Half an hour later, he was still awake and she was simply still. Wyatt favored his left side as he rolled out of bed. He didn't bother with a robe this time, loosely tucking the tails of his shirt into his drawers instead. Conscious of frightening her with a sudden, silent appearance, he made no special effort to be quiet as he crossed the floor and even rattled the knob as he opened the door.

When he saw Rachel slumped in a chair at the table, her head bent so far forward that her chin rested on her chest and one of her arms dangled over the side, he realized he could have tossed firecrackers in the stove and she wouldn't have moved. He didn't see a bottle on the table, nor an empty glass, which meant that she was just bone weary.

Tuckered, they called it here. Plain tuckered out.

Wyatt bent beside her chair and carefully looped one of her arms around his shoulders. He straightened slowly, lifting her at the same time. He felt a twinge of pain in his chest at the site of his wound, but it disappeared quickly when he shifted his weight and got a better hold on her.

"It's bed for you, Rachel," he said quietly. "The bed you should have been in all along." She murmured something that almost sounded agreeable, and Wyatt was encouraged. "Can you help me?"

"Mmm."

"Good." He knew she never really woke, but some memory for motion existed in her sleeping brain, and she matched his steps, though never took the lead.

Wyatt maneuvered her to the bed and set her on the edge. She immediately lay back and began to draw her legs up. "Oh, no," he said, tugging on her ankles. "You're not sleeping sideways, and you're definitely not sleeping in these clothes."

"Go away." She brushed ineffectually in the direction of his hands as he began to remove her shoes. "Go. Away."

Because her next breath was an abrupt little snuffle, Wyatt ignored her. He tossed her stockings beside her shoes, then regarded her gown with a critical eye. There were at least a dozen tiny cloth-covered buttons at the front of her close-fitting jacket. He could find no better place to start. She batted at his hands when they reached her waist, but there was no intent in the gesture. He imagined that if she was aware of him at all, she found him more of a nuisance than a threat.

He struggled with the jacket, finding it difficult to ease off her shoulders, and when he was done he felt a sense of satisfaction that was out of all proportion to his actual achievement. He made relatively short work of her skirt, shirt, underskirt, and bustle, and then he confronted her corset. It looked as hard as a carapace and covered her just as closely.

"You'll thank me," he said quietly. And he hoped it was true. He unfastened the tabs and closures, pulled it out from beneath her, and flung it away. It landed on the chair on top of her other clothes.

Now that she was finally down to her chemise and drawers and looked as if she might have prepared for bed herself, Wyatt lifted her legs back onto the bed, turned her gently so she was positioned lengthwise, and wrestled with the sheet and blankets until they covered her. He plucked the combs out of her hair and set those on the nightstand; then, as an afterthought, he returned to the sitting room and retrieved the quilt she'd brought from home. It gave him another opportunity to survey the couch, measure it against his height and requirements for comfort, and reinforce all the reasons he wouldn't be sleeping on it.

It was only as he was covering Rachel with the quilt that he realized he'd surrendered his side of the bed to her. He considered pushing her out of the way to secure his place, primarily so there'd be no doubt that he didn't walk on water, but then he felt another twinge, this one on account of conscience, not injury, and walked around the bed to the other side.

The sheets were cold. He yanked on part of Rachel's quilt for added warmth and burrowed deeper under the covers. In moments, he was asleep.

"You drugged me."

Groaning softly, Wyatt turned his face into his pillow. He put out an arm to stay the attack he felt certain was coming. Rachel had wakened with an accusation on her lips, just as if she'd been entertaining this argument all night.

"You drugged me," she said again. "Because the only other explanation is that you lost your mind."

"Pick that one." He compressed the pillow near his mouth to make certain she could hear him. "Is it morning?"

"Just."

"Go back to sleep, Rachel."

She jabbed him on the shoulder with the heel of her palm. "Ow!"

Her hand went to her mouth. "I'm sorry. I forgot. Are you all—" She lowered her hand and jabbed him again. "That's your right shoulder. You're lying on your left. And if I'd really hurt you, you would have grunted. That's what you do."

He grunted.

Rachel's lips twitched. "Too late."

In every way possible, Wyatt thought. He slipped one arm under his pillow and eased more fully onto his side. Opening his eyes, he was startled to see how close she was. She was also lying on her side, her position mirroring his. The quilt covered her up to her shoulders, but her heavy sable hair lay on top of it, not under it. Her eyelids were at half mast, and she stared at him through a fan of dark lashes. She did not have the vulnerability of sleep about her, but neither was she guarded and prickly.

"Good morning," he said.

"Mmm."

There was no longer any lamplight in the room, but a narrow band of the pink and mauve colors of daybreak slipped through the drapes and spilled across the floor. "You fell asleep in the chair."

She had a vague recollection of sitting at the table after he left the room. It explained the stiffness she felt in her neck upon waking. "I don't suppose you considered helping me to the couch."

"Considered. I realized I'm just not that cruel."

"Then you didn't consider it for yourself."

"Too short. Too narrow. Too hard."

Rachel smiled. "It's all of those things."

"You shouldn't have been sleeping there."

She didn't reply, merely continued to study him.

"It's the couch that gave you away," he told her. When she frowned, he went on. "The fact that you were so careful to put away the linens each morning before anyone arrived, it made me realize that you didn't want anyone to know that we weren't sharing this bed."

"It could have been because I didn't want someone to pick up after me."

"No. In the beginning, when it made sense for you to sleep elsewhere because I was so fevered, you didn't bother."

"I slept in a chair, Wyatt. Your memory isn't entirely reliable."

He shrugged. "It doesn't matter where you slept then. It matters what you were trying to hide later. I'm right about that." He gave her an opportunity to deny it, but she offered nothing. "Why didn't you tell me that everyone knew we were married, Rachel? Why did I have to figure it out on my own?"

She stared at him. "You really don't know?"

Wyatt said he didn't, but as soon as the words were out, he wondered if he'd lied. "You wanted to avoid this."

"This?"

"This." Edging closer, he brushed her lips with his. "And this." His fingertips ran along the length of her thigh, and his palm came to rest on her hip. "Is that right?"

"Yes."

He had to strain to hear her. "But you didn't leave when you woke."

She shook her head. "I seem to be of two minds."

"Which one wants to kiss me?"

"This one." Then she leaned into him and gave him her mouth.

He kissed her with great care, testing them both with the gentleness of it, with the slow exploration. Her lips were pliant under his, sensitive to the slightest flicker of his tongue or change in the angle of his mouth. He tasted her at his leisure, drawing on her moist lower lip, running his tongue along the ridge of her teeth. He rubbed his lips against hers. She made a pass across his upper lip with the tip of her tongue that made him shudder.

"Wyatt?" She inched away to gauge his reaction.

He drew her right back. "Fine." His voice was thick and a little gritty, like honey poured over sand. "I'm fine. More than fine."

"Mmm." She kissed the corner of his mouth, worked his lips open with her tongue. She fed on him, sucking on his lower lip, feasting on his mouth. Under the covers, she found his hand on her hip and lifted it to her waist. It settled there warmly but didn't move. She determinedly deepened the kiss, acting first as the aggressor, then as an equal in their play.

He turned his head slightly, and his lips pressed against her cheek. He kissed her jaw, her neck, and sipped on the tender skin of her throat. She edged closer, blindly seeking the fit that she knew was possible. Her knees bumped his. She nudged him again, more insistent this time, but he frustrated her efforts.

"What do you want, Rachel?" His mouth was at the curve of her ear. He felt the tremor in her body, the catch in her breathing. His teeth caught her earlobe and tugged. "Hmm?"

"Closer," she said on a thread of sound. "I want to be closer."

Wyatt's palm slid from her waist to the small of her back and jerked her hard against him. Her hips came flush to his, cupping his erection with the natural cradle of her thighs. There was room suddenly for one of her legs to move between his. Her breasts flattened against his chest. His hand moved from her back to the curve of her bottom. He pressed her closer, and her hips stirred, circled, and finally arched into him.

She bit her lip to keep from crying out. He caught the movement and turned his attention to her mouth again. The kiss was long and slow and deep. He fought back urgency in favor of savoring the sweetness in each of her languorous kisses. Her lips were wet; her mouth warm. All of her moved against him with languid, liquid ease.

He rolled onto his back and turned her so that she lay full against him. Her hair fell forward over her shoulders. Strands of it caught in the stubble of his beard and tickled his neck, and for no particular reason that he could name, this tangle of hair and inconvenient tickle struck him as oddly amusing.

Rachel felt the vibration in his chest before she felt it against her lips. She broke the kiss, lifted her head, and stared down at him as his mouth twisted in a wry smile. The laughter was silent.

"I'm doing it wrong, aren't I?" she said.

"Wrong? No. Lord, no." He blew away a tendril of her hair

that swept across his mouth when she turned her head. The puff of air wasn't all that was required, and he had to brush away some of the strands with his fingertips. "Come here," he said. "Bend your head a little." When she did, he threaded his fingers deeply into her hair and deftly braided it into a thick plait. He tossed the rope of hair back over her shoulder, raised his head, and pressed a swift kiss against her bewildered smile. "It'll hold," he whispered. "Give me your mouth."

She did. Cautious of his healing injuries, she made a careful exploration with her fingers across his shoulders, but what she was really doing was holding on. Her fingers pressed into his upper arms, while he palmed her buttocks and squeezed.

Her stomach retracted as the cadence of her breathing changed. She eased away from the kiss to press her lips against his throat. She felt the thrum of his pulse against her lips. His hands were under her chemise now and sliding slowly up her spine. It was as if he were urging her on, though she didn't know to what exact purpose. She raised herself up, her knees falling to either side of his hips, and stared down at him. His fingertips glided up and down her spine. He said nothing.

Rachel reached for the hem of her chemise and pulled it over her head.

Chapter Ten

Rachel's bold, almost defiant gesture was of the moment. Shock followed, and she immediately crossed her arms in front of her breasts. Wyatt's gaze didn't veer from her face. She stared back at him, uncertainty mingling with regret.

He lightly curled his fingers around her wrists. "It's too cold outside the covers," he said. "Come here." Then, instead of drawing her arms out of their shielding position, he drew her down. She dropped her guard and clung to him, and when they rolled together, this time she was on her back.

Wyatt supported most of his weight using his good shoulder and arm, but his injured side held him with little strain. He raised himself enough for Rachel to unfasten the buttons on his shirt. She slipped her hands under the material. The muscles in his back tensed as she ran her palms along either side of his spine.

Wyatt bent his head, teased her lips once, then worked his way to the hollow of her throat. He followed the line of her collarbone to her shoulder. Her fingers stilled on his back as he moved lower. When his mouth closed over her pink-tipped breast, he felt her breath seize. Her nipple budded as he flicked it with his tongue. He worried it with his lips until she drew deeply on the air she'd been denying herself.

Her back arched, and her heels dug into the mattress. She drew her hands out from under his shirt and caught him at the back of his head. Her fingertips stroked and fluttered in his hair. She closed her eyes. Ribbons of heat that had wound tightly in her breast began to uncurl. Her flesh swelled. He laved her areola with his tongue, then drew a damp line to her other breast. She tugged on the curling ends of his hair, guiding him, then holding him. The hot suck of his mouth made her womb pulse. She felt herself responding to him from the inside out, learning things about her body because of what he made her feel.

The contraction between her thighs made her aware not of how he would claim her, but of how she would welcome him. And she would welcome him. She was already damp, and his erection was pressing for entry. Her hips ground against him as she sought relief in the most elemental way. She raised her knees on either side of him and crossed her ankles over the backs of his thighs.

The position was achingly familiar. She could almost feel the scaly patches of bark at her back and catch the lingering scent of pine. Lying under him was infinitely more comfortable, more secure, and ultimately, more satisfying. She tested their fit, pushing against him.

He pushed back.

Rachel pressed her lips together; her moan remained trapped at the back of her throat. Wyatt reared up, abandoning her breast in favor of her mouth, urging it open under his and kissing her until she gave up the cry that was meant to be his.

"That's what I want," he whispered against her mouth. "But not all that I want." He tore at the tabs on her drawers, loosening them. Her fingers were searching for the drawstring to his. Each time she rubbed her knuckles against his skin he felt as if he might come out of it. "God, Rachel. Oh, sweet . . ." Behind him, her ankles unlocked. Her fingers scrabbled to tug at his drawers. He caught her hands, pushed them aside, and breathing hard, reined himself in.

Rachel caught fistfuls of the sheet to keep her hands from wandering. It was all she could do to restrain herself from touching him. "Are you going to leave me?"

He blinked. His voice rough, he said, "A twenty-mule team couldn't drag me out of here."

"Oh." She started to reach for him again, but he blocked her.

"I need a moment, or I'll—" He stopped, just shook his head. "Trust me."

She had to. She had no experience to draw on. "You know I was never Mr. Maddox's mistress, don't you?"

"I know." He brushed her lips. "You could have told me when I asked."

Rachel averted her eyes, shrugged.

"It's all right." He kissed her again. "Later." He slipped his hand under her drawers, felt her inhale sharply, and cupped her mons. His fingertips slid easily between her damp lips. She made a grab for his wrist, but when he didn't move again, she let her hands fall away. He watched her face, saw the shadow of uncertainty that crossed it. He waited her out, as he always did, and with the same deliberation and exquisite timing that he applied to drawing his gun, Wyatt drew his fingers across her clitoris.

It might as well have been a trigger.

She jerked, sucked in a breath. Her hands fisted in the sheet again. Her mouth parted. The steady stroking of his fingers was a caress, and something more. His touch was insistent, relentless. There was pressure, almost infinitesimal at first, then gradually increasing and unavoidable.

Rachel felt the inexorable rise of tension in her body. It swept her up; caused her to lift her hips, press herself against his hand. There was heat there, and the first inklings of pleasure.

He slipped two fingers inside her. She might have cried out except that his mouth found hers again. The thrust of his tongue matched the rhythm of his fingers. He felt the give of her body, the thrum and twitch of arms and legs vibrating with pleasure.

He gave her no time to wonder at it. Removing his hand, he moved over her and settled solidly between her thighs. He fumbled with his drawers, released his cock. Taking her by the wrist, he drew her hand between them. Her fingers splayed and curled tentatively around his erection. She regarded him warily, her eyes a fraction wider than they'd been a moment earlier.

He pressed forward, nudging her open. She hardly knew that she was guiding him. His entry startled her. She wanted to draw a deeper breath; wanted a moment's respite. He gave her neither.

Rachel released him. Her hand settled at his back. Her fingertips pressed whitely against his skin as he seated himself inside her. She sucked in her bottom lip and caught it with her teeth. Her dark eyes captured her wince.

Knowing that he hurt her, Wyatt held himself still. She held him so snugly that it was almost impossible not to move. An involuntary tremor seized him, a sharp pleasure response that made him think he would not be able to wait any longer for her to accommodate him.

Rachel saw the restraint he imposed on himself in the taut line of his jaw and the muscles working in his lean cheeks. His eyes were heavy lidded, yet watchful. The centers were dark and wide, stamped with desire. His beautiful mouth was slightly parted as he drew uneven breaths. The familiar, vaguely secretive smile was absent.

"You can have me now," she whispered.

And so he did.

Wyatt's hips lifted. He withdrew, thrust again, and rocked her back. She clutched his shoulders and pressed her knees against him. He carried her with his movement, and she rose and fell, matching his rhythm. She contracted around him, trying to hold him each time he drew back, blurring the distinction between pleasure and pain. He groaned softly, drove deeper.

Rachel felt heat spark and spin. Certain now of where it would lead, she wanted more. His face hovered above hers. His body strained. Her breasts were achingly tender, the rosy aureoles puckered around her nipples. When he touched her, it was almost too much to bear, and she found that it wasn't yet quite enough. Short of being inside his skin, making his experience her own, she didn't know what would be enough.

She grasped at the pleasure he seemed to keep just beyond her reach, certain this time she would not be denied.

She wasn't.

Her back arched. Her heels dug deep. Every part of her body was engaged in free fall as Wyatt pushed her over the edge. He followed her almost immediately, and she felt his response shudder through her, and knew it to be as powerful as her own. He buried his face in the curve of her neck as his injured shoulder finally gave way. His hips still stirred against her. She cradled him with her body, and there, between her thighs, she held him closer.

Only moments passed before Wyatt was aware of his weight pressing on her. He remembered the clumsy way he had collapsed when his shoulder couldn't support him. Biting back a curse, he started to draw back.

At the first indication that he was going to leave her, Rachel's hands tightened. The movement was merely a reaction, but it became purposeful when he tried to ignore her. A sound that she recognized as distress rose from the back of her throat.

"I'm crushing you," Wyatt said.

She shook her head. "You're not." It wasn't entirely true, and if there had been more light in the room he would have seen her flush at the lie. She didn't want him to leave her just yet, though the explanation for it was not fully formed in her own mind. She couldn't have offered it to him.

What he did was turn on his side, pulling her with him so they remained joined. The swiftness of his move startled Rachel. There was a moment of awkwardness as their legs tangled and their arms sought new positions. He kept her hips flush to his by pressing one hand just below the small of her back.

Wyatt shut his eyes as an unexpected shudder swept through him, this one riding the knife's edge of sweet pain. "Don't move."

The guttural roughness of his voice had an effect on Rachel opposite of his words. She could not stay the quiver that began at the back of her neck, tripped lightly down her spine, and radiated outward to her fingers and toes.

He clamped down on the curse that came to his lips and kissed her hard instead. When he drew back, they both needed to catch their breath.

"Are you all right?" Rachel asked, carefully exploring his shoulder with her fingertips.

It should have been his question to her, he thought, but she found her voice first. "Fine." He tried to shake off her hand, but she was insistent.

"And here?" she said, slipping her hand between their bodies and laying her palm over his chest wound.

"I'm fine, Rachel. You won't have to stitch me up again." He regretted his terse, clipped tone even before he saw the shadow cast by hurt cross her features. His apology didn't come quickly enough. She'd withdrawn her hand as though scalded and was offering a hasty apology that also should have been his.

He let her go on because it seemed important to her, but when she fell silent, he simply shook his head. "Is it so different now?" he asked. "You used to stand up to me."

Searching his face, her own expression uncertain, she didn't respond.

"I don't like to be coddled, Rachel. No, don't apologize again. Tell me I'm an ass, or at least that I've been behaving like one, and we'll be done with it."

"Until the next time," she said. "You'll be an ass again."

He smiled with only one corner of his mouth as if it pained him to lift the other. "I'm sure I will." This time when he began to ease away from her, she let him go. He found it strangely disappointing.

Wyatt tugged at his drawers, righting himself, and threw back the covers. He slipped out of bed and went to the bathing room. When he came out a few minutes later, carrying a basin, pitcher, and washcloth, Rachel was already sitting up in bed. She looked at what he had in his arms and immediately got to her feet. Correctly gauging his intent, she crossed the room and took possession of everything.

"I don't like to be coddled, either," she said. She walked determinedly past him into the bathing room and shut the door sharply with the heel of her foot.

Wyatt stared at the closed door for a full minute after she was gone, then shook his head, largely in admiration, and returned to bed. When Rachel reappeared she was wearing a nightgown and her braid had been neatly replaited and secured with a narrow emerald-green ribbon. Her cheeks were rosy from the scrubbing she'd given them, and her eyes were bright. She met his gaze unwaveringly, though he thought she might have held it to prove something to herself as much as to him. Her smile, slight as it was, seemed forced.

He watched her veer toward the armoire. "Leave your robe," he said. "Come back to bed."

"Sir Nigel always sends someone to inquire about breakfast." She opened the doors of the armoire. "They'll be here soon. I'd prefer to be decent." Her fingers hesitated on the shoulder of her own flannel robe; then she passed it by, and on impulse, selected his. The sleeves fell almost to her fingertips. She rolled them back as she crossed to the window, aware of Wyatt watching her. She hoped he was confused by her choice. She certainly was.

Rachel blinked, facing daylight for the first time as she drew back the drapes. She secured them, then belted the robe. "What would you like for breakfast?"

"You're going to allow me to choose?" he asked, arching an eyebrow at her.

"As long as it's griddle cakes, applesauce, and a boiled egg."

"That sounds about right. Coffee?"

She nodded. She was already halfway to the bed when the knock came. "I'll only be a moment."

Wyatt watched her go. He heard her talking softly, thought he recognized Mary Beatty's voice repeating Rachel's order. There was some lingering conversation, none of which he could make out, and a high-pitched girlish giggle that he knew was certainly Mary's.

"It's a good thing Will doesn't laugh like that," Wyatt said when Rachel returned. "I'd have to put him down."

Rachel understood and sympathized. "Is Mary one of Will's sisters? I've never asked."

"Next to the youngest. A little silly still, but good-hearted."

"She noticed I was wearing your robe."

"Ah. That explains the giggling, then." He turned back the covers and patted the space beside him. "Come here. There's time before she comes back."

Rachel stared at the place he'd made for her. It was different now. If she went, she was choosing it. It had been easier when she'd simply awakened there.

Wyatt shook his head. "Don't do this, Rachel. Don't make it so difficult."

Was that what she was doing? "I'm trying to be practical."

"Practical?"

"About us. About our situation."

"It's a situation now?"

"Well, what would you call it?"

"Our honeymoon."

Rachel made a dismissive sound at the back of her throat. "You know very well that's supposed to be the sweet first month of marriage. That hardly describes our experience."

"I didn't plan to get shot."

"And I didn't plan to go to bed with you."

They stared at each other, neither willing to give way.

The absurdity of their predicament made Wyatt's mouth twitch first. Her composure already strained, Rachel couldn't hold her own against that wicked, ironic smile. The light of humor touched her eyes.

"Oh, very well," she said. "But I'm prickly. And if you think I'm not, just try to touch me." She approached the bed and waited for him to remove his hand from the space he meant her to occupy. When she was seated beside him, her back to the headboard, she drew her knees toward her chest and held them there by locking her arms around them.

"You're like a pill bug with spikes."

It was a uniquely unattractive description. "Some people would say I'm like a hedgehog."

"Sir Nigel would say that, but that's because he likes to remind folks he's a Brit. I'm not. You're like a pill bug with spikes."

"You're not winning me over. Is this how you charm Rose LaRosa?"

Wyatt folded his pillow in half and slid his arm beneath it to raise his head another few inches. It was a delaying tactic only. When he was done making himself comfortable she was still waiting for an answer.

"I don't exactly charm Rose," he said.

"No? She likes you."

"And I like her, but I pay her the same as every other man that she takes to her bed." He watched Rachel struggle with his answer. "That's what you wanted to know, isn't it? How long has that been sticking in your craw?"

"In my *craw*? If you keep sweet-talking me like that, Wyatt, I'm going to ask you for money."

He chuckled. "All right. How long have you wanted to know?"

Rachel shrugged. "I suppose since I saw you standing on her balcony. I don't remember when that was. A few weeks before we were married, I think."

"You could have asked me any time."

"No, I couldn't. I'm not certain I have the right even now." She smoothed his robe over her knees, fiddled with the trim. "She talks about you sometimes when I'm fitting her for a gown. Small things. Like how you brought her back a picture frame from Denver one time, or how you're just about the best dancer in Reidsville."

"Just about?" asked Wyatt. "Who's the best?"

"I don't know. I didn't ask."

"I bet she thinks it's Will. She likes him."

"That no-account Beatty boy?" Rachel shook her head. "No, you're wrong. She doesn't have a nice word to say about him."

"Don't you think that's peculiar, considering she's got a kindness for everyone else? She even talks nice about Estella behind her back."

Rachel realized he was right. It was peculiar. "Will Beatty and Rose LaRosa. Why didn't I know that?"

"You study other things," he said. "I bet you could tell me all about that fabric you're fiddling with."

Startled, she glanced down at her fingers. She drew them in, self-conscious. "I could," she said, "but I'll spare you."

Wyatt reached up and covered his hand with hers. "Ask me what you really want to know about me and Rose." He squeezed her hand lightly when she hesitated.

"Are you going to have reason to pay her again?" she asked.

"No."

"What if you and I never . . . that is, what if I don't want to . . ." Her voice trailed off. "We don't have a real marriage," she said finally.

"We don't? I told you, Rachel, I've been married. This is what it is."

She mulled that over, then shook her head. "You loved your wife. This isn't like that, Wyatt. I'm not comfortable with your comparison, but I'm also realizing that I'm selfish. I don't like the idea of you going to Rose's bed. Or the beds of any of her girls."

"That's not something you have to worry about."

Rachel expelled a long breath, satisfied with his answer. "Good. It's settled, then. You'll go to Denver when you want a woman."

Wyatt gave her no chance to avoid him. He dragged her down beside him. The struggle she gave him at the outset quickly vanished, just as he knew it would. She'd put too much time and effort into healing him to see all of her good works undone now.

He pinned Rachel to the mattress, holding her wrists in check at the level of her head. "I suppose you have a spe- cific brothel to recommend."

"The Fashion," she said. "Rose says that it's—"

"You need to stop listening to Miss LaRosa." He silenced the bubble of laughter that came to her lips by kissing her. When he drew back, she was smiling. "You think you've gotten precisely what you wanted, but you haven't, Rachel Cooper. Not yet."

He kissed her again, more deeply this time. She pushed a little against his hands, testing his strength. He held her easily but threw one leg across hers for good measure. "Denver," he whispered against her mouth. "You must have enjoyed saying that."

"If you'd seen your face . . ." She couldn't finish the thought for laughing again.

Wyatt gave her a mock growl, nuzzling her neck. It was the knock from the hallway that interrupted their play. He released Rachel reluctantly and sat up. "I'll get it," he said. "Don't move."

Not for a moment did he imagine she would listen to him, so he was pleasantly surprised to find her still in bed, if not lying down any longer. He set the tray on the bed, climbed in, and crossed his legs tailor-fashion. "I smell bacon," he said, staring at the covered plates as if he were about to place a bet in a shell game. He sniffed out the right cover and lifted it. Six strips of crisp bacon neatly lined the plate. "Aha. I refuse to believe this is all for you." Just to make sure that it wasn't, he stole a strip and bit into it.

"Very well," she said. "You may have that one." She plucked another off the plate. "And this one, I suppose." Because he looked as if she'd handed him manna from heaven, she waved another in front of him. "This, too."

"All in good time," he said, directing her to put one of them back on the plate. "This deserves to be savored."

Rachel returned both and uncovered the rest of the dishes. There was a plate of griddle cakes for them to share. She took the boiled egg for herself and gave him the ones that were scrambled. The applesauce was for both of them, but she put hers on top of her griddle cakes while he soaked his in maple syrup.

"I suppose you'll want to go out today," she said.

"I don't know. Is one of my choices to stay in bed with you?"

"No."

"Then I'll be getting out. Finally." He looked at her curiously. "What makes you think I'm ready?"

"Your appetite, for one thing."

"I thought it might be my appetite for two things."

She snorted delicately. "Eat. We are still negotiating the other."

Wyatt gave her a steady, knowing look, though he was far from certain of the outcome of any deal they struck, or even if there would be one. He turned away and applied himself to his breakfast.

"Where will you go?" she asked after a time.

"Hmm? Oh, you mean when I go out." He shrugged. "To my office, first. See what Will's made of it in my absence. Then to the livery to check on Raider. He'll have missed me, and I owe Joe Redmond for keeping him."

"I paid Mr. Redmond. He said he could wait until you got around to it, but I didn't think there was any reason that he should." She caught his slight frown. "Was I wrong?"

His face cleared. "No. I'm not used to someone paying my way." He cut into his griddle cakes with his fork. "I'll walk down to see Artie. Probably go by the depot and see how Abe's doing."

"He seems to have it all in hand. He was a good choice for the Calico."

Thinking about Abe made Wyatt recall the last time he'd spoken to Rachel's most persistent suitor. It had been at Longabach's the same morning that Rachel had offered Abe the job, and it wasn't long after that Wyatt had confronted Morrisey and Spinnaker making their escape.

"What were you doing in my office, Rachel?"

"What?"

"On that Monday. What were you doing there? Come to think of it, I've never asked."

She'd been very aware of his lapse. It came to her from time to time, and she tried never to dwell on it. "I was there to see you, obviously." His look told her that he wanted something more than that. "If you must know, I wanted to speak to you about our target practice the day before."

"What about it?"

"Well, I was wondering how Mr. Dishman knew about it. At the time, I thought we'd agreed not to make any association between us known to others."

"I don't recall agreeing to that. We agreed we would keep our marriage a secret." He put up a hand, staying her reply. "I know. I know. I was the one who spilled it, but you must admit that the circumstances were extraordinary. As for the other, I imagine Abe found out from Will. I'm fairly certain I told him why I was leaving with the Colt."

"Didn't you consider how he might interpret that?"

"There was nothing to interpret. I was on my way to teach you to shoot. Will's fairly straightforward in relating information."

She sighed. "Abe found out from Ned, by the way, and I don't know where Ned came by it, but when Abe told me about it I had the distinct impression he thought you were courting me."

Wyatt's face cleared of confusion. "And that's when you decided to march down to my office and tear a strip off me. Is that right?"

"Yes, but none of that matters now."

"Maybe. Maybe not."

"Now, what does that mean?"

He shrugged. "What if I was courting you?"

"Were you?"

He waggled his fork at her. "I asked first."

Rachel sipped her coffee as she considered his question. "I suppose if I'd considered it in that light, it would have made me wary. I don't know if I'd have gone with you."

Wyatt nodded, satisfied. "That's what I thought."

"So you *were* courting me."

"I didn't say that. And you were right, none of that matters."

Rachel's mouth flattened momentarily. "So now you agree with me."

"I do."

She gave him a narrow look. "Of course you do." She picked up a strip of bacon and broke off one crisp end. "Did you court Sylvianna?"

"Yes."

"How?"

"In the usual fashion. Flowers. Asking her to write my name on her dance card. Letters. Carriage rides along the Charles."

"That *is* usual."

"I told you."

"I think I'd like to go shooting again," said Rachel.

Wyatt was careful not to smile. "I thought you might."

There was no point in remaining at the Commodore once Wyatt was substantially on the mend. If word of their marriage had never gotten out, Rachel would have returned home alone, but because there was no one in Reidsville who didn't know the truth, she felt she had no choice but to allow Wyatt to come with her.

She never issued a formal invitation, but she never indicated that she expected anything else. Wyatt did point out that there were certain advantages to remaining in the hotel. The conveniences of the Commodore meant there would be fewer chores for each of them, but Rachel preferred privacy and was adamant that she didn't mind hauling water or preparing her own meals to secure it.

Johnny Winslow, Ned Beaumont, and that no-account Beatty boy helped with the move from the hotel. Sir Nigel Pennyworth looked as if he might cry when the wagon pulled away from the Commodore's wide front porch, but then Wyatt had been his longest and most reliable tenant, and there was always peace of mind for the guests and gamblers when they learned the sheriff boarded there. Wyatt's presence kept all but the most foolish troublemakers away.

Rachel had always found her home to be on the large side when she was rattling around in it by herself. It was true that each room had functionality, and there was none that she didn't use, but they were all generously sized and easily accommodated her. The same space became proportionately smaller once she was sharing it with Wyatt.

She could not even point to the fact that he had a lot of possessions. When the wagon was loaded, nearly half of what it held belonged to her. In two short weeks, she'd managed to bring almost the entire contents of her workroom to his suite, while in seven years at the Commodore, he didn't have much more than what he wore or what he could carry.

Still, it seemed to Rachel that his clothes crowded hers. The addition of his books stuffed the shelves. His clock looked ridiculous on the mantelpiece beside hers. There were boots with spurs in the mudroom and a leather strop hanging from the washroom door. His comb, razor, and lathering brush and cup were jarringly out of place among her pots of cream, atomizers, and delicately scented soaps.

He was always in her way or around when she wanted to be

alone. They had worked better in the kitchen when he was only a visitor. Then they'd managed to skirt direct confrontation. Now she felt as if she had to watch her step constantly or risk bumping into him. It was inevitable that several times each day she would put the wrong foot forward, and they always danced awkwardly when that happened.

When she regarded the pantry with a critical eye, it looked inadequately stocked. Wyatt Cooper ate as if each meal was his last, and he never missed one. He was never even late. What did it matter if she had plenty of firewood if there was nothing but water to boil?

It was a mercy that he left the house each morning. On Sundays, he got up earlier, went to his office, then met her at church. It was his shortest day out unless someone came to him with a problem that demanded his personal attention. If that happened, it was usually something at the saloon that took him away, and she could depend on him to be gone for the better part of an afternoon but arrive home for supper as though he were tracking it.

He still rode out on Thursdays, taking a sack of biscuits with him. It was the only day she ate breakfast and lunch alone, but that was only if she bothered eating. His absence from the house meant that she could sew undisturbed, and she did not waste the opportunity. It wasn't that he interrupted her work with questions, or even that he spoke much. It was simply that he was there and his presence loomed large.

He overwhelmed her, but nowhere more so than in the bedroom. She was the one who had defined what their relationship would be there, and she didn't want him to join her harboring any misconceptions about her view of their marriage. It stunned her at the time that he hadn't argued, but in retrospect, she viewed his agreement as unflattering. Recognizing that there was a certain perversity to her thinking did not help her change it.

She had some sleepless nights in the beginning, not trusting him to honor the bargain they'd struck. She hugged her side of the bed, putting herself so close to the edge that she was in danger of falling out. He noticed it, because it was his nature to notice things, but whatever thoughts he had about it remained unspoken. While she slept fitfully, he slept like the dead. While she occupied a distinctly narrow portion of the bed, he sprawled across it.

Their experience in bed had more in common with range wars than a marriage. It was fences against wide-open spaces, the farmer opposing the cattleman. Rachel had no idea how to alter the terms of their agreement, or even if she wanted to, and it seemed unlikely that it would be changed serendipitously.

If she ever rolled to the middle of the bed, she was unaware of it. Sometimes she dreamed that he was holding her, but when she awakened, she was always just out of his reach. More often than not, she was the one staring at his back. His natural inclination seemed to be to sleep on his right side, which kept him turned away from her. She couldn't very well suggest they switch sides.

Rachel keenly felt their strained intimacy, though it was unclear to her whether Wyatt sensed the same thing. She credited the fact that he'd been married before with his ease for accommodation. He sometimes left the door open to the washroom when he was shaving or completing his morning ablutions. If he woke with an erection, he didn't present it to her, but neither did he try to hide it. He wore a nightshirt to bed, although she suspected he preferred to sleep in his drawers alone. He didn't intrude on her when she was dressing, but more than once in passing, he'd absently fasten a button that she'd missed or tuck a wayward strand of hair behind her ear.

He drew water for her bath, helped her heat it, then disappeared while she undressed. He'd return to the kitchen once she was in the tub and linger at the far side of the table until she needed help with rinsing the soap from her hair. When she reminded him that she had managed it alone for some time now, he merely asked her why she would want to go on that way. His point was well taken, and having him tip the pitcher so that water trickled, then cascaded, over her head, her face, and her shoulders was the one pleasure she could not bring herself to deny.

Her monthly courses came and went, and came again. The first time, Rachel accepted it as evidence that she wasn't pregnant and felt a measure of relief. The second time, it was a reminder that given the conditions she'd set, she'd never be pregnant. What she felt then was something closer to resignation.

Wyatt kept his promise to take her to one of the open mines. He chose a mare for her from Redmond's Livery that didn't mind her lack of experience in the saddle and cared only about following Wyatt's gelding. They rode in tandem on the trail; then he stopped and waited for her when they reached the summit.

The gaping hole in the ground startled Rachel and looking down into the massive crater caused her insides to turn over and her heart to sink. Fear of falling had little to do with her reaction. The pockmark on the land was like an obscenity. She'd never considered how the gold and silver were mined. She knew about panning, of course. One could hardly be born and raised in California without learning something about panning, but that was a rudimentary first step when gold-bearing gravel was in the shallows of a stream. To access gold and silver buried in ancient riverbeds deep in the heart of a mountain required more than a miner with a pan.

She had her eyes opened that morning to the larger consequence of Clinton Maddox's rail spur. Monitors, some as long as eighteen feet, shot powerful jets of water from their nozzles. These cannons were aimed at the mountainside and tore into it with a terrible force, separating rock and earth. Gravel was carried through sluices in one direction, while the remaining dirt and debris were washed toward creeks and rivers. Some miners operated the giants, adjusting the nozzles to change the water pressure or swinging them to aim at a new location, while others stood at the bottom of the sluices where the riffles had been placed. Gold and silver ore fell out of the water, separated by the grooves in the boards. It was a panning operation of enormous proportions, as impressive in its ingenuity as it was hideous in its execution.

Wyatt took her to see the smelters where ore was melted to extract the gold or silver. The miners oversaw every part of the operation, including guarding it by setting up tent stations with a good view of the countryside and arming the men who took turns staying in them. The bricks were transported to the train by way of a trail that was so narrow two men could not navigate it walking abreast. Even mules were too smart to use it as it hugged the mountainside at a precarious angle.

The precious metals were not transported daily. The bricks were kept deep inside a mountain vault that was also guarded. The day they were moved to the train was always selected at random, and it occurred at varying frequencies but never more than three times in a month. It fell to Sid Walker to choose the day, and he did so by selecting one of two colored marbles from a chamois bag. The aquamarine cat's-eye meant yes, and the black-and-yellow solid meant no. Bricks might be transported three days in a row one month and only one day during the next. Choosing the men to carry them was also done at random.

Rachel learned there had never been a robbery attempt on the trail and only one at the mine. The train was more vulnerable, but it had been two years since anyone had tried to stop a shipment and that had ended badly for the thieves.

It wasn't merely the randomness of the operation or the deterrent that the guards represented that kept the mine safe, it was the fact that the extent of its success was virtually unknown outside Reidsville. Rachel could hardly fathom that an agreement forged more than twenty years earlier to keep the breadth of the discovery a secret was still being honored. It was the general opinion outside Reidsville that the gold and silver had been dug out of the mountains hugging the town long ago. Inexperienced miners never arrived in droves entertaining dreams of the mother lode, and as a result, there was never a massive exit.

Wealth might be gouged from the mountain in a torrent, but it only trickled out of the town. Rachel could not conceive of the size of the underground vault and how much of the town's wealth still resided there. Wyatt had offered to take her inside, but one look at the sagging timbers shoring the entrance and the great yawning blackness in front of her made Rachel decide she did not need to see more. Even after he explained the adit was safe and only appeared otherwise to make it seem unimportant, she refused his offer.

"I have a great deal of money now, don't I?" she asked one evening. They were sitting near the stove in the parlor, he with a book in his hands and his feet resting on a stool, and she with yards of lilac sateen spread over her lap. He had *The Three Musketeers*. She had Virginia Moody's wedding dress.

Wyatt didn't look up from his book. "Is that really a question in your mind?"

She held up the portion of the gown she was working on to the lamplight and examined her stitches. Finding them acceptable, she continued hemming. "It's more that I'm looking for confirmation. It doesn't seem quite real."

"Then, yes, you do. A great deal."

"Do you?"

"Yes. I didn't marry you for your money."

"What about the Longabachs and the Walkers and Mr. Beaumont and—"

He glanced at her. "You're not going to name the entire town, are you?" Before she answered, he said, "They do all right. Everyone does."

"But they don't have what I've been given."

"Millions? No." Wyatt closed the book around his index finger and regarded her curiously. "You've been doing a lot of thinking about the mine."

It was true, but it didn't follow that he should have known. "I have."

"Do you wish I hadn't taken you out there?"

She thought about that before she answered. "No," she said finally. "It's better to know." She glanced up, saw he was still looking at her. "I mean, it's better that I understand where my wealth comes from. Exactly."

"You hated looking at that gouge in the mountain."

She nodded. "It was . . . unexpected. I thought the ore was brought out from the inside."

"Sometimes it is. There are areas in the Front Range riddled with tunnels, places where veins were dug out by driving a steel drill with a jack so the powder could be set. A man might be fortunate to move six or eight feet of earth a day, and that was if the tunnel didn't collapse on his head. No one wanted to cut timber for shoring when they could be digging for gold, so the mines trapped men all the time. Owners didn't care. Men cost less than timber."

That was chilling. "So hydraulic mining is safer."

"Comparatively. There are still dangers. Landslides. Flooding. Ned got hurt because a hose broke and the brass nozzle snapped around like a whiplash and struck him in the leg."

Rachel shivered as the image crystallized.

"What's this about, Rachel?"

"I don't know exactly. I've just been thinking about that

open wound in the mountains. I can't quite get it out of my mind." She bent her head again. "It's savage."

"You're not thinking about shutting down the operation, are you?"

She blinked, staring at him. "Could I?"

"Well, not because you're an owner. You'd need me or the town to side with you and that's never going to happen."

"But there's the spur," she said.

"I really don't want to have this conversation with you."

Rachel pursed her mouth to one side. "I'm not going to do anything foolish, Wyatt. I know better than to bite the hand that feeds me, but it doesn't mean I can't do *something*. How many craters are there like the one you showed me today? How many acres does the mine own?"

"Acres? I have no idea. The property covers some forty square miles."

Her lips parted. It was enormous beyond her comprehension.

"Would you like to see more of it?"

The way he asked the question, pushing slightly toward the edge of his chair, made her think he meant to take her outside this very minute. "Now?" she asked, disbelieving.

He nodded. "Give me a moment." Wyatt set the book down and stood. "That chest that I brought from the Commodore . . ." He held up his hands to indicate width, depth, and height. "Do you know where—"

"Under the bed," she said. "Johnny Winslow shoved it there."

"That's as good a place as any."

Rachel stared after him, mystified. Not long after he disappeared, she heard the trunk scraping the floor as he dragged it out. The chest had been a curiosity when she'd first seen Johnny carrying it in. Wyatt wasn't around at that precise moment to tell her what to do with it, and the fact that it had been locked prevented her from opening it. Johnny told her it came from under Wyatt's bed at the hotel, so they agreed it should probably just rest there again. Until Wyatt brought it up, she'd forgotten all about it.

Wyatt returned to the parlor, carrying the chest on his shoulder. It was crafted of dark cherry wood with brass fittings on all of the corners. When it was polished it fairly gleamed, but sitting under the bed for the last six weeks had dulled it with dust. Wyatt set it down on the rug and hunkered beside it. He used a handkerchief to wipe it off, then dug the key from a pocket and unlocked it.

Curious, Rachel found herself leaning forward and inching toward the edge of her chair. When he opened the lid, it blocked her view of the contents. Frustrated now, she pushed Virginia Moody's gown to the side and joined Wyatt on the floor. As soon as she dropped to her knees, he turned the chest so she could see its treasure.

Photographs. Hundreds of them. Some of them spilled over the top when he simply nudged the chest.

Rachel sat back on her heels, pressing her hands to her knees to keep them from sifting through the pictures before he gave her permission. "You're the photographer for all of these?"

He nodded. "Most of them are old."

"May I?" she asked.

"Yes, of course."

She picked up several from among the fallen and looked through them. They were on heavy stock, so they felt thick in her hands. Some of the edges were slightly yellowed. The mountains loomed large in the pictures. On each of the three that she examined, the day was particularly clear and sunshine made the snow cover fairly gleam above the timberline. Two of the photographs were almost identical, but Rachel could see the shifting shadows and recognized the differences were a consequence of time. The third was taken at a different location; the camera's aim was lower on the mountain.

Setting them aside, she picked up others. Wyatt began sorting through the pile and passed more to her as she finished one group. Occasionally, he offered explanations for what she was seeing.

"That range represents the edge of the mine property. There's no mining that far away yet. No one even knows if there's any gold or silver there. Here, look at these. This shows some of the digging and the aftermath of the explosions. You can see the veins."

Rachel looked them over carefully, following the progress of the miners in photograph after photograph as they uncovered the mountain. It was not as delicate as peeling back the layers of an onion. Miners squatted on the banks of a stream, panning the water, looking for evidence of color in their pans. This process of watching the float helped them determine where to sink their shafts. The goal was always the same: to find the main vein.

Even more intriguing to Rachel were the faces of the miners who scored the mountain with their water cannons. There was an intensity of expression but a lack of animation. Wyatt explained it was partly an effect of photographing them over the course of a long exposure to the camera lens. If they moved or failed to hold their smile, their features appeared faded when the photograph was developed.

"Haven't you ever sat for a photograph?" he asked. "There must be dozens of studios in Sacramento."

"There are. I sat for one once. Foster insisted. He told me he thought his grandfather would appreciate it. I was reluctant, primarily because it was Foster's suggestion, but rather than argue, I agreed. It was such a lot of fussing, and in the end, none of the photographs turned out well enough to suit Foster. It was a disappointment all around." She held up a photograph of Sid Walker hunkered on the bank of a stream. He had both hands on his pan in front of him, his profile a perfect study of concentration as he stared at the contents. "You have a talent for it, though. You set your camera to capture the most telling moments."

"Hardly moments," he said. "Minutes."

She smiled. "Well, minutes, then. It's still remarkable." She pointed to a photograph of a waterfall cascading over the lip of a rocky incline. Water droplets refracted sunshine and glistened like a thousand diamonds spilling out of the earth. "This is beautiful. The camera's captured images that seem other-worldly."

Wyatt thought she had described it exactly right. "I had a mule named Toad that could climb just about anything. He carried all the photographic equipment for me. That's a tripod, camera, glass plates, chemicals, and the tent I used for a dark-room. Easily about a hundred and fifty pounds. When he couldn't reach a tight spot, I'd carry it myself. Several trips, of course. We'd go up into the mountains for a few days at a time, mostly in the spring, but sometimes in the summer. It's . . ." He hesitated, searching for the right word, and upon finding it, let it spill softly, reverently, from his lips. ". . . spiritual."

Rachel was drawn into the crystalline blue that were his eyes, knew a feeling of being cleansed by his vision, and remained a captive of his voice. Moved off center, she didn't try to fill the lingering silence, and slowly began to riffle through pictures near the bottom of the chest. The pastoral scenes alternated with rocky crags and sharp ledges, the deep forests with the naked beauty above timberline. The gouges made by the miners were a startling contrast to the ones made by the natural erosion of wind and water. There were photographs of men traversing the mountainside, wading deep into a river, and gathered in small groups to pose with pickaxes, shovels, and a couple of barrels of black powder. A series of photographs were taken from a vantage point somewhere northwest of the town and showed progress on the construction of the

Commodore Hotel. Wyatt had captured not simply the history of the community in his work, but the industry of its citizens. What he'd done was nothing less than a labor of love.

It wasn't the camera's eye she was admiring. It was his.

"I didn't think you would ever let me know you," she said quietly, carefully replacing the photographs. She raised her eyes to meet his and simply held his gaze. "But this is your soul."

He said nothing, gave nothing away.

Rachel leaned over the chest and took his hand in hers. "Come to bed with me, Wyatt."

Chapter Eleven

Rachel led Wyatt into their bedroom. She lighted the lamp on the table closest to her side of the bed and drew the curtains closed. "Is this all right?" she asked.

Watching her closely, he made no reply except to nod his head.

Rachel stood in front of him and angled her face upward. She slipped her hands under his suspenders and slid them off his shoulders, then laid her hands flat against his chest. His heartbeat drummed against her open palm.

Wyatt caught her wrists, held her there. His voice was rough, husky, the words escaping through lips that hardly moved. "Don't do this if you don't mean it, Rachel. I won't go back to living like some damn monk tomorrow."

In answer, she moved her hands to cup his face and raised herself on tiptoe. "I don't want that, either," she whispered. "I never wanted it."

In any circumstance in which her lips were not a hairsbreadth from his, Wyatt would have argued the point, but that was not among the twelve or twenty things he wanted to do right now. Still, he held his ground and let her close the distance to him.

Rachel's mouth settled softly on his, kissing him first at one corner, then moving across his lips until they parted. Taking her time, she nibbled at his lips. Their mouths bumped, clung, then parted damply. She teased him with the tip of her tongue, running it along the sensitive underside of his upper lip. She felt a tremor in his solid frame and drew back. Her hands fell away from his face to rest on his shoulders, then slid lower so her thumbs flicked the buttons on his shirt.

"May I?"

He offered a jerky nod.

Her fingers moved deftly over the front of his shirt, unfastening the buttons and parting the material just enough to make equally quick work of his union suit. Her hands stilled only after they were flush to his skin, and even then it was a temporary state. She traced the puckered scar at his shoulder and the longer one on his chest wall. His skin was warm, the flesh firm and smooth. When she pressed against him with her fingertips, he leaned into her, and his strength was comforting, not overwhelming. Not frightening.

Rachel's fingers trailed to the waistband of his trousers. Her knuckles brushed his hard belly and when he sucked in a breath, there was just enough room for her to slip her fingertips between his skin and his fly. She made a half circle, ending at the small of his back, then brought her other hand around in the same fashion. She stepped as close to him as she could, inching her soft kid shoes between his boots. His erection pressed against her. She pressed back.

Rachel searched his face. He was watching her just as intently, but his gaze didn't look like curiosity. He was guarded with her, even mistrustful, and he wasn't prepared to engage her. Faint lines creased the corners of his eyes, as though somewhere inside he was wincing. His lips, in spite of being slightly damp from her kisses, did not invite more of the same. There was nothing in the mildly reproachful set of his mouth that suggested he ever smiled.

She rose up on her toes again and kissed him anyway, making a pass up his spine with her fingertips. "The boots, I think," she said against his mouth. "Sit down."

Wyatt's legs folded under him when she applied two fingers to his breastbone and gave him a gentle push. Rachel did not suppose that she'd had any real impact on that outcome and did not believe his cooperation was a foregone conclusion. She knelt in front of him, took his boot by the heel, and wrestled him out of it. The boot flew out of her hands when she finally got it free, and the momentum carried her backward. She thumped to the floor just before the boot thumped against the wall behind her.

She stared at her empty hands, took account of her awkward, unflattering sprawl, and sighed deeply; then she got back on her knees and braced herself to take off the other boot. She glanced up just as she was gripping the heel and thought she saw Wyatt's mouth twitch. If it wasn't her imagination or wishful thinking, then that mere suggestion of humor was an improvement over the wariness of moments before.

Rachel found the second boot far easier to remove. When it didn't fly out of her hand, she simply tossed it over her shoulder to join its mate. Standing, she brushed off her hands, then turned and disappeared into the washroom.

Wyatt stared at the door she closed behind her and wondered if she intended to leave him long in this state, or even if she was prepared to finish what she'd begun. He quickly dismissed the idea of going after her. He couldn't see himself backing away easily if she'd changed her mind, and it was difficult to imagine a worse ending to six weeks of restraint.

Some nights he lay awake wondering why he denied himself. Forbearance could easily become frustration, and he would turn on his side and look at Rachel huddled on the edge of the bed. He'd listen to her breathing softly; watch the way her hand sometimes drifted toward her mouth as she slept. Sometimes she made faint, incoherent sounds in her sleep. A protest. A murmur. A moan.

She never reached for him. Wishing that she would, willing her to do so, could not make it happen. He was careful not to touch her, although there were times he extended his arm across the divide and his fingers strayed close. She was so unaware; her vulnerability was the fence that she'd drawn around herself, whether she understood it or not. While she was perfectly capable of standing toe-to-toe with him during the day, sleep exposed her as defenseless.

He let her be.

So now he sat on the edge of the bed, his fingers curled tightly over the side, and waited yet again. To his way of thinking, for his patience to be finally and fully rewarded, Rachel would have to appear stark naked on the threshold. And she'd have to do it in about ten seconds.

The door opened.

Nothing that came to his mind was appropriate to say out loud. Some of the sentiments, like *oh, sweet Lord* and *hallelujah*, were suitable for church but not for this moment. Others, like *damn* and every variation on that theme, did not express the reverence he felt. Still other words were just too coarse and could not be softened, no matter that awe was all he wanted to convey.

Rachel shifted uncomfortably when Wyatt merely stared at her. He didn't move, didn't speak, didn't even blink. She wasn't naked, but the sheer lawn nightgown she was wearing certainly suggested she could be. And very easily, too.

Wyatt almost launched himself at her when he saw her falter and thought she was going to retreat into the washroom. She stepped over the threshold, though, gaining confidence as she approached him, and he stayed his ground.

She stopped at the point where his knees presented a barrier, but as soon as he opened them, she stepped into the breach. Taking his hands, she placed them on her hips, then slipped her own hands into his hair. She ruffled the overlong, curling ends and lightly stroked the back of his neck with her fingertips. She held his gaze as he looked up at her.

"I'm not wearing a corset," she said.

Wyatt's mouth had gone dry when she stepped between his splayed legs. He wasn't sure he could spit, let alone speak, and removing his tongue from where it cleaved to the roof of his mouth required a conscious effort. "I noticed that right off."

Rachel was encouraged by the rasp in his voice. "There's not much that gets past you, Sheriff."

He wasn't so certain that was true. He hadn't seen this coming. His fingers tightened a fraction on her buttocks, just enough to tilt her pelvis toward him. His nostrils flared slightly as he became aware of the moist, musky scent of her sex and the subtle fragrance of her lavender soap.

Rachel cupped his face, brushed the pad of her thumb across his lower lip, then allowed her hands to drift lower as she slowly dropped to her knees between his thighs. His palms grazed her waist, her rib cage, the underside of her breasts, and came to rest lightly on her shoulders before he gripped the silken rope of her braided hair in his right hand.

She turned her head, kissed his knuckles while her fingers strayed to the button fly of his trousers. She heard his harsh intake of air, but he didn't try to stop her. Sparing him a glance, she asked, "You don't mind?"

"Only if you stop." Her faint smile was enigmatic, maddeningly so from Wyatt's perspective. "Rachel?"

"Mmm?" She didn't look up, concentrating on the buttons instead. She opened one after another along the revealing ridge in his trousers.

"Have you been talking to someone?"

Rachel parted his fly. His erection pressed hard against his drawers. She reached inside, circled his cock with her fingers, and drew it out.

"Rachel." Caught in the constriction of his throat, her name was barely audible. He saw her eyes widen infinitesimally. In other circumstances he might have been flattered, but not when she seemed to need to prove something to him, and perhaps to herself. "It's not—"

But her mouth was already closing over him. She pulled back on his foreskin, her tongue flicking around the sensitive head of his cock. He held her thick plait of hair as if it were a lifeline. The moist suck of her mouth drew him in. She cupped his balls, fondled them. The gentle manipulation of her fingers elicited a groan. His skin was suddenly too small for him, the fit of it unnaturally tight against muscle and sinew that were now defined by tension.

Her tongue swirled. She took him deeper. Her fist on the root of his shaft made it feel as if she was taking all of him. He watched her, his blood surging and thrumming, making him so hard that he thought she would draw back. Her fingers merely tightened. Her jaw relaxed, and what she did was swallow.

Wyatt's own jaw clenched and unclenched, the muscle in his cheek jumping in the exact rhythm that his cock was pulsing. The cadence of his breathing changed. He drew in an uneven draught of air, held it. All of his senses sharpened, and there, where she held him, the pleasure was so finely honed that he thought it might cut him.

He closed his eyes, the image of her kneeling between his thighs burned into the back of them. His head fell back, exposing the taut cord in his throat. He released her hair and clenched the edge of the bed again. His knuckles were almost bloodless.

The words that had seemed out of place earlier were the only ones he could voice now. They felt raw in his throat, part need, part prayer, expressive of pleasure that was almost too painful to bear.

It was Rachel, though, who softly gasped. Wyatt caught her by the upper arms, holding her as tightly as he'd held the edge of the bed, and lifted her away from him. He drew her up, urgency defining his jerky movements and rough handling, and pushed her back on the bed. He followed her down, covering her, grabbing fistfuls of her nightgown until the hem was bunched around her waist.

He was between her thighs now and moments later buried deep inside her. Her back arched. She cried out, not from the force of his thrust, but from the intensity of feeling. She clutched his shoulders, dug her heels into the mattress. Her pelvis tilted. He rocked her back, stroking her, making her take him as completely as she'd done before, demanding that she commit all of herself.

He moved powerfully but not for long. She made that impossible with her sounds of sweet surrender. Smooth and sleek and slippery, she contracted around him. His strokes shortened, quickened. He gave a shout of pure relief as he came, shuddered hard, and released his seed.

It seemed an eternity passed before he could move. Occasionally, his muscles twitched, but that was outside his control, aftershocks of the quake. He levered himself away from Rachel, feeling the resistance she applied with her arms and legs, the murmur of protest that came to her lips, and turned over on his back in spite of what she wanted. He fixed his drawers and trousers, drew his shirt down.

He lay there for a time, aware of nothing so much as the sound of his own breathing and the vaguely unsettled feeling that was cradling his heart.

Rachel straightened the hem of her nightgown and drew it down over her thighs. She curled on her side. Raising her head on her elbow, she stared at his profile. Lamplight lent his features a warmth that she wasn't certain was there. Except for the light rise and fall of his chest, he was still. His eyes were open, but he stared at the ceiling without blinking. He turned his head suddenly, startling her with the razor-like sharpness of his gaze.

"Did I hurt you?" In spite of his intentions, it was more accusation than question. He watched her closely, his eyes narrowing, almost daring her to lie to him.

Rachel merely sighed. "No."

He grunted softly.

She didn't know how to interpret the sound that came from the back of his throat. It could have been satisfaction or skepticism. "Your concern is touching, Wyatt, but it's unwarranted."

"I was rough."

"Did it seem as though I minded?"

"I came at you like—"

Rachel laid her index finger across his lips, stopping him. "Like a man who had been thinking about it for a long time." She withdrew her finger and reminded him, "I invited you, Wyatt."

He grunted again.

"Does that mean you agree?" she asked.

Searching her face, he nodded.

"Good," she said, edging closer. "It seemed as though you'd forgotten."

"Not likely." His voice still sounded rough to his own ears. "It was a hell of a greeting, Rachel." The lamplight was sufficient for him to see her cheeks grow warm with color, but she didn't look away. Her candid regard, even if it was a little forced, was still intriguing. "Where did you learn to *invite* a man that way?"

She shrugged.

Wyatt saw her eyes dart away, though it happened so quickly he'd have been willing to believe he imagined it if they had been talking about almost anything else. "Seems like something you might remember. I'm inclined to believe you didn't learn it from your mother." A chuckle vibrated deep in his throat when Rachel's eyes widened and the warmth in her cheeks became real heat. He cocked an eyebrow. "Your sister, maybe?"

She shook her head quickly. "Sarah wouldn't. She's . . . well, she wouldn't."

"Wouldn't do it? Or wouldn't tell you?"

"Either." She dropped her elbow and let her head fall to the pillow. The rest of her reply was slightly muffled. "Both."

"So not your sister." A particularly ugly thought removed the hint of teasing from his voice. "Rachel?"

She was immediately aware of the change in him, though unaware of the source of it. Tension was suddenly palpable. She lifted her head a fraction. "What is it?"

"Was it Foster Maddox?"

At first she truly didn't understand what he was asking her. "Foster? What about him?" Then she realized the direction his thoughts had taken him. "No, Wyatt," she said firmly. "Foster only talked about wanting me in his bed. He was never more explicit than that. His attempts at forcing me were just that. Attempts." She felt the tension that had set his frame so rigidly begin to ease. "If you must know, and it seems you must, I came upon an informative book at Miss LaRosa's."

Wyatt felt as if he had legs under him again. He pushed Foster Maddox to the back of his mind. "Informative?"

"A primer, one might say."

"I doubt anyone would say that."

"Well, I would. It was filled with illustrated lessons."

"Is that right? I imagine you felt compelled to study it."

"Of course. Virginia was mortified when she saw me examining it, and she really didn't want to answer my questions, but I explained that I would put my questions to one of the other girls and that decided her. I don't think she wanted me to have a conversation with Miss LaRosa."

"Probably not," said Wyatt.

"There would have been some awkwardness there, I think."

"You don't say." Death Valley was not as dry as Wyatt's tone.

"Well, it didn't come to that. It also could be that Virginia was worried I'd keep her wedding dress hostage, though where she would get an idea like that, I can't imagine."

"Strange, I'm not having that same problem." Wyatt rubbed his chin with the back of his knuckles. "You want to tell her that she did a damn fine job explaining things or should I?" He managed to avoid the fist Rachel thrust in his direction, catching her by the wrist and pulling her across the small distance that separated them.

She settled quickly and hugged his side, resting her head against his shoulder and securing him with an arm across his chest. "I was nervous," she confessed, whispering.

"I couldn't tell."

"Really?" That pleased her ridiculously. "I thought you'd hear my heart pounding."

"Above my own? Not likely."

Rachel smiled, content. Not long after, she fell asleep in the middle of a thought.

Wyatt supported her until his shoulder went numb; then he eased out from under her. He didn't think he could get her under the covers without waking her, so he drew the quilt up from the foot of the bed. Giving her a last look, he moved quietly to the adjoining washroom. When he came out, barefoot and stripped to a pair of drawers, it was apparent that she hadn't stirred. Wyatt padded to the kitchen to add wood to the stove and adjust the flue and damper. He did the same in the parlor, ensuring that the house would remain relatively warm until shortly after he rose in the morning. He turned back the lamp beside his reading chair and the one where Rachel had been sewing, then wandered to the front window and drew back the lace curtain. The sky was milky, an effect of a full moon and a cloud cover. The flagstone walk and gated entrance were visible, but beyond that everything was a dark gray silhouette.

He hadn't seen Sid Walker today, but he didn't require the old miner's rheumatic bones to know that a storm was on the way. There'd been an odd lull in the snowfall that everyone had come to expect in late autumn, and some folks were moved to say that it was downright balmy. As a Boston native, Wyatt didn't think he had ever experienced balmy, so he listened to the talk without comment. He'd noticed that a certain foreboding accompanied all the discussion, the general feeling being that the weather would turn on them hard.

Looking at the sky now, Wyatt suspected it was about to happen.

He wandered through the darkened room, stubbed his toe on the chest of photographs that had been left lying on the floor in the wake of more important matters, and cursed under his breath as he hobbled off to the bedroom.

Rachel was still sleeping, although she had apparently roused herself long enough to put herself between the sheets. He noticed that while she'd stolen all the covers for herself, she was at least still in the middle of the bed. He wouldn't have to drag her back from the edge.

Wyatt left the lamp burning on the dresser but turned it back so that light merely flickered inside the etched glass globe. He slid into bed beside her and tugged some of the blankets over him, although she was the real source of warmth. It was not unpleasant when she turned on her side and attached herself to him. He pressed his lips to the crown of her dark hair. He thought he heard her sigh, but it could have been his own.

Sleep claimed him.

* * *

Rachel was sitting cross-legged at the foot of the bed when he woke. The lamp that he had been careful to turn back had been given a twist in the other direction and the wick glowed brightly, casting light over her shoulder. Her concession to the room's persistent chill was the quilt she'd tucked around her. Only the upper portion of her face was visible above it. From Wyatt's vantage point, her hands were hidden behind the open lid of the chest she'd retrieved from the parlor. She appeared to be studying more photographs, her concentration so centered on her task that she failed to notice that he was watching her.

He took shameless advantage of it, doing nothing to call attention to himself.

Her head was bent slightly forward, her eyes lowered. He could tell, though, when her gaze shifted between photographs because the shape of her mouth invariably changed. Sometimes her lips parted. Sometimes the tip of her tongue rested at one corner. Sometimes she simply smiled. Occasionally her eyebrows would lift, or she would rub the bridge of her nose with a knuckle, but mostly it was the expressive tilt of her mouth that he watched.

That was how he knew when she finally came upon the photograph that he'd been alternately hoping and dreading that she would find.

It was not merely the suggestion of a frown that gave her away, but the quick indrawn breath that followed. She caught her bottom lip between her teeth and worried it absently as she made her study, angling her head, not the photograph.

"That's Sylvie," he said quietly.

Rachel looked up, startled. He'd spoken her precise thought. "How did you know?"

He didn't think he could explain it properly, and after a moment, said, "Something in your face, I suppose." He thrust an arm outside the covers and held out his hand. "May I?"

Nodding, Rachel leaned forward and extended her arm

over the open chest lid and placed the photograph between Wyatt's fingertips. "When did you make the picture?"

Wyatt stared at the photograph. The sepia tones softened Sylvianna's features, making her seem more amenable to sitting for her portrait than she'd actually been. "A few months after I brought her here," he said. "We had wedding portraits made in Boston, but they were in a trunk that didn't follow us here. We never recovered it, and Sylvie . . . well, she never forgave me."

He returned the photograph to Rachel, pushed upright, and leaned against the headboard. "She wanted to go to Denver for another portrait, but I convinced her to allow me to make one first. If she didn't like it, I promised to take her to Denver."

Rachel's eyes fell on Sylvie's heart-shaped face. Her chin was small, but it jutted forward at a sharp angle, hinting at her resentment. Her lightly colored eyes were steady, even compelling. The bridge of her nose was narrow, but the line of her mouth was full. She had high cheekbones and finely arched eyebrows. Her hair curled softly across her forehead and was coiled in a loose knot at the crown of her head. Red? she wondered. Perhaps strawberry blonde.

"I don't think she wanted to like it," Rachel said. "But it's beautiful all the same. *She's* beautiful."

"Yes," he said. "She is." It did not seem strange to think of Sylvianna in the present tense. "And you're right. She didn't want to like it. She didn't want to like anything about being away from Boston. I should have sent her back, but I wouldn't make the decision for her, and she wouldn't leave. If you're thinking that was admirable, that her reluctance was because of the vows we took, then—"

"I was thinking she stayed because she loved you and that being away from you was more difficult than being away from Boston."

"That was part of it," he said quietly. There was regret in his eyes and a faint, rueful tilt to his mouth.

"Then what was the other part?"

"Punishment."

Inwardly, Rachel recoiled from the notion. "You don't mean that." But even as she said it, she saw that he meant exactly that. She hardly knew what to say, so she fell back on an inadequate "I'm sorry."

"Not for me, I hope," he said roughly. "Sylvie deserves it. You shouldn't forget that I punished her. That was the state of our marriage almost from the beginning, impossible to reconcile."

"But you loved her."

"Yes, I did. It made both of us miserable."

Rachel was quiet, contemplative. It made a terrible kind of sense that neither would allow themselves to be happy at the expense of the other, but that they also could not live apart. Was it love that truly kept them together or something else? She looked at the photograph again and decided that perhaps the thrust of that small jaw wasn't resentment at all, but determination, and the gaze was more gently persuasive than compelling.

"What happened, Wyatt? In the end, I mean. How did Sylvianna die?"

"I killed her."

Rachel could have understood if he'd hesitated, or offered it reluctantly, but his flat declaration surprised her and revealed the certainty with which he had come to accept it. She said quietly, "I doubt that it's true in the way you intend for me to believe."

He shrugged. "It's straightforward, Rachel. I was in the mountains making photographs, and she was at home. She hated when I left her, especially when she knew I'd be gone for days at a time, so we argued as I was leaving. I invited her to come with me. She was a good, confident rider, and sometimes she would accompany me. But not this time. She was insistent about staying back, more insistent than usual that I remain with her. She wouldn't explain herself, so I thought we were repeating one of those arguments we had from time to time, the kind that start in a fog and end up clearing the air for a while."

"So you left," said Rachel.

He nodded. "I was gone four days. I wasn't sheriff then. I didn't have responsibilities to the town, only to Sylvie. And I was gone four days."

Rachel slowly closed the lid on the chest. She still held the photograph in her hands, but didn't glance toward it. Her eyes remained on Wyatt's.

"Grace and Estella had her laid out on our bed when I got home. It was Ned and a couple of Sid's boys that rode out to find me. I was heading back by then, but that hardly mattered. Sylvie didn't know I was coming home." He took a steadying breath, absently rubbed his palm over his knee. "She was taking a walk with the pastor's wife. There was a disagreement over cards at the Miner Key between a couple of sharps. Rudy Martin told them to take it into the street. He just didn't want his place busted up in a brawl. He didn't know they were going to shoot it out with their fancy derringers.

"Sylvie was hit when the first shot went wide. It nicked an artery in her neck. She bled to death in Mrs. Duun's arms. Doc never had a chance with her."

"That's a tragedy, Wyatt, but you aren't responsible."

"Some days I'm almost convinced of it. Most days, not. I brought her here, remember. That's the part that always sticks. And I know, too, that if I'd been the one walking with her that day, there would have been a different outcome."

"You can't possibly know that."

"But I do. I would have been walking on the street side of the sidewalk, and Sylvie would have been on the inside. That's what a man does for a woman. He protects her by providing escort on the outside. That bullet should have been mine, Rachel. I would have taken it in the back, not the neck, and I might not even have died, but I wasn't there, and Sylvianna was."

Rachel closed her eyes momentarily, remembering the evening they'd left the Commodore together. Wyatt had moved immediately to the outside, the time-honored way of making certain a woman wasn't splashed by carriages rollicking through puddles or wasn't accosted by clumps of mud thrown up by a horse's hooves. Or, in Reidsville, wasn't the victim of a stray bullet.

"It's not important that you say anything, Rachel. You looked at my photographs and thought you knew my soul, but you didn't know this. It seemed to me that you should."

"Then say it all, Wyatt."

Perhaps she did know his soul, even the darkest regions, because she was pressing him to say the thing that always stuck in his throat, the thing that was known to one other person at the time of his wife's death and only shared with him afterward with the greatest reluctance. But he had pressed Doc Diggins just as Rachel was pressing him, and he wondered if the time finally had come to say it aloud. To say it all.

"Sylvie was pregnant," he told her. Tears burned, first at the back of his eyes, then along the rim of his lashes. They hovered there. "She was carrying our child."

Although it was the answer Rachel had expected, it was difficult to hear, more difficult yet to look upon the despair shadowing Wyatt's face. The photograph fell from her nerveless fingers. She threw off the quilt and crawled across the bed toward him. He opened his arms, took her in, but she was the one who offered shelter.

She hugged him to her, pressing one hand to the back of his head, the other to his back. He didn't sob, but she felt his tears dampen the thin fabric of her gown. She offered no words. He would have fought those. It was her silence that broke him, and her silence that kept him sane.

He shuddered once, then was still. She stroked his hair, waiting him out the way he often did with her. When she felt his shoulders bunch, she let her arms fall away. He sat up and rubbed his face with his hands. When he came out from behind them, his eyes were clear and his features were no longer shuttered.

"When I look back," he said, "I wonder if I suspected, and that's why I resisted her pleas to stay behind. She was going to tell me, I think, and I didn't want to hear."

Rachel sat back on her legs and reached for the quilt. She dragged it toward her and wrapped it around her shoulders. Wyatt looked as if he couldn't feel the room's chill. "What would a child have meant?"

Her ability to go straight to the heart of it no longer caught him off guard. "Boston," he said. "We would have returned. I know that. Her family. Mine. It was like swimming against the tide. I'd have sold my interest in the mine to the town and settled into a law practice."

Rachel ached for him. She imagined there had been a moment, something even smaller than a moment, when it had crossed his mind that Sylvie's death, and the death of their child, meant he didn't have to go back to Boston, and in that infinitesimal span of time he had known relief. Guilt had been crushing him ever since.

"Do you think it's wrong to be selfish?" she asked.

Wyatt blinked. She'd pulled him suddenly from a very dark place. He regarded her, thoughtful, but uncertain. She peered at him with the intensity of his most formidable law professor, the one who insisted that questions be considered from all angles, like a jeweler admiring the facets of a diamond, looking for flaws with his loop.

"Wrong to be selfish?" he repeated. "No, not wrong. Not in the abstract, at least."

"And when it's concrete?"

He was silent.

"Perhaps it's that you and Sylvie weren't selfish enough. Maybe it was the marriage that needed to be sacrificed, not one of you for the other."

Wyatt let his head fall back against the headboard and briefly closed his eyes. "You may be right," he said at last.

"I don't know, Wyatt. There were no simple choices, not one among them that would have made things right for everyone."

He nodded faintly. "You're the only one besides Doc and me that knows about the baby. I made Doc tell me, but sometimes I wish I hadn't."

"I understand."

Wyatt studied her face for a long moment. "I believe you do."

Rachel leaned forward and kissed him softly on the mouth. She felt his arms come up, but before he could embrace her she moved outside his reach. She held up her index finger to indicate she needed time, then scrambled out of bed. Gathering up the photographs that lay scattered at the foot of the bed, including Sylvie's portrait, Rachel put them in the chest, then moved the chest to the floor, this time putting it beside the dresser, not under the bed.

Wyatt lifted the blankets for her when she was ready to return. They slid down together, each seeking the other for warmth and comfort. She rubbed her feet against his legs.

"Are you trying to start a fire?" he asked.

Rachel's laugh stayed at the back of her throat. "If only I could. Quick. Take my hands."

He did, placing his own firmly around them. "Better?"

"Mmm." She stopped fidgeting. "Infinitely."

Much later it occurred to her that perhaps she had started a fire, but that didn't come to her mind when Wyatt began to make love to her. She was overwhelmed, first by his tenderness, then by his hunger. He demanded nothing from her in the beginning, took everything in the end.

It suited her exactly, this long spiraling climb to pleasure. His mouth followed the trail of his hands. He lingered as he pleased, and he was often pleased to do so. His kisses were by turns deep and drugging, then tempered by his teasing, and he always drew a like response from her.

The damp edge of his tongue dipped into the hollow of her throat and darted over her nipples. He made a track from her breasts to her navel, then lower, lifting her knees and settling his mouth between her thighs. Her fingers threaded in his hair, then splayed stiffly as he flicked her swollen clitoris. She released him, and her hands fisted in the sheets on either side of her.

She came noisily, though she was hardly aware of it. He told her once he was seated deeply inside her, and her doubt became his challenge. She heard herself the second time in spite of pressing the fleshy ball of her hand against her open mouth.

What began sweetly ended on a decidedly different note, one that was deeply and abidingly satisfying. They fell asleep in a tangle of limbs that was only comfortable because of its novelty. By morning, they were cramped or numb, depending on which one of them had a limb trapped under the other's. It was the stiff climb out of bed and the first hobbling steps to their respective destinations that made them collapse back on the mattress in paroxysms of laughter.

That their laughter was out of all proportion to the experience only made it seem that much richer. Rachel found herself gulping for air. Wyatt's need to breathe was equally severe. They had tears in their eyes and lay sprawled on top of the covers as their breathing eased. His hand found hers, and he squeezed it lightly. She turned her head sideways to look at him, a question in her eyes.

"Thank you," he said.

Rachel didn't ask why he was thanking her, understanding it in a way that was not easy to put into words for either of them. She simply nodded.

Wyatt let go of her hand and sat up. He made furrows in his hair with his fingertips. "I'll see about putting some wood in the stoves. You go ahead and use the washroom first." He could see that she was starting to shiver. "You know, Rachel, it's cold mornings like this that I wish we hadn't left the Commodore."

She crossed her arms in front of her. Her sigh was wistful. "Maybe we could have hot and cold running water here, like at the hotel. It wouldn't be an extravagance."

That made him smile. "Come spring," he said, standing up. "It's at the top of my list." He tilted his head toward the washroom. "Go on. Get going before I regret my offer."

Rachel rolled to the edge of the bed, but she wasn't quick enough to escape the flat of his hand on her rump. She jumped up, cast him a withering glance over her shoulder, and darted for the washroom before he changed his mind and blocked her path.

Wyatt enjoyed the view, brief though it was. Chuckling softly, he pulled on a pair of woolen socks and a shirt, then padded to the mudroom for a short stack of wood. He caught the parlor stove before it was cold, but he had to fire up the kitchen stove. He started by setting the covers on top, closing the front and back damper, and opening the one to the oven. He turned the grate, let the ashes fall, then carefully removed the pan.

It was when he opened the back door and took notice of eight inches of fresh powder that he truly regretted leaving the Commodore. Bracing himself, he stepped out onto the protected porch just long enough to fling the ashes. They were carried by the wind in a wide arc, mingling with the falling snow. In a matter of moments, the gray and blackened residue was covered.

He was on the point of turning back into the house when he saw movement at the corner of the house. In spite of the cold, he stayed where he was, instantly recognizing the tall bundle of dark wool and leather that came trudging through the snow toward him.

"What the hell do you want?"

"Coffee," Will Beatty said. "Biscuits, if your wife has any fresh."

Wyatt held up the ash pan in mock menace. "You'll take day-old biscuits the same as me. Come on in. Mind your boots. Rachel's particular about the floors." He lowered the ash pan and ushered Will inside, barely avoiding the shower of snowflakes that his deputy shook off like a wet, frisky puppy.

He pointed Will to a chair at the table while he set about building the fire. "So, what brings you here? It's early for a social call."

Will looked over his shoulder toward the alcove. He raised an eyebrow.

Wyatt understood. "She's still dressing."

"Artie woke me up first thing. There was a message this morning from John Clay that Foster Maddox is in Denver. He'd be on his way now if it wasn't for snow blocking the tracks at Brady's Bend. Depending on how much we get, it could take a few days, maybe as long as a week, to break through. He thought you'd want to know."

Wyatt swore. "I was supposed to know if Foster arrived in Cheyenne. You're sure he's in Denver?"

"I'm not sure of anything, but that's what Artie got from John Clay's message."

"Well, there's nothing much to be done about that now. What's Sid saying about the storm?"

"Last I heard, he was talking a two-day whiteout."

Wyatt considered that. "Do you think we could get better than a week out of the blockage?"

"Probably. I don't know anyone who hasn't made provision for it. Sir Nigel might suffer a bit with the train not running, but he'll keep the guests he has, so I guess it evens out. Why? What are you thinking to gain by a couple of extra days?"

"Time to hide the mining equipment, for one thing. Shut it all down."

"Shut it down? That's going to happen anyway, on account of the snow burying us." It was not much of an exaggeration.

"We need to make it look abandoned. If he knows about it, he's going to insist on seeing it. It would be good if folks don't look too prosperous, either."

Will glanced around the homey kitchen, then fixed his stare on Wyatt's sooty hands and the pair of split logs in them. "I'll tell them they should follow your example."

Wyatt shot him a wry look, then tossed the wood in the stove. "They could do worse," he said, opening the dampers. "They could follow yours."

Not offended in the least, Will grinned. He stood up and waved Wyatt away from the stove. "Go get dressed. I'll finish. It's like diving headlong into an avalanche in here."

Will had coffee ready by the time Rachel appeared in the kitchen. "Mornin', ma'am."

Rachel smiled warmly at him. "Wyatt says you came for biscuits."

"And coffee," he said, holding up a dainty cup, his little finger extended.

She laughed. "I have mugs, you know. You don't need to affect airs."

"I'm not sure what that means exactly, but I'll take a mug."

Rachel got him one from the back of the china cupboard, then took another out for Wyatt. She chose one like Will had used for herself. "Is everything all right?" she asked, handing over the mug. "Not that I mind you coming for biscuits, but I happen to know that Estella's are better than mine."

"You aren't getting me to say one way or the other. Wyatt

would trade my ass for a mule—pardon the expression—if I got caught in that trap."

"Is that right? So how many days is it exactly before Foster Maddox gets here?"

"About seven, maybe nine." That no-account Beatty boy clamped a hand over his mouth in dramatic fashion. His eyes went almost perfectly round.

"Too late." She called to Wyatt in the bedroom. "Seven to nine days." His chuckle drifted back into the kitchen just ahead of him. "That," she said to Will, "is the sound of my husband preparing to trade your ass—pardon the expression."

Wyatt grinned. He caught Rachel by the waist, tipped her back, and kissed her with such thoroughness that she *and* Will were blushing when he set her on her heels again. "Better than washing your mouth out with soap." He glanced at Will. "You, I'll use soap."

"I didn't mean to tell her."

"No one ever does."

"You already said something to her anyway," Will said defensively.

"Yes, but you didn't know that."

Rachel set her hands on her hips. "Stop it. You're like children." That had the desired effect of bonding them immediately. "Like brothers," she said for good measure. She watched them grin at each other, evidently satisfied with this comparison. "Set the table, Will. Wyatt, pour us some coffee. I have biscuits and sausage gravy to warm."

They resisted saluting her and took up the tasks as she directed, trading good-natured barbs and asides until the meal was hot on the table before them. That was when they sat down to the business of what to do about Foster Maddox.

"I suppose it depends on what he's learned," Rachel said, when Will asked her if Foster would be coming alone. "If he knows anything at all about the mine, then he'll have surveyors and engineers with him. People he trusts."

"Cromwell?" Will asked Wyatt. "Do you suppose Ben will come up from Denver?"

"Couldn't say. Lawyers?" he asked Rachel.

"Yes. Probably Mr. Davis Stuart to advise him, perhaps another to review Colorado law. Foster would have gotten rid of his grandfather's private attorney by now. There will be at least one accountant. I can't say who that might be. George Gravely was the one Mr. Maddox trusted the most. He's had the position since my father's death."

Will tucked into his biscuits. "That's good. He'll arrive like the cavalry. No surprises there. We can be ready."

Wyatt didn't share his deputy's easy confidence. He glanced at Rachel on his right and saw his caution was warranted. "How about getting a list of the Commodore's guests from Sir Nigel? Do the same at the boardinghouse. I don't imagine it would hurt to inquire after Rose. I assume you'll want to do that, too. She's speaking to you, isn't she?"

"Sure, but mostly she spits exclamation points at me. It's like she has a mouthful of darts."

Rachel lifted her cup to hide her smile. Over the rim, she saw Wyatt check his.

"Maybe you can sweet-talk her, Will," said Wyatt. "And if you can't, tell her it's because of Rachel that you need the names of anyone new in and around her establishment. She'll give them to you."

"If it's all the same," Will said, "I think I'll start by mentioning Rachel."

"Do what you think's best."

Will lifted a forkful of biscuit and gravy to his mouth. "Can Maddox take back the spur?"

"Not without a fight."

"Saloon?"

"Court," said Wyatt, quelling the gleam he'd seen in his deputy's eyes. "Not as viscerally satisfying perhaps but more widely respected."

Will took the bite hovering at his lips, chewed slowly as he considered how a court battle might favor them in Colorado. "What about the mining?"

"Harder to say. I'm not certain what he knows about it, but I'll be talking to Sid and Henry. Rachel, too, obviously. We'll reach consensus about the best way to protect our investment. Making it all look played out is only a first step."

"The weather's going to slow us down, too," Will told him. "And if there's not a new layer of snow laid down, every trek the men make out there will be visible to anyone who goes looking for a trail."

"We can't do anything about the weather," Wyatt said. "We'll do what we can and hope for the best."

Rachel had been eating quietly during this exchange. Now she looked up and asked carefully, "What happens to the spur and the mine if I die?" She noted they shared a similar reaction, although that was hardly surprising. They both recoiled, very nearly to the same degree. Wyatt's face was the paler of the two, and after last night's confession, she knew something of the pain he was experiencing. "I think there must be a clear plan," she said. When they remained silent, she added, "For inheritance. We have to think about that."

"You're Wyatt's wife," Will said. "Doesn't that mean it will go to—" He stopped, shook his head. "I don't like talking about this, and I'm not sure it's any of my business. I'll just finish my meal and go back out and get to work. You'll be in the office later, Wyatt?"

"I expect. To clean my guns, if nothing else."

Will nodded, bent his head, and wiped up his plate in record time. The silence at the table unnerved him, and he was glad to be heading out before the shouting started. He thought about seeing Miss Rose first, maybe try to dodge a few of her darts before he spoke to Sir Nigel; then he decided to save her for last. Could be that she'd let him escort her back to his room above the sheriff's office, maybe let him take her to bed. He sure wasn't going to bunk down with her in a brothel, at least he was pretty sure he wasn't. It was hard to say which one of them was going to give in first.

"Will?" Wyatt said. That no-account Beatty boy was staring at his empty plate. "You want seconds?"

Will's head jerked up. "What? No. Oh, no." His chair scraped the floor hard as he jumped to his feet. "Sorry about your floor, ma'am. Wyatt says you're particular." He failed to take note of her puzzled expression but saw her start to rise. "No. No point in you gettin' up. I know the way out. Thanks for breakfast." He continued his nervous chatter as he backed out of the kitchen and fumbled with his jacket, scarf, boots, and hat. "Damn fine biscuits," he said, opening the door behind him. Wind and snow swirled into the mudroom, and his very last words were lost in an eerie howl.

Wyatt and Rachel stared at each other, then shook their heads in unison. "You scared him off," Wyatt said. "Scared me, too, for that matter."

"But you're still here."

"That's right. I am." He stood slowly. "You want to pick a fight with me?"

"Kitchen?"

"Bedroom."

Her smile appeared slowly. "Not as viscerally satisfying perhaps but more widely respected."

Wyatt yanked her out of the chair and tossed her over his shoulder; then he headed for the bedroom to prove precisely how wrong she was.

Chapter Twelve

Rachel wrapped a cardinal-red woolen scarf around her head, face, and neck, forgoing a bonnet entirely, and braced herself to entertain the cold. Other than short trips to the spring, the woodpile, or the outhouse, she hadn't been outside for three days. It was easy for Wyatt to say that she was better off indoors because he was getting out daily. He'd spoken to nearly every household about Foster Maddox's impending arrival, but he'd have made rounds to check on folks whether or not he had an agenda. He and Will Beatty were not only the intermediaries for news and gossip during the storm; they also helped people get around when it was essential for them to do so.

One of Sid Walker's granddaughters survived a breech birth because that no-account Beatty boy was able to bring the midwife in time, and Wyatt stopped a drunk and staggering Bud Fuller from leaving the Miner Key in nothing but his union suit after literally losing his shirt.

Rachel appreciated Wyatt's entertaining stories when he returned home each evening, but she felt a desperate need to get out herself. She'd always left the house regularly, even when she was discouraging visitors. During those first fifteen months in Reidsville, her isolation was on her own terms.

It was another thing entirely to have it imposed on her by the weather.

And Wyatt.

She understood why he was discouraging her from leaving. In the main, it was simply dangerous. Several times during the storm, the snowfall reached the whiteout conditions that Sid had predicted. The potential was there for someone who hadn't taken proper precautions to get lost on their way to the outhouse. To prevent that, Wyatt had run ropes to the only places he decided Rachel needed to go.

It was helpful and appreciated, but it wasn't enough. Rachel wanted a guide rope that stretched all the way to Artie Showalter's, and not having it wasn't going to keep her from leaving home—not any longer.

Wyatt's trail was easy for Rachel to follow. He had cleared a path in the snow all the way to the end of the flagstones. Beyond that, he'd simply pushed his way through. She did precisely the same, although her passage was made easier by his earlier ones. Snow fell lightly but steadily, and Rachel had no difficulty seeing where she was going. She'd fashioned a pack for herself from scrap material and carried it on her back. It was stuffed with two gowns in different states of completion, one a traveling dress intended for Virginia Moody, the other a pink-and-white sateen tea gown that Gracie Showalter had ordered for Molly's birthday.

Rachel paused to catch her breath when she reached the corner of Aspen Street. Most of the shop owners had cleared the sidewalks in front of their businesses, not that there was much in the way of pedestrian traffic. Stepping up to the walk, Rachel suddenly felt conspicuous. She was entirely alone.

It was a sharp reminder of the other reason Wyatt did not want her venturing out alone. She made a clear target. Erring on the side of caution, Wyatt did not want to suppose that Foster Maddox and his companions would arrive at the same time. He had to consider that Foster might have sent some of his men ahead of him. Even when the names Will collected at the Commodore, the boardinghouse, and the brothel revealed none that were familiar to Rachel, Wyatt remained stubbornly wary.

Rachel lifted her scarf a fraction higher so that only her eyes were visible. Glancing at her reflection in the emporium's large window, she was hardly recognizable to herself. That gave her the confidence to continue.

It was late in the afternoon by the time Rachel finished with her errands and arrived at Wyatt's office. She stood in the door and stamped her feet. No one was in the front, and no one came from the back to greet her. She called for Wyatt and Will, but neither answered. Fully expecting that one or the other of them would appear soon, Rachel unwound her scarf and draped it over a chair. She unbuttoned her coat, but didn't remove it, and stood in front of the stove warming herself for a few minutes before she took off her kid gloves and shrugged off her backpack.

There was a pot of coffee on the stove, and she poured herself a cup. It was slightly bitter—the last of the morning brew, no doubt—but it was warm and satisfying. Since the news of her marriage to Wyatt had become known to everyone, she visited his office at least once a week, occasionally bringing him something to eat, but more often because she liked to see him sitting behind his desk with his long legs stretched out at an angle, his boot heels perched on the lip of a drawer. She never shared the reason that she made a point of dropping in, but she never tried to deny it to herself.

The unvarnished, and sometimes uncomfortable, truth was that he could make her heart stutter.

By way of an experiment, Rachel took up Wyatt's position at the desk, swiveled in his chair exactly as he did, and propped her feet on the edge of a drawer that she'd opened for just that purpose. She clasped her hands together over her abdomen and tilted her head at what she thought of as a mildly inquisitive angle. She lowered her eyelids to that sleepy, vaguely bored position at half-mast in which he often contemplated the comings and goings of nearly everyone in town.

"You planning on running for office?" Wyatt asked from the doorway.

Rachel didn't flinch. Conversationally, she asked, "Did you know you can see right through a crack in the back of the roll-top when you sit like this?"

"Is that right?"

"While you're just about invisible back here to anyone passing by or coming in from the street."

He grunted softly, tapping his snow-covered boots against the doorjamb before he closed the door behind him.

"I imagine people are always surprised how you know who's coming to see you."

"They're not surprised at all. They think I'm prescient."

Rachel laughed, dropped her feet to the floor, and rolled the chair out from behind the desk. "You, Wyatt Cooper, are a fraud."

"Only if you reveal the well-kept secrets of my trade. Otherwise, I'm prescient."

She stood, crossed the distance to him in a few long strides, and flung her arms around his neck. "Hello, Sheriff." She gave him a loud, smacking kiss on the lips.

Wyatt's arms circled her at the waist. When she would have skittered away as quickly as she'd come, he had a good grip on her. One of his eyebrows shot up. "I bet you think that kiss answers for everything."

"I have no idea what you're talking about."

"Which means you know *exactly* what I'm talking about. What are you doing here?"

"I thought it might be nice if we walked home together."

"Rachel."

She made a face at him. "Oh, very well. If you must know, I couldn't stand being confined to the house a moment longer. I couldn't work on Virginia's traveling dress without another fitting, so I went to see her, and I thought if I was walking that far, I might as well stop at Gracie's with the tea gown that she ordered for Molly's birthday. I just finished a little while ago. *Then* I thought it might be nice if we walked home together."

"We agreed you wouldn't go out."

"No. You said I shouldn't leave. I didn't agree to anything." She noticed that his hands had dropped to his sides. She removed any lingering temptation he had to shake her by backing away from his easy reach. "I know what you wanted, Wyatt, but really, it was becoming intolerable."

He wasn't the least sympathetic. "I'd think you'd find that being abducted by one of Maddox's men is not to your liking, either."

"You have no proof that anyone in his employ is here already. And where would they take me? The bend's still blocked, and the trains aren't running. The snow's made it almost impossible to get from here to anywhere except by sled and pack mule. I think you're being overly cautious."

"You're merely convincing me of all the reasons Foster might find it more convenient to kill you."

She sighed. "I should never have mentioned making a will. Foster's never made that kind of threat against me."

"He never had so many reasons. Millions of them."

Rachel held up her hands, palms out. "Please. Don't."

Wyatt exhaled slowly, nodded once. "I was just going to look over some papers. I'll be ready to go in a few minutes."

"All right." She stepped out of his way. "Where's Will?"

"With Jake Reston at the bank. He's helping Jake close." He sat at the desk and began going through the papers scattered across the top.

"No one's locked up in the back?"

"Not a soul. I thought I'd have to bring in Ezra Reilly for drunk and disorderly. Virginia's got him spinning in circles about the wedding. He doesn't believe she's not working over at Rose's since she's still living there. He made some threats to shoot up the place, but we got his gun, and Rudy agreed to let him sleep it off in the back of the saloon. That seemed kinder than throwing him in here for the night."

Rachel opened the door to the cell area and poked her head in. It was the first time she'd looked back there since the shoot-out. With some trepidation, she glanced at the floor, breathing easier when she saw it had been scrubbed clean. "What's behind that door on the left?" The right one, she knew, led to the alley. "Is that where you keep your guns?"

"Yes, and it's also a broom closet," he told her, squaring off the papers and setting them aside. "I used to use it as a darkroom."

"Really? May I look?"

He shrugged. "Help yourself but be careful. You'll need a lamp."

She smiled, recognizing it as an invitation to leave him alone. She took the lamp from the shelf behind his desk, slipped into the narrow corridor, and closed the door.

Shaking his head, amused, Wyatt lighted another lamp for himself and continued working. He studied the descriptions provided by the detectives' association that Artie had received over the wire, aware all the while that Rachel was rummaging through his things. He could hear her moving crates around, rearranging his perfectly settled clutter. He'd be fortunate if he could find the mop and broom the next time he went looking for them.

Wyatt found himself wincing when he heard the clink of glass jars being knocked together. Or was it his photographic plates that she'd found? Then there was the scrape of something wooden against the floor. His tripod? There was a thud. Lord, but he hoped that was a broom.

He closed his desk and stood. "Rachel? Don't make me sorry that I'm coming back there." He thought he heard her chuckle, which was hardly a good sign. When he stepped into the hallway, he caught her in the act of hoisting his camera and tripod over her shoulder. He stayed where he was and held his breath, afraid a movement of any kind would upset the precarious balance she'd managed to find.

Rachel carried the equipment carefully, making certain she didn't bang it against the door frame as she left the darkroom. "It's heavier than I thought. Do you want to take it now?"

Wyatt didn't require a second invitation. He quickly removed it from Rachel's shoulder and put it on his own. "There's a plan, I imagine."

"I want to take it home. You can teach me how to make photographs."

"And that's all?"

"Well, as long as it's there, I thought you might like to use it yourself."

"Hmm."

"When the weather's improved you could take it with you. It had *cobwebs* on it, Wyatt. That's really a very sad state for something that can capture so much beauty."

"Are you thinking I'm going to argue with you?"

"Well?"

"Get the lamp, Rachel. I'll carry this home today, but the other things I need will have to wait."

"Tomorrow?"

"We'll see. I need some sort of darkroom."

"All right. We'll think of something."

He believed her, but if she thought he was going to mix chemicals in the pantry, she was mistaken. "The lamp," he said again, jerking his chin toward the door behind her. "And then home."

The meeting took place around the dining room table. Abe Dishman was present to report on the progress of clearing the pass, and Sid Walker and Henry Longabach each had information on various aspects of the mining operation. Wyatt came with notes on what he and Will had learned about every stranded stranger in town, and Rachel had a journal with questions that she'd scribbled down since their last meeting.

"Have you considered that Foster Maddox will attempt to buy the answers he wants?" she asked.

Henry took out a handkerchief and cleaned his wire-rimmed spectacles. "Sid and I discussed it. We don't think there's anyone that's likely to be tempted."

"They'd be givin' up more than they'd be gainin'," Sid said, absently rubbing his shoulder.

"What about Miss LaRosa and her girls? They're relatively new to town. It's my understanding that none of them have been here more than five years. They don't have the same investment in the mine as the families who have been here better than twenty. Could they be bought?"

Every man at the table simply stared at her.

"What?" she asked. "Did I misspeak?"

Abe, Henry, and Sid all swung their heads in Wyatt's direction.

Wyatt's mouth twisted wryly. "Now I know how Caesar felt in his final moments." He shook his head at them, feigning disgust at their cowardice. "I guess it's up to me." He saw that Rachel was looking at him expectantly, and he addressed her. "The town supports one brothel. Only one. It began in the days when there were hardly any women in Reidsville. The men, well, the men got lonely and . . . they . . . well, they decided they—"

"They decided they would operate their own establishment," Rachel said. "Is that right?"

"More or less," Wyatt said. "They built the house and furnished it; then they hired a madam to run it. Paid her good money to keep a nice place and fill it with girls that were friendly and accommodating."

"I'm sure." Rachel wasn't certain how she managed to appear unaffected by what she was hearing. It helped that Abe, Sid, and Henry were all blushing deeply. She supposed one or two of them had been accommodated by that first wave of friendly girls. "I imagine those women are all married now."

"I imagine they are," he said carefully. "And the ones that came after them."

"And so on," said Rachel. "Yes, I see how it works. Like Virginia Moody and Ezra Reilly. They eventually marry and end up with a claim in the mine."

"That's right."

"So the short answer is precisely what Mr. Walker said about everyone else in town: they'd be giving up more than they'd be gaining."

Wyatt nodded, and this time he was joined by the other men as they sharply turned their heads in unison toward Rachel.

"You might have just said so." Rachel coolly checked off one of the questions she'd jotted in her book and continued with another. She didn't dare ask publicly which of the town's upstanding women first made an impression on their husbands when they weren't standing up, and she wasn't even certain that she wanted to know. She was reminded again of Wyatt telling her that whether a woman was once a man's mistress just didn't matter a lot in this town. Here was the proof of it, in spades. "All right, gentlemen, if people can't be bought, can they be threatened?"

The meeting went on for several hours as they parried questions and answers. Determining their preparedness to have Foster Maddox in town without hinting at the mine's success demanded a certain amount of deception, and they all agreed that Reidsville was peculiarly suited to carry it out. The citizens had been engaged in an elaborate charade for more than a score of years, making certain their wealth was sustainable, not, as they liked to say here, a flash in the pan.

By the time Rachel and Wyatt saw their guests out it was after ten. They stood arm in arm on the porch until the men were through the gate. Snow flurried in front of them, most of it being swept up from the existing drifts. Sid had warned them not to expect another storm that would delay Foster's arrival. The snow that they could anticipate would be measured in inches, not feet.

"What do you think?" asked Rachel as they stepped inside. "Are we ready to welcome Foster Maddox?"

"Welcome him? I don't think I would say that. Weather him is more like it."

"Weather him. Yes, that suits."

"Do you still have doubts?"

Rachel considered that. "No, not really. I only wish I knew more about what he wants."

"That's not much of a question in my mind. He wants everything."

She moved closer to Wyatt. His arms went easily around her. "Well, he can't have it," she said quietly. "I won't let him."

Wyatt rubbed his chin against the crown of her hair. "Let's go to bed."

They went through the house together, extinguishing the lamps and setting the fires in the stoves. Rachel removed cups and dishes from the table while Wyatt wiped it down. She drew the curtains, he checked the doors, and then they took turns in the washroom preparing for bed.

Rachel was shivering by the time Wyatt joined her. She immediately rolled into him and fairly hummed with pleasure as she warmed herself.

It wasn't an unpleasant experience for Wyatt, either. "Better?" he asked when she finally settled.

"Warmer, anyway."

Wyatt's deep chuckle had a wicked edge. He turned on her, tickling her until she was gasping for breath and beyond helpless to defend herself. Hovering over her, he asked, "Better?"

"Much warmer."

He kissed the smug smile off her face.

His playful teasing was a revelation to Rachel, not only for what she learned about him, but for what she learned about herself. It seemed to her that this turn in bed was more representative of their relationship outside it. She almost told him then, but he was making a sweep of her neck with tiny, lapping kisses that made her want to laugh and bat him away like a pesky puppy.

He nuzzled her throat, then pressed his open mouth against her skin and blew hard. His lips vibrated and the noise was like a bugle blast.

"Wyatt!"

He raised his head, both eyebrows lifted innocently. "What?"

She set her mouth primly, the whole of her expression admonishing. It had absolutely no impact. "Oh, very well. If you must."

"I really must." He grinned, unrepentant, and began working his way along the neckline of her nightgown. It was tempting to tear it right down the middle, but he used what sense he had left to unfasten the tiny mother-of-pearl buttons.

Rachel pushed herself up on her elbows and watched his fingers flick over the front of her gown. She let him keep going because he planted a kiss on every patch of skin he revealed. He didn't necessarily do it immediately. Sometimes he made her wait. He'd run his index finger over her skin, circling a spot for no apparent reason except that he could. Sometimes he'd press the tip of his fingernail just hard enough to make a crescent, branding her, she thought, then placed his lips flat against the tiny mark.

"Wyatt." She whispered his name this time.

"Hmm?"

"You're taking a lot of time."

"There are a lot of buttons, Rachel. Each one deserves attention."

"What if I helped?"

That brought his head up. "I think I'd like that just fine." He slid onto his side and propped himself on an elbow, prepared to watch. "I wish you'd offered earlier."

Rachel rolled her eyes as she sat up.

"Oh, no." He put one hand on her shoulder and pushed her back to the mattress. "Now you can help."

It should have been cold with the covers thrown off, but Rachel discovered that her skin was deliciously warm. She walked the fingertips of one hand between the narrow opening in her gown until she reached the button below her navel. It wasn't necessary to watch what she was doing. Watching Wyatt's eyes darken was enough to know that she was doing it exactly right.

She teased him a little by taking her time, slipping her fingers under the fabric so he couldn't quite see how they were engaged. She did it again and again until her gown was open and her hand lay over her mons. Then she surprised them both by tentatively touching herself.

Wyatt's elbow collapsed, and his head hit the pillow. His breath almost seized. Both actions were only slightly exaggerated. "You're trying my patience."

"Am I?" She was ridiculously pleased by the notion. "That's good, isn't it?"

Growling softly, dangerously, Wyatt slid over her. His face hovered inches above hers. "In this case, maybe."

They never quite abandoned their play or their laughter, even when the tenor of their teasing changed. It was always there, just beneath the surface as they began to learn about each other in a way they hadn't done before. They fell into new positions, sometimes by accident, sometimes by design. They appreciated the awkwardness of certain moments when they grappled but never quite fit. The tangle they could make amused them both. Wyatt's leg cramp amused only one of them.

They were swept up separately and climaxed within moments of each other. This time it was Rachel who fell weakly across Wyatt. He clasped his hands behind her back just above the curve of her buttocks. She hugged him.

"Don't move," he said.

It wasn't possible to be perfectly still. Small contractions still tugged at her, but he didn't seem to mind those. Her breathing quieted. He released her long enough to pull the blankets up to her shoulders.

After a few minutes, they parted and got comfortable together, finding their fit easily. His arm slipped around her waist, and she laid her hand over it, keeping it in place.

Rachel closed her eyes. She thought about what she'd wanted to tell him earlier, and she hesitated again, wondering how it would be received.

"What is it?" he prompted.

She didn't ask how he knew to nudge her. It was something she could simply accept now. "I've been thinking . . . we're friends, aren't we?"

Wyatt didn't answer immediately, giving what she said the consideration it deserved. "I suppose we are."

Rachel remained quiet, stroking his forearm with her fingertips, content with his response.

Wyatt couldn't recall that he and Sylvie had ever been friends. They had too many expectations, perhaps, while he and Rachel had almost none. He thought about what Rachel had said, that his marriage to Sylvie was often about sacrifice. He couldn't think of anything he'd given up for Rachel. He couldn't think of anything that she'd asked him to.

The corner of his mouth kicked up as he recalled the six weeks of celibacy he'd managed to endure with Rachel always in arm's reach. Even that wasn't strictly a sacrifice. It had always seemed more of a strategy. He'd imagined turning the tables on her, wearing her down in so many small ways that she wouldn't be able to tolerate the limits she set. It hadn't occurred to him once that she was the weather to his mountain.

Looking back over those weeks, he was struck by how often she'd given him opportunities to talk about himself. Almost reflexively, he turned her questions back on her. He always found ways to change the subject or answer a query by using someone else as an example. She never pressed, never pursued. He thought he was being clever.

And all the while she was simply waiting.

Wyatt nudged Rachel's hair with his chin. His stubble rasped softly against her scalp, and he breathed in her fragrance, at once exotic and familiar. He felt her push her bottom back against him, fitting herself snugly into the cradle he made for her. He couldn't tell if her slight movement meant that she was still awake or if it was sleep that made her settle closer.

"Rachel."

"Hmm?"

"Nothing. I just wanted to say your name."

* * *

Rose LaRosa resisted placing her hands on her hips. Her impatient energy found an outlet in the tattoo she beat against the floor with the toe of her ankle boot. "You can't sit here all night, Will. Maybe they let you do that in Denver, but here, you've got to choose a girl." She pointed to the plate of ginger cakes on top of the piano. "Besides, you're making a little too free with the samplings."

"But I like ginger cakes." To prove it, he rose from the piano stool and snagged another one. He took an enthusiastic bite as he sat down. "Anyway, I've chosen a girl."

Rose glanced around the salon. Except for Adele Brownlee and Virginia Moody, who were sharing the chaise, the room was empty. Her girls had their heads bent close together as they examined swatches of fabric for Virginia's ever-expanding trousseau. They didn't even glance up to observe her exchange with that no-account Beatty boy.

Frustrated, she turned on them. "Which one of you is making the deputy wait?" she asked sharply.

Their heads came up simultaneously. They shared the same blank look.

Rose frowned. "Did the deputy ask one of you to take him upstairs?"

"No, ma'am," Adele said. She looked at Will. "That's right, ain't it? You didn't change your mind?"

Will's deep, crescent-shaped dimples appeared as he grinned. "Didn't change my mind at all."

Relieved, Adele and Virginia went back to fingering the swatches.

Rose crossed the room to stand at the piano. "Who are you waiting for, then? Sally's going to be a while. Margaret usually entertains her man most of the night. Jenny's feeling poorly so I excused her, and Abigail's singing at the Miner Key."

"Quiet night for you," Will said.

She sighed. "You're not good for business."

"First I heard of it."

"Well, I'm telling you. The regulars don't pay you any mind, but strangers tend to wonder why you're hangin' around."

Will unpinned the star from his vest and slipped it in his pants pocket. "Better?"

"Hardly. Better would be if you were upstairs with one of the girls or on your way home."

"Is it the money?" he asked. "I don't mind paying. How much you figure these ginger cakes are worth?"

Rose ignored the titters from Adele and Virginia. They were still examining the fabric swatches, but now they were attentive to her every word. "What do I have to do to get you out of here?"

He didn't hesitate. "Walk me home."

"That's ridiculous."

Will shrugged. He spun the stool to face the piano and began playing. The intricate strains of a Chopin etude emerged from an instrument that was generally used for tentatively picking out the melody of "Oh! Susanna" and "Camptown Races."

Rose stared at him. Out of the corner of her eye she saw that Adele and Virginia had picked up their heads. "You can't play that here," Rose said stoutly. "No one knows the words."

Unperturbed, Will continued to run his fingers nimbly over the keys. "There are no words."

"That's worse," she snapped. It didn't matter to her that it was the most beautiful thing she'd ever heard. It *couldn't* matter. "You'll run people off with that kind of music."

He looked over his shoulder, first to the left, then the right. "Seems they were run off before I started playin', and them that are here seem to like it just fine. You being the exception."

Rose considered dropping the lid on his fingers, but the truth was that she couldn't bring herself to do it. Watching his hands was mesmerizing. "Where did you learn to play like that?"

"Same place most kids here do. My ma's been teaching piano for just about forever. Thought you would have known."

She looked at her girls for confirmation. They both nodded. Rose's generous mouth became a flat line that communicated her disapproval. "Well, I didn't know."

"Not a problem," he said. "Now you do."

If he could play like this, she supposed, it stood to reason that he'd memorized dozens of pieces—none of them with sing-along words. "All right," she said. "I'll walk you home."

Only Will knew that his fingers fumbled on the keys and that for a moment he couldn't feel the pedals with his feet. "That's real nice of you, Miss Rose."

Turning with an abrupt flourish and an unladylike snort, Rose stalked off to get properly dressed.

It was a clear, crisp night that Rose and Will stepped into. Moonlight glanced off the snowbanks, making their route perfectly visible. Music drifted toward them from the saloon, but neither one of them suggested going in to hear Abigail sing. In fact, they didn't talk at all, a circumstance that amused Will and annoyed Rose. Her stride was long, vaguely impatient, and she never glanced at him. He loped beside her good-naturedly, hands thrust in his coat pockets, his collar turned up to keep the cold off the back of his neck.

When they reached the foot of the stairs that led to his rooms above the sheriff's office, they stopped simultaneously. Rose's dark eyebrows lifted, and she put out a hand to direct him up the stairs.

"I know the way," he said.

"Good for you." She started to turn only to be brought up short when he moved to block her path. Her head snapped up. "What are you doing?"

"Can't let you walk back alone. Wouldn't be mannerly."

"I won't tell your mama."

"Doesn't matter. I'd know I'd done wrong."

"You're about as dumb as a stump, Will Beatty."

"There are some that say I'm dumber."

She stared at him for a long time, searching his face for craft and cunning. She saw neither. His slight smile was mischievous, not mean, and he looked as if he just might be able to wait for her forever. Still, she had to ask, "Are you looking to have me for free?"

"I haven't decided if I'm going to have you at all, Miss Rose, but I know I won't be inviting a whore to my bed."

It took her a moment to understand what he was saying, and she found herself both insulted and oddly pleased. "Well," she said finally, "I suppose I could see you inside your door, maybe have a cup of tea."

"That'd be just fine." Now he turned out his hand and indicated that she could lead the way.

Will was roused to wakefulness by the first footfall on the stairs. The steps creaked with different pitches and groans, and he'd lived above the office long enough to be able to identify the peculiarities of all of them. By the time he heard his visitor reach the halfway point, he was already out of bed and grabbing his pants. He had just finished tucking in his shirt when the knock came.

Glancing over his shoulder, he saw that Rose hadn't stirred. He took the time to tuck the covers, kiss her sleep-flushed cheek, and sweep aside the heavy ebony curl that wound around her throat. He allowed himself one last look before he hurried out of the room and closed the door quietly behind him.

Artie Showalter stood on the landing, shoulders hunched, warming his hands under the armpits of his coat. Will stood back to let him inside.

"Go warm yourself at the stove," Will told him. "I can't believe Gracie let you out the door without your gloves."

"Gracie doesn't know I'm gone," Artie said, rubbing his hands together over the stove. "Leastways, she didn't. I couldn't sleep, so I got up and thought I'd do some work on the press, tinker with a couple of stories I've been working on for this week's paper."

Will casually removed the two empty mugs from the table and set them in the washtub. He noticed that both chairs were pushed out, so he sat in one and nudged the other back into position while Artie was still turned away. He thought about Rose in the other room. He hoped she didn't snore.

"So I was doing this and that," Artie went on. "And a message starts coming in over the wire. Now, that's real unusual. I could have been sleeping and never heard it. I don't stay up for transmissions unless I'm expecting a reply. Folks at the Denver office know that."

"Who's the message from, Artie?"

"George Eller."

"He's with the detectives' association."

"That's what I thought, and that's why I'm here. A message like this, well, it generally comes to the attention of the sheriff, but this one didn't. Just says 'On their way.'"

"What the hell does that mean?"

Artie shrugged. He removed his spectacles and wiped off the condensation on the lenses with a handkerchief. "I thought you'd know. The message repeated a few times, then stopped. Cut off between *their* and *way*."

Will made a sweep of his hair with his fingers, leaving it only marginally less tousled than before. "That happen often?"

"Hardly ever."

"George Eller," Will repeated, more to himself than Artie. "Could be almost anything. I don't want to assume it's about Foster Maddox."

"Wyatt did ask the Denver city marshal to keep an eye on Maddox."

Will nodded. "Could have something to do with Morrisey and Spinnaker, though. We have to keep that in mind." He got to his feet. "I suppose I better go see Wyatt."

"I don't envy you that."

"I know. Otherwise, you'd have gone there straightaway."

Artie's grin was sheepish but not repentant. "I have to get back. Let me know if you need anything. I don't mind riding out to check the lines, if that's what's called for."

Will thanked him and saw him out, then returned to the bedroom to wake up Rose and tell her he had to leave. The only thing that made it less than painful was that she didn't seem to be any happier about it than he was.

Wyatt kept an open mind about the cryptic message, but he leaned toward the idea that the intention behind it was to warn them that Foster Maddox was on his way.

"I thought we would have heard from John or Sam Kirby," said Will. He got out of the way as Wyatt grabbed his boots and proceeded to jam his feet into them. "What about you?"

"That's more or less what I was hoping." He stamped his feet, settling into his boots, and then took his coat off the hook. "But we know Maddox has the ability to get another train and hire another engineer. Maybe he got tired of waiting for the bend to be cleared and decided to take care of it himself."

Rachel appeared in the doorway to the kitchen, stifling a yawn with the back of her hand. "What's going on?"

Will told her while Wyatt continued to get ready.

"Why not wait until morning?" she asked.

Wyatt finished pulling on his gloves. "Because if he's got his own train on the spur, then it's trespass. Abe sure as hell didn't approve it. If he doesn't turn back, I have reason enough to put him in jail. The bend's not clear. We know that. Whoever's coming has to deal with that from their side. We can get around on horseback, but a train's caught. By morning, I can't guarantee the same."

Rachel nodded. "Very well. What can I do?"

The question didn't surprise Wyatt. "I think you should stay with someone while I'm gone."

"It's awfully late, Wyatt. I just can't appear on someone's doorstep at this hour."

"Go to Rose's," Will said. "She'll take you in." He felt the tips of his ears grow hot when they both looked at him, a similar question in their eyes. Trying to forge ahead, he heard himself stammer slightly. "She . . . well, that is, she might have heard . . . actually, I told her what Artie said on account I had . . . on account I had to leave her to come here."

One of Wyatt's brows lifted while the line of Rachel's mouth relaxed and became a gentle smile.

"Artie found you at Rose's?" asked Wyatt.

Rachel shook her head as she stepped forward and slipped her arm into Wyatt's. "Rose was at Will's," she corrected. "Finally."

Now Will's face went as ruddy as his earlobes. "She walked me home. Stayed for tea."

Rachel spoke quickly before Wyatt felt the need to clarify what Will had been careful to avoid saying. "That's lovely." She squeezed Wyatt's arm lightly. "Go on. You need to leave. I can get to Rose's safely on my own." She saw that neither of them particularly liked the idea, but the press of time forced them to accept it. She followed them out the back door and kissed Wyatt good-bye, then returned to the bedroom to dress and collect a few things to take with her.

Wyatt and Will didn't ride out alone. They got two men from the Miner Key who'd come for the singing, not the drinking, and roused four others out of bed. Ezra Reilly, Sid Walker's son

Sam, Andy Miller from the bank, and three from the Beatty clan were all deputized and given tin to pin on their coats.

They rode out of town three abreast, then followed the track in pairs, one on either side. They carried lanterns on their mounts but found the half-moon provided sufficient light for them to move with relative ease. There was little conversation. What discussion was necessary had happened when they all came together.

It was first and foremost a scouting mission. Whoever was coming mattered less than the fact that they *were* coming. Depending on the manner of their arrival, the spur itself was at risk. Improperly set charges might trigger an avalanche, or worse, bring down a section of the mountain, and rebuilding the track at Brady's Bend was just about the last thing anyone wanted to do. The old-timers remembered the toll it took on men and animals to create the pass. They liked retelling the stories but had no wish to relive them.

It took them the better part of the night to reach the bend. There was a small camp set up on the Reidsville side of the snow blockage. Six men shared three tents. A couple of mules and a half dozen horses occupied a makeshift corral. A handcar was on the track about twenty yards from where they were digging. Wyatt could see they'd made good progress without using powder.

Wyatt sent Will and Andy in to alert the miners to their presence, then led the others up the rocky, snow-covered incline to make their way cautiously around the block. Before they reached the halfway point, they were already aware there was no train immediately ahead of them. If one was on the way, they'd clearly beaten it to the bend.

They rode on for a couple of miles before they heard the distant rumble that signaled that an engine was straining to make the first rise. That was their cue to retreat to the block, corral their horses with the mules, and take up posts on either side. They were joined by the miners, who all carried Henry rifles now instead of pickaxes and shovels.

The break of day gave them their first glimpse of smoke curling from the engine. By gauging the distance between the points where the black smoke rose, they could estimate the speed of the engine and realized it was moving too quickly to be pulling more than a few cars. Because there was nothing else they could do, they all settled back and waited.

Foster Maddox was lean to the point of being gaunt. The slight hollowness in his cheeks was largely disguised by his full sideburns, but there was no hiding the sharp ridge of his brow, or alternately, the deep set of his green eyes. In startling contrast to the narrow nose and jaw, his lips were sensual in their plumpness. His hair was sandy at the crown but ginger at the tips. His sideburns were full on red.

He stepped out of the cab of the engine where he'd been riding and jumped easily to the ground. He landed lightly, without stumbling or sliding, and turned to confront the wall of ice and snow that blocked his way.

Daniel Seward appeared before he was summoned. He was a broad, bulky man whose only sharp feature was his mind. His work for C & C went back years, and he was one of the very few men Foster retained on the payroll after Clinton Maddox died. Daniel could build a bridge, but he also knew exactly how to destroy one.

"I don't recommend blasting," he said, surveying the blockage and then the mountain peaks that cradled it. He walked ahead, past the snorting engine, and dug out a handful of snow and ice, testing the crystals as if he were sifting dirt or sand. When he turned to face Foster, it was to discover the man was almost on his heels. He backed up a step. He outweighed the owner of the California and Colorado by a solid forty-five pounds, but Foster was a head taller and had the eyes of a mountain lion. In spite of the fact that he was saying things Foster Maddox didn't want to hear, he persevered. "The mountain's fragile. There's a lot of new powder and I don't like the way the rocks are set." He pointed to the timberline much higher up. "The snow's just sitting there, waiting for a tremble, and even if we can shake this loose, we still have to clear it." He dug into the snow again and showed it to Foster just as if he could appreciate it. "Once we dig this out, I recommend taking it very easy through here, or it's this train that's going to be buried."

"Why'd they snake the track through here? Why not bring it around the side of the mountain?"

"I imagine they couldn't stake the supports deeply enough. It would have required a lot of blasting to get a decent ledge and a grade a single engine could make. This pass, even with this horseshoe bend, was the best choice they had."

Foster looked it over, not liking what he saw. "How long to get through it?"

"If they're working on the other side like the reports say, then a couple more days."

"What about pushing the engine through? That's why we have a plow, isn't it?"

"It's too narrow. There's nowhere for the snow to go." Seward offered this information politely while he privately thought the answer was painfully obvious.

"I don't like it," Foster said. "She's behind this, Seward. I can feel it. She's got someone dancing to her tune, and she's holding us up."

"Yes, sir. Seems like that might be true."

Foster speared his man with a sharp glance. "What do you know about it?"

Realizing he'd just overstepped, Seward fell silent.

"Keep your opinions to yourself," Foster said. "Get your men together. Set the charges. We're going through."

"Yes, sir." He was tempted to shake his head in disgust at the hubris of the man, but he stopped himself. It was the sort of gesture that had led to the firing of more than one employee at C & C.

Andy Miller jabbed Will in the ribs with his elbow. Four men jumped out of the train's middle car when summoned by a bellow from the man standing front and center of the blockage. "How many men do you think are on that train?"

Will shrugged. He kept his voice low just as Andy had, conscious of the way sound carried in the bend. "Hard to say. One private car, one passenger car, and one freight car. I suppose there could be upwards of forty." He saw Andy blanch and couldn't resist adding, "That's if the freight car isn't packed with men. Might be forty more if they're standing balls to butt."

"Jesus," Andy said. "Don't joke about it."

Will took pity on him. "Don't worry. They'd all be climbin' over each other to get out and take a piss. I reckon we'll get a good count in the next ten minutes or so." Will looked back over his shoulder and farther up the mountain to where Wyatt, Sam Walker, and Ezra Reilly were huddled behind a rock. They'd brushed out their tracks so their path to the post wasn't easily visible. He watched their spot long enough to see Ezra poke his head up a few inches and make his own count of the men loitering around the freight car.

"Looks like Foster brought a baker's dozen with him," Andy said after no one new appeared from the cars for a while. "About the same as we have."

"Wyatt's not lookin' for a gunfight," Will reminded him. "We're here to protect the spur." Movement around the freight car caught his attention. "Aw. Damnation. Does that look like dynamite to you?"

Andy watched someone passing bundles to each of the four men standing on the ground by the freight car's open door. "Probably not a box lunch."

Will was thinking the same thing. Looking back, he saw Wyatt step out from behind the rock and hold up a hand, palm out. That was their signal that he was going down to talk to Maddox and that they should hold their positions. "What do you think, Andy? Does a man with that much dynamite ever negotiate?"

Andy didn't reply. He found himself thinking that maybe being poked and prodded by the six-shooters Morrisey and Spinnaker had put to him wasn't the worst thing he ever faced.

Chapter Thirteen

Foster Maddox was the first to see Wyatt approaching. He leaned out of the engine cab and pointed up the hillside. That simple gesture got the attention of his men, and they turned from conversation or the work they were engaged in and followed the direction of Foster's fingerpost.

Wyatt saw heads turn abruptly almost as soon as he began his descent. He didn't pause then, nor when he passed within a few feet of Will and Andy. He'd purposely left his Henry rifle with Sam and Ezra, but his Colt remained holstered at his side. None of the men below were armed, though Wyatt fully expected there to be rifles on the train. His decision to approach Foster Maddox on his own seemed a good one.

Snow and small rocks slid and tumbled out in front of Wyatt as he disturbed everything in his path on the steepest part of the descent. He angled his boots sideways to slow his progress and keep from stumbling ignominiously all the way to the bottom. Jumping the last two feet to avoid a sharp-edged rock, he landed as lightly as a mountain cat.

"Who's in charge?" He saw that enough of the men immediately surrounding him had taken notice of his star. He didn't feel the need to explain who he was.

Foster Maddox made himself visible by stepping out of the cab, but he didn't climb down. "That piece of tin says you're in charge, Deputy. What can we do for you?"

Men parted, making room for Wyatt to approach the engine. He didn't correct Foster for addressing him as deputy, sensing it was intentional and meant to assert his own authority. "Who's in there with you? Is that Jack Gordon you've got driving for you?"

"As a matter of fact, it is," said Foster. "How does that concern you?" Foster motioned behind him and Jack appeared in the open window.

Wyatt looked over Jack's craggy face and his thick shock of white hair and just shook his head. "You lost your mind, Jack? I have to believe you talked to John and Sam. You must have known this bend was still blocked."

"Sure did, Wyatt," Jack said. "Told this gentleman, too. But he's payin' me a lot of money to drive his train, so I guess I ain't completely lost my mind."

"I'll ask you again after they bring down this snowpack on your head." He lifted his chin in Foster's direction. "Is the dynamite your idea?"

"It is."

"It's a real bad idea."

"Then it's excellent that you happened upon us, isn't it? Tell me, exactly how does that occur?"

"Got a message that someone was coming just before the lines went down. We had a bank robbery a couple of months back, and it seemed like I should get a good look at who might be making the trek from Denver."

"Do we look like bank robbers?"

"I never understand that question. Bank robbers look like everyone else, so yes, you look like you could be a poster on my office wall. It would go a long way to relieving my mind if you told me your name and your business here."

"Well, certainly I want to relieve your mind. I am Foster Maddox, the owner of the California and Colorado. My business is in Reidsville, and that's where I'm taking it."

"Not if you're of a mind to blow up that snow dam, Mr. Maddox. Who's setting the charges for you?"

Foster gestured to Daniel Seward to come forward. "This is Mr. Seward. He's the man directing the operation."

Wyatt held out his hand to Seward. "Wyatt Cooper," he said. "Come with me. I want to show you a couple of things." He saw Seward glance at Foster Maddox for permission. Wyatt didn't wait to see if he got it, he simply started out and left it up to Seward to follow.

"I know the dangers," Seward said, coming abreast of Wyatt. "I've explained them to Mr. Maddox. He wants to get through today."

"There're men from Reidsville working on the other side. They've been at it for days."

"I figured there probably were. Mr. Maddox thought there should be something done from this side as well."

"Abe Dishman is in charge of managing the spur, and he didn't want a couple of engines stranded up here. Reidsville's a quiet town. No one's in a hurry much. A thing like this, it's better if everyone takes the time to do the job right."

"It's different for Mr. Maddox. We've already had quite a few delays."

"Hard for it to be otherwise, this time of year."

"He didn't want to wait. As owner, that's his prerogative."

"Do you know his business in Reidsville?"

"Yes, sir. I sure do. But it's not my place to tell you. That's for Mr. Maddox to say."

"Fair enough. Are you planning to do as he orders?"

"I am. I also plan to be standing about a hundred yards to the rear of the last car when the charges go off."

Wyatt appreciated that. "All right. I have a suggestion that might suit all of us."

"I'd like to hear it."

"Then stand close enough to listen to what I have to say to Mr. Maddox. It sounds as if decisions begin and end with him." Wyatt turned back to the engine cab. He noted that Foster was still standing just outside the cab, refusing to yield the high ground. Tipping his hat back with his forefinger, Wyatt tilted his head in Foster's direction.

"Mr. Seward seems to appreciate the dangers, even if you don't," he said. "I told him there're men digging from the other side, but he doesn't think that's fast enough for you."

"It's not."

"I'd like to propose that you consider coming with me. I can get you around the slide and take you on horseback all the way to Reidsville. You can bring a few men with you, if you like, but only a few because there's not nearly enough animals to carry everyone. The men you leave behind can start clearing the track. By clearing, I mean digging. Unless you want to risk being trapped in Reidsville until the spring thaw, you won't insist on blasting."

Foster's sandy eyebrows knit, and he stroked his jaw, considering. "How many men?"

"Three. The rest will be able to join you shortly."

"How long to get to Reidsville?"

"That depends on your stamina. It's a different kind of riding in this country than you're probably used to. I imagine it'll be well after dark before we get to town."

"I'm not worried about keeping up," Foster said. "I'm not my grandfather."

Wyatt thought it best not to comment.

"I like your proposal, Deputy."

"Thank you, sir. Happy to make the offer." Wyatt glanced

around. "How much time you reckon you'll need before we go?"

Foster's smile did not quite meet his eyes. "I *reckon* that'd be about ten minutes. Do you have another appointment, perhaps?"

"Not at all, Mr. Maddox. I'm dressed for the weather. I can wait as long as you need me to."

"Then wait over there." Foster pointed to the spot where Wyatt first landed when he came off the hill.

Wyatt kept his tone perfectly civil. "Don't mind if I do."

Foster made eye contact with the men he wanted to step forward. They complied quickly. "Did you hear the suggestion he made?" When all three nodded, he went on. "Can you do the kind of riding he's talking about? If you can't, tell me now, because I won't hesitate to leave you on the trail."

No one spoke up, not even Randolph Dover, the C & C's accountant, although he did swallow visibly.

"Very well." Foster's question had been primarily aimed at Dover. He hadn't decided if he'd really accept the man's defection, but his hand hadn't been forced. Dover's fear of him was apparently greater than his fear of horses. It would make for an interesting journey.

"Get your guns," Foster told the other two men. He wasn't worried about their ability to ride or shoot. He'd hired them for their talent at each of those things when he got to Denver, and they'd already proved their worth. They weren't loyal to him through long association, but they were loyal to his money. In many respects, it was a better arrangement.

Wyatt merely raised an eyebrow when he saw that two of Foster's party had strapped on gun belts. The quartet approached him after Foster had given direction to Seward about clearing the track. "The horses are on the other side," Wyatt told them. "We have to climb first."

"Lead on," Foster said, his mouth twisting wryly as he made a slight bow. "We're prepared to follow."

Wyatt thought about the rifles that would be aimed at Foster and his group if he just gave the signal. It helped him shrug off Foster's condescension. He started to climb, never looking back to see how the pack was faring.

He didn't take them past Will's post, nor past any of the others. It made for a winding route, but he avoided the possibility that his own men would be seen. By the time he reached the other side of the snow dam, the miners were back in position, working in a steady rhythm as they cleared away ice and debris.

Wyatt couldn't have asked for a better response. They'd read the situation perfectly, and when he asked if he could have some of their horses to take Mr. Foster Maddox and the others back to Reidsville, they didn't blink an eye.

It took them a little while to saddle up, especially with Mr. Dover being more skittish than any of the animals. Wyatt suggested that he stay behind, but he wouldn't hear of it, and Wyatt supposed that had a lot to do with the fact that Foster Maddox wouldn't have approved.

They rode out in silence for the first five miles. Wyatt led some of the time, but fell back when he needed to so he could make sure Dover didn't drop too far behind them. It was out of concern for the accountant as much as it was a practical decision. Wyatt was very aware that Will and the others were following at a cautious distance. If he allowed Dover to hang back, it was more likely they'd be discovered before they were in their proper positions.

"Sorry to hear that your grandfather passed," Wyatt said as he rode up to Foster. "There's a lot of admiration for him in this part of the country."

Foster glanced sideways, grunted softly.

"You ever been this way before?"

"Never."

"Not much for conversation, are you?"

"You seem to be loquacious enough for both of us."

"Loquacious. Now, that's a four-dollar word. I make a study of words from time to time. Read up on their meaning. You're sayin' I talk too much, is that right?"

"In a nutshell."

"Huh."

Foster Maddox reined in his horse and let Wyatt go ahead of him. He missed Wyatt's grin entirely.

Wyatt stayed out in front as they came upon the Hancock Creek tunnel and led them through. The rails gleamed like silver ribbons at the far end where light appeared at the opening, but the middle third of the tunnel was just about pitch-black. Rather than light his lantern, Wyatt talked to his companions as they rode through the darkness and bored himself with the inanity of his chatter.

It did the trick, though, and when they emerged from the tunnel, Will and the rest of the men he'd handpicked were only twenty yards behind them. He pulled Raider up and swung the gelding around so he could face Foster, Dover, and the two guard dogs. "Let's break here, gentlemen. Stretch your legs." He smoothly reached for his Colt and held it up, pulling back the hammer in the same motion. "This is as good a place as any for you to get rid of your guns. Don't pretend to do anything else. My men will shoot you in the back. You, too, Mr. Maddox. Ease that derringer out from under your coat sleeve."

Wyatt wasn't surprised when they hesitated, but none of them looked back. They were all watching him warily and wondering if they could trust what he'd just said. "Ezra. How about firing off a shot and show these men that you're really back there?"

Ezra Reilly raised his Henry rifle and fired it into the trees. Snow fell in clumps from the highest branches, and the sound echoed in the narrow pass.

"The guns," Wyatt said. "Now."

The Colts were thrown wide of the horses first; then Foster

Maddox removed the derringer from the leather strap affixed to his arm and let it fall to the ground.

"Mr. Dover?" Wyatt regarded the accountant gravely. "Do you have a weapon?" Randolph Dover was quick to shake his head, and Wyatt believed him. "I want you to dismount and pick up the guns. Take care not to shoot yourself."

Mr. Dover stumbled a little when his feet touched the ground, but he straightened and gamely went to gather the weapons.

"So you're not the law after all," Foster said, "If your intention is to rob us, then you're going to have to make do with very little."

"That's not my intention," said Wyatt. "And I am the law. So are the men with me." He watched Mr. Dover gingerly pick up the guns, then gestured to him to hand the weapons over to Will. "Back on your horse now, Mr. Dover. Sam, give him a leg up if he needs help."

Foster Maddox stirred impatiently in his saddle, causing his horse to move restlessly.

Wyatt gave him a sharp look. "Control your animal, Mr. Maddox, or I'll tether you to mine." He went back to ignoring the C & C owner and made certain Mr. Dover was settled. "Let's go." He turned Raider and let him lead the way.

That no-account Beatty boy slapped his snow-dusted hat against his thigh as he stepped into Rose's salon. On any other evening, that would have been greeted with a lecture, but Rose was feeling warm toward him because he'd come back to her in one piece. She allowed that she might have overestimated the danger when he set out with the others to meet Foster Maddox's train, but she simply didn't care if her glad cry at his appearance was out of all proportion to the situation.

It helped that no one else was in the salon to see her.

Will caught Rose as she approached and pulled her into his

arms. He kissed her hard, relished the warmth of her embrace, and for a few moments allowed himself to forget that it was business that brought him.

"Is Rachel here?" he asked, finally drawing back.

Rose's immediate disappointment gave way to concern. "She's here. Probably sleeping. Is everything all right? Wyatt?"

"He's fine. No one's been hurt. He needs her over at the office. We've got Foster Maddox in a cell."

She stared at him, eyes wide. "You *arrested* him?"

"He took a swing at Wyatt. Pretty good one, too. If it had connected, Wyatt would have gone down hard. We mostly put him in the cell to keep him out of trouble—and because Wyatt was feelin' a mite ornery." His eyes darted in the direction of the hall stairs. "Will you get Rachel for me?"

Rose nodded, kissed him again. "Help yourself to the applesauce cake."

Rachel took a steadying breath as Will opened the office door for her. Her heart still hammered in her chest, but she mastered the short, panicked breaths that had made her light-headed earlier.

Wyatt stood up from behind the desk immediately and held out a hand to her. "It's all right," he said gently, beckoning her forward. "Thanks for escorting her, Will."

"Do you want me to hang around?"

"You'll be upstairs?"

Will nodded.

"That's good enough. Appreciate your help."

Rachel waited until Will backed out the door; then she took Wyatt's face in her hands and examined it for bruises. "Rose said Foster hit you."

"*Tried* to hit me. Sam Walker saw it coming and blocked it with his arm." He caught her wrists and drew her hands away.

"You're cold. You could have taken the time to put on a pair of gloves."

She ignored the admonishment and just let him rub her hands. "Where's Sam now? And everyone else for that matter? I heard you had seven men with you."

"I let them all go except Ezra. He volunteered to sit in the back with our guests."

"Foster's really behind that door?"

"Behind the *bars* behind that door," he corrected. "He's sharing a cell with his accountant. The two men he brought along to provide protection are in the adjoining one." He studied her worried face. "What is it?"

She hesitated. "I wonder if it was wise to arrest all of them."

"Even Mr. Dover attempted to throw a punch," he said. "It was more for show, to prove that he stood with his employer, so I obliged him by putting him with Mr. Maddox. The other two had more serious intent. Ezra got the worst of it before we settled them down, that's why he volunteered to stay with the prisoners and why I didn't send him to Rose's to get you. Virginia wouldn't let him out of the house if she saw his face."

"Does he need attention?"

"Doc's been here and gone. He'll be fine. He packs a little snow over his eye now and again to keep the swelling down."

"Why did they start fighting?" Rachel's gaze became narrow, suspicious. She removed her hands from his. "What did you do, Wyatt?"

Her question was more in the way of a scold, and Wyatt was inclined to grin. He tempered that inclination, suspecting that she would fail to see the humor right off. If he even hinted that she was being wifely, she'd think he was patronizing her, whereas he believed it was simply an acknowledgment of how well she knew him.

He offered up a less provocative response: he shrugged.

"Wyatt?"

"I told him you and I are married." He held up his hands. "I swear. That's all I did."

"Then it must have been the way you said it."

"No, I'm pretty sure I was just matter-of-fact."

Still skeptical, Rachel sighed. "Very well. May I see him?"

"That's why I wanted you here. I don't think it's a good idea, Rachel, but it's also your decision."

"I understand."

"Do you? He was unflattering in his description of you."

"I'm sure he was. Can you listen to him say those same things to my face?"

"Without flattening him?"

"Without showing any reaction. That's what he wants to provoke. He'll want to gauge your intentions, observe your weaknesses. He's a master at it."

"He threw the punch, Rachel. I didn't."

"Yes, and he'll be looking to settle the account. To his way of thinking, he came up short in that column."

"Not surprising, then, that he chose to travel with his accountant instead of his lawyer."

Rachel smiled at his dry tone, but her message didn't change. "I'll see him alone if you don't think you can bear it."

"You aren't seeing him alone."

She understood that he hadn't agreed to anything, but she nodded as if he had. "Where can we talk?"

Wyatt would have preferred that Foster remain behind bars, but there was no privacy in the jail area. He made his offer reluctantly. "I'll bring him out."

Rachel unwound the scarf she'd loosely thrown over her head and shoulders, but she didn't take off her coat. If she had to leave, she would rather it were done quickly, without scrambling for her outerwear, or worse, going without it. Every conversation she'd ever had with Foster Maddox tested her mettle. Her caution to Wyatt that he should not reveal any reaction was also a caution to herself, and she hoped she could heed it.

She was standing on the far side of Wyatt's rolltop desk, taking advantage of the barrier it presented, when the door opened. Her features remained perfectly still as Foster stepped into the office.

He had changed very little. There were perhaps a few more lines at the corners of his eyes, and the crease across his brow appeared now to be permanent, but on the whole he looked as fit as she remembered. Where her memory had failed her was in the true accounting of his size. She'd forgotten how fine-boned he was, how slender his shoulders were, how sharply pointed his knuckles could be when he clenched his fists. She had misrepresented the angular nature of his features in her mind, making him broader and bulkier when in fact, he was lean and taut and wound like a spring.

He stood slightly taller than Wyatt, but the correctness of his posture and the narrowness of his frame seemed to lend him additional height if no more authority. He breathed in his own air of superiority, and as often as Rachel had wished he might choke on it, he never did.

He crossed to her quickly, and Rachel was hard-pressed to hold her ground. It was only because she anticipated that he would try to crowd her that she was successful.

"Step back," Wyatt said. "Stand over here." He tapped the side of the desk.

The small smile that Foster offered Rachel was both apologetic and regretful. "It's an unsatisfactory manner in which to greet a dear friend."

Rachel offered no comment, and she was careful not to look to Wyatt. She hoped the relief she felt when Foster retreated was not palpable.

"You are looking very well, Rachel."

"As you are."

His eyes made a second examination of her, this one more thorough, slightly insolent. "Very well, indeed."

Rachel could do nothing about the blossom of heat in her cheeks. Far from being flattered by his study, she felt as if fire ants were crawling helter-skelter across her skin.

"Well," Foster said, looking around the spare office. "A stove. May I? Your husband's jail is cold. I could stand to warm my hands."

Wyatt was not sympathetic. "Rub them together. Or better yet, blow on them."

Foster chuckled, and he continued to address Rachel. "I suppose he is telling me I'm full of hot air. Not a terribly subtle allusion. He is not at all the sort of gentleman I thought you might choose, Rachel. Is it really true that you're married?"

"It's true."

He glanced pointedly at her hands. "No ring, though. Why is that?"

His observation startled Rachel. She glanced at Wyatt for the first time and saw he was similarly struck.

Their brief exchange was not lost on Foster Maddox. "As I suspected. You're not married at all. Why the ruse, Rachel? What purpose did it serve?"

"It's not a ruse. Wyatt is my husband."

"I don't believe you. I saw how you looked at him. You were surprised. So was he."

"We were surprised because neither one of us has ever given thought to a ring." She wondered how to explain that without revealing the unusual circumstances of their marriage. "It was a civil ceremony, Foster."

"Now I'm certain you're lying. Do you imagine I never paid attention to the things you said? I know there was very little that you wanted as much as to be married in church."

"My life is different here."

"Reidsville has churches, doesn't it?"

"This is not a conversation I care to have with you. I can offer the proof of our wedding certificate, but that seems excessive. Believe what you like. I can't see that it matters one way or the other."

"Oh, it matters," he said softly. "I always said I would find you."

"So you did, and so you have."

"If it's true that you're married, Rachel, it seems especially providential that you married this particular man."

"I don't understand."

"He's what passes for the law in this town, isn't that right?"

"He's the sheriff, yes."

"The sheriff." Foster laid his hand lightly on the top of the desk. His fingers were long and tapered, the nail tips buffed and squared off. "Have you told him about yourself, Rachel? *All* about yourself?"

Rachel's gaze remained focused on Foster, but she was acutely more aware of Wyatt in her peripheral vision. Although Foster's question was directed at her, she understood his intent was to raise doubt in Wyatt's mind. When Wyatt didn't turn by so much as a hair in her direction, she felt the trust he'd extended to her as a tangible thing.

Rachel sidestepped Foster's question by asking, "If there is something you'd like to tell my husband, then you should do so."

Foster rubbed his jaw. "He took violent exception the last time."

"Actually," Wyatt said, "it was Ezra."

Rachel's right eyebrow lifted a fraction as she addressed Foster. "Then you must have said I was a whore. That would raise Ezra's hackles."

"To be perfectly correct, I said you *are* a whore. I was particular about the tense."

She nodded. "Is that something you think I should have told Wyatt?"

"Don't you?"

"It's really only ever been your opinion, Foster, and it seemed to concern you more that I wasn't your whore."

Foster Maddox's lips twisted in a slight smile. "It won't surprise you that he spoke of you at the end. His last words were for my grandmother, but he was crossing over by then. His last lucid thoughts were for you."

Rachel refused to snap at the bait he dangled. "You were with him, then."

"Yes, of course. So was my mother."

She closed her eyes briefly against the sting of tears.

"We didn't abandon him, Rachel."

It was too easy for Rachel to hear the accusation that went unspoken. She had abandoned Clinton Maddox, allowed him to die with family at his side, but no one who had ever loved him as she had. "I miss him terribly," she said quietly. "He was a good friend to me. An extraordinary mentor."

The line of Foster's mouth became disapproving. "I am endlessly fascinated that you are able to describe your relationship with him as anything but what it was."

She sighed deeply. "And here we are, returned to this single argument. I can't imagine that there is one thing to be gained by going over it again. We're done here, Foster."

When Rachel started to turn away, Foster reached for her. He had extended his arm only half the distance when it was abruptly caught and pulled hard behind his back. He grimaced, clenching his jaw.

Rachel's eyes flew to Wyatt's. "It's all right," she said, backing up another step. "Please, let him go."

Wyatt did, and Foster carefully brought his arm around. He shook it out and made a particular point of tugging on the sleeve of his jacket, then brushing himself off. "Does he always do as you tell him, Rachel?"

She ignored the barb and addressed Wyatt. "Shall I wait for you outside or at home?"

"At home. I won't be much longer, but there's no point in you waiting in the cold."

"One moment," said Foster. This time he did not put out a hand to stop her. "I have something to show you." He glanced over his shoulder. "Both of you, actually."

Wyatt indicated that Rachel should stay where she was. "Where is it?" he asked.

"Inside my jacket. May I?"

Nodding, Wyatt moved to the side so he had a better view of Foster's hands.

Foster showed his amusement. "It's not a weapon."

"I know it's not," said Wyatt. "All the same, I'll watch."

"Of course."

Rachel frowned slightly, suspicious of the turn in Foster's demeanor. There was a certain civility to his tone that made her brace for the blow.

"Right here," Foster said, producing a folded document from his pocket. He held it up with his fingertips. "Sheriff?"

"Why don't you just tell us what it is?"

"Naturally, if that's what you want, but I don't flatter myself that you'll believe me." He placed the paper on top of the desk and tapped it lightly with his index finger. "It's a warrant. It authorizes me to take Rachel back to California, specifically to Sacramento."

Rachel's stomach clenched. She stared stonily at Foster. "Why would any judge authorize that?"

"I imagine because my lawyers presented a compelling case."

"They lied for you, you mean."

"I don't mean that at all."

Wyatt stepped in and asked calmly, "What are the charges?"

"Theft and attempted murder."

Rachel blanched, but Wyatt went on without blinking. "Tell me about them."

"If Rachel has revealed anything of her true nature to you, they should be painfully obvious. She took advantage of my grandfather's bedridden state and stole a great many items from his home when she left. Most of the things were gradually secreted away in preparation of her departure. Furniture. Jewelry. China. Silver. I left behind a full accounting of the items on the train. I expect to find most of them here in Reidsville."

Wyatt's expression remained shuttered. "And the attempted murder?"

Foster shrugged lightly. "I confronted her about the thefts, and she tried to kill me." He lifted his hand slowly and rubbed the back of his head near the sandy-colored crown. "Twenty-two stitches."

"You waited a very long time to bring your charges forward."

"Two reasons. I did not want to distress my grandfather, and I didn't know where Rachel was. His death finally eliminated the first impediment and eventually provided me with the answer to the second."

"I see." Wyatt did not argue either of Foster's points. He turned his attention to Rachel instead. "Go on home. I'll be along directly."

Rachel was sitting on the edge of the bed, brushing out her hair, when she heard Wyatt come in. She called to him to let him know where she was but didn't get up to greet him. She continued to apply the brush, counting out the strokes, while she listened to him preparing the stoves for the night. For the first time, she found herself wishing these last chores took longer to complete than they did. No amount of brushing could diminish this final vestige of dread.

She looked up in anticipation of his entrance as the last lamp was extinguished in the parlor. Her smile was in place when he appeared on the threshold.

Wyatt looked her over and shook his head, unconvinced by what he saw. "Foster should have charged you with fraud."

Rachel's smile faded, but there was some relief in knowing that she hadn't fooled him. "I didn't know what to expect from you."

"You should have," he said, unbuttoning his vest. "I was thinking earlier that you knew me at least that well." He approached the bed, took the brush from her nerveless fingers, and set it on the nightstand. Bending, he kissed her cheek. "It's going to be fine, Rachel."

"How can you know that? He has a warrant."

He straightened, shrugged out of his vest, and laid it over the top of a ladder-back chair. "He has a document that he's calling a warrant. It's signed, but there's no raised seal to attest that it's from the court. To execute it in this state, it requires at least that much authenticity, and as I am the person charged with serving it, I have to be certain of its origins."

"But you track men all through these mountains with no more than a telegraphed notice from the detectives' association."

"That's entirely different. I trust every member. I don't trust Foster Maddox." He sat down to pull off his boots. "Are you trying to talk me into sending you back to Sacramento?"

"No!"

The right side of his mouth lifted. "He could have written that document himself, Rachel. I don't believe he did, but I don't think it has the authority of the court, either. I imagine he had an attorney draw it up for him. It's just a ruse to justify his appearance here."

Rachel remained silent, thoughtful.

"He would be happy, I think, to have you accompany him back to California, but happier yet if he can wrest control of the spur from you on the return."

"I didn't understand what he meant when he said it seemed providential that you were the man that I married. He thought he would have the cooperation of the town's sheriff when he came here." Her smile was wry. "It explains why he tried to hit you when you told him we were married."

Wyatt pushed his boots aside and began removing his socks. "Imagine how angry he'll be when he learns that his own grandfather arranged the match."

"Does he have to know?"

"I don't see how it can be helped. He's going to ask to see the papers." Wyatt stood, unfastened his shirt. "What about that concerns you?"

Rachel hadn't realized her distress was so transparent. She paused in turning back the covers. "He'll think our marriage isn't real."

That caught Wyatt's attention. "Are you saying it is?"

She was quiet.

"Rachel?"

"Isn't it?" she asked softly.

From memory, he quoted her, "A marriage is generally defined by the usual practices of sharing a common dwelling, coital relations, and raising children together. That's what you told me. Do you remember?"

She did, and the recollection pained her. "I was as ignorant as I was arrogant."

Wyatt moved to sit beside her. "You were terrified." He caught her chin and tilted her face toward him. "And arrogant."

That made her smile, though the edges of it wobbled a bit. There was an aching press of tears behind her eyes. "I love you, you know."

He released her chin and let his hand rest lightly on her knee. "How about that."

She laughed a little at what she thought was his quiet conceit. "I suppose you thought it was inevitable."

"Inevitable?" Wyatt shook his head. "Maybe you remember exchanging vows differently than I do."

"No, I've come to recall every word I barely spoke." She laid her hand over his. "I wish now that I had been able to say them with my heart."

"It was honest," he said. "Was Foster telling the truth? About you wanting a church wedding?"

She shrugged, and then because he waited her out, she nodded. "He must have overheard me talking to Mr. Maddox. Foster wasn't part of the conversation. It was just idle talk while I was working on someone's bridal gown."

Because it was clear that she did not want to make too much of it, Wyatt let it go. "Under the covers. You're starting to shiver."

Rachel's hands and feet were still cool to the touch when Wyatt finally joined her. She tucked them under his body to warm them and sighed agreeably. "This was unexpected," she said, cozying up to him. "No one told me about this part of marriage. It's really quite nice."

"It's lumpy."

Unperturbed, she left her hands and feet where they were until she judged them sufficiently warmed. "Better?" she asked.

"I never said it wasn't good." Wyatt turned onto his back and took Rachel into the crook of his shoulder. "I've been thinking about this matter of a ring." He felt Rachel begin to lift her head to look at him, but he threaded his fingers in her hair and drew her back gently. "Hear me out."

She nodded, though not without a sense of unease.

"I have one of my grandmother's rings," he said. "That's my grandmother Cooper. She died shortly before my father and had already made provision for him to have her ruby. I'm not entirely sure why. She was as unhappy about the decisions he made as anyone in my mother's family, but lately I've been thinking that perhaps the ring represented a change of heart. And if that's the case, then there's no one who deserves to wear it more than you."

She hesitated. "I'm not sure I understand."

"Don't you?" he asked. "You changed my heart, Rachel."

She felt her throat constrict, making any reply impossible.

"Rachel?" Her silence rarely made him uncomfortable, but this time he had no clear view of her features and no way to gauge her reaction. He wondered if he should have made a more straightforward declaration. "Did you hear me say I love you?"

She turned her cheek into his shoulder. "I heard you."

He gave her a corner of the sheet to dab at her eyes. "Are you going to cry when I give you the ring?"

"Probably." She sniffled. "Why?"

"Just wanted to make sure I have a handkerchief."

Wyatt produced the ring at breakfast, having awakened Jake Reston at dawn to open the safe at the bank. Rachel stared at the ring for several long moments before she extended her hand and allowed him to slip it on her finger. The ruby appeared flawless to her eye, resting in an exquisite platinum filigree and raised a mere fraction so that it seemed to float above the setting.

Turning her hand this way and that, Rachel admired the deep claret color through eyes that watered just enough to lend the stone a dozen more facets than it had. She only accepted Wyatt's handkerchief when he dangled it in front of her.

Throughout the meal, her eyes strayed to her hand so often that Wyatt had to tap his fork on his plate to focus her wandering attention. "Would you like more coffee?" he asked when she finally lifted her eyes to him.

Rachel was surprised to see that he was holding out the coffeepot so that it hovered over her cup. "Please." By way of explanation for her distraction, she added, "I don't recognize my own hand."

Wyatt leaned back to set the pot on the stove. "My grandmother didn't wear it all the time, probably for the same reason."

"I'd rather get used to it," she said, "though I don't imagine it's practical when I'm washing dishes or working with lace."

He grinned. "Probably not." Reaching in his pocket, he produced a black velvet bag no bigger than his palm and handed it to her. "This is for those times, so you don't lose it."

"Perish the thought." She placed the bag beside her plate and smoothed the velvet with her fingertips. "Where were you keeping this?"

"The bank." He told her about rousing Jake Reston from his slumbers. "I sent Sylvie's jewelry back to her family, and I buried her with her wedding ring, but this was never hers. I couldn't think of a better place to keep it than the safe at the bank." His tone became wry. "Men like Morrisey and Spinnaker aside."

Chilled at the reminder of those men, Rachel wrapped her hands around her coffee cup. "I don't imagine Mr. Reston opens the bank early for just anyone," she said, changing the subject. "There are certain advantages to being sheriff, I suppose."

"Perhaps, but nothing is more persuasive than owning the bank." When Rachel's stare went from blank to accusing, Wyatt held up a hand as though he could deflect it. "Not me. I don't own it. That would be my family." He saw this announcement had no palliative effect. "I know I told you they're all bankers on my mother's side. They wanted me to become one of them, remember?"

"You might have said something like that," Rachel said

slowly, drawing on a maddeningly elusive memory. "Perhaps when you told me about Sylvianna's expectations that you would remain in Boston, but you never hinted that the Reidsville Bank had anything to do with you."

"That's because I have very little to do with it. My father established the bank right after the first gold strike. It was more than merely practical. He saw it as a way to get my mother to join him. He even named the town after her."

"Reid," Rachel said softly, mulling it over. She blinked as it came to her. "You're a Reid."

He nodded, frowning slightly. "You've heard of them?"

"From Mr. Maddox. They were investors in his eastern rails before the war."

"That's right. It's one of the reasons my father turned to Clinton Maddox when he needed a railroad to join Colorado to the rest of the country."

"And a line that would join Reidsville to the rest of Colorado." She shook her head slowly, trying to take it in. "I had no idea how long you and Mr. Maddox had been engaged in these enterprises."

"Not me," said Wyatt. "But yes, his association with the Reids goes back to when he was first putting down rails in the East."

"Then what is it that your father did that so disappointed everyone? He struck gold and silver, founded a town, created a bank, established what amounts to a sustainable trust for the citizens, and helped bring in rails to make it all viable. How is any of that disappointing?"

Wyatt's shoulders settled heavily. He held his mug in both hands and stared at it. "Matthew Cooper's sin was that he never returned."

It was then that Rachel truly understood the depth of Wyatt's own struggle. "Your mother lived here for a time, didn't she?"

"Now and again. You have to remember that the town was considerably less developed. It had a bank and not much else. She had five children, no help, and a good memory for the amenities she'd left behind. She came west expecting that my father would manage the bank and assume a position in the town that was more fitting of his accomplishments. Instead, he continued to mine and explore the mountains, and was as much a stranger to her as he'd been when she was in Boston. He even hired someone else to keep the bank's affairs in order.

"I don't know how they arrived at the decision that she should leave. No one ever talked about it. My father came with us as far as St. Louis, and I think he hoped she'd change her mind every step of the way. She never did, though, and he stayed until we boarded the train. Nicholas begged to remain behind, but my father refused. For himself, I believe he would have been pleased to have Nick, but there are few things so clear in my mind as my mother's distress when she thought Nick would leave her."

Wyatt took a sip of his coffee and then set the mug down. "My mother did see my father one more time. It was during the war, not long after Nick's death at Chickamauga. My father got leave, and they met in New York."

"I imagine it was a bittersweet reunion."

He nodded faintly. "My brother Morgan was born nine months later."

"Really?"

Wyatt smiled. "Really. He's just eighteen now."

"Did your father ever see him?"

"Photographs only. They wrote regularly."

"And you? Do you write?"

"I do. Not as frequently as Morgan would like, but that's because I have to be cautious of every word. He's been hinting at coming west, and I can't encourage him."

Rachel thought about what he'd said earlier about his

mother's distress. "What if he did come? Would your mother hold you responsible?"

"For a while." He considered that, and added, "A long while. Morgan's been at the center of her life for a lot of years. When he goes to Harvard, she'll have reins that stretch from Beacon Hill to Cambridge."

"Was it like that for you?"

"When I went to school, no. But earlier, when Nick left with the regiment from Boston, and I ran away to join him, it felt as if I was straining at a bit."

"You were twelve, Wyatt, and you were running off to a war. Your mother should have had you hobbled."

"I'm sure she wished she had."

Rachel stood to clear the table. "Would you do any part of it differently?"

"No, not if I were twelve again. I don't think I would be able to help myself, even if I knew what lay ahead. I was . . . *am* . . . curious. There's at least that much of my father in me. I regret the pain I caused my mother, but then . . . *then* I had no real understanding of it."

"Yet you had already seen how she felt about losing Nick."

"And I never thought once that she might feel the same about me."

Rachel carefully placed the dishes in the washtub. "Perhaps you didn't want to."

"Could be." He held on to his coffee cup to keep her from taking it off the table in her second sweep. "It probably made it easier for me to leave."

Rachel wiped the table. "Just the same, when our boy is twelve, I'm going to hobble him."

"Good idea." He watched Rachel straighten at the table and turn to the sink. She looked rather grim, scraping plates with more ferocity than was called for. "Are we going to have a twelve-year-old boy, Rachel?"

His question broke her concentration. Her hands were still in the tub, and she turned her head to regard him sideways. "I haven't decided. If I have to worry about giving him up at twelve to wanderlust, I just don't know."

Wyatt quickly raised his cup to hide his smile. "Aren't you putting the cart before the horse?"

"Maybe we should only have girls."

"So I can worry about boys like Johnny Winslow trailing after them?"

"That wouldn't happen until they're fifteen or sixteen."

"If they look like you, it'll happen a lot sooner."

One of Rachel's eyebrows lifted. "Flattery?"

"Ma Beatty would say it's honest speak."

She didn't miss the gleam in his eye. It wasn't there solely because he was amused. "Sly, lawyer speak is more like it. I think you want to go back to bed."

"Could be I want to get to that third part of our marriage."

At first she didn't follow, and when it came to her, she couldn't help but smile. Share a dwelling. Engage in coital relations. Raise children together. Rachel removed her hands from the tub and dried them on a towel. She crooked a finger at him as she deliberately skirted the table. "Why don't we have the party of the second part first?"

Chapter Fourteen

"I'm going to let you out, Mr. Maddox." Wyatt turned the key and opened the cell door a few inches. Will Beatty stepped aside to make room. "You, too, Mr. Dover. I didn't like leaving you here last night, but there wasn't a room available at the Commodore."

"And today there are two," Foster said, tugging on his jacket and running his fingers over the buttons. "How convenient."

"For you. Otherwise you'd have to take a room at the boardinghouse, and I don't think you'd like the accommodations as well as what you'll find at the hotel." Wyatt ushered them out.

Foster glanced back at the men in the adjoining cell, the pair he'd hired in Denver. "What about them?"

"I'll get to them. There's something I want to show you and Mr. Dover first." He indicated they could wait by the stove while he leafed through papers on his desk. "Here we are. You recognize either of these gentlemen?" He passed the flyers on to Will, who passed them to Foster Maddox. "Because I have to tell you, they bear a startling resemblance to the two in the back."

Foster looked over the rough drawings while Mr. Dover strained to see over his shoulder. "I'm afraid I don't see it." He handed the posters to his accountant and stepped sideways to put some distance between them. "It says their names are Franklin and Ross. I hired a Mr. Ford and a Mr.—" He paused, trying to recollect the name. "What was it, Randolph?"

"Richards."

"Yes. Richards."

"You hired cattle thieves, Mr. Maddox. Scratch them just a little and you'll likely find they're killers underneath."

"I don't think so. They were walking free in Denver."

At this confirmation that the men were hired in Denver, Wyatt and Will exchanged glances. "They were hiding in plain sight," Wyatt said. "Blake Street? Larimer? Along with Holladay, they make up the tenderloin district." When Foster didn't say anything, Wyatt turned his attention to the accountant. "Do you know, Mr. Dover? Was it somewhere in the tenderloin?"

"A gambling house. Chase's Cricket Club. I don't recall the street." He ran his fingers nervously along the edges of the papers, turning them in his hands.

Will took the posters from Mr. Dover and returned them to the desk. "We'll keep Mr. Ford and Mr. Richards awhile longer. Just to be sure."

"But you're free to go," Wyatt said. "Sir Nigel has two rooms ready for you. You'll have a suite, Mr. Maddox. A change of clothes has been made available, and Sir Nigel will see that what you're wearing is laundered. You can settle up with him when the train catches up to you. If we don't get another storm—and no one's expecting one—that'll be another day or so. If you eat at the hotel, you can put your meals on your room. If you want to eat anywhere else, you'll have to have money. No one extends credit to strangers."

"I have money," Foster said coldly.

"Good. Then you might want to visit the Miner Key. There's a show tonight. Who's singing, Will?"

"That'd be Adele. She has a real nice voice."

Watching Foster's complexion turn ruddy provided Wyatt

with a certain amount of pleasure, but he recognized that he'd pushed him about as far as he could. "Do you want an escort to the hotel?" he asked.

"I'm sure we can find it."

"I'll stop by this evening, make sure you're settled in."

Mr. Dover took a step forward, only to be stopped by the arm Foster extended like a gate. Foster thrust his chin in Wyatt's direction. "You're not going to do anything about Rachel Bailey, are you?"

"What would you like me to do?"

"Perhaps she should spend a few nights in jail waiting for the train. That seems to be your plan for my two men, and you're not certain they're the ones on your posters, while I harbor no such doubts about Rachel. I *know* what she did."

Wyatt scratched his head and made a point of only marginally containing his amusement. "She sure got you riled up, Mr. Maddox. I can't think of maybe two, three men that would make a journey like you set for yourself on account of a woman taking some furniture and clobbering him so he needed a few stitches. Most fellas would be saying good riddance. At least that's been my experience. What about you, Will?"

That no-account Beatty boy offered a careless shrug. "Same for me."

"Will's spent more time in Denver than I have, so I'd count his experience as superior to mine."

Setting his jaw, Foster Maddox crossed the floor to where his coat and hat hung by the door. He took both down, laid them over his arm, and left without putting either on. Mr. Dover hurried to follow but couldn't get through the door before it swung shut on him. He bumped into it awkwardly and had to open it again, fumbling with the knob several times before he could do so.

Wyatt and Will held their breath until the accountant was

out of earshot; then Will broke first, sucking in his laughter so that he choked on a lungful of air.

"Easy," Wyatt said, clapping him on the back. "Show some compassion for poor Mr. Dover. Unless I miss my guess, he'll be spending the evening listening to Foster Maddox rail against just about everyone on this side of the Continental Divide."

"Good guess." Will caught his breath and sidestepped Wyatt's cheerful blows. "You sure did get under his skin. Foster Maddox's, I mean. I don't think Dover has any. Maddox stripped it clean off a long time ago."

Wyatt was inclined to agree. He sat behind his desk and propped his feet up. "Maddox hasn't mentioned the spur. Not a word about the mine, either."

"We have two of his men in the back, Wyatt, and no intention of putting Rachel in jail. He's probably not feeling so confident right now. I imagine he wants to wait for the rest of his men."

That made sense to Wyatt. "I didn't see Ben Cromwell among the men at the train. Did you?"

Will shook his head. "It surprised me. Maybe he couldn't get to Denver to meet them."

"What do you think about Ford and Richards?"

"You mean Franklin and Ross?"

"The very same." Wyatt picked up the wanted posters and looked them over again. "Do you suppose there are more like these two ready to roll in with Foster's train?"

"Jesus," Will said softly. "I don't want to think about it."

Neither did Wyatt, except that it was his job. "We should tell some of the others. Rudy at the Miner Key. Sir Nigel, but only if we're certain he won't panic. Artie. Sam at the land office."

"Rose," Will said.

"Yes. Rose. Certainly Rose."

Will mentioned a few other names that Wyatt agreed to.

They didn't want to alarm the town, but they also didn't want the citizens to be unprepared. They were making a list so Will could make the rounds when Artie came in. He crossed his arms and clapped his shoulders, warming himself until he got to the stove. The fire was too meager for his tastes. He tossed in a few sticks of wood to get it blazing again.

"Make yourself at home," Wyatt said.

Artie ignored him and gave the stove his backside. "I came to let you know that I haven't received a message since yesterday morning. That'd be the same message that was interrupted. I have to believe a line's down."

"Weather?" asked Will.

"Couldn't say. You rather it was?"

"Than being brought down on purpose? Yep. That's always my druthers."

"Mine, too," Artie admitted. His spectacles fogged, and he took them off to clear them. "You didn't notice a downed wire on your way to the slide, did you?"

"No," said Wyatt. "We went a few miles east of the blockage. I didn't see anything like that."

Artie grunted softly. "Must be closer to the city, then. I suppose someone will get around to looking for it when no one hears from us. Abe was thinking of sending out a crew to find it, but I told him I wanted to talk to you first."

"It's good you did," Wyatt said. "Leave it be. I don't want anyone leaving town except to relieve the men working the slide." He told Artie about the pair sharing a cell in the back. "If that's a sample of what Foster's brought with him, I don't like the idea of sending anyone past the slide. We're better off just waiting for the train to come to us."

"All right, then," Artie said, collecting himself. "Makes sense. You need any help?"

"Would you mind picking up breakfast for our thieves at

Longabach's?" asked Wyatt. "Don't know when we'd get around to it otherwise."

"Sure."

"Oh, and don't mention where the prisoners came from. Maybe you should just tell Estella that I offered lodging to a couple of drunks. She makes a spare breakfast if she thinks they've got a hangover."

Wyatt found his photographic equipment set up in Rachel's workroom when he arrived home for lunch. Rachel wasn't immediately visible in the same area, and his heart thundered hard against his chest until she stood up suddenly from behind the mannequin.

"Mmm," she said, trying to greet him around a mouthful of pins. She plucked them out from between her lips and stuck them in the pincushion on the table. "I didn't hear you come in. That's a first. Were you trying to be quiet?"

"Not in the least. You must have been deep in your work."

"I suppose I was. What time is it?"

When he told her, she shook her head. "It can't be. I don't have anything prepared."

"That's all right. I won't starve. You might, but I won't."

Rachel sighed. "It's a good thing you have so few expectations."

"Oh, I have a few." To prove it, he closed the distance between them and kissed her soundly. "It's so much better without the pins."

Rachel's mouth curled, and she pushed him away. "I was thinking that I'd like to make a photograph."

"I see that. Have you solved the problem of a darkroom?"

"I think so. What about the woodshed?"

"Too cold."

"Oh. Then, no."

"Let me think about it, and we'll work on it this evening. I'll bring home the chemicals we'll need. Chet has everything. I think I can get the proper paper at Morrison's. There won't be enough light to make a good photograph, but you can get the feel for it and try it on your own tomorrow."

"I'd like that. Maybe we can use the parlor. I could hang black fabric at the windows." She looked critically at the pile of folded remnants that occupied one corner of the room. "I'm sure I have enough there."

Wyatt pointed to the gown on the form. "Is this what you want to photograph?"

"Yes. I thought I might like to have a more exact record of the gowns I design than my own sketches. This is the last dress for Virginia's trousseau, or at least it's the last that I'm making. She'd have me be her personal dressmaker if I allowed her. I keep reminding her that she can only wear one at a time."

"I know Ezra will be pleased to hear you're done. As I understand it, this matter of the trousseau was the last obstacle."

Rachel's smile was sympathetic. "Poor Ezra. What about his sore head? Did you see him today?"

"Oh, he's fine." Wyatt fiddled a little with the tripod, setting the legs so they supported the camera better. "I didn't see him. Will told me he has a good shiner and a lump on his forehead. I'm fairly certain he punished everyone by not letting them sleep much last night. They all looked bleary-eyed this morning."

"They're out now, aren't they?"

"Maddox and Dover are. I let them go first thing." He told her about setting them up at the Commodore. "Sir Nigel is supposed to let me know if Maddox leaves the hotel."

"What about the other gentlemen?"

"I'm not so sure that's how I'd describe them. I'm keeping them locked up a little longer. Will and I think they're both wanted for rustling cattle. I'll know more once the telegraph line is repaired, and I can get a message through to Denver."

"The line's down?"

Wyatt nodded.

"I don't think that's happened since I've been here."

Not wanting to alarm her, Wyatt said, "There's nothing unusual about it. Ice can snap the wire." He plucked a piece of material from among the remnants and used it to clean the camera lens. "I was thinking that I'd send Molly up to help you this afternoon."

"Now, why would you do that?"

"Couldn't you use her?"

"Yes, but she'll be here the day after tomorrow, same as she always is." Rachel stooped a little to catch his eye as he worked on the camera. "Stop that," she said. "You're not fooling me." She took the cloth from his hand and tossed it on the table. "If you don't want me to be alone, then just say so."

"I don't want you to be alone," he said. "And I can't spend my day here."

"I understand." Her brow puckered as she weighed his concern against her own desire to be undisturbed. What tipped the scales in his favor was not wanting him to be distracted with worry. "All right. But ask Virginia to come by. I can finish pinning and hemming her gown, and she can take it with her."

"What about the photograph you wanted to make?"

"We'll do another."

"You're sure?"

"Don't press me, Wyatt. I'm liable to change my mind and bar the door to everyone." She pointed in the direction of the foyer. "Go. Get something to eat at Longabach's. I'll be fine."

"Did I know you were this bossy when I married you?"

Rachel gave him a playful push toward the front door. "You must have. You notice everything."

* * *

The rolling boil of water in the kettle finally caught Rachel's attention, and she put down her work to make a cup of tea. She mocked herself with a wry smile when she felt the lightness of the kettle and realized most of the water had boiled away. Here was further proof that she was oblivious of most everything while she worked. It wasn't that difficult to understand why Wyatt thought she required a keeper.

She sat at the kitchen table while she drank her tea and looked over the list of items she wanted to pick up at Morrison's. She idly tapped her pencil against the table as she thought about the contents of her pantry. After some consideration, she added tea to the list, then returned to her absent tapping.

The knock at the door blended seamlessly with the tattoo she beat against the tabletop. She never heard the door open nor felt the presence of anyone in the house until Foster Maddox spoke from somewhere behind her.

The pencil flew out of her hand and hot tea splashed her knuckles. The chair scraped the floor as she jumped to her feet and spun around. At her side, her fingers were already curled like talons.

"I knocked," Foster said. "I thought I heard you invite me in. I see I was mistaken." His mouth twisted in dry amusement. "Stand down, Rachel. You look feral. I mean you no harm."

Rachel's immediate struggle was for composure, and it was hard won. "You have to leave." Even to her own ears, her voice sounded unnaturally strained. "You should never have come."

"To Reidsville?" he asked. "Or do you refer to your home?"

"Both. You can have no real business in either."

"I do, though. I thought we should speak privately, and your husband seems set against it."

"He has good reason. So do I. I want you to go."

Foster removed his hat and hooked it on the ear of a ladder-back chair. Watching her closely, he began to unfasten the buttons of his coat. "I wouldn't mind a cup of tea. I saw a sideboard in the other room. Do you have any whiskey?"

Rachel remained mutinously silent.

He shrugged. "You don't mind if I look for myself, then." He laid his coat over the rung of the chair and went in search of something to add to his tea. He opened the sideboard and moved bottles around. "You haven't asked me anything about your mother or sister. Frankly, that surprises me." When she didn't respond, Foster ducked his head back into the kitchen. Rachel was already at the back door. She had a heavy woolen cape drawn across her shoulders and was pulling on her gloves. "Where are you going?"

"Out." She laced her fingers and pressed her hands together to give the gloves a good fit. "If you won't leave, I will."

"You're being ridiculous, Rachel. There's no reason that you should go."

Rachel didn't step into the kitchen, but she also didn't retreat to the door. "Wyatt's going to learn that you left the hotel," she said. "He asked to be told. It would be better for everyone if he didn't find you here."

"But no one knows I'm gone, apart from Dover, and he's unlikely to tell anyone. He's in my suite, you see. I took his room. A minor inconvenience to provide a simple confusion."

Rachel was skeptical that it had been so easy or as successful a ruse as he thought it was.

"You don't believe me," said Foster. "It makes no difference, but I will tell you that if your husband meant to keep us apart, then he should have posted himself at the hotel, not put the responsibility in the hands of that effete Brit."

"I'm expecting a visitor, Foster."

"Really? I would have thought you'd have mentioned that at the outset."

She sighed. He only ever believed what served him. "What do you want?"

"Tea." He returned to the sideboard to collect a bottle. "And conversation."

Rachel glanced at the door behind her, wondering how foolish it would be to hear him out. She had things she wanted to tell him as well, and there might never be a better opportunity. Wyatt's presence would invariably change the tenor of any discussion she and Foster had. She slowly removed her gloves.

Foster paused on the threshold, watching her a moment, then set the bottle on the table. "Is the water still hot?"

Rachel didn't answer his question directly. "I'll make your tea." She didn't want him moving about her kitchen, asserting his presence. Further, she wasn't going to permit him to sit at her table. "Wait for me in the parlor, Foster. You can pass the time taking inventory of all those items you claim I stole."

He surprised her with his acquiescence, although he did return almost immediately for the whiskey. Rachel supposed that tea was a secondary consideration, but she went about making it anyway.

She found him standing with his back to the parlor window, rocking slightly on the balls of his feet as he surveyed the contents of the room. She set the tray on a side table and poured him a cup, stopping short of inviting him to sit. Taking nothing for herself, she chose a side chair and perched on the edge

"Have you finished?" she asked.

"Indeed. I don't believe there's an item here that I don't recognize from my grandfather's house." He walked to the table, placed the bottle on the tray, and poured a cup of tea. He sat on the long upholstered bench. "I think he would have given you the moon if you'd asked for it."

"I never asked for anything."

"That was your cleverness, Rachel. You demonstrated

restraint. I always admired you for it." He sat back, sipped his tea, and regarded her from the remote vantage of his deep-set eyes. "I don't know if you heard me earlier. I mentioned that I was surprised you haven't asked me about your family."

She *hadn't* heard him. "I hoped you would have nothing to tell me."

He lifted both eyebrows. "That strikes me as strange. Why wouldn't I have news for you?"

"Because I hoped you would allow them to be. No one knew where I was, Foster. They must have told you that."

"They did. Many times. It just didn't seem possible that you would leave them with no word for so long a time."

Rachel tightened the leash she'd drawn around her emotions.

"Your mother is well," he said, just as if she'd inquired. "She remains employed as a housekeeper for the Carrols. There was some discussion that she would move to that residence, but with your sister breeding again, the greater need was in her own home."

In spite of her intentions, Rachel felt the press of tears at the back of her eyes. She blinked hard and set her lips together. She couldn't bear to ask him a single question.

"You really didn't know, did you? I was fairly sure there were no letters, but knowing how attached you were, it was difficult to imagine." He raised his teacup. "Sarah is teaching a Wednesday evening Bible class and regularly takes in mending. The children grow like Topsy, of course, so the money she brings in must be welcome. There was some support for them while my grandfather lived because his attorney saw to it, but that's gone now. I offered, but they refused."

"Refused to give me up," she said.

"Yes, well, I didn't realize then that they didn't know anything. Had I understood, I would have been prepared to be generous. Your brother-in-law remains employed at a good wage, so they are doing well, if not well-to-do."

"You hounded them. I'll never forgive you for that."

"I didn't imagine there was anything I could do to put myself in your good graces, Rachel. I wish you'd told me."

His cool sarcasm grated. She rubbed her arm absently. Every place he'd ever struck her seemed to blossom heat under her skin.

"Grandfather had another stroke," Foster said. "It happened a few days after you disappeared. Did you know?"

Rachel shook her head. She squeezed her hands into white-knuckled fists and waited for him to go on.

"There was no announcement. We decided it was in the best interest of the railroad to keep it quiet. People knew he was ill, but not the full extent of it. He rarely spoke and most of what he said was unintelligible. Except at the end. I told you that he asked for you at the end, didn't I?"

"Yes."

"I thought I did. The old goat spoke clearly enough on that occasion. I swear he did it to spite me."

"Did you kill him?"

"My own flesh and blood? Am I really such a monster in your mind?"

"Yes."

He set his cup down. "Why would I kill him, Rachel? For all intents and purposes, I was in charge of the Maddox holdings after his first stroke."

"As long as he was alive, there was oversight."

"The advisers, you mean?" He shook his head. "They were a nuisance, nothing more. Their own interests made them entirely malleable." Foster's eyes narrowed slightly. "Did you and my grandfather believe I intended to murder him?"

"You told me you would."

"I think you are unclear in your recollections, but even so, I never threatened my grandfather. Did you tell him I did?"

"He *heard* you, Foster. He heard *us*. Our arguments carried down those hallways. He knew every time you struck me, whether or not you left a bruise. Your grandfather was bedridden, but he wasn't deaf. You threatened all of us."

Foster's features were set sympathetically. "I am generally thought to be a man of my word, Rachel. It stands to reason that I would have carried out one or two. I never did, though, and certainly none against my own beloved grandfather."

"The old goat."

"One and the same," he said pleasantly. He reached inside his vest and withdrew a photograph. "I carry this with me, Rachel. Do you recall?" He turned his open palm so she could see what he held.

Unable to do otherwise, she drew in a sharp breath and stared back at her sepia-toned image, a reflection of herself that she might have glimpsed in a dark pool of water. She had no words.

"I see that you do remember. Grandfather never saw it. That would have been cruel, I think, to taunt him in such a way. I carry it for resolve."

Agitated, Rachel rose from her chair and went to the stove. She was cold to her marrow. "I think there was nothing about Mr. Maddox's last stroke that was real," she said. "The ruse kept him alive for fifteen more months, and he was watching all the while. He was infinitely more clever than you thought, Foster."

"Do you think so?"

Feeling him close behind her, Rachel flinched. The hair at the back of her neck stood up. She turned, needing to face him before he was toe-to-toe with her. "I want you to leave. I told you I'm expecting someone."

"So you've said."

. "If Wyatt finds out that you were here, you'll spend another night in jail."

"If?" asked Foster. "That sounds as though there's a possibility that you won't tell him. Would you do that for me, Rachel?"

"I don't want trouble."

"Your husband has my gun. He has my hired gunmen. I have an accountant with a head for figures and a dull pencil. If there's trouble, it won't be because I've done anything."

"Except provoke it."

"Oh, I see. It's your husband you want to protect. From himself, apparently, because he has nothing to fear from me." Foster returned the photograph to his pocket. "I don't care about the furniture, and I can forgive you for the gash in my scalp, but you'll have to turn over operation of the spur, Rachel. It's C & C property."

"It's not, though. It's mine. Your grandfather wanted me to have it."

"My grandfather would have signed anything you put in front of him. I saw him do it, remember? The letters you gave him for his signature. The invitations you declined on his behalf. He hardly glanced at what you handed him."

"Is that what you think happened?" She shook her head. "Until I came to Reidsville, I had no knowledge that the Calico Spur existed. How would I?"

"He told you everything. The fact that you came here after you left Sacramento speaks to that. You must see that the spur belongs with the rest of the Maddox holdings."

"It's only a spur," said Rachel. "Seventy-three miles of track. That's nothing—less than nothing—compared to the rails that you own. Why is it so important to you?"

Foster was silent a few moments, shifting his weight from side to side as he regarded Rachel closely. "It's important to me because it was important to him," he said at last. "My accountant? The one with the dull pencil? He thinks he understands my grandfather's interest, and I am sufficiently intrigued to want to discover if he's correct."

Rachel pressed her hands together to keep them still. Unease made her heart hammer and color rise in her face. She made a quarter turn, hoping Foster would conclude it was her proximity to the stove that warmed her cheeks. She did not foresee that this small movement would goad him to reach for her. His hand was on her forearm before she had any opportunity to step aside. The stove blocked a full retreat.

She resisted the urge to yank away. "Please, Foster, do not be difficult."

"My feelings for you haven't changed."

"I'm aware of only one feeling," she said flatly. "Enmity."

"How can you say that?" His fingers tightened so his square-cut nails dug deeply into her sleeve. "You have frustrated me certainly, and provoked me to act in ways that I have often regretted but that you know you deserved. Still, it doesn't follow that I despise you."

That he was blaming her again for the blows he'd struck left Rachel unable to speak.

"Are you still so haughty, Rachel? It no longer seems as if you might be. You look unexpectedly fragile." His hand wrapped more tightly around her wrist.

Rachel twisted. His fingernails dug deeper. "Let me go, Foster."

"Of course." In spite of his words, he didn't release her. "In a moment." He slipped his free hand around her waist and pulled her against him. "There's been no proper greeting, Rachel. I mean that to change."

She twisted hard again, ignoring the pain. When he swooped, she gave him her cheek and not her mouth. He set her off balance so that she had no leverage to push him away; then he slid the hand at her waist up her spine until it pressed hard between her shoulder blades. Rachel felt herself being pushed against the stove. Only moments passed before she was aware of the heat penetrating the fabric of her gown. Pain tore a cry from her, but rather than release her, Foster seized on it as an opportunity and caught her mouth with his. Tears came to her eyes. She stumbled a little as she attempted to stand on her own and found the toe of his shoe with her foot. She stomped hard, missing most of him at first, but she struck again, and quickly, and ground her heel sharply when she caught him. The angle of his hold changed, finally giving her the purchase that she needed.

Rage lent her strength. She used one hand to free the other, pulling through the weakest point of his grip on her arm between his thumb and fingers; then she thrust her shoulder into his chest and leapt sideways when he staggered back. She didn't wait to see what he would do. She ran to the front door and pulled it open.

Virginia Moody stood squarely in her path, one hand curled and raised to shoulder height in preparation of knocking.

"Did you hear me coming up the steps?" asked Virginia. "I thought I was quieter than—" Virginia's pleasantly rounded features took on a distinctly sharper edge as she looked at Rachel more closely. "Are you all right? You don't look well." She stood on tiptoe, trying to see beyond Rachel's shoulder. "I'd like it better if you'd say something. I'm liable to fetch the sheriff otherwise."

"I'm fine. A bit harried, I expect. I've been pressing myself to finish your gown."

Virginia's diminutive bow-shaped upper lip was pulled taut by her frown. She ducked suddenly, trying to see under the arm Rachel had spread across the doorway. "Is someone in there?"

Rachel shook her head and hoped it was true. She'd given Foster at least enough time to get to the back of the house. "Come in. Wyatt said he was going to ask you to come by. I hope it was no inconvenience for you."

"Not at all." Virginia dusted snow off the hem of her coat

before she gave it to Rachel. She held out her bonnet and gloves a moment later. "It's quiet at the house today, and I couldn't bear looking at Ezra any longer. Poor thing's got an eye like a pounded steak and a lump on his head as big as his left ball." Her hand flew to her mouth. "Forgot where I was."

Rachel laughed softly, hoping that only she heard the thread of unease running through it. "It's all right. Why don't you come into the dining room? It's where I work." Rachel tried to gently steer Virginia in that direction, but it was the younger woman's first visit and she was openly curious. It was inevitable that she'd see the tray in the parlor.

Virginia giggled as her eyes alighted on the bottle of whiskey beside the dainty teacup. "So you enjoy a nip now and again." She cast a conspirator's smile at Rachel. "I don't mind it myself, though Rose is stingy with the drinks. Waters everything down for us girls, insists on it, in fact."

Rachel actually felt a little giddy. Foster was indeed gone, and Virginia had misinterpreted the evidence that he, or anyone else, had been there. Relief and a need to calm her own nerves prompted her to make Virginia an offer. "Why don't I get you a glass?"

They were a little worse for wear when Wyatt and Ezra came upon them several hours later. Wyatt looked them over, took note of the mostly empty whiskey bottle between them, and pointed Ezra toward the parlor so they could set down the chemicals and glass plates they'd carried in. He cautioned Ezra, "This is probably something you and I should forget, or at least save until we do something equally foolish."

Ezra gingerly touched the lump on his head. "I suppose that gives me about a day or so. I should be able to keep it to myself for that long. You?"

"About that. Maybe less with Maddox in town."

Ezra looked over his shoulder at where the women were sitting at the corner of the dining table, their heads bent close together as they whispered like thieves. "Are you going to tell Mrs. Cooper about Maddox disappearing this afternoon?"

"I don't know."

"Probably isn't that important. He wasn't gone long enough to set out for the mine. Somebody out that way would have seen him."

Since Foster shouldn't have been able to leave the hotel at all without someone noticing, Wyatt wasn't interested in Ezra's thoughts on what he might have done. The truth was that no one knew when he left his room, and Wyatt blamed himself for that. He should have made certain that Sir Nigel knew which man was Maddox and which was Dover. If he hadn't sent Will over early to be sure they were settled in, they wouldn't have known about the deception.

Foster reappeared at the hotel before they had time to begin a search, and his explanation of a walk around town rang hollow. He further denied there had been intent to deceive and said that after he and Dover saw the rooms, he preferred to be on the lower floor. Randolph Dover registered for both of them but used Foster's name. The accountant had nothing to say that helped explain his employer's absence or established the time for it.

"I'm glad Virginia was here," was all Wyatt said.

The snow dam was cleared two days later, and the train arrived at the station at dusk. Abe Dishman heard the whistle when the engine was still rising out of Brady's Bend and made certain that Wyatt and Will knew it was on its way. They were at the depot to greet it, looking over every man that alighted, comparing them against the flyers littering the top of Wyatt's desk.

Foster Maddox was also there, Randolph Dover at his side. He directed some of his employees to the hotel, others to the boardinghouse, and the last of them to rooms for let at the saloon. He lingered in front of the station house after he dismissed his accountant and walked up to Wyatt and Will, tipping his hat politely.

"Sheriff. Deputy. Is there a problem?"

"No problem," Wyatt said.

"Then you greet every train."

"It's a friendly town."

"My lawyer and I will be paying a call on Rachel tomorrow. I want to see the documents that give her possession of the spur. You will want to make certain she has them. Delays are pointless." A glimmer of a smile touched his mouth. "Still a friendly town, Sheriff?"

Wyatt watched him go, but it was Will who spoke. "You sure we got no reason to lock him up?"

Grunting softly, Wyatt clapped Will on the back. "C'mon. I have a few stops to make on my way home."

Rachel spread remnants of black velvet and damask across the parlor window and secured the ends so that no light came through. "It's dark outside," she said. "I don't understand the point of a darkroom at night."

"Humor me."

If he'd asked her to trust him, she might have pressed her point a little harder, but the idea that he just wanted to be humored left her without resources to deny him. "I thought we needed more light to make a good photograph."

"That's why I'm putting all the lamps in the kitchen." He picked up the one he usually read by and another on the mantel and headed out.

Rachel finished tacking the velvet, then began working on

the drape she'd quickly made to hang over the entrance to the parlor from the foyer. Wyatt returned in time to help her hang it. She rose on tiptoe, holding the heavy fabric as best she could while he fastened it to the lintel. When he was done, she stood down.

"Should I take the last lamp?" she asked.

"No, I still need to mix the chemicals and prepare the paper and plates. I have to see to do that."

Rachel looked at the pans on the tables, each one of them partially filled with water. Bottles of silver chloride, silver nitrate, and pyrogallic acid stood nearby. "What should I do?"

"You can set up the drying rack. That's it against the wall. I'm going to move the camera and tripod into the kitchen."

Rachel listened to him moving things around in the kitchen while she tinkered with the rack. She finally set it down beside the table where the bottles rested, but not so near the stove that heat would not permit the colloid solution to set; then she went to see what Wyatt had done in the kitchen.

"Surely there must be a better way," she said, examining the lamps he'd set out around the room.

"Flash powder. That's magnesium powder and potassium chlorate, but I don't know the proportions, and I don't think I want to experiment with them tonight."

Rachel was quite sure she didn't. "Your equipment is rather old. Will it work?"

"I don't see why not. The leather bellows are still supple, and the lens isn't scratched. The camera uses the wet-plate process, and that still makes a good photograph. That's all I need." He looked around the kitchen. "And better light."

Rachel made her own survey. "What about a mirror to reflect what we have? There's one above the mantel and another in my workroom."

Wyatt caught her by the shoulders and kissed her hard. She was still wavering on her feet when he disappeared.

It took them half an hour to set the mirrors where they would do the most good, and then ten more minutes to re-distribute the lamps. Wyatt had to adjust the dampers on the stove to reduce the heat in the room.

"I think we're ready." He adjusted the tripod one more time, lowering the camera another inch. The lens was aimed at the tabletop. "If this doesn't work tonight, I can try again in the morning. I just don't know if there will be enough time. Each one of these plates will take between twenty and thirty minutes. I sent word to Foster at the hotel that we'd meet him at our lawyer's office. If we're late, I don't know that he'll wait around."

"If we're late, Wyatt, he can't get in."

"True."

Rachel thought she saw a smile edging his mouth. "You're taking him seriously, aren't you?"

He straightened and turned to her, and there was no hint that he'd ever been amused. His features were sharply defined by their gravity. "Don't ever doubt it," he said. "Even if I didn't trust myself to recognize him for the kind of man he is, I trust you."

She nodded faintly, her eyes straying to the documents spread out across the table. "He's good at negotiation," she said. "Better, some would say, than his grandfather. It's easy to forget that because he was only ever a bully with me."

"Have you wondered why?"

"Because I'm a woman," she said, surprised that he didn't understand. "A whore, according to him."

"Maybe," said Wyatt. "And maybe it's because he's never been able to negotiate a satisfactory arrangement with you. I imagine he didn't approach you with threats at the beginning."

It was so long ago, Rachel could barely remember. "I don't suppose he did, no." She frowned, thinking. "He might have asked me to accompany him to the theater. I can't recall now.

Whatever it was, I had to honor a commitment I'd made with Mr. Maddox. I'm sure I explained that. Regardless, the idea that Foster wanted me to go anywhere with him made no sense. He's never liked me, Wyatt, and his invitation would have been in defiance of his mother."

"How do you know?"

"Cordelia disapproved of me. It was not a secret. As for Foster, he was always watching." She didn't miss the arch of Wyatt's eyebrow. "Do you think I don't know that you watched me, too? It was different. I didn't know quite what to make of you, or your interest, and certainly your attention made me uncomfortable, but I truly never had the sense that you meant me harm. I know I swung the bucket at your head and might have stabbed you with my shears, but what I did was because of Foster Maddox, not because of you." She rubbed the back of her neck, massaging away the tight cords of tension. "Perhaps you're right, and I should have given in to him."

Wyatt took her firmly by the arms. "I never said that you should have given in, Rachel. Is that what you heard?"

She lowered her hand, almost crying with relief when he began to knead her shoulders and slowly work his fingers toward the base of her neck. "I don't know," she said, weary. "I want it to be done. I want it as much as I've ever wanted anything."

He pulled her into an embrace and ran his hands up and down her back until he felt her relax against him. "The kind of man that Foster is," said Wyatt, "doesn't make him evil. Pathetic, perhaps, even petulant, certainly cunning, but not evil. To view him through that lens gives him power that he's never earned and doesn't deserve. It makes opposing him more difficult, not less, because how does any one of us face evil?"

"Besides knocking it down and giving it twenty-two stitches, you mean."

He chuckled. "Besides that."

Closing her eyes, Rachel breathed in Wyatt's scent. She clasped her hands behind his back and rubbed her cheek against his shoulder. "I don't know," she said softly. "In the end, I ran away."

Wyatt's law office was crowded. Sam Walker carried chairs up from the land office to accommodate Foster's entourage. Wyatt and Rachel had asked only Ted Easter to join them. As the mayor of Reidsville, he could represent the town's interest and provide witness to the proceedings. He also acted as the scribe because Wyatt didn't trust that Foster's recollection of the meeting would be the same as his own.

Foster Maddox brought four men with him. His accountant sat on his right with a stack of squared-off ledgers in front of him. On Randolph Dover's right was Daniel Seward, the surveyor and engineer who knew all the reasons that dynamite shouldn't have been used at the blocked pass and had been willing to abandon his superior judgment in favor of Foster's interests. Davis Stuart and George Maxwell were both attorneys, and they huddled together at the foot of the table, comparing notes that they shared by holding up leather portfolios so no one else could see.

Wyatt glanced sideways at Rachel. Her desire to appear indifferent was already taking a toll on her. He suspected that Foster would see that soon enough and use it to his advantage. He dropped his hand under the table and found Rachel's thigh. At the first touch, her lips parted a fraction to take in a breath, and when his fingers tripped lightly up to her hip, her mouth revealed a sliver of a smile. Her own hands were clasped together on the tabletop, and Wyatt watched as her fingertips went from bloodless to pink.

He slid his palm over her thigh so that it came to rest in her lap. She'd chosen to wear one of her most tailored gowns this

morning and the dark ruby fabric was stretched so tautly that
there was no cradle for his hand. He had to be satisfied that
she would remember the one she'd made for him earlier,
when they were still lying in bed and awake only in the sense
that they'd ceased to dream.

"Shall we begin?" Foster asked, raising one eyebrow in the
direction of Stuart and Maxwell. When they set their notes
down, he turned his attention to Rachel. "I'd like to hear why
you think my grandfather, from among all of his many holdings, separated the spur from Denver to Reidsville so that he
could place it in your hands."

"I couldn't possibly speak for the workings of Mr. Maddox's
mind."

"Come. You must have wondered. What did you conclude?"

Wyatt interrupted. "I don't see how that's relevant. From
the nature of your question, one can infer that you are not
challenging that Mr. Clinton Maddox did indeed intend for
Rachel to take possession of the Calico Spur."

Davis Stuart tapped the nib of his pen against his papers. He
had a broad face with craggy features that were only moderately softened by a full wiry beard. "The intent of the question
is to establish the state of Clinton Maddox's mind. The fact that
he did it doesn't mean that it was either right or reasonable."

Rachel said quietly, "I imagine he did it because he wanted
to ensure that I had a means of income. When my father died,
Mr. Maddox made certain that my mother had a way to care
for herself. He would have given her an allowance for the rest
of her life if she would have taken it, but that wasn't her way.
She accepted a position in his home instead and would have
remained there if my sister hadn't left."

"You stayed," said Foster.

"I did. Your grandfather offered me an opportunity to meet
women who would buy my gowns and eventually help me
achieve success independent of him. The plan was always that

I would establish myself first, and then establish my own place of business. I wore only things that I made for myself, and there was no better method of having my designs seen than by going out with Mr. Maddox."

"And what became of that plan?" asked Mr. Maxwell. He nudged his spectacles downward and squinted at Rachel over the thin gold rims. "It seems that you abandoned it when you left Sacramento. Whose idea was that?"

"I left at the suggestion of Mr. Maddox. Mr. *Clinton* Maddox." Her eyes remained steady on Foster, and he looked away first. "He invested in my business and settled some things on me, including the furniture that I allegedly stole."

"We're prepared to forget that," Stuart said. "What is more difficult to reconcile is the idea that Mr. Maddox thought you could have a successful business here."

"Success is relative, I suppose. The women in Reidsville are as eager to be made fashionable as any Sacramento debutante. He was capable of foreseeing that I would be able to make a comfortable living."

"Yet he still carved out the spur to place it in your control."

Wyatt pushed the documents in front of him toward the lawyers at the end of the table. "He certainly did," he told them. "And he arranged it before she ever heard of Reidsville. His intent is clear. He wanted to ensure that she would be able to care for herself and her family. He owed her father a great deal more than what he could repay by settling the spur on her."

"Oh?" asked Foster. "How's that?"

"William Bailey helped him secure an empire during the war. Without him, Clinton Maddox would have lost everything."

Chapter Fifteen

For several long moments the only sound in the room was the scratching of Ted Easter's pen. Davis Stuart and George Maxwell glanced at the papers that Wyatt had pushed in front of them, but neither moved to pick them up. Randolph Dover's attention didn't stray from his ledgers, and Daniel Seward tapped the thumbs of his clasped hands together.

Rachel met Foster's glare without flinching even though she'd been unprepared for Wyatt's revelation. She'd been certain the documents he'd given over were the same ones they'd photographed last evening. Now she didn't know what he had put in front of the attorneys.

"My grandfather never came within a hairsbreadth of bankruptcy," said Foster. "And your assertion about William Bailey is equally false. He only remained employed because he was my father's best friend. The war broke him." He looked at Rachel again. "I apologize, but I must speak frankly. It was commonly known that your father was unwell and depended upon the charity of my grandfather and others to manage his position."

Rachel set her jaw and said nothing. It seemed to her that offering any sort of defense merely lent weight to Foster's words. There was also a thread of truth to what he said, making it difficult to pick apart his argument.

Wyatt reached for the papers that the attorneys still had not picked up and started to slide them toward Randolph Dover. "Too late, gentlemen," he said when they simultaneously made a grab for them. "I think Mr. Dover will understand their significance more quickly." He turned his attention to the uneasy accountant. "If you will, Mr. Dover. Please."

Rachel could not miss Dover's reluctance to take possession of the papers. It was as if he and the attorneys expected they might have to deliver disturbing news, and no one wanted to do that. She hadn't understood until this moment how little support Foster had in this pursuit. He held them by virtue of his money and position, not his principles.

Randolph Dover pushed his pen and ledgers in front of Daniel Seward to make room for the documents. He drew them closer and began to read, aware that Foster Maddox never glanced in his direction and merely waited to hear what he had to say. It didn't take long for him to make his review, but he looked everything over a second time while he considered his words carefully.

"These are letters from the Reid Bank of Boston. All of them were written between February 1861 and September 1862. They are demand notes. The bank owners were requesting immediate repayment of all debt."

Foster frowned deeply. "Why would they do that?"

"The first note would have been in anticipation of war. Recall that succession had already taken place, and Mr. Lincoln was prepared to make his inaugural address in March. I can only surmise that the Reids were attempting to collect on as many loans as they could in order to have sufficient capital to invest in more solvent enterprises. The Colt factory, for instance. Cotton mills. The foundries. Certainly, the railroads, but it seems not the Maddox line. One can suppose they had information that made them question Mr. Maddox's financial situation. Perhaps they suspected he had unreasonably extended himself."

"He had millions."

"Millions in credit, it would seem." Dover handed the notes to Mr. Maxwell when the attorney thrust his arm forward. "I would have to examine the financial records for those years, of course."

George Maxwell quickly examined the notes and passed them one at a time for Stuart's review. He asked Wyatt, "Where did you get these?"

"From Mr. Jake Reston. He's the bank manager."

"It's a Reid bank?" he asked, incredulous.

"You're in Reidsville, Mr. Stuart. Or did that escape your notice?"

Rachel quickly put her hand to her mouth and turned her strangled, nervous laughter into a credible cough.

"I only present them," Wyatt went on, "to support Mr. Clinton Maddox's decision to give the spur to William Bailey's daughter." He turned to Ted Easter, nodded once, and the mayor began to look through his sheaf of papers.

"This the one?" Ted held it out to Wyatt.

"That's it." Wyatt took the document and slid it across the table. "The proof of repayment," he said. "October 1862. That would be five short months after William Bailey secured a contract with the Union to put down fifteen hundred miles of track from Chicago to points west and south. Clinton Maddox's fortune turned on that contract and land grant. William Bailey managed supply lines for the Union generals, and they advocated for the plan he put before them. You can verify all this in the archives in Washington."

Wyatt waited until they reviewed the last item before he continued. "There is one other matter I wish to address, and that goes to the soundness of Mr. Maddox's judgment."

"How could you possibly speak to his judgment?" asked Foster. "He was under the care of several physicians, and all of them are prepared to give testimony to the fact that his faculties were impaired."

Wyatt made a steeple of his fingertips and tapped them lightly together, his demeanor in every way that of a cautious man on uncertain ground. "During what period?"

"If I may answer that," Davis Stuart said. He made a note that he showed to his partner, and when Maxwell nodded, he went on. "For three months prior to Mr. Maddox's first stroke, there were signs that he was suffering memory loss and given to making nonsensical statements."

Rachel sat up even straighter. "That's a lie," she snapped. "He never showed the slightest inclination toward—" She reined herself in sharply when she saw one corner of Foster's mouth lift the smallest of fractions. Her passionate defense only amused him, and she did not dare look to Wyatt to rescue her. "I spent a great deal of time with Mr. Maddox," she said quietly, "and never witnessed what you are describing."

Wyatt didn't wait for anyone to respond to Rachel's outburst. "Let us suppose that it is fact," he said. "And further, allow me to make the time period more generous. Say, two years. Can we agree that Clinton Maddox's reasoning was intact two years in the past?"

The attorneys hesitated, exchanging glances. It was Foster that breached the silence. "Yes," he said impatiently. "I can agree to that."

"And three years?" asked Wyatt.

"Of course."

"Four?"

"Just say the number you have in mind and be done with it."

"The number is six and one-half, and the year is 1876. That is the year Rachel Bailey celebrated her eighteenth birthday and the year Clinton Maddox decided she should inherit a portion of the Maddox holdings. It is immaterial how often Mr. Maddox revised his will subsequent to that date. He made provision for this years before his passing."

George Maxwell quickly opened his portfolio and began leafing through the papers contained in it. A moment later, Davis Stuart did the same. With their heads bent, they were able to avoid Foster's sharp glance.

"You have proof, I suppose," Foster said.

"I do." He turned to Ted Easter and nodded.

Ted produced the papers and put them on the table. "Have a care with these, gentlemen. No one wants to see anything happen to them."

Wyatt watched the attorneys pick them up. Foster expressed no immediate interest. "I remain curious about your need to see these," Wyatt said. "Mr. Maddox assured me that he was specific in his will. I find it odd that you're not familiar with it."

"I am very familiar with his will," said Foster. "And it's a thorny document where the succession of property is concerned. At issue is the breadth of the estate and what constitutes its real property."

Wyatt heard what Foster *didn't* say: namely, that he was preparing to challenge the provisions of his grandfather's will. Foster's charges against Rachel were precisely what he had supposed: They were meant to provide leverage to encourage her testimony.

Foster went on. "I am also familiar with the Maddox holdings, or at least I believed I was until this matter of the spur was revealed. I had to ask myself, of all the assets that my grandfather could have bestowed on Rachel, why the spur to Reidsville? That's when I requested Mr. Dover to make a thorough examination of the financial ledgers. Not, I must add, only of the Maddox public holdings, but of my grandfather's private assets and records. Would you like to know what Mr. Dover discovered?"

"I would." Wyatt waited for the accountant to speak, but the man had swept his ledgers toward him again and merely fidgeted with the stack. It was Foster who responded.

"After unraveling what seemed to be a Gordian knot of bookkeeping entries, Dover was able to show that the spur is profitable beyond what can be reasonably predicted."

"Is that right?" asked Wyatt. "This bit of track?"

"Hmm. I was surprised also. Beyond the financial sleight of hand, there was an organized conspiracy to keep it from me. This was managed by a small circle of men that I also inherited from my grandfather, but who are quite sensibly no longer in my employ."

"Understandable."

"Yes, it is." Foster laid his hand on top of the ledgers at his right, effectively stilling Randolph Dover's twitching fingers. "There remains the question of what makes the spur so profitable."

"Aside from efficient management," Wyatt said dryly. "And the labors of men and women who depend upon the work for their livelihood."

Foster's smile did not touch his eyes. "Aside from that," he said without inflection.

"You have a theory?"

Foster nodded. "I do."

Wyatt waited, but Foster Maddox was not inclined to share it. Wyatt didn't press and hoped Rachel would remain silent as well. Out of the corner of his eye, he saw that the attorneys were finished shuffling the papers he'd given them.

George Maxwell adjusted his spectacles and peered at Wyatt over the rim. "Is this everything?"

"It is."

"It sets some rather unusual terms." He looked past Wyatt to Rachel. "You agreed to these terms?"

"I did."

Foster leaned forward. "What terms? What did you read?"

Davis Stuart stroked his wiry beard with his knuckles. "You were correct, Mr. Maddox. The real property that your grandfather meant to conceal from you is a mining operation." He quickly went on to explain the details of the corporation and the distribution of shares among the holders. "While she was made a shareholder of the mine outright, the spur is Miss Bai—pardon me, Mrs. Cooper's—because she met Mr. Maddox's terms by marrying Mr. Cooper."

Foster's deep-set eyes darted between Rachel and Wyatt but gave no hint as to his own thoughts. "Marriage? That certainly is unusual, even for Grandfather. It explains a great deal, though, doesn't it?" He pressed his lips together and shook his head, at last demonstrating a trace of wry humor. "I did not foresee that. But, really, what person could?"

Stuart went on. "Your grandfather does not explain his reasoning here, nor I suspect, anywhere else."

"He did it to make certain she stayed right here," Foster said. "That is easy enough to comprehend." His attention swung back to Rachel. "Did you hesitate? Or did you think that your many calculating kindnesses to my grandfather were about to pay you handsomely?"

Rachel returned his regard but didn't respond.

"Are you truly married?"

Ted Easter did not wait for Wyatt to hold out his hand. He had the marriage license ready. "Who would like it?" he asked. When no one answered, he stood and leaned across the table to set it in front of Foster.

Foster glanced at it and pushed it aside. "Tell me about the mine. What is your share worth, Rachel?"

"I couldn't say precisely. Ten to twelve, I think."

"Ten to twelve *million*?"

Laughter parted Rachel's lips. "Ten to twelve *thousand*. Millions? I can't imagine it. The property is virtually played out, Foster." Her regard shifted to the accountant. "I certainly mean no offense, Mr. Dover, but I do wonder if there is any possibility you could be mistaken in your conclusions? Reidsville depends on the spur, but it is not mining that sustains the town. Your acquaintance with its attractions has been severely limited, but I can assure you that the Commodore rarely has a vacancy. Citizens from Denver make the journey regularly. There is gaming, of course, and if I may speak with unbecoming frankness, there are certain other entertainments that are known to be finer than what is available in the tenderloin district. There are also the mountain springs, which are said to have restorative powers. Naturally, at this time of year they are unavailable, but our druggist uses the water in his liniments and elixirs and cannot keep up with the demand from the city. I could go on, but I invite you to look around and see the true source of the town's success."

Wyatt's hand slid under the table and came to rest just above Rachel's knee. His gentle squeeze was a caution.

Rachel continued quietly. "I know little enough about the figures you work with, but as a seamstress I've had to follow more threads than I care to think about. It's possible to tug on the wrong one. I think, Mr. Dover, that you may have done just such a thing."

Everyone's eyes went to Randolph Dover. Tiny beads of perspiration appeared on his upper lip, and he swallowed uncomfortably. Before he spoke, he looked to his employer. Foster Maddox merely stared back.

"Well," Dover said, clearing his throat. "As I explained to Mr. Maddox, the accounts suggest that the spur is profitable, though I never put that figure in the millions." He smiled uneasily. "Profits of that magnitude simply could not be concealed. I agree that the figures you mention, Mrs. Cooper, are more congruent with my findings. Regardless, Mr. Clinton

Maddox went to some trouble to obscure these profits and that made them interesting enough in their own right."

Foster's eyes slid in Rachel's direction. "You can appreciate the irony, I hope."

Rachel ignored Foster and addressed Mr. Dover. "How many years did you include in your review?"

"Five."

Wyatt asked, "And what did you observe over time?"

"Small fluctuations from year to year but steady income."

Wyatt nodded. "Mining is boom to bust. Ask the men who were here when placer gold and silver were discovered. They'll tell you what it's like. People have had to find other ways to make a living."

The accountant nodded faintly while Foster Maddox's expression remained implacable.

Holding out his hand, Wyatt asked for the documents he'd passed around to be returned. He collected them and gave them over to Ted Easter.

"I'd like to transcribe the originals," Davis Stuart said.

"Of course," said Wyatt. "I'll want to review the copy. Mr. Easter is able to witness and certify the document."

"Tomorrow?" asked Stuart.

"Sunday? No." He glanced at Ted. "It should be at your convenience."

Ted Easter shrugged. "Monday's fine. Bank opens at nine. Jake will let us use the back room."

"Does that suit?" Wyatt asked. At Stuart's nod, Wyatt looked back at Foster, his eyebrows raised. "Is there anything else?"

Foster didn't answer immediately, resting his chin on his knuckles in a deeply thoughtful pose while he fixed his remote stare on Rachel. "No," he said at last. "It seems you have an answer for everything."

* * *

Rachel accompanied Wyatt and Ted to the bank, where Jake Reston was waiting for them. The corporation papers and Clinton Maddox's directions regarding the spur were returned to the safe. Ted took his notes, and Rachel kept her marriage license.

"Foster never mentioned my ring," she said after parting ways with the others.

Wyatt plucked the license from her, folded it carefully in thirds, and placed it inside his coat. "That can't be because he didn't notice it. You flashed it often enough."

"Not intentionally. I hardly knew what to do with my hands. I was nervous."

"I couldn't tell."

Rachel didn't miss his dry tone. "Liar." She slipped her arm in his. "Why do you think he let it go unremarked?"

"I suspect it was on the advice of his counsel. He was careful in his language where you were concerned."

"Do you think so? He characterized my kindnesses toward his grandfather as calculating."

"That's my point. In other circumstances he certainly would have called you a whore." He gave her arm a small squeeze, softening the sting. "I have to know," he said. "Where did you come by this notion of a spring with restorative waters?"

She glanced at him, her smile both guilty and apologetic. "Was it too much, do you suppose? It just seemed that the town should have more to recommend it than gambling and brides of the multitude."

Wyatt's eyebrows lifted. "Brides of the multitude? Where did you hear that expression?" Even as he asked the question, he knew the answer. "Never mind. I suppose as long as you're going to make gowns for Rose and her girls, you're going to hear things."

"I certainly am." Her smile turned sly. "And I certainly am."

He chuckled, shaking his head.

"Did it sound convincing?" she asked. "About the springs, I mean."

"I was convinced. In fact, I thought I would stop by Chet's and ask for a bottle of his liniment."

She sighed, slowing her steps as they approached the drugstore. "Perhaps we should go in and mention my deception to Mr. Caldwell."

"The least we can do," he said mildly. "In the event that Foster and his men show more interest in Chet's foul concoctions than either cards or the brides."

Joe Redmond was waiting for Wyatt in the churchyard before services began. He tipped his hat to Rachel and asked for a moment of Wyatt's time.

"Go on," Wyatt told Rachel. "I'll be in shortly."

She looked at the grim set of Joe's mouth, the concern that he couldn't conceal, and told Wyatt, "I believe I'll just wait by the steps."

Wyatt not only waited until Rachel was out of earshot but also turned so that his back would be to her. "What is it?" he asked Joe.

"Seven of them came by the livery this morning." Joe thrust his hands deep in his pockets and rocked back and forth on his feet. "A man named Seward took that many of my horses. Paid what I asked for them, and I charged them plenty just to see how serious they was to have the mounts. He didn't blink."

"Seward's the surveyor and engineer. The demolition man, too."

"Ah. That explains the equipment."

"Explosives?"

"I didn't see anything like that. There were a couple of tripods. I thought they were for cameras. You know, like you used to do."

Wyatt nodded. Seward might be planning to take photographs and make a survey. He described Foster Maddox to Joe and asked if he was among the riders.

"Sorry. Don't recollect seeing anyone like that."

"It's probably better that you didn't. Did they say where they were going?"

"I tried to ask real delicate-like, on account they weren't exactly inviting questions. Not one of them acted like he heard, so I let it pass."

"Good idea. Do you have a guess?"

Joe's mouth twisted to one side as he thought. "They went toward the depot. I figure they want it to look like they're following the tracks out of town, but it's likely they'll double back. Can't imagine they're riding out today for any reason 'cept to try to find the active mine."

"How long ago?"

"Forty minutes give or take. I have a mare getting ready to foal. Had to tend to her first before I could get away to find you."

"Did you see Will?"

"Pounded on his door, but if he's there, I couldn't rouse him."

"That's all right. I think I know where he is." He clapped Joe on the shoulder. "Thanks. I appreciate the information. Take care of that mare."

Rachel was talking to Molly Showalter and Johnny Winslow when Wyatt stepped to her side. Molly and Johnny excused themselves and hurried into the church just as the bell called the congregation to worship. Rachel turned to Wyatt and knew immediately that he wouldn't be joining her.

"Where do you have to go?" she asked, steeling herself for the answer.

"Just out." He repeated Joe's story quickly. "It doesn't look as if Foster tagged along, so I'd feel better knowing you aren't alone while I'm gone."

"I'll go to Rose's," she said.

He could think of half a dozen other places he wished she'd go, but he also had no grounds for objecting. Sunday afternoon at Rose's was likely to be quiet. "That's fine but stay put."

"Yes, sir."

Her easy compliance made him look her over carefully. "I mean it, Rachel."

"So do I." She wished she'd told him earlier about Foster's unannounced visit to their home, but telling him now was out of the question. "Truly," she said. "I'll be fine. And what about you? Are you taking that no-account Beatty boy?"

"As soon as I yank him off from the piano stool at Rose's place."

Rachel nodded, satisfied. At least he wasn't setting out alone. "What do you think they're doing?"

"Just poking around."

"I don't like it," said Rachel.

"It will be fine. Think of it this way: when they don't find anything, Foster's likely to abandon this nonsense about challenging your right of ownership. It's only worth his while if there's something to gain. His attorneys know that he has almost no chance of winning, especially if he can't make his case in a California court."

"Have you heard anything from Judge Wentworth?"

"No news to or from Denver. The line is still down somewhere. We'll have to wait to see if the Admiral arrives tomorrow. John Clay can't know the bend's been cleared. If he comes, we'll send out a message to the judge on the return."

Rachel had a sudden urge to touch her husband, and she didn't hesitate to give in to it. Stepping closer, she laid her hand on his upper arm and rubbed gently, then fussed with the lamb's wool collar of his coat. Even as she did it, she appreciated that he allowed her. If he was worried about his own safety, it wasn't readily apparent. It seemed his only concession to the fact that there might be trouble was to have Will with him. "You'll be careful?"

"Yes."

Reluctant to back away, she fiddled with the buttons on his coat. "You tell Will to be careful, too."

"I'll be sure to do that."

Rachel searched his face. "I love you."

Wyatt's throat tightened as he covered her hands with his. "I'm coming home, Rachel. I love you and I'm coming home."

She held on a moment longer, then turned away abruptly and hurried into the church, the beginnings of a prayer already forming on her lips.

Molly and Johnny insisted on escorting Rachel home after the service. She gave in, not because she was particularly concerned about herself, but because they so clearly wanted an excuse to remain together a little while longer. She sent them on their way when they reached the flagstone walk and watched them wander off, fingers tentatively intertwined and heads gently angled toward each other.

She was still smiling as she walked in the door and removed her bonnet and gloves. It was only as she pivoted in the direction of the parlor that the turned-up edges of her mouth collapsed.

"Adele?" Rachel's brow puckered as she hurried into the adjoining room. Adele Brownlee sat perched with the delicacy and stillness of an injured bird on the edge of one of the damask-covered side chairs. Her legs were tucked slightly under the chair, and her arms rested flush to her sides so she occupied as little space as she possibly could. Her narrow, oval-shaped face was turned so it was revealed in only three-quarter profile, but

even then as Rachel got closer she could see the beginnings of
a bruise on the delicate line of Adele's jaw. "Let me look at you."
She placed three fingers under Adele's wobbling chin and gently
nudged her head. "Who did this to you?"

Tears swam in Adele's leaf-green eyes. She tried to look
past Rachel to the front door. "Is Sheriff Cooper coming?"

Releasing Adele's chin, Rachel shook her head. "He had to
ride out. I don't know when he'll be back."

Adele fumbled for a handkerchief in her reticule. She
pressed the crumpled ball of linen to each of her eyes, momentarily stemming the tide of tears. "I'll just go, then. Don't
know what I expected he could do anyway."

"Come into the kitchen, Adele. Let me look after your face
and give you a cup of tea; then you tell me what happened."
Rachel could see that Adele was reluctant, but she didn't give
the girl a chance to refuse. She took Adele firmly by the
elbow and insisted she rise. It was immediately apparent that
Adele's face was only the visible evidence of injury. There
was a definite favoring of her left side as she began to move.

Rachel said nothing about this but made Adele comfortable
in the kitchen, taking her outerwear and hanging it in the
mudroom. She set the kettle on the stove for tea and put out
cups and saucers and a small plate of almond cakes. While
the water was getting hot, she went to the bedroom and removed her coat, then searched the cupboard in the washroom
for liniment. When she returned, Adele was nibbling carefully
on one of the almond cakes.

Rachel pulled the glass stopper from the bottle of liniment.
She wrinkled her nose at the strong, pungent odor. "Turn your
head this way," she told Adele.

Adele recoiled as the scent reached her. "Pardon me for
saying so, but that smells like cat piss."

Rachel didn't blink an eye. "I prefer 'woodsy.' And I can't
say that this will improve the look of the bruise, because it

seems they must all run the full course of color, but it will ease the pain in your jaw. You can take it with you if you like and apply it at your convenience to your ribs." When Adele looked at her sharply, she simply said, "Well, that's the other area that's injured, isn't it? You weren't wearing a corset."

Adele's smile was a bit uneven, but there was finally a spark of humor in her eyes. "No," she said. "I wasn't."

Rachel applied the liniment gently but still had to brace herself against Adele's wince. Her own experience with this sort of injury told her that it was very recent, probably just early this morning. "You haven't told me who did this to you," said Rachel. She corked the bottle and placed it on the table at Adele's side. While Adele wrestled with what she wanted to do about that, Rachel washed her hands. "You came here to tell Wyatt, didn't you?"

Adele shrugged uneasily.

Rachel began to prepare the tea. "Adele, does Rose know?" Out of the corner of her eye, she saw Adele shake her head. "Did this even happen at the house?"

Adele was a long time in answering. "No, ma'am," she said finally.

Rachel sighed. "I thought you girls didn't go out on your own."

"Don't usually. But Rudy offered me a good wage for entertaining at the Miner Key. Singing, I mean. Not the other."

"I knew what you meant. You have a lovely voice." Rachel put the teapot on the table and took a chair herself. "So you met someone at the saloon. Someone from town?"

Adele could barely hear herself when she replied, "No."

"I didn't think so," said Rachel. "Someone from the train, then."

"Oh, he was very nice," Adele said quickly. "Polite. A bit shy, I would say. He kept looking away. Not sneaky, not at all, just like he was out of practice talking to a woman."

"You were charmed." Rachel watched color creep int Adele's cheeks and was reminded that Adele's experience di not make her less vulnerable to matters of the heart. In truth the very opposite was probably true. "I suppose he wa charmed as well."

"I think so, yes. He complimented my performance severa times and invited me to the hotel for dinner."

"I see. It must have been very late by then."

She nodded. "It was, but I was hungry. My insides get al twisted up before I sing, so I can't eat more than a couple o salted crackers. And besides, he was . . . well, he was . . ."

"It's all right," Rachel said when Adele couldn't find th proper adjective. "I understand." She poured tea and pushe a cup and saucer in front of her guest, then gently encourage her to drink. "You went with him, I take it."

Adele gripped her cup and offered a shade defensivel "We had dinner in the dining room. It was . . ." Again, sh struggled for the right descriptor. "Lovely," she said at las "Yes, it was lovely."

"Did he tell you his name, Adele?"

She was slow to answer, but eventually said, "Pennwa James Pennway."

Rachel hardly knew what to make of her own relief. It wa undeserved and seemed strangely like a betrayal, but she' been so certain that Adele's path had crossed Foster's tha relief was the first emotion to wash over her. "Was he stayin at the hotel?"

"Yes. We went to his room after dinner." She hesitate slightly. "At least I thought it was his room."

"What do you mean?"

"I think it might have belonged to someone else."

Rachel still didn't understand. "Why do you say that?"

"A man came in much later, close to dawn, and ordere James out. He was very angry."

"James?" asked Rachel. "Or the man that sent him away?"

"The man. I tried to leave with James, but I had more clothes to gather and no wish to be tossed into the hallway in my drawers, so it took time and I was clumsy and the gentleman just got more impatient."

"Is that when he hit you?"

Adele nodded. "I was half in and out of my dress. I couldn't lift a hand when he struck me. He knocked me off my feet." She absently raised a hand and touched the back of her head. "I fell against the nightstand."

"A fist to the jaw," Rachel said quietly. "Then a kick to your ribs?"

Adele regarded her with surprise. "How did you know?"

Rachel didn't answer. "Your hip?"

"There, too."

"When you curled up to protect your ribs."

"That's right."

Not wanting Adele to see that her fingers were trembling, Rachel quickly set her cup down and folded her hands in her lap. Her heart hammered, and she closed her eyes briefly. "I'm so sorry, Adele."

"Why should you be sorry? You didn't do anything."

Shaking her head, Rachel said, "But I think I did." She carefully described Foster Maddox and saw in Adele's increasingly curious expression that she had drawn the correct conclusion. "Did he hurt you in any other way?"

"Rape me, you mean?"

"Yes, that's what I mean."

"No." Adele's fingertips whitened on her teacup. "For a moment . . . his hands were on his britches like he meant to take them off; then he looked at me real odd, sort of puzzled, sort of sickened, and told me to get out. To get the hell out."

"Sickened?" asked Rachel. "Do you mean remorseful?"

Adele's laughter was bitter. "I mean like I was something he wanted to scrape off the bottom of his shoe."

"Oh, Adele." Rachel knew that look, remembered to clearly what it was like to be on the receiving end of a glanc that ran both hot and cold. She'd always suspected that Foste was more satisfied using his fists on her than he would hav been if she'd ever once surrendered. He might revile whores but they also darkly fascinated him. Uncertain she would eve understand, Rachel sighed. "Finish your tea, and I'll walk yo back. Wyatt asked me not to stay here while he was gone."

"Because of him," said Adele. "We were warned abou Foster Maddox."

"That's right. Rose wouldn't have allowed him in. She knev who she was looking for because Will gave her a description.

"Rose told me to do my performance and leave." Adel hung her head. "I suppose she trusted me to listen to her. Sh might not even know I didn't go home last night."

"Well, I'm sure she's worried sick now, and with Wyatt an Will both gone, there's no telling what she's planning to do t find you. I think we should get you back as quickly as possi ble. But first, we're going to make a photograph."

Wyatt slowed Raider to a walk and waited for Will to com abreast. "We should stay here awhile. We're close to catchin up with them."

Will nodded. "I was thinking the same thing." He pointe to the narrow trail ahead of them. Pine trees cast their shado across the snow. "They're not making it difficult to follov Why do you suppose that is?"

"Could be because they don't know we're back here." ·

"Maybe."

"Could be because they expect us to follow and want t make certain we can."

"Maybe."

"Or," Wyatt drawled, "it could be that they just don't know any better."

"I like that one best."

"Thought you would, but I wouldn't count on it being right."

"They already passed the open mine," Will pointed out. He leaned forward to pat his mare when she started nudging Raider.

"There're still places up ahead where they can get a good look at it." He turned his face toward a small patch of sunlight through the trees and squinted into the blue sky overhead. "Good day for photographs, though. C'mon. Let's go. If we take Potter's trail, we can follow their route from above."

"I hate Potter's trail. It's like climbing a steeple."

"It sure is." Grinning, he urged Raider to veer sharply to the right. "Let's go."

Sighing heavily, but still game, that no-account Beatty boy followed.

They sighted the surveying party an hour later and from a couple of hundred feet higher. They removed their mounts to a place of safety behind an outcropping of rock and concealed themselves fairly well by hunkering down in the midst of some scraggly limber pine. Wyatt took out his field glasses to observe the movement of the riders below.

"How many did I tell you there were?" asked Wyatt.

"Seven. You said Joe told you they took seven mounts."

Wyatt passed the glasses. "You see seven down there?"

"I'm counting four."

"That's what I saw." He fell silent as he considered what that meant. He recognized Daniel Seward among the riders. The other men made no particular impression on him except that none of them was Foster Maddox. Joe Redmond had been right about that. Wyatt traveled over the trail they'd

taken, this time in his mind. The entire time he and Will had
followed their exact path, no one had left the trail. Had three
riders broken away later or never set out with the others? And
if they hadn't set out, why did they need mounts in town?

"I don't like this." Wyatt tipped back his hat with his forefinger and broadened his view to include more than the surveyors. Sunlight glinted off the virgin snow. There were no
trails leading away from the group.

Will turned and focused the field glasses farther up the
mountain. Only animal tracks disturbed the crust. "No one's
above us."

"Look," Wyatt said. "They're stopping."

Will brought his attention around. "Why there?" The rider
dismounted beside a shallow stream. Two of them waded in
and began poking among the rocks. Daniel Seward started
loosening the ropes on the equipment strapped to his horse.
"That's definitely for surveying. He's taking out the chains."
He handed back the field glasses.

Wyatt only needed to raise the glasses for a moment to see
that Will was right. Seward appeared to be speaking to the
man at his side. It wasn't long before a map was removed from
a saddlebag. The pair began poring over it and pointing to
where they wanted to set up the equipment for triangulation.

"There's no reason for them to survey here," said Wyatt.
"This area is clearly within the property borders. If they're
looking to confirm the northern perimeter, then they're six
miles short. Seward has to know that."

Will drew his muffler a fraction higher to cover his chin.
"Do you think the men with him know?"

"Hard to say." Wyatt rose slowly from his crouch, raising
the field glasses one more time. "There're two reasons I can
think of why Seward would ride out this far, then make a mistake like this. The first is that he has plans to deceive Foster

Maddox. The second is that he was sent here to draw us away from town."

Will stood and shook out his cramped legs. Without a word, he began moving toward his mare. He took up the reins and mounted. He didn't have to look back to know that Wyatt was right behind him. The second reason that Wyatt had provided was too compelling to ignore.

Faint, but unmistakable in pitch and the sustained power of its initial blast, the sound of an engine's whistle traveled through the mountain pass. Wyatt and Will both paused, cocking their heads. Even the horses stilled to listen.

"Can't be the Admiral," Will said. "Nothin's scheduled until tomorrow. Kirby doesn't make a run until Tuesday. Anyway, No. 473 has a whistle that's pitched half an octave higher."

Wyatt hadn't felt the need to say it aloud, but his line of thinking was exactly the same. "It's Foster's train. He's preparing to leave." The pronouncement was somehow as mournful and hollow as the whistle that preceded it.

Ezra Reilly had no chance against the trio that stormed the jail from the alley side. They backed him up against the wall, stuck the barrel of a Remington pistol in his belly, and took the keys to the cell, then felled him with two sharp blows to the head that left him unconscious and bleeding on the floor. Once Franklin and Ross were free, they took it upon themselves to move Ezra to a cell. Ross kept the keys.

Now five in number, the men moved quickly up the alley from the jail to the bank. Two of the horses were teamed to pull a sled. The third horse carried supplies. When they reached the bank's rear entrance, one of the men removed black powder charges from a saddlebag and placed them carefully around the door. They backed up and turned away after the fuse was lighted. The door did not explode out of its frame but splintered at the hinges and lock so that it was easily removed.

Franklin and Ross remained in the alley, alert for anyone who heard the noise and came to investigate the cause. They had assurances that a lot of folks were attending late services and wouldn't hear a thing above the Bible thumping, but their recent turn in jail made them cautious just the same.

They were both braced for an explosion from inside the bank, so when time passed without any noise, they grew increasingly restless and traded talk about taking two of the horses and bolting. They were on the verge of separating the team when the other men emerged from the bank, straining like draft horses pulling a loaded wagon. The pair of cattle thieves and occasional guns-for-hire stared openmouthed as a Hammer & Schindler safe crashed down the stairs behind them.

They didn't wait to be told what to do. They moved the team hitched to the sled closer to the entrance and then helped right the safe and roll it through the door and onto the sled. The leather straps that had aided in the removal of the safe were transferred to the sled to hold it in place. The horses required very little encouragement to get under way.

One of the men consulted his pocket watch. From storming the jail to removing the safe, the time was under twenty-two minutes, well within the parameters that had been established for success.

Rose LaRosa was having none of it. She set her hands hard on her hips and stared fiercely at the two men who had entered her establishment against her wishes. The fact that they both produced badges held no sway with her.

"If you are who you say you are, then you should have

identified yourselves to Sheriff Cooper. Pinkerton men have no authority here."

"Afraid we do, ma'am." The fair-haired gentleman regarded her with some sympathy. "We have a warrant."

Rose's hands dropped to her sides, where they balled into fists. "That warrant means as little as those badges. I don't believe either of them, so go shake them at someone else."

"Afraid I can't do that," he said. "Now go and fetch Rachel Bailey. Mr. Pennway and I need to talk to her."

Rose didn't give ground. "There's no Rachel Bailey here."

"Rachel Cooper, then."

"She's not here, either."

James Pennway took over when he observed his partner's frustration. "You'll have to excuse Mr. Barlow. He's used to people being impressed by his credentials. We know Mrs. Cooper's here. We watched her walk in from across the way. She was accompanied by one of your girls. A young woman named Adele, I believe."

Rose's features revealed nothing except her frustration. "Then you confused her with another of my girls." Rose went to the foot of the stairs and called up. "Adele, can you come down? Bring Virginia with you." She turned to wait, effectively blocking the Pinkerton men from advancing. "I don't appreciate you disrupting our Sunday."

Neither man spoke, though they acknowledged the admonition with a mildly apologetic smile.

Adele held the banister as she made her way down the steps. Virginia watched her, prepared to assist her if she faltered. Rose stopped them before they reached the bottom and then addressed her visitors.

"Are these the women you saw?"

Barlow pointed to Adele. "That's Miss Brownlee. I recognize the hair. And she was limping. But that's not the woman who was with her. That's not Mrs. Cooper."

Rose glanced over her shoulder and regarded Adele. "Do you have anything to say?"

Adele merely shook her head.

Frowning, Rose asked, "You don't know either of these Pinkerton men?"

Adele looked them over closely. "I might have seen him before," she said, pointing to Pennway. "I think he was at the Miner Key last night, bucking the tiger."

"Is that right, Mr. Pennway? You play faro?"

Before James Pennway could confirm that he did indeed like to make wagers on the game, Adele's knees were giving way. She lowered herself to the stairs, ignoring Virginia's efforts to keep her upright. "That's not James Pennway," she said, drawing back her hand. "He's not the man I had dinner with."

Pennway regarded Adele more closely, seeing the bruise on her cheek for the first time. "Indeed, I'm not," he said. "But I am James Pennway." He exchanged a glance with Barlow, communicating an understanding that was not necessary to share aloud. "This isn't getting us anywhere, Miss LaRosa. I have my orders, a warrant, and the means to enforce it." He opened his coat so she could see his gun. A moment later, Barlow did the same.

"Wyatt took your weapons," Rose said, staring at the Colts each man had strapped to their thighs. "He took everyone's weapons from the train."

"And we took them back," Mr. Barlow said.

Rachel appeared at the top of the stairs. "That's enough, Rose. I'm going with them."

"Why didn't you leave by the rear door?"

It was Pennway who answered. "She probably saw the men we put there." He stared up the steps. "A wise decision, Mrs. Cooper."

Adele pulled herself to her feet again. "Who the hell was

he?" she snapped, pointing at Pennway. "If you're James Pennway, then who the hell was he?"

Pennway merely looked past her and gestured to Rachel. "Come down, Mrs. Cooper. It's time to go."

Rose backed up onto the stairs to make certain that Adele didn't fall forward. Virginia also looked prepared to haul her back if she stumbled or leapt. "You're cowards," she accused the men. "Coming here to take Rachel when her man isn't around."

"Not cowardly," Barlow objected. "Just smart. No one gets hurt."

Rachel started down the steps. "That's what I want as well, gentlemen. No one getting hurt." She paused when she reached Virginia and Adele and waited for them to part so she could get through. In the end it was Rose who blocked her way. "Don't, Rose. I need to go with them."

"No, you don't."

"He'll never stop. You don't know what he's like. He believes this makes sense. He believes he's right."

"Doesn't make it so."

Rachel placed her hand on Rose's shoulder. "Let me pass. You tell Wyatt that I went willingly so he doesn't lose his mind thinking I was forced."

Rose exhaled deeply and set her spine stiffly. "Virginia, you tell Wyatt what she said. Adele, you tell Will that I went along to keep her company."

Chapter Sixteen

Wyatt and Will met a crowd at the depot when they returned to town. The men had already been discussing the best way to proceed and shouted out their plans while Artie Showalter began whispering in Wyatt's ear as soon as he dismounted, trying to tell him the whole of what they'd confronted in his absence.

That no-account Beatty boy finally took matters into his own hands and held up his gun, threatening to shoot if they didn't start talking one at a time.

The story came out in bits and pieces, but this time Wyatt and Will were able to follow the thread that held it together. Wyatt thought Will would be sick when he first heard that Rose had gone with Rachel, but just as quickly, the pallor of Will's complexion changed, and he stood straighter, his eyes clear and sharp and unnaturally calm.

Wyatt's attention was caught by Adele Brownlee standing at the center of a clutch of concerned women, and he moved toward her. "Are you sure you're all right, Adele?"

She quickly put her hand on her jaw, covering the bruise, and nodded. "Rachel put some liniment on it," she said because she felt as if she needed to tell him something. "And she took photographs."

"Did she?" Wyatt said quietly. He felt his throat tighten again. "She doesn't miss a trick."

"Not one," said Adele. "They're on the rack in your parlor."

"Thanks for getting help, Adele." He patted her forearm, then addressed Gracie Showalter. "Ezra?"

"Doc's sewing him up. Virginia's with him. He's going to be fine, Wyatt. A safe's harder to crack than that boy's skull, Doc says."

Considering that Foster's men had fled with the bank's stronghold rather than try to open it, he supposed that might be true. Wyatt simply nodded and walked off toward the depot's platform. He held up his hand, signaling for quiet, and got it immediately.

"I need some men to ride out to the basin northwest of the number-two mine. That's where Daniel Seward and three others were surveying. There was no point in it that Will and I could see, but they should be followed all the same and brought back when you have the opportunity." Hands shot up immediately and Wyatt selected five. "Now I need at least six, no more than ten, to ride out after the train." Men came forward and stepped up to the platform to stand beside Will. Wyatt looked them over, nodded, then pointed to Abe Dishman standing in the crowd beside Artie Showalter.

"Abe, tell us all again how we're going to catch that engine before it gets to Denver."

Abe thrust his lantern jaw forward and folded his arms across his chest. He nodded once, firmly. "It's like I was sayin' earlier. I never did like Jack Gordon driving that engine up here on our track. He had no right to do it, no matter what Maddox was payin' him, so I figured that we was owed something. Could be that something's wrong with that engine's boiler."

"Could be?"

Abe shifted. "I don't imagine they'll be getting much more pressure than forty pounds per square inch. That'll slow them, even on the downhill."

Wyatt thought nothing could ease the tightness around his own heart, but his rival for the affections of Rachel Bailey did just that. "Abe, I could kiss you, but I'll step aside for Rachel to have a turn at it when we get back."

Abe Dishman's face reddened, but he looked overwhelmingly pleased at the prospect.

Wyatt called out for the supplies they would need, and men scattered quickly to secure their horses, saddlebags, weapons, and explosives. He and Will stayed behind to reassure everyone else as best they could, though reassurances were returned to them in equal measure, and when the two posses reassembled, he deputized them and ordered them out.

Rachel and Rose sat side by side on a leather bench in Foster Maddox's private car. They no longer whispered to each other, having been given the directive several times to stop talking, the final one being accompanied by a threat to throw Rose from the train when they reached the first drop higher than fifty feet.

Foster was supremely unhappy that Rachel arrived with a companion, and nothing Pennway and Barlow offered in explanation satisfied him. He plucked their badges from their coats and pitched them out a window; then he sent the Pinkerton impersonators to sit in the common passenger car with the other men.

Rachel's eyes strayed often to Randolph Dover. He sat alone on one of the benches, his head mostly turned toward the window as though he had a genuine interest in the scenery and wasn't merely trying to avoid facing her. Davis Stuart and George Maxwell shared a bench near the door of the car. The attorneys spoke occasionally to each other, but their voices were pitched low. Rachel observed that Foster had almost no use for them, and she wondered how deeply they were involved in his scheme. The few times that one or the other glanced back at her, however, she saw nothing in their expressions but indifference.

Foster Maddox sat behind a large desk in a heavily padded red leather chair that reminded Rachel of a throne. There were papers spread out before him, and he leaned forward in the chair, supporting his head by pressing his thumb and fingers against the sharp ridge of his brow. He looked as if he had a powerful hangover, but since she knew that he rarely drank to excess, Rachel thought it was more likely that he was suffering from one of his migraines. The way his hand was set across his brow, it seemed possible that he was not merely supporting his head but also shading his eyes. When he snapped at his accountant to pull the shades, she knew she was right.

"Is this everything that was found in the safe?" he asked, shuffling the papers on the desk.

The attorneys turned as one, twisting their heads to address Foster. George Maxwell deferred to his partner. "Everything that pertains to your case," said Stuart.

"What about the rest? There was cash, wasn't there? Stocks and bonds, perhaps."

"All back in place."

"No one took anything?"

In spite of his attention seeming to be elsewhere, Randolph Dover had been following the conversation. He pulled down the last shade and returned to his seat. "I made an inventory of the contents. Besides the papers you wanted, there was $4,850 in cash, seven deeds, thirteen stock certificates, and a locked box containing various pieces of jewelry. All of it was returned to the safe after your items were removed."

"If you're here, who's minding it now?"

"Ford and Richards."

Foster removed his hand so that Dover could see one of his eyebrows arching. "The men that the sheriff says are cattle thieves? Did you consider that at all?"

"I did. And I recalled that you weren't troubled by it. You also ordered their release from jail, so it seemed that you trusted them. I felt I could do no less."

Rachel felt Rose's fingers cover hers. She glanced sideways and saw a glimmer of a smile touch Rose's mouth. Rachel suppressed the same tug on her lips. Mr. Dover's clever reply gave Foster little recourse but to accept it.

"In any event," Dover went on, "the man that was finally able to open the safe is in the other car."

Nodding faintly, Foster said, "Give them the order to push the safe out."

Dover frowned. "Push it out?"

"I'm not a thief, Randolph. I only want what belongs to me." He pointed to the papers, then looked in Rachel's direction and gave her a slight smile. "Tell them to get rid of the safe and make certain it can be recovered."

"Very well." The accountant nodded and left the car to enter the one to the rear.

"I think I surprised you," Foster said to Rachel. "Am I right?"

"It's only in the broadest strokes that I've ever been able to predict what you will do," she said. "The details are always a surprise."

"Really? I believe you mean to flatter me."

"I'm sure I don't."

He chuckled and then winced, touching his fingertips to his temple and revealing again how much he was pained by the migraine.

"Do you have any headache powders?" asked Rachel. It was not sympathy that moved her to raise the question, but common sense suggested that if he was not in pain, he might deal with her and Rose more fairly. "I don't mind mixing them for you."

He looked her over, his regard suspicious. "There's nothing like that in the car."

Rachel pointed to the pocket of her coat. "May I?"

Annoyed by the question, he waved his hand impatiently. "Yes. Yes, of course."

Rachel stood and withdrew a small cobalt-blue bottle from her pocket. "Do you recall that I told you people come to Reidsville for the mountain springs?" She didn't wait for him to comment but continued blithely. "This particular elixir has been found to be efficacious for pain, and most people swear it is because of the spring water. I'm not in the habit of carrying it with me, but I had need of it only this morning because a young woman presented herself at my house after she had suffered a beating." Rachel did not expect that Foster would blink an eye, and he didn't. "She's rather small and delicately boned, so she had no use for more than two teaspoons. You will perhaps have to finish the bottle, but I believe you will find it as helpful as she did."

"Let me see it." Foster held out his hand.

Rachel approached but kept the desk between them. She placed it in his open palm and waited for him to take it. His fingers closed around it slowly, deliberately brushing her hand. She did not smile, but neither did she look away.

"There's no label," Foster observed, turning the bottle. "What's it called?"

"Coldwell." When Foster merely stared at her, she explained. "Cold. Well. Our druggist, Mr. Caldwell, perceives it is clever wordplay. I'm told that he originally recommended it as a cold remedy, but it has since proven its worth in regard to general pain."

Foster stared at the bottle a moment longer, then at Rachel. "You are not generally so amenable." He removed the bottle's stopper, sniffed, and reared back his head. He shoved the stopper back into place. "Jesus! What's in it? It smells like cat piss."

In response to having her offer so bluntly spurned, Rachel tried to snatch the bottle back. Foster held it out of her reach.

"Not so quickly," he said. He moved a little in his chair so he could see past Rachel to Rose. "Have you used this before?"

"Often enough to know that you're right," said Rose. "It smells like cat piss."

Rachel watched Foster's eyebrows lift a notch and wondered if he would lecture Rose on her language. It was his strongly held opinion that a man could say what he liked, but a woman who repeated it was coarse and common. She carefully released the breath she was holding when she saw Foster was going to restrain himself.

Foster gestured to Rachel to step aside so he didn't have to crane his neck around her. "Miss LaRosa, is it?"

Rose nodded. "That's right."

"You're a friend of Miss Bailey's?"

"I am."

He considered that. "Then you wouldn't mind supporting her claim about this elixir."

"I thought I already had."

"Not to my satisfaction. Come here, Miss LaRosa."

To her credit, Rose did not hesitate even though she suspected what he was going to ask of her. She went directly to his side, swaying provocatively in concert with the motion of the train. "Do you imagine that she's trying to poison you?" she asked, extending her hand to take the bottle. "If so, the blame must lie with Chester Caldwell. I've maintained he's been trying to poison all of us for years."

Foster regarded her, then her open hand. "What is the most effectual dose?"

"I couldn't say. I've never measured. I pour."

Holding up the bottle, Foster examined the amount of liquid inside. "A full swallow, then," he said, removing the stopper again. "Just so that I can be sure."

Rose took the bottle and put it to her lips. Her nose wrinkled a little, but it was a mild reaction compared to Foster's earlier one. She tipped the bottle and her head and swallowed. Her features puckered as though she'd sucked on a lemon, and she shivered slightly in the aftermath, but she remained standing and presented herself as no worse for wear.

Foster took the bottle back and dismissed Rose. He watched her walk away from him, then turned his attention to Rachel. "I thought you would stop her," he said.

Rachel had been on the verge of doing just that, but she doubted Rose would have forgiven her. "Why would I? There's hardly a person in Reidsville that doesn't use it regularly this time of the year." Affecting indifference, Rachel returned to her seat. She smiled coolly at the lawyers, both of whom had turned in their seats to observe. Confident now that Foster had been sufficiently challenged, and could hardly do less than follow Rose's example, Rachel surreptitiously sought out Rose's hand and squeezed it.

Foster lifted the bottle in the manner he might lift a wineglass in preparation of a toast. "Cheers." Then he drank.

Rachel tried to gauge how much of the liniment he swallowed, but it was difficult to see through the cobalt glass at her present distance. It seemed to her that he had taken enough to begin to notice the effects within the half hour.

Foster stoppered the bottle and put it in a drawer. He drew a handkerchief from his jacket and touched it to the corner of each watering eye.

Watching him, Rose was moved to say, "It settles better in the stomach than it does on the tongue."

Grunting softly, Foster shoved the handkerchief out of sight and sat back in his chair. He closed his eyes momentarily and massaged the bridge of his nose with his thumb and forefinger. The sway of the train was like being rocked in a cradle. "Why the hell aren't we picking up more speed?" he demanded of no one in particular. "It's downhill to Denver, isn't it?"

Wyatt and Will drove the posse hard. Not everyone who volunteered was used to riding at the pace Wyatt set, but no one complained. They had been chosen for more than their riding skills. Catching the train was only the first step. Stopping it, holding it, and getting Rachel and Rose off it accounted for the whole of what they had to do.

Occasionally a thin cloud of smoke would rise in the distance, evidence of the engine's progress through the mountains. Wyatt and others gauged their own advance against where they believed the train to be. As the eddy of smoke and ash became thicker and darker, they were able to judge the number of miles that separated them.

They traveled routes that no train could, trails that were familiar to Wyatt and Will from their weekly rounds of the vast mining property. While Foster's engine was forced to sometimes take a meandering path because of the steepness of the grade, the posse was able to take a more direct course. They lost time going around the trestle and made it up when they carefully picked their way through an abandoned tunnel.

"Can we get ahead of them before Brady's Bend?" Will asked. He anxiously watched a curling ribbon of smoke rise above a long stretch of pines.

Wyatt tugged on his scarf, tucking it under his chin so Will could hear him. "I don't think so. Just beyond it, though, we might."

"The Bend's better."

"I know."

"Let me take a few men. Some of us can ride harder. Faster."

"And do what when you get there? You don't know anything about explosives. You could bury the train. Derail it. We need everyone, Will. Everyone."

Rachel and Rose huddled together, sharing their body heat as best they were able. The private car had a stove, but Foster was warm and decided everyone else must be as well. When Mr. Maxwell suggested adding coals for the comfort of the women, Foster ordered him to the next car. His quick departure seemed to indicate that he did not mind going.

Mr. Dover returned to report that the safe would be ejected from the train when they reached Brady's Bend. Foster merely raised his hand to indicate approval of the plan and gestured to the accountant to return to his seat. Dover glanced around, his mildly questioning look directed first to Mr. Stuart, then to Rachel and Rose, to provide some indication of what had transpired in his absence. No one spoke.

With the shades drawn, the gloomy interior of Foster's private car accurately reflected the mood of the passengers. Rachel did not find herself heartened by the beads of perspiration that she observed on Foster's upper lip. He was uncomfortable, not unconscious, and it was the latter that had been her goal. Occasionally he would close his eyes, but for the most part he watched her and Rose with an intensity that she found unsettling.

"Why did you agree to come?" Foster asked suddenly.

Rachel blinked, surprised that he was addressing her after so long a silence. She couldn't fathom why he was asking the question now. "I didn't realize that you were offering me a choice."

"Pennway and Barlow said you didn't argue." He jabbed a finger in Rose's direction. "Your fellow whore, on the other hand, raised a number of objections."

Rachel felt Rose's gloved hand press lightly against hers, and she understood it as a warning that she needed to remain reasonable and restrained. She drew a short, calming breath. "I'm weary, Foster. Weary of the conflict between us. My decision to come with you is not motivated by anything more than that and the small, lingering hope that you can be saved from yourself."

"Saved? What can that possibly mean?"

"You've surrounded yourself with men who have subjugated their best judgment to your whims." Out of the corner of her eye, she saw Mr. Stuart cock his head to better hear the conversation. Across the way, Mr. Dover sat up straighter.

"I have no idea if you chose them for that weakness in their character or merely eroded their will over time. I am actually sympathetic to their position, having found myself in a similar one where you are concerned. The decision to leave rather than surrender my soul was difficult and not without sacrifice, and I certainly do not hold myself up as an example for others to follow. I merely point it out because I've had reason to wonder if leaving was the right thing to do. It was clearly the prudent thing, but perhaps it wasn't right.

"When Mr. Pennway and Mr. Barlow informed me that I had to accompany them to the train, I knew they had no legal standing to force me. I also knew they would do it because you'd ordered them. Your willingness to resort to abduction, to face charges of the same, was an indication to me of how impaired your thinking had become. The fact that no one among your advisers was stepping forward to put a hold on your actions was equally alarming. I have not been able to determine if their silence is because they've abandoned the last vestige of good sense or if they've conspired to abandon you."

Foster's gaze rested briefly on his attorney, then moved to his accountant. Neither met his eyes. He returned to Rachel, who met him squarely. "You're saying that they wanted to see me charged with abduction?"

"It's a possibility, isn't it? But I came willingly, and there are witnesses to that fact, so there can be no charge. The same cannot be said of the bank robbery. Do you see now, Foster? You bought and bullied your closest advisers into saying and doing nothing, but what does it mean? Who can you trust now that everything's been turned on its head?"

Foster rubbed the back of his neck and rolled his shoulders. Neither action relieved the tightness in his skull. "You make a compelling argument, Rachel, but then you studied at the feet of the master."

She sighed and ignored the barb. "I want a resolution to this matter of the mine and the spur. We both know what your grandfather wanted, but if you must have it settled in court, then I have no objection to having the case heard."

"Really?"

"Really," she said flatly. "You have no tolerance for waiting, Foster. For anything. If you had been willing to remain in town a few days longer, Judge Wentworth would have arrived from Denver to listen to the arguments. We would be done. Done with all of it."

"You mean everything would be settled in your favor."

"I mean it would be settled. I don't pretend to be able to predict the outcome, but I believe the law favors my case."

He snorted, then winced. He pressed one hand to his temple again. "We'll see what the court in Sacramento has to say."

Rachel shook her head. "No, we won't. That's what you've failed to understand. I'm not going that far with you."

Foster's mouth thinned, but he did not take issue with her assertion. Instead, he growled a directive at his attorney. "Find out why the hell we're going so goddamn slow."

* * *

Will held his mare to a walk, falling back from the others, and raised his field glasses to examine a section of the track below them. Lying not four yards from the rails in the midst of a cluster of boulders and three feet of snow was something that simply didn't belong. Its flat black color among the gray stone and virgin snow was what caught Will's eye, but it was the sharp, clean lines of the object that roused his curiosity. It could only be man-made.

Holding the glasses to his eyes, he tipped his head to the side to study the thing at another angle. It wasn't entirely visible, but there, just above the snow line, he could make out the first two distinctive gold letters of the Hammer & Schindler safe.

He dropped the glasses and called to the rest of the posse to hold. He pointed down the hillside and told them what they were all straining to see.

Andy Miller shook his head in disbelief. "Now, why the hell would they do that?" No one answered what each one of them supposed was the bank teller's rhetorical question. Their silence prompted him to ask another. "Do you have any idea how much that weighs?"

"How much?" Sam Walker asked.

"Dunno."

Wyatt intervened. "We have to leave it for now. They're through the bend. That okay with you Andy?"

"Sure. It's bound to be empty."

"All right," Wyatt said. "Let's go." He started out, Will beside him again. He glanced over at his deputy. "Good eye, Will."

Will shrugged. "I'm thinking I want to go down there and take a look at it."

"Why?"

"I got a bad feeling is all."

"Neither Rose nor Rachel is in that safe."

Will looked at him, startled. "How'd you know that's what I was thinking?"

"Because it went through my mind, too."

"So how do you know one of them's not in it?"

"Foster needs Rachel," he said. "And she'd throw herself from the train before she'd allow him to use Rose against her."

As soon as Davis Stuart left the car, Rose stood and crossed to the accountant's side. She put herself on the bench beside him, close enough that her thigh rubbed his as the train turned into another curve.

Foster observed Mr. Dover's discomfort but left it to him to do something about it. "Why are you here?" he asked Rose.

"I fancied a trip to Denver."

He didn't smile. "How are you acquainted with Rachel?"

"I know just about everyone in town."

"I'm sure you do, but I wonder if you would choose to accompany all of them in similar circumstances."

"Denver's real nice."

Foster addressed Rachel. "She thinks I have an endless well of patience. Perhaps you should explain."

"I thought I had. Perhaps she wasn't listening when I said you have no tolerance."

"I heard you," said Rose. "I didn't realize he had no sense of humor."

"None at all, I'm afraid."

Rose sighed and gave Foster Maddox her most pitying glance. "That *is* unfortunate. A sense of humor is perhaps a man's most attractive feature. After the size of his . . . bank account."

Rachel quickly stifled nervous laughter with the back of her hand. Feeling Foster's sharp glance, she cleared her throat and settled her hands back in her lap.

Foster shifted his eyes to Rose. "If you believe that," he said, "then you certainly have misjudged the character . . . and bank account . . . of the man beside you. Isn't that right, Randolph?"

Mr. Dover raised his head. He offered a faint nod and did not engage anyone's eyes.

"Rubbing up against him won't start a fire, Miss LaRose," said Foster.

"LaRosa."

"Pardon me. Miss LaRosa." He ran the knuckle of his forefinger across his upper lip. "I only thought it fair to point out that your effort to turn him is wasted. Randolph is loyal to me."

Rachel managed to catch Mr. Dover's eye. "Is Foster right?" she asked. "It seems as if he might be. You gave him Adele Brownlee easily enough. Did you even hesitate?"

"I don't know what you mean."

"Adele Brownlee," Rachel repeated. "The pretty young woman who sang at the Miner Key? I believe you invited her to have dinner with you at the Commodore. Was your interest earnest, Mr. Dover, or were you expressing the interest of your employer? Acting as a procurer, perhaps."

Rose clamped her gloved hand hard just above Mr. Dover's knee. "Is she right, Randolph? Did you pimp my girl?"

Affronted, Mr. Dover's head snapped up.

"Oh, it's no good affecting insult at this juncture," Rose said. "You pimped Adele and then didn't protect her."

"I didn't know he was going to hurt her." He seemed late to realize that not only had he spoken aloud but his words damned him. Rattled, he went on quickly. "There was no plan, not the way you make it seem. The invitation to dinner was my own, and she accepted. What happened afterward was—"

"Shut up, Randolph," Foster said mildly. He rubbed his eyes. "It's done with, isn't it? Let it be. My mother could tell you, that little girl was no better than she—"

The explosion was loud enough to make the remainder

of Foster's sentence inaudible. He stood clumsily, grabbing the desk for support with both hands while he tried to get his legs under him. His head was finally clear, but his feet felt like anchors.

Rose was knocked sideways against Mr. Dover, momentarily pinning him to the window. She recovered first and reached around him. Her fingers fumbled for the string on the window shade. She had to shove him forward before she found it. She yanked once and it snapped open.

"Holy Mother of God," she whispered.

Ignoring Foster's command to stay where she was, Rachel was at Rose's side in seconds. She set one knee on the bench and bent so she shared the same angled view of the mountain up ahead. She was in time to see the first cascade of white powder slide over the packed snow. It billowed like a summer cloud but moved with the speed of a storm, not merely covering everything in its path, but gathering it to its center so that its power increased exponentially. Rocks appeared like so much flotsam, then were sucked under. Scrub pines lost their mooring and were set adrift.

Foster lurched to one of the windows and tore the shade aside. His ears registered the sounds as a series of explosions, but his eyes saw that it was the rending and tearing and sliding of the mountainside that was the source of the noise. He searched for something to hold on to when he felt the train begin to shudder as the engineer applied the brakes. He clutched the back of the bench where Mr. Dover and Rose sat and set his feet apart in a sailor's stance.

Rachel lost her balance and stumbled sideways before she could grasp the hand that Rose thrust out to her. The train's momentum carried her forward, and after a few awkward attempts to halt her progress, she fell to her knees. She managed not to slide into the stove, missing it by inches as she threw herself flat to the floor.

Her body continued to slide as the train vibrated and the brakes screeched. Outside the private car, the avalanche thundered and rolled. She squeezed her eyes closed and protected the crown of her head with her hands, expecting at any moment to be pitched against the wall.

Rachel waited for her world to still before she opened her eyes. Rose was also on the floor, but she had managed to stay on her knees by hugging the legs of the bench seat. Mr. Dover was slumped forward so that his chin rested on his chest. His spectacles perched crookedly on the bridge of his nose. Blood trickled from his scalp. Tiny shards of glass dusted the shoulders of his coat. Only a few dangerously sharp pieces remained in the window.

Foster was still on his feet, though visibly shaken. She watched him recover his bearings, then begin to carefully look around. She saw immediately that his concern wasn't for any of his fellow passengers. He was scanning the floor, searching for the documents that had disappeared from his desk.

Rachel thought he would fall when he stooped to pick up one of the papers, but he managed to retrieve it without toppling. She rolled on her side and pushed herself up. Rose was crawling on all fours toward her.

Rachel rose up on her knees and reached for her. They clung together. She whispered in Rose's ear, "They've come for us."

Rose nodded. Tears clung to her lashes. She pulled back and gave Rachel a watery smile. "I'll see to Mr. Dover. You look after Foster Maddox. You certainly have that right."

They got to their feet together. Rose leaned over the accountant and began her ministrations while Rachel went to Foster. He was still crouched on the floor, sweeping his hand under the desk to collect more of the documents.

"Leave them," she said. "They can't possibly be so important."

He didn't lift his head to look at her. "You're wrong."

Rachel got out of his way. He was moving with a certain frenzy that she found curious and more than a little alarming. Skirting the desk, she opened the drawer where she'd seen him put the bottle of liniment. It was lying on its side between a ruler and a compass. She pulled it out and shook it a little as she held it up to the light. He had indeed drunk most of it, a fact that led her to believe he had the constitution of a horse.

She returned the bottle to her own pocket just as Foster stood. He counted the pages in his hand and began another search.

"The train's stopped, Foster. We're not going anywhere."

He ignored her. His eyes alighted on the last of the papers. Rose had captured them with the toe of her left shoe. She was bent forward, picking glass off Mr. Dover's coat with one hand and pressing a handkerchief to his head with the other. He was moaning softly.

"Foster," Rachel said. "Leave it."

He stooped, shoved Rose's foot aside, and grabbed the papers. She teetered on one foot and then righted herself. She held up one hand to show Rachel how she'd cut herself on the glass. Blood trickled down her palm.

Rachel gestured to her to step out of Foster's way and gave her a warning look not to provoke him. "What are you going to do with those?" she asked Foster as he counted them again.

He didn't answer.

Rachel recognized his intent when he began moving toward the stove. His steps were heavy and slightly faltering, but he only had a short distance to cover to reach his destination. She called out to him as he opened the door to the stove. "We photographed the papers, Foster. We have everything. You can destroy them, but I'm telling you it won't matter. I photographed Adele's face, too. All of her bruises, in fact. There's evidence now. People will learn the truth about you."

He turned sharply, holding the documents in front of him. His eyes accused her before his words did the same. "You're lying."

Rachel saw that he was weaving slightly. "Sit down," she said. "You're going to fall. Do you have any idea what's happening?" When he merely stared at her, she pointed to the shattered window. "The avalanche didn't happen by itself. Miners brought that down. My husband's out there, Foster. So is that no-account Beatty boy. They're coming for us. They're coming for you."

"What?" He frowned. "What? No."

"No one's come forward," she said. "You haven't even noticed that no one's come forward to find you. Wyatt's rounding them up. Like cattle." She smiled faintly, wryly. "Like sheep."

For the first time since the train stopped, Foster listened to something outside the drumming in his own head. He heard the snuffling of horses, the deep timbre of masculine voices, and the thud of firearms being tossed to the ground.

"Please, Foster, won't you sit down?" She pointed to the bench the attorneys had occupied and prayed that he would take it.

"It's the elixir, isn't it?" he said, closing his eyes briefly.

"I'm afraid so."

His hand wavered as he pointed at Rose. "You drank. I watched you."

Rose shrugged. "You saw what I wanted you to. That's the nature of my business, Mr. Maddox, and I'm very good at what I do." She smiled sweetly, if insincerely. "Besides, there wasn't a chance in hell I was going to drink something that smelled like cat piss."

Rachel braced herself for Foster's response. His eyes were not so glazed that she could miss the annoyance that Rose

parked there. She imagined that in his own mind he
saw himself as charging forward. What he did in reality was
stagger.

Rachel turned sideways, blocked his path, and put her
shoulder hard into his chest. He stumbled backward against
the stove and dropped the papers as he tried to regain his balance. He stared at them for a moment, frowning as if he were
struggling to recall how they'd come to be there; then he
raised his head and fixed his attention once more on Rose.

Watching him, Rachel realized that he had but one target
now. Rage had chipped away at his peripheral vision, narrowing his focus so that Rose stood alone at the end of the tunnel.
Rachel pushed her out of the way just as Foster sprang out of
his crouch. It hardly mattered that he lacked the gracefulness
of a mountain cat. He was tall and lean and fit and had a
reach that extended well beyond Rachel's own. His fingertips
grazed Rose's shoulder, but Rachel took the full force of his
rash leap and was slammed to the floor and pinned under his
suddenly dead weight.

That was how Wyatt found her. Standing over her, he took
stock of her situation and simply shook his head, the faintest of
admiring grins tugging at one side of his mouth. Out of the
corner of his eye he saw that Will was already all over Rose and
that the hapless Mr. Dover had been left to fend for himself.

"Took your breath away, did he?" Wyatt asked his wife. He
reached down, grabbed Foster Maddox by the collar of his
jacket, and jerked him off Rachel. Holstering his gun, he hunkered beside her, and placed a restraining hand on her shoulder.
"Give yourself a moment," he said. "He took you down hard."

She made a strangled, gasping sound as she tried to fill her
lungs with air. In the end, she mostly mouthed the words.
"You saw that?"

"He was already in the air."

"He wanted Rose."

Wyatt's fingertips grazed her cheek. "Did he?" he aske softly. "I couldn't tell."

She nodded. Her wary glance went sideways to whe Foster lay.

"He's out cold." To prove it, Wyatt gave Foster's shoulder hard jab. "You cushioned his fall, so that doesn't explain What did you do to him?"

Rachel reached in her pocket and drew out the cobalt-bl bottle. She held it up for Wyatt to see.

His brow puckered. "Liniment? I don't understand. Ho did that work?"

"He drank it."

Wyatt's expression clearly betrayed his revulsion. "Dra it? Why would he do that? It smells like cat piss." He took t bottle, examined it, then regarded Rachel's innocent smi with suspicion. "It's all right," he said, pocketing it. "I'll he about it later, though I'm inclined to think target shooting w mostly wasted on you." He slid an arm under her shoulde and helped her sit up. "Better?"

Her eyes darted to where Will and Rose were still lock in a smothering embrace. "Better if you kiss me."

His eyes followed hers. That no-account Beatty boy had come up for air. "You just got your breath back," he remind her.

She raised her arms and slid them around his neck. "I nev mind when you steal it away."

Wyatt caught Rachel by the waist and drew her up as stood. His hands moved to the buttons of her coat. He unfa tened them and slipped his arms inside, drawing her flush his body. It still didn't seem close enough, but then he did know what would. It was only now, with the assurance t she was safe, that he could admit to all his fears that s wouldn't be.

He touched his forehead to hers. "Oh, God, Rachel,"

hispered. "You can't know. You can't possibly know." His
outh found hers. He kissed her hard, deeply, and took the
eath she offered him.

At their feet, Foster Maddox stirred. Sensing the move-
ent, Wyatt placed a boot heel hard in the middle of his back.
e ignored Foster's soft moan and kept him pinned underfoot
ntil he could set Rachel safely away. She didn't make it easy
r him to leave her. Her lips clung, and even when he raised
s head a fraction she leaned into him and pressed her mouth
the corner of his.

"Go on," he said. "I need you to be outside."

Rachel did not try to conceal her worry. Her eyes darted to
ster, then back to Wyatt. "You won't . . ." She didn't finish
r sentence, couldn't really.

"Go on," he repeated, more firmly this time. It wasn't a
ggestion and he didn't mean for her to take it as one. "Rose.
 with her."

Rose's only response was to point a finger at Will behind
s back.

Wyatt barked at his deputy, "For God's sake, Will, propose
 let her go. Better yet, do both."

That made Will's head snap up. He stared at Rose. Twin
ins of ruddy color appeared in his cheeks as she stared right
ck. "I—that is, I—well, Rose, it's a fact that I—see, Wyatt
ows how I feel about—"

She took pity on him, patting his shoulder. "I'll just go,
ill. Give you some time to work on that proposal." She
pped out of his embrace and dodged him when he would
ve made a grab at her, then made a wide arc around Foster
addox's outstretched arms. "C'mon, Rachel. We're in the
ly now."

Rachel understood that her presence was a distraction and
mpromised Wyatt's choices and his ability to act. It should

have been easier to leave than it was. She backed away fr͏
Foster and Wyatt and waited for Rose to reach her side.

"He wanted the mining agreement," she said, pointing
the papers littering the floor. "And control of the spur. He w͏
like a dog with a bone. I told him you'd made photograph͏
but he had his mind set on destroying them anyway."

"He convinced himself that you'd take everything." N͏
Randolph Dover sat up a little straighter as every eye w͏
drawn to him. He touched his tender scalp and found a fold͏
handkerchief still pressed to his bloody wound. He left͏
there and laid his hand over it. With his free hand, he brush͏
bits of glass from his coat, clearing most of it before he rais͏
his head again. "He thinks you're his aunt," he told Rach͏
"No one could tell him differently."

"His aunt?" Rachel stared at him, incredulous. "But th͏
would make me—"

It was Wyatt who put what strained her belief into wor͏
"Clinton Maddox's daughter."

The accountant nodded. "It was his mother that planted t͏
seed, and her parents that nurtured it. They might even ha͏
believed it. I can't be sure." He paused, working his jaw ba͏
and forth. "And it doesn't change anything. They poison͏
him. There's no other way to describe it."

Rachel shook her head. "No. He couldn't have thought th͏
He accused me of being his grandfather's mistress. He want͏
to make me his—" She bit off the last words and protectiv͏
crossed her arms in front of her. This last gesture didn't s͏
her from shivering. "It's not true," she said. "Mr. Madd͏
wasn't my father. I know he wasn't. He never hinted as mu͏
to me, and my mother . . . my mother would never have . . . s͏
loved my father."

Rose stepped back as Wyatt left Foster and moved
Rachel's side.

"Mr. Dover knows it's not true," Wyatt said gently. "So do You don't have to convince us."

Groaning in pain, Foster Maddox rolled onto his back. He aaded his eyes from the light coming in the window, and hen he spoke, his words were slurred but understandable. She's trying to convince herself. Isn't that right, Rachel? You ondered all your life, the same as I did."

"You're wrong," she said. "I never wondered."

"Same as I did," he repeated. "He sent your father off to e, just like he did mine. He wanted your mother again. veryone knew."

Rachel realized he was only repeating the things he'd been ld by Cordelia and her parents. She discovered that in spite f all that he'd done, and all that he'd tried to do, she could ill feel pity for him.

Randolph Dover swept glass off the bench and moved to e end of it. "You can't tell him he's wrong," he said. "I atched two of my predecessors try. He dismissed both of em. He thinks there's evidence somewhere that will prove so he's destroying everything. The attorneys can't reason ith him. He's certain you know you're his aunt because you fused all his advances."

Rachel flushed, but her embarrassment paled in compari-n to Mr. Dover's. He fiddled with his spectacles while his es remained fixed on the floor. He had to clear his throat fore he could go on, and then rushed through the last of his planation as though every word of it was distasteful to him.

"He couldn't imagine that anything other than the sin of cest would make you deny him. And that was the trap, you e. Even if he had to force you, it would ensure your silence. was always his fear, that you or Clinton would publicly knowledge your blood tie. That's why he approved of e rumor that you were Clinton Maddox's mistress and why was so important to him to get you into his bed. He was

certain you'd never come forward if he had carnal knowledg
of you."

Rachel pressed the back of her fist to her mouth b
couldn't quite stifle her moan. Wyatt was the one who put
stop to it.

"For God's sake, that's enough. Rachel, get out of here."

Mr. Dover hung his head. "I thought she would want
know," he said quietly. "I thought after doing nothing, I owe
her that." At his feet, Foster Maddox had managed to pus
himself up on his elbows. Randolph Dover stared at hir
"But I might owe Miss Adele Brownlee more."

He lifted his palm and revealed the four-inch dagger
glass resting on his knee. Before anyone could react, he use
it to open Foster Maddox's throat.

Epilogue

"Did you finally get your sister settled?" Rachel dipped wer in the tub as soon as she heard the back door open. She /ore she could feel an eddy of cool night air slip into the use along with Wyatt. Even with the tub pulled close to the ove it was hard to keep the bath warm enough for her tastes. e'd already added as much hot water as she dared, and ere was little maneuvering that could be done without shing it over the sides.

Wyatt knocked mud off his boots and brushed rain spatter om the shoulders of his coat before he stepped into the chen. A grin tugged at his mouth when he saw Rachel in e tub. He leaned back against the wall, folded his arms in nt of him, and gave her the benefit of his full, appreciative gard. "Am I in time to wash your back?"

"Already done."

"Then your front."

"I don't even think you're supposed to see me on the night fore our wedding day."

"I'm not supposed to see you in your dress or some such

nonsense. According to your mother and mine, I'm suppose
to be in Wyoming. But I don't think those rules apply whe
the couple is already married."

"An insignificant detail." She squeezed water from th
sponge and let it trickle over her shoulders. "Did you hear n
when you came in? I asked if you got Julianna settled."

"I did." He unbuttoned his coat and hooked his thumbs
his pockets. "It would have been easier if I'd put my sister ar
her brood in jail for the night. Her children would have er
joyed the adventure, and Julianna and her husband woul
have been assured of receiving breakfast in their room."

Rachel laughed, though not without sympathy. "Sh
cannot have been so awful."

"Even my mother was out of patience with her. She r
minded Julianna that everyone else has been here since Tue
day and that if Julianna was unhappy with the arrangemen
she should have arrived before all the suites were taken." H
shook his head, sighing. "Of course, Mother did not offer
give Julianna her suite and take a room instead. Your moth
made the offer, but my sister had the good sense to refuse it

"Were you pointing your gun at her?"

"It was tempting, but no." He pushed away from the wa
removed his coat, and hung it up. When he returned to th
kitchen, he pulled out a chair, spun it around on one leg, ar
straddled it. He laid his forearms over the top rung of th
ladder-back and rested his chin on the back of his hands.

Rachel glanced up. "I wish I had been able to spend mo
time with your sister. I liked her. She is very direct."

"That's one word for it."

"What do you call her?"

"Rude."

Rachel threw the damp sponge at him. He batted it awa
easily, and it fell back into the water, splashing her. She swip
water from her eyes and then settled back. "I'm glad she a

rived in time, Wyatt. With the exception of your grandparents, who would certainly have found the long train journey a hardship, you have your entire family here. That's satisfying, don't you think?"

It was, but he wasn't prepared to admit it so easily. "They're here because they're curious."

"There's nothing at all wrong with that. I don't mind their examination; it seems perfectly natural given the circumstances. And you must have noticed that my mother's inspection of you has been equally thorough. I think they feel compelled to be cautious in their judgment, perhaps even a bit critical, because in the end, their good opinion is merely gravy on the biscuit."

Wyatt chuckled. "I'll keep that in mind tomorrow morning when I'm waiting for you to join me at the chancel rail. Of course, no one pays much attention to the groom. They'll all be looking at you." He watched Rachel lose a little color in her cheeks as she absorbed the truth of that. "Gravy on the biscuit," he reminded her.

Rachel slipped a little lower into the tub. Water lapped at her chin. "Maybe we should elope. I could still wear the dress."

He pretended to think about it. "Well, I suppose if you promised to wear the dress . . ." He grinned as she flicked water at him. "All right. No. Absolutely not. We're getting married in a church this time around."

"Thank you," she said. "For a moment, I thought you were wavering."

"You're confusing me with that no-account Beatty boy."

She stared at him from under her long, dark lashes, her expression wry and amused. "Now, there's a mistake I'm not likely to make."

Wyatt knew better than to assume she was complimenting him. He proceeded cautiously. "Is that right?"

"Will Beatty's asked Rose to marry him more times in the last three months than Abe Dishman ever asked me, so his hesitation to keep spinning that wheel is understandable, but my point is—"

"So you have one. I wondered."

She threatened him with the sponge again. "My point is that you've never proposed to me."

He regarded her with surprise. "Of course I have."

"You showed me some papers and we negotiated a settlement. That's what I remember."

Wyatt thrust his fingers through his hair as he thought back. "That's a hell of a thing to tell me now."

"Could be it's your last chance to get it done."

"Hell of a thing," he said again, more to himself than to her. He fell silent for a while, watching the water lap gently against the side of the tub as Rachel sat up a little straighter. He reared back in his chair suddenly and began patting down his vest and searching his pockets.

Watching him, Rachel simply shook her head. She doubted that a carefully penned proposal was what he was looking for.

Wyatt finally produced a folded piece of paper and tipped his chair forward so he could put it in Rachel's hands. "Telegram. Artie found me at the hotel after you left."

"And you're just recalling it now?"

He gave her a frank look, his cool blue eyes dipping significantly to the white curves of her breasts. "I can't imagine what distracted me."

"If you keep looking at me like that, say, for the next fifty years or so, I might just get annoyed." Ignoring Wyatt's unrepentant grin, Rachel unfolded the telegram. "Well," she said after reading it through once. "Jay Mac Worth has finalized the purchase of the C & C. I'm sure it isn't right to say so, but it feels as if he's given us a wedding present."

Wyatt had to agree. He accepted the telegram back and

looked it over. "It's done, then." There was a certain amount of satisfaction in finally being able to say the words. Foster Maddox had proved to be almost as difficult in death as he had been in life. He died intestate, thus leaving the door open for his mother to continue his claim that the Calico Spur was legitimately his. Cordelia Maddox made a fight of it simply because she was sufficiently rich in both resources and resentment. She made the journey to Reidsville to bring back her son's body and stayed to watch Randolph Dover hang for his death.

The accountant's trial was a subdued affair, unlike the ones where cattle thieves and land grabbers were the defendants before the court. The gallery was filled every day and remained largely quiet as the facts were put before the jury. Adele Brownlee was the exception to the peace and dignity of the proceedings. She had convinced herself that she was in some way responsible for Mr. Dover's actions and cried so loudly and copiously on the first day of the trial that Judge Wentworth ordered her removed. He told Wyatt later that he would have liked to remove Cordelia Maddox as well, but other than her coldly penetrating stare she gave him no cause.

The accountant posed no problems during his brief stay in jail. Although he had nothing to say in his defense, he was willing, even eager to talk at length about the fragile solvency of the empire that Clinton Maddox had built. Certain decisions made by Foster in the eight months before Clinton's death had placed the California and Colorado in a vulnerable financial position. It was Dover that suggested contacting John MacKenzie Worth of the powerful Northeast Rail and hinting that the C & C could be acquired at a very reasonable thirty-nine cents on the dollar.

Wyatt glanced at the telegram one more time before he set it aside. Jay Mac's negotiations for the C & C included the contested spur and property around Reidsville, but now that the purchase was complete, both would be returned to the rightful owners. The contract that Wyatt and Jay Mac's attorneys had drawn up assured it.

It was satisfying to see justice applied in such a fashion, and the timing could not have been better.

"The town's going to have a good deal more to celebrate than our wedding," he said. "This news will ensure that the dancing and drinking goes on all night."

"Debauchery, too, I suspect."

Wyatt gave Rachel a frankly carnal look. "Lord, but I'm counting on that."

Her laughter was short-lived as she aspirated some water and began to cough. Wyatt seized on the opportunity and left his chair so that he could hunker beside the tub. He slipped a hand under Rachel's arm, pulled her up, and gave her a solid thwack between her shoulder blades. The sound of it was out of all proportion to the actual force he used and very nearly echoed in the small kitchen. Afraid that he had really hurt her, Wyatt reared back and threw up his hands.

"Are you all right?" he asked. He angled his head, trying to catch her eye. He couldn't tell if the trail of water on her cheeks was the result of splashing or tears. "I swear I didn't mean to—" The sopping wet sponge she pushed in his face served to effectively cut him off and answer his question at the same time.

Wyatt wrested the sponge from her hand and wrung it out over her head. She protested more for form's sake than out of any sincere outrage. It was only when he stood and removed his jacket, then began to unbutton his vest that her objections took on a more genuine tone.

"There's no room in here, Wyatt."

"Sure there is."

"There'll be water all over the floor."

He tossed his vest over the back of a chair and started on his shirt. "I'll mop it up."

"No, you won't."

One corner of his mouth edged upward. "How well you know me."

She snorted lightly. "I know every man at least that well."

Wyatt lifted his left eyebrow and gave her an arch look.

She decided to take another tack. "I put lavender in the water."

He already had his shirt half off, and now he paused to regard her suspiciously. Bending at the waist, he waved one hand over the ribbons of steam rising from the tub and sniffed. The fragrance was definitely floral. He considered the consequences to his manhood and announced, "I'm partial to lavender."

Rachel looked pointedly at the bulge in his trousers, then even more pointedly at him. "You'd be partial to skunk if I'd put it in the water with me."

He held up his thumb and forefinger separated by a hairsbreadth. "You could be flattering yourself just this much."

Rather than risk choking on her laughter again, Rachel pressed the sponge against her mouth to suppress it. His single-mindedness was both maddening and disarming. "Did I know you were incorrigible when I agreed to marry you?"

Wyatt sat down again to remove his boots and socks. "You're a fair judge of character. I'd have to say you had your suspicions."

"Hmm. I wonder what made me put them aside?" The knowing, slightly wicked smile he turned on her warmed Rachel from the inside out. "No, that wasn't it." His deep chuckle, though, made her shiver. "It might have been that."

Wyatt stood up, shucked his trousers and drawers, and tested the water with his fingertips before he committed.

Amused, Rachel asked, "Isn't it a bit late to decide that my bath is too hot to suit you?"

"Not at all." He put one foot in. "I can always lift you out." He stepped in fully and began to gingerly lower himself into the tub. Water started to spill over the sides before he got his thighs wet.

Rachel made as much room for him as she could, but when the waterfall began she levered herself to her feet like a jack-in-the-box. She was out of the tub before Wyatt understood her intention. "Stay where you are," she told him as he started to rise. "I'll scrub your back." She pointed to the water when he hesitated. "You won't be sorry."

Wyatt watched her put on her robe. He was already sorry, and the fact that robe clung appealing to her damp skin only improved his mood marginally. Still, he eased himself into the tub. The promise of a back scrub was a powerful inducement, and in truth, they both knew she'd merely won a temporary stay.

Rachel wrung out her wet hair and loosely plaited it while Wyatt attended to his bath. She stood over him with a pitcher of warm water when it was time to rinse the soap out of his hair, and he sighed with sybaritic pleasure as she tipped the pitcher and trickled water over his head and shoulders.

Rachel set the half-empty pitcher on the table and knelt beside the tub. "There's not a dry spot left on this floor," she told him. She folded a towel and put it under her knees, then gave him a gentle push to lean forward. "How do you manage that?"

"Couldn't say." He handed her the soap and sponge and presented his back. "Take your time."

She gave him a little jab with the sponge. "You aren't that patient." Lathering his back, she felt his chuckle more than heard it. "I've been thinking about what I want to tell my mother and sister about the mine," she said. "I'm not certain they need to know everything."

With Rachel's hand moving hypnotically across his back, Wyatt had some trouble following the abrupt turn in her conversation. He knew she'd been struggling with keeping the town's secret from her family, but since her mother and sister had no intention of settling in Reidsville, she had gone back and forth with not only what was fair to reveal, but what she could live with. He crafted a careful reply. "Tell me more."

"Well, it didn't seem possible that the true wealth of the town's mine could stand so much scrutiny and not be revealed. Attorneys. Accountants. Engineers. Cordelia Maddox was as certain as Foster that there was something worth finding."

"She wasn't wrong."

"I know," she said quietly. Rachel had often wondered if Cordelia suspected Mr. Dover of keeping his own secrets. The accountant had not only lied to Foster Maddox about his grandfather's private records; he'd also created a separate set of ledgers to keep the originals from being examined by anyone else. Randolph Dover had known all along there were millions of dollars associated with the mine production, not thousands. "It certainly helped that Daniel Seward and his men never located the underground vault. They had nothing at all to report to Cordelia. I still find it odd, don't you?"

"Sid and Ned blew the charges in the shaft and buried it," he reminded her. "There wasn't anything to find. Now that Jay Mac has the C & C, we'll be at least six months digging out the bullion."

"That's my point. So much effort has been expended to keep the secret that it seems wrong, even a betrayal of the town's trust, to explain all of it to my family. I only want to see them comfortably set, Wyatt. I can manage that without telling them everything." She hesitated, resting the damp sponge at the curve of his shoulder. "I've been thinking about what I'd like to do with my profits, and I know now that I want to invest in the land."

"You mean the mine?"

"No, I mean the land. I want to see if it can be returned to something like it was. I keep thinking of the images in your photographs, the beauty that you captured. As the mines play out, it should be like that again. I don't know what's possible exactly, but I'd like to try."

It moved him powerfully that she would want to. He reached for his shoulder and laid his hand over hers, rubbing it gently. "So what will you tell them? Your family, I mean."

"That I married into money." Slipping her hand free, she ran the sponge along his back again. "It's the most reasonable truth."

Wyatt lifted his head to look around the modest, functional kitchen. He was still waiting for the thaw that would allow him to put in running water, and they didn't have room to spare for even one of her family or his. "Not an obvious one."

Rachel's tone was dry. "My family's met yours, Wyatt. It's obvious to them now." Leaning forward, she kissed him at the nape of his neck. "My mother asked me this afternoon if you were the black sheep."

"Wonderful."

She kissed him again, this time on the shoulder. "It's all right. I explained you were a wolf in black sheep's clothing."

He shot her a wry glance. "That must have eased her mind."

"Oddly, it did. She thought I was being humorous."

Wyatt wasn't certain how he was supposed to interpret that, but with Rachel's mouth hovering near his ear and her tongue poised to lick his wounds, he chose not to take issue. When her teeth caught his earlobe and tugged, he thought he would come out of his skin.

What he did was come out of the water. Shaking droplets and lather left and right, he rose from the tub like the titan

Oceanus rising from the sea and made a grab for Rachel. She danced out of his reach and showered him with what remained of the rinse water. For good measure, she tossed the pitcher at him as well. He caught it easily and made a threatening gesture to fill it up and toss it back. That was enough to make Rachel bolt from the kitchen and charge toward the bedroom.

Wyatt followed her damp footprints. They ended about four feet from the bed, proof that she'd covered the last bit of ground in one impulsive leap for the safety of the covers. Now she was cocooned in them. He caught the outer edges of the blankets in two places and yanked hard. Laughing, Rachel obliged him by rolling out of them until she reached the far side of the bed. She loosened the belt of her robe and teased him with a glimpse of her breast and the smooth, creamy flat of her abdomen.

The bed shook as he flung himself across it. He captured her easily, pinning her wrists back and drawing himself up on his elbows so he didn't crush her. "Did I know you were incorrigible when I agreed to marry you?"

She smiled up at him, unapologetic, and gave him back the response he'd given her. "I'd have to say you had your suspicions."

Wyatt touched his forehead to hers. "You're right. I did. It's what made me fall in love with you." He lifted his head, touched his mouth to hers, then drew back slightly. "You will marry me, won't you?"

"Are you proposing, Sheriff?"

"I love you, Rachel Bailey Cooper. Will you marry me?"

"Nicely done." She made him wait while she pretended to think about it. "I believe I will, thank you."

Growling softly at the back of his throat, Wyatt gave her wrists a little shake and then proceeded to kiss her so thoroughly that a sigh was all that occurred to her when he was done.

Much later, when she had returned every favor, it was all that occurred to him as well.

Standing at the chancel rail, Wyatt turned toward the doors of the church as they opened. The swell of guests followed his example, every head straining to see the view that captivated him.

Rachel seemed to hover on the threshold, ethereal in her white satin gown, sunlight glancing off the long, draping train. Perfectly poised, she glided toward him without escort, her head held high, her slender throat exposed by the scalloped neckline of the dress she'd been crafting in secret for weeks. As always, there was no hint of hesitation in her step, and she looked neither left nor right, but straight ahead, at him, her eyes clear and bright and full of promise.

Wyatt tapped the rail at his side with his fingertips, counting her carefully measured steps down the aisle, just as he used to when he observed her progress through town. Here she was passing Morrison's, then Easter's Bakery from across the way where Abe and Ned were once again engaged in a game of checkers. Johnny Winslow and Henry Longabach tipped their hats as they loitered outside the restaurant. Jacob Reston swiveled in his chair to watch her from the bank window, and the tellers crowded in the doorway. That no-account Beatty boy showed his deep, crescent-shaped dimples when he smiled at her. Ed Kennedy flexed his arms as he straightened over his anvil to bid her a good day. Rudy Martin leaned on his broom in front of the Miner Key when she sailed by, and Artie Showalter waited outside the telegraph office just to greet her.

Wyatt saw that she seemed unaware of the attention she

aroused, except for the attention she aroused in him. If he'd been on the sidewalk in front of his office, he'd never have let her pass, and she wouldn't have wanted him to. She met his eyes, held them, and took another step closer, exactly on the downbeat of his gently tapping finger. He couldn't look away.

Smiling, he counted it out. Four steps to reach him. Then three. Now two.

As always, watching her was a pleasure.

A pure pleasure.

About the Author

Jo Goodman lives with her family in Colliers, West Virginia. She is currently working on her newest Zebra historical romance. Jo loves hearing from readers, and you may write to her c/o Zebra Books. Please include a self-addressed stamped envelope if you would like a response. Or you can visit her Web site at *www.jogoodman.com*.

Romantic Suspense from
Lisa Jackson

See How She Dies	0-8217-7605-3	$6.99US/$9.99CAN
Final Scream	0-8217-7712-2	$7.99US/$10.99CAN
Wishes	0-8217-6309-1	$5.99US/$7.99CAN
Whispers	0-8217-7603-7	$6.99US/$9.99CAN
Twice Kissed	0-8217-6038-6	$5.99US/$7.99CAN
Unspoken	0-8217-6402-0	$6.50US/$8.50CAN
If She Only Knew	0-8217-6708-9	$6.50US/$8.50CAN
Hot Blooded	0-8217-6841-7	$6.99US/$9.99CAN
Cold Blooded	0-8217-6934-0	$6.99US/$9.99CAN
The Night Before	0-8217-6936-7	$6.99US/$9.99CAN
The Morning After	0-8217-7295-3	$6.99US/$9.99CAN
Deep Freeze	0-8217-7296-1	$7.99US/$10.99CAN
Fatal Burn	0-8217-7577-4	$7.99US/$10.99CAN
Shiver	0-8217-7578-2	$7.99US/$10.99CAN
Most Likely to Die	0-8217-7576-6	$7.99US/$10.99CAN
Absolute Fear	0-8217-7936-2	$7.99US/$9.49CAN
Almost Dead	0-8217-7579-0	$7.99US/$10.99CAN
Lost Souls	0-8217-7938-9	$7.99US/$10.99CAN
Left to Die	1-4201-0276-1	$7.99US/$10.99CAN
Wicked Game	1-4201-0338-5	$7.99US/$9.99CAN
Malice	0-8217-7940-0	$7.99US/$9.49CAN

Available Wherever Books Are Sold!
Visit our website at **www.kensingtonbooks.com**

More by Bestselling Author
Fern Michaels